TOXIC

JAMIE DOWARD

CONSTABLE • LONDON

CONSTABLE

First published in Great Britain in 2015 by Constable

Copyright © Jamie Doward, 2015

The moral right of the author has been asserted.

A CIP catalogue record for this book
is available from the British Library.

ISBN: 978-1-47211-559-1 (hardback)
ISBN: 978-1-47212-054-0 (trade paperback)
ISBN: 978-1-47211-560-7 (ebook)

Typeset in Bembo by Photoprint, Torquay
Printed and bound by CPI Group (UK) Ltd, Croydon, CR0 4YY

Constable
is an imprint of
Constable & Robinson Ltd
100 Victoria Embankment
London EC4Y 0DY

An Hachette UK Company
www.hachette.co.uk

www.constablerobinson.com

For Terry and Jack

Chapter 1

According to the local police report, the body was discovered by schoolchildren out combing the beach for fossils on a geology field trip.

The bleak shoreline was a good place to look for traces of the long dead. Petrified truths hunkered in the shingle like sea lice. The beach seemed more prairie than coast, an expanse of lichen-rich flatness that assumed the colours of wet bark when storm clouds blew in across the Channel.

But the day Kate first saw it, when the shoreline spoke to her, impressed upon her how everything, the sea, the land, the sky, was connected, its shingle was bleached white by a stubborn layer of frost.

The vast February sky over the sea seemed to belong more to a continent than a county. The coastline was somewhere a person could feel very small and very alone. Empires could fall, countries implode and economies collapse, but the coast remained immutable. There was security in geology, reassurance in the physical.

The shoreline told of man's failed efforts to impose himself on nature. Hubris was not hard to find. Old fishing boats lay forlornly across the beach, rotting in the winter chill like skeletons of washed-up pilot whales. Derelict huts, where fishermen had once sought refuge against cruel weather, whispered stories from a dead era. The huts were more holes than buildings. Sky poured through the forced spaces, invaded the shadows cast by the decaying structures, their dank timbers splintered by the regular assault of coastal winds.

This smashed-up tableau was played out against the background of a hulking modern presence. A nuclear power station, resembling a decrepit spaceship that had landed millennia ago, loomed large and ugly some 300 metres from the beach. It sat squat at the end of the beach, like a toad.

At first the schoolchildren had thought the body was some soft, bloated sea creature. Its naked grey flesh made it look more marine mammal than human. Their mistake was understandable. The absence of a head and hands rendered the corpse barely recognizable and the lack of clothes had stripped it of any human dignity. It was only when one of the children had dared to poke it with a stick, rolling it over onto its side so an arm flopped out, that their teacher had pulled them away. The children were made to have counselling sessions. But they never forgot what they had seen, the precise moment when the strange sea creature had been transformed into a mutilated corpse. They carried it with them for the rest of their lives, a memory they refused to share.

Kate had read the police report several times, checking it again and again, half hoping that it contained some sort of code that, once cracked, would yield new intelligence. But she knew such an idea was fanciful, bordering on hopeless, so two weeks after the body's discovery she'd made the hundred-mile trip from London to the beach at the very south-eastern tip of England in a bid to convince herself that the murder was not her concern.

The journey was an attempt to close things down, block off one line of wider enquiry that was obsessing her boss, McLure. Ever since the body had been discovered, and clues to the identity of its previous owner had first surfaced, he'd become convinced the corpse could talk, could tell them about its former employer. 'Dead men can give up secrets,' he'd told her. She had her doubts.

The local DCI, who was leading the murder investigation, had been surprised to receive her call. 'You're with MI5? He was a banker, not a terrorist,' he'd told her over the phone. 'But, come to think of it, many would say same difference, these days, hey? In the eyes of the public I guess they're on a par. But, yeah, come on down and I'll show you where we found it. Truly desolate spot. Bring a thick coat.'

So they had walked across the shingle on a freezing February day and stopped at an unprepossessing strip of beach stretched under a taut sky. It looked as if it would shatter if the mercury dropped further. The odd plastic bottle and strip of gnarled driftwood bobbed along the shore. It was not a place for proposals or picnics.

The DCI, who went by the surname Sorrenson – 'I've got Viking blood in me although I'm Kent through and through' – pointed out to sea. Several large supertankers were chugging across the horizon, trailing diesel fumes. 'Busiest shipping lane in the world, the Channel,' he said. 'You've got all that going on out there and then this.' He

3

gestured around him, at the vast flatness of the furry white shingle. 'Get my point?'

She drank in the view, thirsty for big horizons. London offered only the thinnest of perspectives. Her line of vision was normally measured in metres, not miles. Skyscrapers restricted views as much as they made them.

She looked up and down the beach. Something was missing, she felt. She thought for a second, puzzled by her sense of absence, and then she realized. There were no waves. The sea was as flat and untroubled as a lake. There was a calm about the place, as if sea and land had reached a truce. 'You get much washed up here?' she asked Sorrenson.

'Dungeness? No. Further round the coast, yes. The odd seal. Had a whale once. A few abandoned boats. But not here. Nothing happens in Dungeness. This is ghost country.'

She squeezed her hands for warmth. A body could stay preserved for weeks in such a chill. 'What makes you say that?'

The detective waved his arms around him. 'Well, look at it. The buildings are half dead. This whole stretch of coast is like one of those abandoned Western sets. Ha, we've even got an old steam train running through this desert of a place. Some long-dead Victorian's folly, back when the coast earned its keep from fishing. Hardly anyone lives here now. There's no work to be found, except for the odd job at the power station, which they're shutting down anyway because it's so old and dangerous. No one wants to live near a dying nuclear plant. Only animals and not many of them. People say a pride of big black cats inhabits this place. It's certainly not welcoming to humans. Come to think of it, I've hardly ever been called down here in all the years I've been working. Like I said, nothing happens here. Nothing happens in ghost country.'

'Until now.'

Sorrenson nodded. 'Well, clearly, if you guys are here. What's the story?'

She turned to him, gazed at his face. He was similar to a man she'd slept with the previous week, she realized. She couldn't remember his name but vaguely recalled his looks. He'd been tallish, dark hair, mid-forties, grateful for his chance at adultery. That had been a mistake. Another. She shivered in the cold. 'Sorry, can't tell you,' she said. 'And even if I could, there's little to say. Like you, we think we know his name, but that's about it.'

'The tattoo, right? That's how we matched him against missing persons.'

'Yeah. It was of his blood group. He was once in the US Army, we think, special forces maybe. Then he went into the City, made a fortune as a fixer for foreign businessmen and bankers. And then . . .' They stared out to sea. It was a windless day. It would have taken a fierce storm to wash the body high up the beach, she thought.

'And then he ended up here,' Sorrenson said. 'Washed up, handless and headless.'

'You sure about that?'

The detective was surprised. 'What?'

'You sure he was washed up here?' she said.

'Well, I suppose there's a chance that the body might have been placed here. It was so decomposed anything's possible. But it's more likely that it was thrown out of a boat offshore and found its way here. Why go to all the trouble of placing it here?'

It sounded plausible. They turned and walked back to her car across the frost-caked shingle, glistening under a weak winter sun.

'Tell me something,' she said, when the car heater had begun a reassuring purr and she could feel her hands again. 'The toxicology reports suggest there were large traces of alcohol and cocaine in his blood.'

'Equivalent to a bottle of whisky, apparently.'

'That's what I thought.'

'Bankers, hey? They do everything to excess.'

'Yeah, they do.' She nodded at the detective. 'I'll give you a lift back to the station where I picked you up, right?'

'Right. Thanks. I just hope you think your trip was worth it. Nothing really to see.'

'It's helped a bit,' she replied doubtfully. 'Good to see things for yourself, not just read the reports.'

Sorrenson examined the Golf's interior. 'Where are the gadgets, Miss Pendragon?'

She turned the ignition key and glanced at him. No wedding ring, she noticed. Unusual for someone in their mid-forties. She figured he was around five years older than her. 'No gadgets. Cut-backs. Like everyone else. Otherwise, of course, this car would be loaded with spy stuff. It's a company vehicle after all, paid for by the hardworking taxpayer.'

Sorrenson laughed. 'You're not how I imagined an agent from Five would look.'

'You're not the first to say that. And I'm not an agent.' She steered the Golf from its scrubland berth next to the beach onto the single-track salt-bleached road that ran along the shore.

'So I'm not original Not a crime.'

6

'Nope, but what you are guilty of is making a mistake. I'm not even really MI5. I've been seconded to the agency from the Financial Intelligence Unit, part of the Treasury. My job is to follow money, not people. Just as well, really. Money talks a lot louder than people, dead people especially.'

Sorrenson gazed out of the window. 'So why did you come down here, then? Can't have been much use to you. No money on a beach.'

'You're right about that. Still, good to get out of London. I've always wanted to see this remote part of the country. It's a haunting place. The only officially classified desert in the UK, so I read.'

He studied the tall woman with the long, dark curly hair. She was a strange one. Distant but not unapproachable. Clearly liked to do her research. 'Yep. It's a desert, all right. But maybe not for much longer. They're looking to turn a disused airport a couple of miles from here into a major transport hub. Talk of high-speed trains going into London. Two-million passengers a year flying in and out – and that's just the start. It's a money-spinner – it'll bring jobs to the area. Progress, they call it.'

She tried to imagine the coastline's vast skies littered with planes. It seemed impossible. 'Who's behind the plan?'

'Following the money again, hey? Its owners, a Saudi prince and his son. The prince lives nearby. Bought it a couple of years back. He's the only one who uses the airport at the moment. Well, him and the odd cargo plane. It's ex-military. It's got the longest runway in Europe. Americans were going to use it for their bombers in the sixties but changed their minds and went elsewhere. Now it's like the rest of this place. Ghostville.'

She watched the coast disappear in her rear-view mirror. Shingle gave way to tarmac. A line of stone-clad bungalows, with uPVC windows staring out to sea, stretched along the road. A thought looped through her mind, urgent, insistent. At first she couldn't grasp it, was unable to understand its importance. The picture seemed incongruous, had no place in her current thinking. In her mind she saw thousands of people running in front of huge crowds lining London streets. She could tell that the picture was of a warm spring day. She saw water stations and giant electronic clocks. She saw inflatable arches and the names of sportswear sponsors emblazoned on billboards. She saw the London Marathon.

The thought kept blowing around her mind, like a plastic bag in the wind. Marathons, she thought. You didn't run marathons if you were an alcoholic.

'You wouldn't believe how difficult it is to hire a skip in Twickenham.'

She continued studying her newspaper. The obituaries column was proving hypnotically interesting. The writer seemed to be about three steps ahead of her.

'I mean, I can obtain a warrant to intercept someone's phone at the stroke of a pen, I can commission GCHQ to tap submarine cables going out of Land's End to God knows where, but try to get someone to rent you a skip and, well, fuck, it's impossible.' McLure pointed at Kate. 'I don't suppose you have these problems, what with your minimalist city living and your spacious studio loft. God, how I envy you.'

She put her newspaper down and looked at him. His divorce was taking its toll. Every day brought another frustration as he tried to leave his old life behind and start again. Clearing out the marital home was the latest trial, which he'd been performing with ill grace and a sour running commentary.

She was not without sympathy. It was difficult to concentrate on domestic problems when you were personally responsible for monitoring more than two-hundred suspected terrorists at large in the UK. And, besides, she was complicit in his difficulties. She winced each time she remembered what had happened between them the previous year. A huge mistake. There had been just a handful of dismal liaisons between them but, still, it constituted a fairly massive breach of security-service protocol.

And it had escalated so quickly. McLure had started talking about leaving his wife for her and them buying a home together. It had been a horrible, cloying, claustrophobic affair, as far from the escapism she'd hoped it would bring her as she could imagine. She'd struggled to think of a more terrifying future than one that involved living with a colleague who was ten years older. What had she been thinking? It was a question she asked herself regularly. It was an issue that needed to be addressed. But things kept getting in the way. Dead people kept getting in the way.

In the end it had been a relief when Marion, McLure's wife, had found his text messages. An agent who couldn't even keep things secret from his own wife. Farcical, really. The efficiency with which Marion had shut down the marriage and emigrated to Spain with their eleven-year-old daughter had been impressive. It had made Kate think of an exposed sleeper cell scrambling to disband. So much energy had gone into breaking something up. People could be very energetic when it came to destruction.

She poured some coffee from a cafetière and handed it to McLure. Always 'McLure' at work. Never Tony. Despite . . . That would be far too intimate, she felt. 'I take it the great clear-out isn't going too well?'

'It's a fucking nightmare. I've cleared out everything and now I've got nowhere to put it. It's all there in the living room, haunting me. My fucked-up past.'

For a second they looked at each other, the roar of traffic outside their office on the Embankment filling the room. McLure smiled. He raised his mug in appreciation. 'Cheers for the coffee. And sorry for banging on. It's just . . . difficult, you know. Moving on. Fuck, what a mess. But, well, it's good. Necessary.'

She felt herself relax. It was getting easier between them. A few more months, she figured, and things would be back to normal. She'd be out of Five, seconded to somewhere else within the government. Her role in destroying McLure's old life would be barely perceptible. Her fingerprints would be removed from the scene of the crime. 'I'm glad. I'm happy for you. Things will get easier.'

'Yeah, I know. But when I come back next time I'm going into skip hire. There's more demand for it than anti-terrorism. That our man from the beach?' He pointed at the obituaries page of the newspaper.

She nodded. 'Meet Brad Holahon. All-round American superhero, apparently. Both Mammon and marine. According to his obit, he was a former US Navy Seal who became a CIA station chief in Latvia, then went into the City. Made a fortune introducing wealthy people to people with ideas.

Half the dotcom IPOs wouldn't have happened without him, it claims here. The obit says the cause of his death has not been confirmed, although he's believed to have drowned.'

'Right, if headless men can drown. You talked to our American friends?'

'Yep. They're as baffled as we are. Say he wasn't working for them any more. No idea who would have it in for him. He was clean.'

McLure examined his coffee cup. 'They would say that. If their lips move they're lying. That's the special relationship for you. They lie, they lie, they lie. But maybe not this time. For once. Six say they don't believe he was active – no sign he was trading intel with anyone – so we're back to an empty space.' He pointed at a whiteboard on the wall in front of them. A tray fixed next to it offered an array of Magic Marker pens, like votive candles in a church. 'What else does the obit say?'

She returned to the newspaper. 'He was a marathon runner. His colleagues had told me that. The obit says he ran seventeen marathons. Good times, too – sub three hours, many of them. Keep-fit fanatic.'

McLure examined Holahon's photograph. 'Trim for a fifty-three-year-old. But they often are.'

'They?' She saw that at least he had the grace to look embarrassed. McLure was from an era when a person's sexuality had been an issue of national security.

'Yeah, they,' he muttered. 'You spoken to his partner?'

'He was single. His previous boyfriend says they last spoke three years ago. Since then Holahon's life has been devoted to running and making money with near equal amounts of intensity. His computer activity suggests he watched the odd bit of porn, played online roulette occasionally, but nothing particularly spicy. Seemed to have very few close friends. In many ways he's extremely bland. Displayed none of the ostentation that someone with his wealth normally likes to throw around.'

McLure turned the newspaper over in his hands, as if weighing the value of its information. He put the paper down, took a sip of coffee and studied the empty whiteboard again. 'Maybe, but there's the Higgs link. You can't work for Higgs and be an innocent. Everyone touched by Higgs is tainted. And bad things happen to bad people. We all know the rumours about Higgs. We all know about its grubby dealings.'

She nodded, chewed her lip. Her boss was in danger of becoming obsessional again. They had nothing to suggest Holahon's death was linked to his work for Higgs. But McLure was desperate to find something – anything – that might back up his theories about the bank. It looked like he was going to have a long wait. She handed him a sheaf of papers. 'Here's some of the accounts Holahon looked after at Higgs. A few offshore that are interesting. He was co-signatory on several others. A couple of oligarchs, several in the Middle East, the usual characters. You never know, you may get lucky. Your hunch may still turn out correct.'

'Good,' McLure said. 'We haven't got the resources to bring the murderers of dead bankers to justice. It's not our remit. That's for plod. But the murder just might shine a spotlight on what's going on inside Higgs. God, I pray it's not some petty killing. A jealous ex or something. That would be a complete waste. I really hope it's something to do with Higgs. That would be our way in. Thanks for the coffee.'

He walked out of her cramped office, leaving her staring at Holahon's photograph. The obituary didn't mention that he had been very drunk when he died. Wired on coke, too. She studied the bull-chested figure staring out of the newspaper. Five words echoed in her mind. He doesn't look the sort, she thought. He doesn't look the sort.

Chapter 2

Prince Aldud Bin Taleed Sin Abdullah peered out of the window of one of his two Gulfstream jets. Below him he could see the power station nestling beside the coast and, beyond it, his private runway. The power station was such an ugly building, he thought, so utilitarian, so closed. It was an offence to God, really. In fact, the whole of the peninsula was ugly. It was a strange, cold, desolate place of shingle and horrible squat houses that were crying out to be bulldozed to make way for a major new airport. His airport.

Despite the ugliness of his impending surroundings, the prince was in good spirits. His favourite falcon had recovered from a potentially fatal disease, and a horse from his stud was heavily fancied in a race later in the week.

And then there was the airport. Planning permission for its expansion had been granted the previous year but it was only in the last week, when a Judicial Review brought by environmentalists seeking to contest the approval had been rejected at the High Court, that the prince had allowed himself to dream a little about the future.

The airport's development would yield tens of millions of pounds in revenue in the coming years, his coterie of financial advisers had predicted. Although margins were tight, it would turn a profit within a decade, they'd suggested. People were addicted to flying. Runways gave them their fix.

But the prince didn't need the money. Such small sums were trifling, really. He was a billionaire, wealthier than many nation states. It was status that he craved. Even more status than that conferred by his almost unrivalled wealth. He was sixty-eight years of age and the prognosis on his prostate cancer wasn't good. He would be moving to a new place soon, somewhere his wealth would cease to open doors, command respect. He needed to get things in order before his final departure. He needed the airport to be open for business. He needed to secure his legacy. The runway was one part of his strategy for immortality. He almost felt like kneeling down and kissing the tarmac as he descended the stairs of the jet. He nodded at the pack of security goons and assistants waiting to greet him. If only they knew, he thought.

As his chauffeur-driven, bulletproof Bentley sped through the denuded moonscape of the peninsula towards his Lutyens mansion inland, Carlyle briefed him. A waspish, gaunt man with no discernible interests other than making money for his employer, Carlyle had started his business life running a chain of franchised pizza parlours across Eastern Europe. There he'd fallen in with the local Mafia, who were active in shipping guns out of the former Yugoslavia after the civil war. Within weeks, Carlyle had gone from selling Margheritas to AK47s via a series of offshore companies that made the transactions almost impossible to trace. His clients had been mainly African dictators and their opponents, and

he'd often dealt with both simultaneously. The CIA estimated Carlyle had been responsible for fuelling three civil
wars on the continent, conflicts the agency was happy to see
perpetuated as they frustrated China's attempts to own
increasingly large supplies of Africa's mineral wealth.

It was while selling a massive cache of weapons that
Carlyle had met the prince. Terrorists were trying to destroy
his oil pipelines and he needed mercenaries and weapons to
protect his infrastructure. Carlyle was happy to oblige. There
was no shortage of fighters left over from Bosnia and his
contacts in the country were grateful for the work. The
prince was happy too. The mercenaries had been very
enthusiastic in the way they went about mopping up what
Carlyle termed obliquely 'the irritation'.

'The new pool is impressive' Carlyle said, looking out of
the window as hop-fields gave way to the prince's vineyards.
'The builders have placed your family seal in a mosaic at the
deep end as you requested. We had to put down one of your
daughter's ponies, but that's about it. Nothing to report since
you were here last month.'

The prince seemed momentarily troubled. 'Which pony?'
'Panzer.'
There was a pause.
'That would be . . .'
'Your eldest daughter's pony.'
'My eldest?'
'Fatima.'
'Ah, yes, Fatima. A sweet girl. She is . . .'
'Fifteen now. Enjoying life at Roedean, the headmaster
tells me. Wants to become a vet.'

The prince snorted. 'I worry sometimes about my children. An English education is in danger of limiting their horizons. They need to see further. They lack vision. All seven of them. Well, maybe not Faisal.'

Carlyle didn't respond. He kept a close eye on the prince's children. But Faisal – Prince Faisal as he was always referred to, the prince's anointed heir – was a different case. Down the years Carlyle had expended huge effort on covering for the prince's firstborn. In many ways he'd ended up with two masters: the prince and his eldest son. The dual role of serving two men, whose views and lifestyles were not always harmonious, created tensions. Opportunities, too. Carlyle never bothered to tell the prince half of the stuff about his eldest son as it would have distressed him too much. The hit-and-run; the tabloid sting with the fifteen-year-old girl; the destruction of local cattle with an Uzi; the allegations of insider dealing; the jet-ski incident; the arson at a Cambridge college; the paternity suits; the large donations to dubious front groups that scared even Carlyle, who had quite relaxed, non-judgemental views about terrorism. All had been left for him to pick up. It was a litany of carnage that had seen Carlyle assume a unique status as Faisal's trusted fixer. Carlyle had been made privy to deep secrets. It made him useful, dangerous and of interest to others.

It was also exhausting. Faisal was only twenty-nine. He was just starting out on the path to wilful destruction. When his father died, he would be able to do real damage, Carlyle had realized. It would be something epic. Something historic. Something truly memorable.

The Bentley went through the security gates and passed inside the thick perimeter wall that guarded the mansion.

The prince was pleased, but not surprised, to see his staff waiting outside for him. They all sported fixed smiles, he noted. There was something reassuring about the reluctant, forced show of enamel. It made him feel powerful.

Hyde Park was a good place to burn off anger. Kate could feel it melt away as she completed the familiar ten-mile loop, a mixture of small hills and fast flats that she'd created using a GPS watch that monitored her heartbeat and uploaded her running times to her personal computer. She knew that if she gave herself an extended lunch hour she could complete the run and be back at her Whitehall office desk before three. A day without a run and, well, there would be problems. Issues to deal with. Seemingly insurmountable issues that came in the small hours and lingered for days.

She ran past the Peter Pan statue and towards the Serpentine. There was a thin layer of snow dusting the grass and she had only the ducks and geese for company. It was bizarre, she felt, to be in a city of seven-million people and to feel so isolated, to have so much space. But it was the reason she ran. When she was running she felt as if she'd slipped from herself and entered a parallel person. She became immersed in another, lost to all her fears. The sense of blissful release was palpable, chemical. Addictive. Once, sex had done it. To be truthful, sex still did it, still helped her escape. There had been so many escapes and, if anything, they were becoming more numerous. After McLure she'd hit a particularly bad patch. But running – well, running made much more sense. It was less messy and healthier, both mentally and physically. And no small-talk afterwards. No complications. Running turned her into a clean skin every time. It purified her, allowed the toxins to seep away. Whenever she approached other runners she would look at them closely, study their faces, and see that they were just like her. I know what you're running from, she would think. I know what you crave.

She picked up the pace as she ran past the Diana memorial fountain. It always looked so sad, she thought. Few ever seemed to pay it attention. Difficult business, commemoration. It took more than polished stone and running water for an individual to live on in people's memories. Legacies required more than marble.

She thought about the tributes to Holahon in the newspapers' obituaries. The warmest comments had come from members of his running club, the Hampstead Harriers. She knew it well. Her husband, Michael, had introduced her to it – to running, really. Ironic. Now she used it to replace him.

'He was stubborn as an ox,' one of the Harriers had said of Holahon. 'Didn't fear hills. Could beat men half his age. No wonder he was so successful in business, too.'

She'd been surprised that there had been so many obituaries. The number seemed disproportionate to Holahon's profile. There were more than there would have been for a dead athlete, say. It was clear that Holahon had been more than just a fixer: he had been Someone in the City. He had been, if not Square Mile royalty, at least a member of its aristocracy. His death would leave a hole. He would live on in people's memories for good or bad.

She was aware of claims that Higgs had hired private investigators to track down Holahon's killer or killers. But she was losing interest. As far as she was concerned, Holahon was

barely more than a person of interest in the wider Higgs
drama that was obsessing her boss and adding to her work-
load. He had a cameo role, Holahon, but no more. His death
was in all probability down to something simple and ugly: a
toxic relationship that had blown up.

Her iPhone, attached to the elasticated belt in which she
carried fuel gels and water, started to vibrate. She hit receive.

'That you?'

McLure.

'Yep.'

'You running? You sound a little breathless. Or maybe
you're, erm, doing something else.'

She shuddered. She could almost see him leering down
the phone. How had she allowed him to come anywhere
near her? God, he sounded sleazy. But, then, so did many of
his colleagues. For all its progressive talk of subsidized
crèches, maternity leave and flexible working hours, the
security service was still, basically, a place for unreconstructed
public schoolboys, most of whom hadn't been bright enough
to go into investment banking. 'Yes, I'm running.'

'Well, run back to my office. Get a sweat on.'

Yes, she thought, really sleazy. Never, ever again.

'Got something to show you. Those offshore accounts you
found, the ones that were run by Holahon, I think they're
interesting. Might be worth you spending a bit more time
checking them. Maybe his death is linked to his work after
all. Maybe we're getting lucky.'

She felt her shoulders tense. She didn't want to share
McLure's obsession with Higgs. It was just one bank, after
all. But, still, maybe he was on to something. Intelligence,
she was learning, was about joining the dots, understanding

how all things were connected. Numerous internal reports berated the service for being too myopic. Since she'd been seconded to Five it had become clear to her that it was struggling to understand how the world was changing. It didn't seem to realize that bankers could do more damage than bombs. It didn't understand contagion. McLure appeared to be the exception.

She banked around the Serpentine and headed towards Whitehall, building up for a sprint finish that would leave her gasping for air. She calculated that she would have run seven-and-a-half miles by the time she got back to her desk. It wouldn't be enough, she knew. She'd have to be careful. She was dangerous. She had too much energy. She was at risk of losing control.

'Interview commences three-fifteen p.m. In attendance, DCI Sorrenson and DC Hughes.'

Sorrenson flicked a switch on the digital recorder, pushed a cup of tea across the table. 'Here, this is for you. Good to see you, Davey. Been, what, a month since we were here last?'

Davey Stone said nothing. Usually he had a reasonable idea as to why he had been brought in for questioning. But now he was confronted by the unsettling knowledge that he hadn't done anything wrong. The thought scared him. He couldn't lie. Silence, he figured, was his best option. Play dumb, play for time. A poker face would see him through the game.

'My client would like to know why he is here,' said Stone's solicitor, a shrewish woman whose mortgage was practically paid for by her client and his extended family's regular use of her services.

Sorrenson and Hughes looked at the solicitor, then back to Stone.

'Well, that's a very good question,' Hughes said, biting hard on a fingernail. 'A very good question. Why doesn't your client tell us why he thinks he's here?'

'I would like to remind you that my client has voluntarily attended this police station at the request of yourselves. He has not been arrested or charged. He is merely here as a public citizen, obeying a plea for co-operation from the police, which he, as a law-abiding citizen, is happy to do.'

'That's exceptionally kind of him,' Hughes muttered. 'We need more people like Mr Stone. Public citizens. Stalwarts. Obviously not exactly like him. Not people who steal performance sports cars to order and ship them out to China on supertankers. What did you get for that one, Mr Stone? Three, wasn't it? And all those cash-in-transit raids? What was your role in hiding the cash? Remind me again. And how long did the rest of your family get for their part?'

Stone continued to say nothing. He sipped his tea and glanced around the interview room. Its blank walls were familiar, comforting.

'My client's previous criminal record has no relevance,' the solicitor said. 'Now, either you tell Mr Stone what you want to ask him about or, may I suggest, gentlemen, we call it a day?'

Hughes appeared about to say something, but Sorrenson raised his hand a fraction and silenced his junior colleague. He nodded at Stone. 'We just want to pick up where we last left off, Davey. We could have done this informally, you know, over a drink, like we once did. But I'm conscious of what you said last time, that it gave you a bad reputation down in Margate to be seen with me. So, I'm sorry but this seemed the best way to go about things. How's Janine by the way?'

Stone coughed. 'Good, thanks. A boy. Seven pounds. Mother and baby doing very well. They've got really good facilities for jailed mothers in Holloway. My little girl will be out in two years.'

'Great news, Davey,' Sorrenson said. 'That's good to hear. I'm pleased for you. She's a good girl, your Janine. Just fell in with the wrong crowd. Those Vietnamese gangs, well, they take their cannabis cultivation very seriously. Don't want to go falling out with them.'

'She's learned her lesson. She only got in with them because there's no jobs down here, you know that, Mr Sorrenson. Well, no proper ones anyway. She needed the cash for the baby. She felt like she didn't have any other options. Stupid, I know. But she'll just work for her pa in the future. It's safer.'

'Excellent,' Sorrenson said. 'The family way. It's a proud Kentish underworld tradition. Now, look, Davey, thanks for coming in. Not everyone would, you know. I just wanted to go over something you mentioned in passing last time, when we brought you in for questioning over that red-diesel scam. Now, I'm not interested in whether or not you and your family have been skimming off red diesel from farms in the area. Quite frankly, I couldn't give a fuck and, truth be told, given the price of petrol, I'm not unsympathetic, but what I want to know more about is what you saw that night back in January. You remember what you told us before, yeah?'

Stone grinned. There was no reason to be alarmed. They had nothing on him. 'Yeah. I mean it was dark, obviously.'

Sorrenson read from his notes, scrawled on a pad in front of him. 'Yeah, you said it was about ten in the evening. Hardly any moon. You were visiting the smokehouse down on the beach to get some mackerel fillets.'

'Correct.'

Hughes guffawed. 'Bit late for buying fish, wasn't it?'

Stone slurped his tea. 'Bill Henry's a mate. I rang him earlier in the day and told him I wanted some the next day. Me and the boys were going out to fish off the Shivering Sands for the day and wanted to take a bit of a picnic. I explained to Bill that I couldn't pick it up until late. He was fine about it. Ask him. Check my phone records. It's all there.'

Stone liked irritating the younger detective. Sorrenson he respected, even if he was a copper. Sorrenson didn't wear his occupation heavily and, despite his name, he at least came from the same county. But Hughes, well, he was a waste of skin, really. Jumped-up Cockney doing his time before returning to the Met. He should be in Traffic, nicking people for doing nothing, Stone felt. He was the vindictive sort, Hughes, the type who liked to let grudges fester. There were stories being told about him. Stories Stone had heard.

'No need for that sort of thing, Davey.' Sorrenson decided to play peacemaker. He was anxious to place Stone back on the beach, help him refresh his memory. He kept thinking of the female agent. It would be good to have some reason for contacting her. It was her curly jet-black hair that had done it. Sucker-punched him from the start. No wedding ring, he'd noticed. He pointed at Stone. 'So, it was a dark night, no one else around, you said. You were driving back from the smoke-house down the peninsula towards the power station.'

'Right. The gritters had been there a bit before, I reckon, cos there was salt all over the road. They were expecting snow but not a lot came down in the end, as I remember. The grit chipped my fucking Beamer. Nicks all over it. The missus wasn't happy. You know how much you have to pay to get a BMW resprayed? It's criminal.'

'And then, according to the notes I took last time, you were almost forced off the road by a police van, you said.'

'Yeah. It was dark and it all happened in a blur. Going like the clappers it was. No flashing light or anything. Didn't make out any numbers on its side, just the word "Police". But it must have some sort of tracking system on it, I guess. So you guys should be able to find out where it came from. That's why I told you about it last time. If what I'm saying is true and I saw it on the peninsula road just after ten, there's no way I was nicking red diesel from Manor Farm at the same time. And why would I make up seeing a police van? Bloody strange place for one of them to appear, hey? If I was going to lie I'd at least tell you something that sounded more real. Don't see vans like that down here on the coast.'

'Did you catch the number plate?' Hughes said urgently. 'Did you see the driver?' He didn't want to appear to be letting Stone off lightly. Sorrenson was too soft. Gave his interviewees way too easy a ride. Hughes wanted to stress-test Stone, squeeze him of all his knowledge. He really wanted to know what Stone knew.

Stone shrugged. 'I was too busy trying to stop my motor ending up in a ditch. For a moment I thought I'd end up like all the others at Traitor's.'

26

'Traitor's?' Hughes frowned.

Ha, Cockney boy, you don't know your local geography, do you? Stone thought. You really are just biding your time before you go back to the Smoke. 'Yeah, Traitor's,' he said. 'Traitor's Point. Just before the lip at the end of the peninsula. Where they used to hang smugglers and suspected spies in the old days. Napoleon times. They liked to display their traitors in those days. Warning to others. Their way of keeping law and order. More effective than how they do it these days, I guess. Some people take terrible liberties. There's some bad 'uns out there.' Stone nodded at Hughes and grinned again. Hughes glared at him.

Sorrenson seemed puzzled. 'I thought I knew the area but I've never heard it called that before.'

'Well, you'd have to be pretty local, I suppose, but that's what it's called.'

'Wait a moment, will you? I'm getting a map.' Seconds later Sorrenson returned and unfolded a local Ordnance Survey map. 'Show me Traitor's Point, please, Davey.'

Stone indicated a position on the map.

By Sorrenson's estimation it was about a mile and a half from the power station and two from the airport. He remembered the first time he'd seen the body, how it had looked almost alien. Something about it, he realized, had been troubling him. There was a lack of hair. The odd wisp on the arm, but the legs were shaved smooth, like a woman's. Strange.

'Why you interested in this story anyway?' Stone was curious. He could sense the detectives were uncertain about what they were doing. It was a gift, his ability to detect uncertainty. There was opportunity in uncertainty. If he

27

could just figure out what they were after he might be able to dangle something in front of them, use it as a get-out-of-jail-free card for the next time they came calling. 'I mean, maybe it was some copper just driving like a madman to see his mistress or get the takeaway for the boys back at the station,' he said. 'Probably nothing.'

'Probably,' Hughes muttered. He stared hard at Stone.

'That's all I know,' Stone said abruptly. 'Sorry I can't be of any more help.'

Sorrenson stood up. 'Interview terminated at fifteen thirty-nine. Thanks, Davey. Very helpful. We'll be in touch.'

Stone nodded. 'No worries. Glad to have been of help. See you around.'

'Sure will,' Hughes said. He waited several seconds after Stone had left the room with his solicitor, then banged the table. 'We going to let him waltz out like that? Can't we get a warrant? Go over to his and have a rummage? At least fuck him up a bit?'

Sorrenson looked thoughtful. 'He's many things, Davey Stone, but he's not stupid. I buy his story. But the question is, is there something in it? Or, rather, is there a link between the body and the van? The van is seen in the area the night before the body's discovered, but so what? What does that prove? Someone in uniform felt an urgent need for a bit of nocturnal bird-watching? I've heard stranger. Still, Davey Stone was right about the satellite tracking. Some of them have GPS these days. If it was working we should be able to track it. Make some enquiries, will you? Ask for information on police vehicles in the area at the time. Might yield something, stop us chasing a non-lead.'

'You going to tell the spook about the van?' Hughes's face broke into a half-smile.

Sorrenson played dumb. He didn't like the way Hughes seemed to be insinuating something. He shouldn't have told him about her. He didn't like his colleagues knowing what little there was to know about his private life. 'I'm not sure she was that interested in the dead banker. I got the impression from her questions that it was more about what he did for a living, who he worked for, that really interested her. I'll sleep on it. I suppose we could do an appeal for information about the van. But it's hardly likely anyone saw it. Personally, I can't understand all the interest in the dead guy. He was just a banker. Not like he's a threat to national security. Especially not now.'

Sorrenson realized he was talking to himself. Hughes had left the interview room, dragging his anger with him. His colleague didn't buy his soft line on Stone, he knew. There would be trouble there if he wasn't careful. But sometimes, Sorrenson knew, even career criminals told the truth. It was impossible to lie about everything all the time. It was too corrosive.

Chapter 3

Dick J. Reynolds looked out of his office window and down to Ground Zero, some fifty storeys below. It was a freezing March day and snow was falling heavily in southern Manhattan. The city was going to take a battering. Yellow taxis had been blanched within minutes, and New York already resembled a giant dirty wedding cake.

Reynolds felt sorry for the construction workers below. 'Helluva way to make a living,' he would say to his colleagues on the bitterest days, when the light was failing and his thoughts turning to his comfortable commute home to Williamsburg. The colleagues would nod dumbly, then return to their computer screens, leaving Reynolds angry. It was all very well the agency hiring these rocket scientists – and they were rocket scientists, all of them straight out of MIT – but, well, intelligence was ultimately a people game, Reynolds believed, and he was playing it with robots.

In his crueller moments Reynolds wondered just how absent of personality someone had to be to enjoy working in his elite team within the National Security Agency's arcane Financial Intelligence Unit, a specialist division that worked closely with the Central Intelligence Agency and was a core member of EWAN, the Early Warning Alert Network, which produced detailed threat assessments for the Pentagon.

Most of his staff, Reynolds felt, would be single for a very long time – they were introspective, awkward and lacking in people skills. It was frustrating, the lack of camaraderie. God, he missed the Cold War. But, then, everyone his age – he was sixty-two – said that, and he didn't want to become that most terrible thing in the spy world, an object of pity, someone pushing a pen waiting for their retirement. He was better than that.

Reynolds often wondered whether he should have taken another overseas station posting instead of joining the unit. There had been an opening in Poland he'd been quite interested in, but Teri, his second wife, wasn't keen: she was too settled. She had a good network of friends and the twins were happy at school. They had spent years trying for children and the boys had been a tremendous blessing but they came with hefty price tags. His options had been seriously reduced by impregnation. So he was left managing rocket scientists.

'It's a job with great potential,' Carey, the deputy head of the FIU, had told him. 'No one has done this before. You can be a real hero. Take the ball and run with it. Run far. See Dick run.'

Only, as far as Reynolds could tell, in the eight years they'd been operating, his team had achieved nothing in terms of their original aim, a big fat zero, of which he was reminded every time he looked out of the window and down to where the Twin Towers had stood. It wasn't that they were lazy or ineffectual, his staff. It was just that the thing they'd been set up to detect wasn't happening. Probably. It was difficult to detect the non-existent, Reynolds conceded. Even the rocket scientists, the ones who specialized in scarily non-existent stuff – dark matter, for example – had yet to crack how to detect something that wasn't happening.

When Reynolds had tried to explain to Teri what he did he'd found it impossible. But, over the years, he'd developed an efficient, albeit clumsy description. 'I manage a team of very clever people,' he would tell certain people he trusted. 'They build computer programs, algorithms, to monitor unusual trading patterns in the world's stock markets. We believe that sometimes the markets can provide us with an early warning that something bad, something terrible, is coming down the track. And if we can act quick enough, we figure we might be able to stop it. The market is never wrong. It sees everything. It is the most efficient creation in the world. And now, because you've got all these super-computers performing high-frequency trades almost at the speed of light, the stakes are huge. One big player makes a bet and it's immediately picked up by all the others in the market and they pile in. No one can afford to be left behind when the market swings. It can make for huge movements. Lot of volatility, potentially.'

Normally people would nod dumbly and say something like, 'Yeah, I understand.'

And then Reynolds would feel even more frustrated. The more intelligent would say something about 9/11. 'Like the share trading patterns of the airlines before those planes hit the Towers?' they'd say. Reynolds would smile and stroke his ginger moustache, which clashed comically with his grey hair, and say, 'Yeah, just like that. You got it, good on you.

You understand the importance of all this. Next time, they're not going to aim at skyscrapers. They'll aim higher. Terrorism is inflationary, you know. They need to pull a bigger rabbit out of the hat to keep the fear factor alive. Maybe they'll try to hijack a plane full of Chinese and load it up with a dirty bomb. Then they're going to fly it at the White House and the president is going to have make the decision to shoot it down. That'll trigger World War Three. We really don't want that to happen. We want Nine/Eleven to be the wake-up call to end all wake-up calls, something that, in the long run, makes us more alert, safer, stronger. Resilient. You understand?'

It was true. Without 9/11, Reynolds's team wouldn't exist. It was the Pentagon's deep suspicion that key individuals in the financial world had known the attack was coming and had shorted airline shares by unloading them to unsuspecting third parties. Someone had made a killing when the Towers came down. The suspicion had led to the creation of the elaborately titled DOPIPISMA – the Detection of Potential Irregular Patterns In the Stock Market Agency, an acronym Reynolds hated with a passion engendered by decades spent fighting Agency-speak and, in particular, the spying world's love of arcane codifiers.

What Reynolds didn't explain in his little briefings to trusted contacts, however, was that even the combined might of the United States' most powerful security agencies had found it difficult to penetrate the byzantine world of high finance, with its hidden offshore accounts, front companies and taciturn bankers, who were paid so much that it was difficult to turn them into or, indeed, force them to become intelligence assets. In fact, the agencies had found it near impossible to get any sort of oversight of the situation at all. Tracking weapons-grade plutonium they could do. Tracking hot money was far more difficult.

It was, Reynolds eventually decided, a structural problem. When they had started out they had been simply a bunch of men (and they were all men, with bad haircuts, hygiene issues and, for a surprising number of them, an unhealthy interest in Tolkien) who crunched financial data the way others traded baseball statistics. They lacked penetration, Reynolds had told his seniors, in a confidential memo that had somehow found its way onto the front of the *New York Times*. The memo had suggested more resources should be spent on the no-longer-top-secret project, or it would be classed a total failure and a colossal waste of the American taxpayer's hard-earned cash. It would be embarrassing for those who had championed the project, Reynolds's leaked memo implied. It would be difficult for those people to progress further in their careers if things continued as they were.

That had been 2005. No one had heard about Reynolds's team after that. There was speculation that the project had been closed down. It was difficult to confirm, though. The various security agencies' budgets were so impenetrable that no one could be sure where the money passed by Congress was going.

But a more astute observer, Reynolds would concede, might have learned something by tracing the money flowing into the FIU rather than out of it. Now, that might yield some really interesting intel. Because Reynolds and his team had been, for a while at least, the most unusual of things in the spook world. They were a profitable business, a net provider to the rest of the US security-agency apparatus. Almost by accident Reynolds and his team had built a bank. And, almost equally by accident, their bank, Higgs Bank, had quickly become a financial leviathan, the twelfth largest in the US and one that had operations on five continents. It was Reynolds's dirty little secret, Higgs. Ostensibly, Reynolds was a member of the intelligence community. Secretly he was a banker. His late father, once a leading light in the Teamsters Union, would have been dismayed by the revelation, Reynolds knew. Banking was a dirty word in his family.

There was a skewed but brilliant logic in how Higgs operated. With impressive alacrity, Reynolds had grasped the main problem with what they were doing. It was, Reynolds had told his bosses, 'fucking impossible' to monitor chaos. There was so much going on in the chaos, so many things taking place in impenetrable and unlikely corners of the globe, that they had no hope of monitoring what was happening.

So Reynolds had gone old school. Borrowing from his early days in the field, he suggested that the unit consider doing the very things they wanted to observe, just to ensure that they were observable. It was, he suggested, similar to when they had given the Iranians around 90 per cent of the technology they needed to build a nuclear weapon. It meant they pretty much knew where the Iranians were in their nuclear programme so they could prevent them acquiring the vital remaining 10 per cent they needed to seal the deal. The Iranians spent so much time trying to get the 90 per cent to work that they had no time to focus on the remainder. So why not do the same in banking? It was high risk, Reynolds admitted, but high finance was a high-stakes game, from what he'd learned observing the big beasts on Wall Street. There were big rewards for success. He down-played the risks.

His suggestion, as Reynolds predicted, had been greeted with incredulous silence. But Reynolds was not to be deterred. He had his response prepared. He had practised for hours in front of the mirror, hours in front of Teri.

'Just hear me out on this one, OK?' he'd said. 'At the moment we have nothing. We don't know if anyone's doing what we fear they could be doing. We can't monitor it – all these transactions are taking place out of sight across com-puter systems that even the NSA finds it hard to hack into. But if, say, we set up our own system, we can monitor the activity and then we might just get lucky.'

A venture capital firm operated by the CIA found the initial seed capital to set up the bank, which was quietly given a licence by the US Treasury.

And then had come the PR war. A series of strategically leaked stories months after its creation hinted that Higgs was very much the go-to bank for those who wanted to deposit their money with the minimum of questions asked. As a result, many of the Mexican drug cartels started laundering their cash through Higgs accounts. Sudanese, Iraqi and Iranian military leaders also became enthusiastic clients, although most of their money seemed to be spent by their wives in the stores of Fifth Avenue.

Higgs prospered. It gained a reputation as a bank that would go the extra mile to ensure its clients' wishes were fulfilled. With offices in all the main tax havens, including the Cayman Islands, the Turks and Caicos Islands and the

British Virgin Islands, the bank was able to monitor the activities of its more dubious clients, all the while feeding the information back to the FIU, the NSA and the CIA.

But, still, there was little forthcoming in the way of intelligence. There was hefty and prosaic money-laundering, mainly for drug cartels and Eastern European Mafia, but nothing that would have triggered a national security crisis. No one, it seemed, was betting on the apocalypse arriving again any time soon. Or if they were, there was no sign that they were doing it through Higgs. Reynolds didn't know whether to feel relieved or disappointed. He half thought about closing the whole thing down.

But Higgs lurched on, a drunk unable to slake its thirst. It picked fights, became acquisitive. Reynolds had only just managed to prevent it making an offer for Lehman Brothers, such was the hubris of its stooge directors. No one paid much attention to its finances, its capital base. Markets were booming. People were getting rich everywhere. Reynolds started to grow bored with the whole operation.

And then Holahon had turned up on some British beach, headless and handless.

He would never admit it publicly, but Reynolds was actually half pleased when news of the grisly death of a senior employee had come through. If nothing else, it offered a distraction from the tedious world of banking, which, Reynolds had recently learned, was actually in danger of becoming very interesting.

Even to his untrained eye, Higgs seemed to be building up a lot of debt. The rocket scientists had assured him that all banks were being stretched and that, to use their favourite word, 'strategically' it made sense. But, still, something didn't feel right. Anxiety burned inside him like a stomach ulcer. He continued to grill his rocket scientists.

'We need to keep leveraging,' they explained.

Reynolds nodded. 'Right,' he would say. 'Right.'

But the truth was he was too embarrassed to ask what they meant. Reynolds would look out of his window and envy the construction workers below. They had simple tasks that yielded physical, tactile results. He, however, was growing less certain of what he was doing by the day. Leveraging? What the fuck did that even mean?

The murder would help, he thought. It would calm him. Remind him of old times. You knew where you were with a corpse. The dead made more sense than money.

When the news first came in from London that Holahon was missing, Reynolds had enjoyed the flashbacks. He'd known Holahon quite well, once. Both had been active in Eastern Europe during the late eighties and early nineties, although never at the same station. They had swapped intel a few times, he recalled, mainly about arms shipments and smuggled uranium. It was good, clean, dirty stuff, like New York snow.

And look at them now, Reynolds had thought. Both bankers. Except one kept his role hidden. Holahon wasn't even aware that Reynolds was effectively his boss. Reynolds kept a very low profile at Higgs. His name was nowhere to be found in the bank. Everything had to be done through back channels and third parties. He was a puppet master who didn't want to meet his puppets.

But the lines were becoming tangled, confused. It was a giant squid, Higgs. It had so many tentacles that no part knew what the other parts of its anatomy were doing. Bits could be cut off, sold, closed, disbanded, and it would survive. Higgs was like the internet, Reynolds often thought. It was designed to withstand a nuclear war. Well, that was possibly taking it a bit far, but not *too* far. It was a feared, all-powerful organism. The irony, which Reynolds tried not to think about too much, was that Higgs had been created for noble reasons, to protect the citizens of the United States, and yet it had assumed in many people's minds the persona of a comic-book villain: reviled, mocked, feared. No, Reynolds thought, there wouldn't be many people outside the world of high finance who would mourn the passing of a murdered banker.

At first, Higgs's internal security team, a highly remunerated collection of former CIA and Mossad agents, sprinkled with SAS and SBS officers to provide the muscle and the prestige, had simply flagged Holahon's unexpected disappearance as 'Green Three' – their code for a suspected personal breakdown. History suggested that Green Three often ended with a suicide, an exit which, if initiated in London, usually involved the employee leaping off the roof terrace of a well-regarded City restaurant that boasted 'breath-taking views'.

But within days of the security team making discreet enquiries, Green Three became Amber Three as it became apparent that Holahon had not defenestrated himself and was not to be found in any of the country's leading recuperative retreats that specialized in caring for burned-out City types. It was the transition from Green to Amber that had triggered the sending of a message to Reynolds.

'We've got a potential situation over here,' the memo had

explained. 'Brad Holahon gone AWOL. It is a concern, given his position.'

Reynolds had understood what the security team were saying, albeit obliquely. Holahon knew where the bodies were buried. Or some of them. A dead Holahon they could cope with. A gibbering, loose-lipped, nervy Holahon was a liability. And, while Reynolds was confident that Holahon wasn't one of the elite who were aware just how much Higgs was a front for America's security services, he must have had his suspicions, given his background, suspicions that would prove explosive if they ever found their way into the public domain.

Reynolds had drafted the response memo himself. If the balloon ever went up and the emails were sequestered by some NSA computer, they were plausibly anodyne. They were simply the memos of a concerned boss. No fingerprints.

'Do find Mr Holahon,' Reynolds's email had read. 'We must do everything within our power to ensure he gets our support. For his own sake we request that you find him urgently.'

A couple of days later the security team had responded with new information: 'Urgent. We believe we know of Mr Holahon's whereabouts. You may want to come over here to instruct us how best we can proceed.'

Reynolds had flown out the same day. Holahon's body was found on the beach less than a week later. Reynolds wrote Holahon's obituary for the bank's intranet system. It noted that he had been an avid runner.

★　★　★

She ran her hand through her thick black hair and stared at herself in the long mirror running behind the optics and the glass shelves laden with expensive bottles of gin and vodka. She sat on a stool nursing a whisky sour in front of what was reputedly the longest zinc bar in Europe. It was a strange claim to fame, she felt. Who wanted that much bar? That much mirror? Well, Kate knew the answer to that question. She did. She needed perspective.

From her vantage-point, she had almost thirty metres of reflection to appraise. She could spot targets either side with ease, all the while pretending to be immersed in her copy of the *New Yorker* and a hard-earned cocktail at the end of a long day.

Only she wasn't really drinking the cocktail. She needed a clear head if she was to identify a target. She studied herself, studied her targets. The lipstick, she felt, was the give-away. She might as well have put a neon sign above her head saying 'Easy'. Her eyes were so rimmed with kohl that she felt as if she was looking out of a cave. The skirt was far too short for a forty-year-old. She'd had to change in the Ladies' after arriving. It wouldn't be great for her colleagues to see her vamping it up. It was a censorious place, MI5.

But she wasn't embarrassed about her appearance. She looked good, she knew. She had clocked the stares when she'd walked in, taken a seat at the bar. They had given her confidence. Not that she really needed it. The boots helped, gave her an extra three inches so that she was almost six foot two. And, besides, she was just doing what animals did all the time, puffing themselves up, showing themselves off to seek a mate. She really needed a mate. The run hadn't been enough. She had way, way too much energy and it was either sex or a lot of drink, and she couldn't take the hangovers any more. She needed to escape for a while.

She selected targets. Embassy types mainly. Suits but no ties. A smattering of academics who'd been attending one of the foreign-policy think tanks that seemed to cluster around the edge of Hyde Park and acted as a magnet for putative MI6 types.

Her gaze settled on the broad back of a thick-set thirty-something. In a few years he would be all fat. But now . . . Well, now there was potential. He was wearing a wedding ring. Good: it was unlikely there would be any complications.

The man turned round as if scalded by her stare. She held his gaze. It was just like being back at university, really. If they held your eye for more than eight seconds they were yours, she had learned in her first energetic weeks at college. They were so pliant, especially the ones who believed they weren't. They were the easiest, the ones who thought they were in control. Their egos kidded them into believing her interest was inevitable. But she wasn't interested in them. She was only interested in what they could do for her. They were all members of her personal escape committee.

Six seconds. Seven seconds. Eight seconds. She continued to hold the man's gaze. He said something to his friends and walked towards her. She was pleased the others hadn't turned around. That was a good omen. He didn't seem the boastful sort. As he approached she felt a flicker of irritation. He was younger than she had first thought. He had the smooth, untroubled skin of someone born into money. There was a signet ring on the little finger of his left hand. Figures, she thought. It was that kind of bar. But it wasn't the privileged background that was troubling her. It was more his age. She must be . . . what? Thirteen, fourteen years older than him. Still, it was a bit late now. The target had been identified. The launch sequence had commenced.

She wondered which chat-up line he would use. The buy-you-a-drink one was the most obvious, of course, but he didn't seem the type. There was a lightness about the way he walked that suggested confidence. Confident people tended to avoid the worst clichés, she found. It was like they didn't need the comfort of them. They had other stuff to fill the awkward gaps. The comedy approach would be almost unbearable. She imagined the conversation.

'Did it hurt?'

'When?'

'When you fell from Heaven.'

God, no. Comedy wouldn't do. He was just a few metres from her now. He was handsome, very handsome. A broad, strong stag. Got you in my crosshairs, she thought.

'So,' he said.

A Scottish accent. A small thrill surged through her. She collected accents. She had a bedroom full of them. His sounded like it had rolled down from the Highlands. 'So,' she said, staring at him in the mirror.

'I'm figuring you want me to fuck you.'

The direct approach. Bingo. The evening was going well. She continued staring at their reflection. She was imagining him on top of her, behind her. He looked like he had stamina. And he wasn't drunk. Another tick. 'Just don't tell me your name,' she said, still staring into the mirror. 'I'm really not that interested in you.'

He slipped an arm around her back and helped her off

her stool. She left her magazine on the longest zinc bar in Europe.

The prince watched his peacock strut towards the peahen with almost paternal pride. He preferred falcons, but there was something about the ostentation of peacocks that he found charming. And, besides, what good was an English mansion without peacocks? He liked to watch their clumsy attempts at flight. They could barely make five metres before having to land. They were just too big to be airborne. They were like abandoned jumbo jets in the Mojave Desert, he thought. Big old relics from another era. Nothing that proud, that useless, should have survived extinction. And yet they were still going. They endured. Truly remarkable.

The prince examined his BlackBerry and read a series of emails. The thought of jet planes had reminded him of his airport project. Faisal was enthusiastic about it too, he'd discovered. Where that enthusiasm had come from he couldn't say, but father and son agreed that the project had possibilities. The prince smiled to himself. Yes, there would come a time for those possibilities to surface.

But that was months off. There was much work to be done, starting with the repair of the runway. It would need to be reinforced, restructured, if it was regularly to take bigger planes.

Carlyle materialized at his shoulder. 'Sorry to interrupt you, Your Highness.'

'Thomas, no problem. You never interrupt, you know that. My gain is the pizza world's loss.'

It was a joke with which Carlyle had become familiar down the years. He smiled at his employer. 'Too kind. I thought you should know that Brad Holahon is dead. I'm not sure how he died, the obituaries are unclear, but I thought you would want to read this.' Carlyle handed him a two-week-old copy of *The Times*. 'I'm sorry, I've only just learned of this. Otherwise I would, of course, have drawn it to Your Highness's attention earlier.'

The prince raised his hands as if to forgive Carlyle's tardiness. 'This is a grave matter, is it not?'

Carlyle nodded. 'Mr Holahon will be greatly missed,' he said. 'He has been a great help to you and your family. He advised on many of your investments, a lot of those dotcom IPOs, I seem to remember, and, of course, he had personal oversight of your bank accounts. He was a very reliable, discreet man. Totally trustworthy. I've always felt safe knowing your money was with Holahon at Higgs.'

'Mmm, yes,' the prince said, stroking his beard. A flutter of wings signalled the peacock was attempting to fly up to a nearby branch. The two men watched its awkward ascent. 'He thinks he is a king, doesn't he?' the prince said, gesturing towards the bird. 'But he isn't. He is all show. The peahen sees his beauty, sees him high up there on the branch and she is seduced. But she will be less impressed when he comes down. He will crash to earth. It will be ugly. Perhaps Mr Holahon crashed to earth? We all must come down in the end.'

The two men looked at each other for several seconds. Their eyes seemed to be having a private conversation. They turned their collective gaze back to the peacock.

'Yes, a preposterous bird,' the prince said. 'It really has no right to exist in this world when you think of it. But praise be that it does. The world is more colourful for it.'

Carlyle made to walk away. A thin rain had started to fall in the late March afternoon. There had been talk of snow blowing in from the States.

'Please, Thomas,' the prince murmured, 'do me a great favour, if you will. Find out who else knows the circumstances of his death. I hope we understand each other.'

'It will be a great pleasure,' Carlyle responded. He pulled his BlackBerry from his jacket pocket and glanced at his watch. It would be coming up to eleven in the morning in New York. Time to rattle some cages. He knew who he was going to call first.

It was a morning ritual that had still not become familiar. Every time she approached MI5's bomb-proof security doors, the reinforced-glass cylinders that swooshed open and then shut to allow only one person through at a time, Kate was surprised that they granted her entry. Welcome to the covert, they seemed to say to her. Secrets cannot escape from us. We lock them in. When you come through us, you are entering a different world. In here, everything is sealed, everything is recondite.

The guilt from the night before seemed to stick to her, like a stain on her dress. It had been OK at the time. Better than OK, in fact. It had been diverting. But the legacy of the promiscuity, the glow that came after the strangely impersonal intimacy, felt simultaneously alien and familiar. She was grateful that her next quarterly psychological assessment wasn't for another two-and-a-half months. The last had caused her assessor to raise his eyebrows.

'You remind me of a chap we had in MI6,' he had told her. 'Some quarters he would get top marks. The next he would be right at the bottom. He blew hot and cold. Had a breakdown in the end. Not sure where he ended up. Some suggestion he went a bit rogue. That's showbiz, as they say.'

She promised herself she would improve. She would run more, go out less. Maybe rejoin that running club, the one Michael had introduced her to. She would visit her mother that evening. She would take the family album and allow the woman who had brought her into the world to ruthlessly sully the past. Yes, Margaret Pendragon would enjoy that.

But now, as she contemplated a hurried, puritanical lunch of guilt-cleansing steamed greens and soba noodles, all her promises were in danger of evaporating. It had been almost four years since Michael had died, and most days she felt as if she was dissolving, that her entire being was fizzing away to nothing, like an aspirin in water. There would be a little more effervescence and then she would vanish completely.

The doors swooshed open as she returned with her lunch from the noodle bar down the road. She walked into the cylinder and waited for its iris scanners to recognize her. Another swoosh and she was through into the vast atrium that boasted an impressive living wall and a wide, wood-panelled reception desk that wouldn't have looked out of place in the Savoy. Her pumps felt the reassuring brush of a marbled floor. Such grandeur, she thought. And virtually nobody gets to see it.

'Ah, there you are. Thought you'd done a runner or something.' McLure bounded up to her.

She was disconcerted by his enthusiasm. There had been none of that when they had been . . . She attempted to erase the thought. It had been another time, and she had been another self. She was starting again. A clean skin. Year zero. She smiled at him. 'Sorry, needed carbs. Anyway, back now. Why are you so sprightly?'

'Well, could be because the fucking skip has gone at last but it's more likely to be because I've got a trip to the Big Apple coming. I haven't been to New York for years. We went there shortly after our honeymoon, I remember. I wanted to go to the Met, she wanted to do Saks. Total nightmare. Should have known it wouldn't last right then.'

She nodded. 'Business or pleasure?'

'Business.'

'Right. I'm guessing our friends across the water want to talk to you about those Higgs accounts we've been looking at. All the money-laundering stuff in my report? The risk assessment?'

'Yes.'

McLure frowned. She sensed he wasn't enjoying her quick-fire questions. But she had a right to ask them. It was her report that McLure was waving at the Americans. She wanted to know why he was using it as bait. What was he hoping to land?

'They know we're still looking at Holahon?' She watched McLure's face crease further.

'I mentioned he was a person of interest to us, yes. I stressed we were keeping an open mind about whether his death was linked to his professional life. Told them we weren't currently responsible for investigating the murder and that it was incidental to our interest in Higgs. I asked

49

for their help and, unusually, they seemed keen to comply. Very keen, in fact. Maybe I was a bit harsh on them last time I mentioned it. Perhaps the special relationship still exists after all. I mean, it does whenever they want us to turn a blind eye to their movement of high-value terrorist suspects through Diego Garcia. Thank God for the far-flung remnants of the British empire. They're very useful for hiding bad people. Makes us still of some use to the Americans.'

They walked towards the bank of lifts at the far corner of the atrium. A large notice-board carried fliers seeking recruits for the staff football team, discounts on Pilates classes and hypnotherapy sessions for smokers trying to quit. It could be any office in the world, she thought. And, come to think of it, providing security wasn't very different from, say, providing finance. Both were about insurance, risk assessment. It was just about sifting information, really, working out what was good and what had to be rejected. If it wasn't for the bullshit machismo and the ludicrous self-aggrandizing mythology that was attached to working for the security services, her job would be branded dull. Well, she could cope with dull. Michael couldn't cope with dull. That had been his problem. Her problem now. They walked into a lift. She turned to McLure. 'Strange, though, their eagerness to play ball. The Americans.'

'I agree. At first they didn't seem too bothered, but then I mentioned the stuff you found in Switzerland, the Caymans and Liechtenstein and suddenly it was game on. They couldn't see me soon enough. I'll go out tomorrow and tack some holiday on at the end. On our salaries we have to do these things. Pitiful, really. If people knew what we earned beyond the entry levels they'd never join. Not a problem for our American friends, of course. Intelligence is one giant money tree over there.'

The lift door pinged open. She turned. 'I'll do some more checking. Strange coincidence, but Higgs's biggest client, a Saudi prince, owns a mansion just over a mile from where Holahon's body was found. He owns an airport nearby, too. He is what the City calls a whale, the sort of client whose massive wealth can almost make or break a bank, depending on how much of it he pumps through its coffers. Completely unconnected, I guess, but interesting.'

They stopped outside her office. McLure placed a hand on her elbow. He seemed genuinely concerned, she thought. Jesus, she must look bad if McLure was showing her sympathy. 'You OK?' he said.

'Fine. Just coming up to the anniversary. It shouldn't make a difference but it does, you know.'

'I know. I really do. You'll get there. Don't rush things.'

'Thanks. It means a lot.'

McLure smiled at her. 'That's what I'm here for. That's what I should always have been here for. It's only when you rush into things that you make mistakes.'

She watched McLure walk down the corridor. He was contradictory, sleazy, impulsive, petulant, kind, thoughtful, fearful. He was human. There was nothing special about spies, she thought. For all their quarterly psychological assessments, they were just like everyone else. Frightened of being alone. Frightened of making the wrong call. Frightened of not leaving anything behind.

Chapter 4

Sorrenson studied the scene before him. A strong wind was up and the Channel was being whipped into white foam. Gusts battered the peninsula's shore. A brilliant April sun burned down on Traitor's Point and in the distance he could see kite surfers looping in the wind. If he were five years younger he'd give the sport a go, he thought. It was unlike any other activity he'd ever seen. On the windiest days, the surfers could fly for long, fat seconds some ten or so metres above the sea. They rose effortlessly, like they were wearing jetpacks, before sliding down to skim across the waves, trailing arcs of white spume behind them.

But he was almost closer to fifty than forty and it would seem such a cliché to take up the sport – the typical action of a man having a mid-life crisis. He'd stick to running. Running was basically a way of stopping time, resisting entropy. It was a form of insurance, taken out against growing old. The more pain, the more sweat, the better it was for you.

He walked towards Bill Henry's hut. Two wooden fishing boats had been hauled up onto the shore by a rusting winch that belonged in a museum. Bill Henry, the only active fisherman on the peninsula, was sitting in a decrepit canvas picnic chair in front of the shack, looking out to sea. He turned when he heard Sorrenson's trainers scuffing shingle. 'Davey said you might turn up. Surprised you haven't come round sooner.'

Sorrenson nodded at him. 'All right, Bill. Thought I'd pay you a visit while I was out running. I'm in no rush to hassle you. You get enough grief from us as it is. Keep it informal, like. How's the fishing?'

'Useless as always. There's fuck-all for us to catch, these days. Some mackerel, the odd whiting. But, well, there's a reason no fishing boats operate off here any more, Mr Sorrenson. More money to be had working the tills in a supermarket.'

Sorrenson had heard Henry's sob story several times. He knew it was highly fictionalized. Henry was capable of spinning lies longer than fishing lines. 'How come you keep going, then?' Humour him, Sorrenson thought. Let him get comfortable behind his mask.

Henry shrugged. 'Well, I don't really. The money I make is from taking people out on fishing trips for the day. Londoners mainly, happy to catch the odd one with a line.' He gestured around him. 'This . . . well, it hardly pays anything now. I'm doing it more because my father and his father before him did it. Kind of out of respect for them. Not because it pays the rent.' He held up a net for Sorrenson to inspect.

'Lonely place out here.' Sorrenson pointed down the peninsula.

'Depends what you mean by lonely. No shortage of life here. It's got one of the largest, most important bird populations in Europe. Not that the planners gave a stuff when they approved the airport's expansion. I'm not sure why anyone thinks it's a good idea to build an airport next to millions of birds. The chance of bird-strike must be sky high, forgive the pun. Still, could be worse. It might be located next to a nuclear power station. Imagine if a jumbo hit that. It would be Armageddon. Jesus, give me strength.'

Henry offered Sorrenson a cigarette.

'No, thanks.'

'No, you don't seem the type,' Henry said, looking at the detective's running shorts and vest.

Sorrenson cleared his throat. 'You know the reason I'm here.'

'Right. Davey's telling you the truth. He turned up just after ten that night and bought around ten smoked mackerel from me.'

'For what it's worth, I believe him. Did you hear anything, see anyone?'

Henry shook his head. 'Nah. Davey told me about the van but I never heard nothing. Possibly because I was stoned out of my box and playing my music loud. Steeleye Span.'

'Yeah, well, go easy on that stuff. The music, I mean – it can seriously damage your health. Just stick to the drugs. If you think of anything else about that night, give me a ring, OK?' Sorrenson handed Henry his card and turned to leave.

The other man laughed. 'Right you are. I take it this is about the body?'

'What body?' Sorrenson was surprised. There had been no media release to confirm that a body had been found. There had been a news blackout while they attempted to identify the deceased. And then the security services had got involved and slapped a D Notice on the affair and everything had been buried. It was almost as if, officially, it had never washed up on the beach. But, still, too many people knew what had happened, Sorrenson accepted. The schoolchildren would have talked. Most of the coast would know by now. Rumours were a form of currency down there.

'The body they found, down at Traitor's. People at your station talk in pubs, Sorrenson.'

'Well, they shouldn't.'

'But they do. Loose lips and all that. I never saw the body, if that's what you're wondering. I was away when it was found. At my sister's. Check if you want.'

It was Sorrenson's turn to laugh. 'You're not under suspicion, Bill.'

'Well, strikes me I should be. Or at least someone local.'

'What do you mean?'

'Well, if I have it right, the body was found up on the beach, right on the lip of Traitor's Point.'

'Right.'

'I've lived my whole life on this peninsula.'

'OK.'

'And I can tell you for free that nothing washes up on the beach at Traitor's. The tide either takes stuff far out or it drags it round the coast towards Dover.'

'So, what are you telling me? That this was a freak incident?'

'Possibly, but I doubt it. Ask yourself how a body is found metres up a beach that borders a sea that never gives up its property.'

Sorrenson felt uneasy. He had missed something. They had all missed something.

'Because it was never in the sea in the first place.' Henry puffed his cigarette, grinned up at the midday sun. 'Traitor's Point. Interesting place to leave a body, don't you think? Like someone wanted to leave a message. Some sort of memorial or something.'

Reynolds examined the documents laid out on his desk in front of him. He could, he knew, look at them on screen, but it felt more reassuring to have them in a hard copy. And it was hard copy. It was unfathomable, impenetrable, the information in front of him, a seemingly endless list of numbers, codes and letters. Higgs had super-computers that functioned almost at the speed of light and understood it all, Reynolds reassured himself. But, still, the idea scared him. It was like something out of science fiction. We're being run by machines, he thought.

Gelner coughed, cleared his throat. Reynolds looked at his deputy warily. His sixth sense suggested that bad news was hurtling towards him. The collision seemed to be imminent and powerful.

'So, these are the accounts British intelligence have asked us to help them with,' Gelner said. 'Holahon helped set them all up. All in tax havens.'

'Right.' Reynolds braced himself for the explosion.

'Most of the accounts are fine,' Gelner went on. 'Nothing to worry about. Holahon did a lot of work for Russian oligarchs. The accounts launder hot money mainly through Cyprus but nothing that we feel has national security implications. It was, I guess still is, mainly large-scale tax avoidance rather than downright evasion. Quasi-legal. The

Brits won't care about that sort of thing. Pretty low-grade stuff. Nothing revealing. They start messing around with all this, their own tax havens will kick off and they don't want that.'

'Go on.'

Gelner squinted out of the window at the New York spring morning. He was trying to find the right words. The less incendiary the better.

'If it's going to come out at the end it may as well come out at the beginning,' Reynolds snapped. 'Kissinger's maxim is a good one when you're in a difficult spot.'

Gelner pushed his frameless glasses back up his nose. 'OK. Well, bottom line is that one of the accounts they're interested in belongs to an intelligence asset.'

'Which one?'

'Our favourite prince.'

'Aldud?'

Gelner nodded.

'Jesus.' Reynolds felt sick. Over the years the prince had fed the FIU useful information in return for the US authorities taking little interest in his business dealings. It was the perfect symbiotic relationship but it would dissolve if it was dragged into the public glare.

'Yeah, right,' Gelner said, watching his boss's face burn red with fury. 'It's a difficult one.'

'Yeah,' Reynolds said. 'You don't say. What was the Aldud account used for?'

'Two things. It received bribes, kickbacks on arms deals. The prince, you may remember from your intel briefings, was in charge of arms procurement for various Middle Eastern regimes. He arranged a lot of deals for the big US military contractors. His slice of the deal went into the account. Then things got a bit hot and we had to close that down. There was a court case and various arms manufacturers had to pay some pretty substantial fines, if you remember. But the account was also used to buy arms – hundreds of thousands of Kalashnikovs and smaller numbers of pistols, Italian Berettas mostly. They were shipped across Europe from China and various Central Asian countries. Most found their way to Africa. We lost track of a lot of them. Some ended up in the hands of terrorist factions in Iraq, if you recall.'

Reynolds recalled. He'd approved of the plan. It had been genius. By facilitating the arms deals they'd been able to track the shipment of weapons around the globe. It meant they could gauge the scale of imminent bloodshed by the number of weapons pouring into a conflict zone. It had provided useful information.

But it wasn't something many in Congress would have understood, Reynolds knew. There were some things that had to be held back for the good of the nation. The US had enough to worry about, with the economy and global warming and high-school killings. It didn't need to fret about its part in fuelling international conflict as well. And, besides, Higgs wasn't doing anything illegal. The bank and the FIU had a mandate. Somebody had signed off on it somewhere. It was exactly the sort of transaction that Higgs was supposed to facilitate. It was just better not to draw too much attention to it. Reynolds pointed at Gelner. 'What do we tell the Brits?'

Gelner shook his head. 'Don't know. I'm not paid for my foreign-policy advice. You need to get some help with this. Take it up with Carey.'

Reynolds looked out of his window. The morning held the promise of warmth. It was going to be a beautiful day, a fine day to be out of doors. It was a good day to be a construction worker, Reynolds thought.

She studied the artwork with an open mind. She didn't want her knowledge of the artists – or, rather, the condition of the artists – to influence her opinion. That would not be fair to them, Kate felt. That would be a betrayal.

Most of the art exhibited on the corridor's walls took the form of striking oil paintings, large canvases with bold colours. There was little room for nuance, she appreciated. The brush strokes looked hurried. Understandable. When you had only weeks left to live you were unlikely to be too concerned with the minutiae. It was all about the big picture, really. The abstract. You wanted to get something down on canvas urgently. You wanted to have something to leave behind. Anything.

'Mrs Pendragon is ready to see you now.' A nurse materialized at her shoulder. Kate turned her gaze away from the palliative-care art exhibition and walked slowly down the corridor to her mother's room towards the rear of the private hospital. She carried the family photo album. On her face she fixed a smile.

She was shocked by her mother's appearance. Her face was grey and dull, and she was so frail, so small. There was barely anything left of her. She seemed to be disappearing by the minute; her thin wrists looked as if they would snap if she tried to lift a teacup. Her hair, of which she had once been so proud, hung in wisps on her head. It was grotesque.

Her mother was much more dead than alive yet still she clung on. But, then, she had always been stubborn. She had needed to be, given her husband. Kate bent down and kissed her cold forehead.

Her mother groaned and opened her eyes. For several minutes she said nothing while she examined her daughter through half-dead eyes. 'So,' she said at last.

'So I'm here and, like we discussed a couple of nights ago, I've brought the album. The early one of you, me and Dad.'

Her mother remained silent. Kate thought she detected a slight nod, a tremble of affirmation. She opened the album, flicked through the photos, held up the pages for her mother to see. She waited for the onslaught. Even bile was better than nothing.

In the first weeks of her mother's terminal illness, she'd watched with horror as a cocktail of drugs had wreaked their toxic havoc. Her mother had gone from being a strong, dignified woman, proud of her achievements, of her marriage, of her daughter, to a poison-dripping Gorgon whom Kate didn't recognize. Her hazel eyes seemed to have turned almost jet black in the half-light of the room and her teeth had yellowed. Her deathly appearance seemed to become more dramatic with each visit. Kate had come to dread making the trip from her central London flat to the hospital on the edge of Regent's Park.

Her mother, Margaret, known to all as Maggie, pointed at a photo. Kate examined the image. It was of her and her parents in Keswick in the Lake District. They were at a pencil museum, of all things. She'd been fascinated by the special pencils with the hollowed-out insides in which Second World War spies had hidden coded messages. Now such things seemed ridiculously quaint. It was all super-computers and encrypted numbers and codes moving at close to the speed of light. Everything had become so much more complex and less interesting. Spying was no exception. Her mother tapped the photo with a finger. 'I hated that holiday,' she rasped. 'Why did we have to go somewhere dreary? Why couldn't he take us abroad like other families? Somewhere warm.'

Cancer couldn't just kill you once, Kate had come to realize. It could kill you many times as the pain and the drugs polluted your body and mind, turned you into someone else, someone who could hate. Her mother had loved all their holidays, especially the ones in the Lakes. Come to think of it, she'd been less keen on the exotic trips abroad. She'd worried about the expense. She looked down at Maggie and wondered if she should start grieving. Her mother was already gone. She was in a room with a stranger, an unpleasant one. She turned some more pages.

'Oh, you were so pretty as a child,' Maggie whispered, after another several minutes had passed. She waved a bony finger at an opened page in the album. It displayed a photograph of Kate when she was around nine. She was staring impudently into the camera. Her face was boyish, her hair long and sleek. In the background she could make out the sea and brilliant white sand. Must have been taken in the Seychelles, she thought.

Her mother gasped something but it was inaudible. She tried again. 'I had such hopes for how you would turn out. You were such a happy child and now you never seem to smile. I know you have your reasons. Michael, of course. And finding out you couldn't . . . you know, but I think you were unhappy long before all of that.' Her voice trailed off. A wheezing sound signalled that she was sleeping.

It had hardly been worth making the journey. Kate wondered whether her mother's dreams were as jaundiced as her view of reality. She hoped not. Maggie had been a wonderful, inspirational person. But now she was engaged in a deliberate destruction of the past. Well, let the cancer do its worst, she thought. It won't win. You could fight cancer with drugs. But you could also fight it with love. Kate chose love. She loved her mother too much to listen to what she was saying any more.

She walked down the corridor, blinking heavily to claw back the tears. She felt her jacket vibrate. She pulled her phone out and studied the text message. At first she was unsure what she was reading. It had been sent from a number she didn't recognize. Then she realized it was from the DCI she'd met on the coast. She studied the message. It was cryptic. She read it again: *Your banker was never in the sea.*

Chapter 5

The two men walked through the early lunch-hour rush, negotiating the human traffic flowing through Central Park. The sun was out and it would soon be Easter. The city had a relaxed holiday feel, like a sedate Mardi Gras. People were smiling. The icy spring was long gone.

Carey and Reynolds clutched Styrofoam coffee mugs and paper bags containing pastrami sandwiches. Their sullen faces were at odds with the exuberant throng around them. They looked like recently laid-off bankers discussing their job prospects.

The two men made their way to their preferred spot, the baseball pitches of the North Meadow, in the centre of the park. It was where they always came to discuss bad news. The huge public space was about as private a place as there was in New York. It was a city that didn't allow secrets.

'Difficult to talk openly in the office,' Carey said. 'Can't be sure who's listening.'

'You'd need a pretty sensitive microphone to listen in here,' Reynolds said. 'Like that one we use on the UN, I guess. But let's not take our privacy for granted, hey?'

'Right,' Carey replied. 'I hear you. So, you want to discuss what we're going to say to them?'

'Yeah,' Reynolds said. 'I need guidance on how co-operative we should be, that's all. The Brits half believe they're on to something. They've got a dead man who worked at Higgs and had some interesting clients. They can sort of see how things might fit together. They're building their own jigsaw, piece by piece. They're not there yet, but they've got some sort of picture. Their man should be in town tonight and has requested a meeting. It's gone through the official channels. State department's been informed. We can't really say no to it. Special relationship. All that crap.'

Carey broke his sandwich out of its paper-bag wrapper and stared at it for a few seconds, as if he was going to interrogate it. 'Well, it seems to me they probably know pretty much everything we know. They've got the accounts. They've got the names on the accounts. They know there's billions of pounds flowing through them. They just want to know if we know any more than them, that's all. They're fishing. Relax. To them, Higgs must seem like any other bank. It's got some bad clients, a bad reputation and a bit of bad debt. So what? It's no different from any other Wall Street bank.'

Sprinklers hissed into life, fired gleaming droplets across the ball parks. The two men sat in silence for several minutes, observed the glistening grass.

Being around Carey made Reynolds feel uncomfortable. He wondered how long it would be before Carey discovered what he himself knew. When Reynolds spoke next his tone was clipped, cautious. 'We know anything about how Holahon died?'

Carey sipped his coffee, let the question linger. 'I'll ask.'

'You going to take it up to Brandeis?' Reynolds tried to keep his question calm. But he needed to know the answer. There was a grave danger that things would spiral out of control if Brandeis, the boss of the FIU, was dragged into the mess swirling around Higgs. The shit that Reynolds was having to dealing with was becoming weapons-grade. If Brandeis got involved that would be very bad news.

Carey's response nearly destroyed him.

'I guess we should tip him off. The Brits are going to want to talk to someone from Higgs, too. They still keep asking if Holahon was one of ours. They must have their suspicions, given some of his clients. They must figure he was feeding us stuff.'

Reynolds was unable to keep the anxiety out of his voice. 'But he wasn't, was he? I mean, I knew him a long time ago, when he was one of ours, but I thought he was no longer active. I would have known, surely.'

Carey shook his head. 'Well, you'd be entitled to think that. That's how it should be. But that's the problem with our creation. We've been too successful. I've been saying this for years and no one's been listening. Things happen that we just don't know anything about. It's one big fucking sprawl-ing mess that's in danger of spiralling out of control.'

'Just like any other bank,' Reynolds said.

Carey drained his coffee. 'I was talking about the CIA.'

The sprinklers finished their work. Reynolds found that he was struggling for breath. 'Yeah, right,' he said. 'That's what I meant.'

★　★　★

The epic sweeping view of the capital made the burn from the lactic acid worth the effort. It was a 150-metre ascent up Parliament Hill, the imposing mound on Hampstead Heath that looked down on London and afforded views as far away as Crystal Palace.

She allowed herself the luxury of slowing down to drink in the London skyline, then followed the other runners, banking a hard right through a copse before descending to the ponds. Her GPS watch told her she was running seven-minute miles. She turned left and began an urgent climb up the hill to Kenwood House, the stately home that dominated the top of the Heath and was hidden underneath scaffolding and tarpaulin. There had been a donation to renovate the house, she'd read somewhere. Some august philanthropical foundation had made a sizeable gift. The past was to be given a makeover. It would live on. The legacies of important individuals would be assured.

She ran through the dusk of the April evening, through snatches of conversation in French, Russian and German. The Heath had become a multilingual zone, a polyglot place. The world now lived beside it. The world's bankers, at least. They were the only ones who could afford the postcodes that rubbed up against it.

In front of her, wearing their trademark red-and-black vests, were members of the Hampstead Harriers.

'Three more and we'll call it a day,' she heard the front runner call. The group speeded up, and suddenly she found herself struggling for breath. She was trying to keep pace but the other runners knew the Heath far better than she did. They poured past the ladies' bathing pond and were quickly lost to her. She slowed to a more manageable pace and minutes later found herself back at the top of the hill. From above the capital, she looked down on her favourite landmarks: the Eye, a renovated St Pancras, Canary Wharf, the Gherkin, the Shard. Twenty years ago the skyline would have looked very different. The City's wealth had brought huge, visible change. Nothing was as transformative as money.

Her fellow runners were waiting for her, stretching, swapping water bottles and energy gels. They nodded at her.

'Not bad for a newbie.'

It was Brockman, a club veteran she remembered from when she used to run with the club. He was an investment banker from Texas, she recalled. 'Thanks. I'll improve. I hope. Just didn't want to push it too far on my first outing.'

'Wise,' Brockman said.

'Anyone got one of those blueberry protein chews?'

Another banker she remembered. Ennis, a Scot. The group shook its collective head.

'Nope,' Brockman said. 'Holahon used to bring those. Got 'em from a supplier on the internet, I think. They were the business. Really boosted recovery.'

Kate was startled to hear Holahon's name. She'd almost forgotten about him. 'Holahon?' she said.

The runners looked at her.

'Um, yeah,' Brockman said, assuming the role of group spokesman. 'He was a member of the club. But no more, sadly. He died recently. Real tragic.'

She played dumb. She'd told them she was an accountant. 'What was it? Heart attack?'

Ennis shook his head. 'No.'

She waited for more information.

Finally, Ennis spoke again. 'No one knows. His body was found on the coast. Washed up on the shore. Suicide, maybe.'

'Gonna miss those chews of his,' Brockman said. 'And him, of course. Helluva nice guy. Horrible to end up like that.'

'Like that?' Kate said.

'Alone and dead.' Brockman gazed down to the running track at the bottom of the hill. He gestured approvingly at a relay team practising their sprints. 'Every time I watch 'em they get faster. Takes real dedication, that. You've got to keep putting in the hours. There are no short-cuts. You pay with pain.' He glanced around his fellow runners, then ran a wristband across his glistening forehead. 'Yeah, we'll miss Brad. Although I think he would have ended up leaving us anyway. I heard he'd developed a drink and drug problem.'

She studied Brockman, who was staring hard at Ennis. She thought she saw a half-smile hover on his lips. He caught her eye and his face soured. 'Yeah, too bad,' he muttered. 'Like I said, one helluva nice guy.'

She waved at the other runners. 'See you next week,' she said.

'Count on it,' Brockman said. 'But what's the hurry? We usually go for a drink after we shower. We've earned it.'

'Meeting a colleague in town.'

'An accountant, like you?'

Curious question, she thought. There was an edge to it. But that was bankers for you. Hungry for information. She turned to go, prepared to run down the hill, then paused. 'You could say we're in the same field, yeah.'

★   ★   ★

Sorrenson felt out of place. He glanced at his watch for what seemed the seventeenth time, bored by the chatter around him. In the old days, when you could smoke in pubs, he would simply have lit another cigarette and contemplated the world through a contented, guilty fug. But no more. He hadn't smoked for years. It had gone the way of most of his vinyl collection and was now confined to memory, a ritual he had performed long ago. He drained his pint of Guinness and looked around the bar. Not the sort of place he would choose to come. A lot of mirror. Way too much reflection. Still, it made for a pleasant view. Some of the women were sensational. Where did they all come from? Did the capital suck all the beautiful ones in? Or maybe cities illuminated people differently.

He ordered another Guinness and waved at Kate as she approached him.

She flashed him a smile that was reflected all along the bar. 'I've booked us a booth further up the bar. It's quieter and we can get something to eat,' she shouted above the din.

Sorrenson followed her tangled mass of curly black hair through the crowds to a roped-off section at the back. She thrust a large menu at him as he sat down. 'This is on me. Grateful to you for coming up here. Least I can do is buy you dinner.'

'Cheers.' He turned the menu over. Far too many choices.

'I'm hungry,' she said. 'Just been running. I suppose it should be something involving chicken, but . . .'

They ordered burgers and a bottle of Côte du Rhône.

'Weird thing,' Kate said, when the wine arrived. 'It's a coincidence but I was just out with some of our late friend

Holahon's running club. They miss him. Or, at least, the protein bars he used to share with them.'

'So you're a runner.' Sorrenson sipped his wine. She seemed the sort, he thought.

'Yes – look.' She held up her left arm. Her GPS watch was still on her wrist. 'I've got quite obsessed with uploading all my runs to my computer,' she said. 'You can track where I've been on every one. Worse luck.'

'Makes you pretty competitive, having one of those things on you all the time. I've got one myself.'

She nodded. 'I'd like to see Holahon's GPS watch. He was quite something apparently. Head of the veterans' rankings. But what else would you expect from a former US Navy Seal?'

'His running explains something that was bugging me,' Sorrenson said. 'I couldn't figure out why his body was almost hairless. But I guess he shaved his legs to keep them as cool as possible. Lot of runners do it, I read somewhere.'

'Yeah, that figures. Although the running obsession seems to conflict with all the drugs and drink in his bloodstream. That makes no sense. It's like he's two people. Massive contradiction. Anyway, tell me about your text message. Very cryptic.'

'I thought it was the sort of thing you people liked to hear.'

She laughed, and Sorrenson found himself staring at her lips. 'If you realized how dull our job was you wouldn't say that,' she told him.

The burgers arrived.

'Well,' Sorrenson said, becoming embarrassed by his clumsy attempts to impress her, 'there have been two developments. Both a bit murky, and they come from single sources, so treat them cautiously, but . . .' He took another swig of wine. He looked at her hands. Yes, he'd been right. No rings.

She saw the glance, allowed herself a private smile. Not tonight, she thought. I've run way too far for you to be in with a chance.

'Go on.'

Sorrenson was conscious of the half-smile that had formed on her lips. He felt she was studying him, playing him. Stands to reason, he decided. All MI5 employees were trained to read body language, even the IT workers and the secretaries. He was conscious that sweat was breaking out on his back. The bar had become very hot.

He swirled some wine round his mouth for reassurance. Then he told her what Davey Stone had said about the van, and what Bill Henry had revealed about the tides at Traitor's Point. 'No record of a police van being taken without permission or stolen. It's a strange one. And it's probably a coincidence, the appearance of a body at the exact spot where they used to hang people.'

She wiped her mouth with a napkin. He found himself staring at her lips again.

'Mmm. Maybe. But if Bill Henry is correct, someone placed the body there. And, given they could have placed it anywhere along the peninsula – or, indeed, anywhere at all – there's a chance it was put there deliberately. But, then, what do I know? Like I said when we first met, I'm paid to fol-low money, not dead people.'

Sorrenson gulped more wine. He really could use some air. Or a cigarette. He felt out of his depth. 'Well, if you're right, it reminds me of that Italian banker murder,' he said. 'Calvi, wasn't it? Found hanging off Blackfriars Bridge? That was where they used to hang traitors centuries ago. The bridge was picked deliberately to send a warning to others. I saw a documentary on it once. All sorts of weird suggestions that it involved some sort of conspiracy between the Vatican and the Mafia.'

'It sounded fantastical when the claims were first made but it all came out later on.' Kate smiled. 'But I really don't think our man was paying the ultimate price for double-crossing the Pope. It's much more likely to be something mundane. The usual murder motives: lust, envy or, perhaps, good old wrath. Well, that would be my best bet if television detective dramas are anything to go by.'

Sorrenson laughed. 'Fair enough. But, then, what's your interest in the case? Why bother checking something out if you thought it was just a mundane murder?'

It was a fair question, she acknowledged. But she couldn't tell him the truth. She couldn't tell him that the security service was concerned about endemic money-laundering at Higgs and that an asset had suggested some of the money was flowing to an Islamist terrorist cell. GCHQ had picked up vague talk of an attack that would eclipse 9/11 in the terror stakes and that the plot had London links. Holahon, they knew, managed money for clients who were potentially interesting from a national security point of view. Therefore his murder was potentially interesting to the security service.

But only up to a point. They'd checked all the accounts Holahon had created. There was some interesting stuff: a huge amount of Russian Mafia money was being washed through London, buying up property it seemed, but there were no signs that money was being diverted for a potential terrorist attack. They were reaching a dead end. It was down to McLure now, she thought. He needed intel from the Americans. She didn't fancy his chances. 'I'm sorry,' she said.

Sorrenson smiled. 'I understand.'

'Thanks. It's not that I don't want to put you in the picture, it's that I'm not allowed to.'

'Yeah, I know.'

'I could buy you another drink.'

Sorrenson checked his watch. There was plenty of time to catch the last train back to the coast. 'That'd be good. But this place is stifling. And I can hardly hear you.'

She stood up, thought for a second or two. 'Come on, then. I know somewhere else.'

They walked out of the bar and into a calm London night.

'Thursday night before Good Friday,' she said. 'No wonder that bar was rammed. People were preparing for a four-day weekend. I should have suggested we met elsewhere, but I don't know that many bars in London. The only place I know quite well is where we're going.'

She stood still. She hadn't been to the pub since Michael was alive. The ghost pub, they had called it. It was down a cobbled street off Hyde Park Corner. You had to walk down a side alley, negotiate several huge restaurant wheelie bins, then enter a gate in a private mews. If you didn't know it existed you'd never find it. The best Bloody Marys in London was the pub's USP. On Remembrance Day queues of immaculately dressed service personnel from the nearby barracks spilled out into the mews. After they'd gone, the private road was littered with poppies. The Grenadier was something of an army institution. It was even reputed to have its own ghost, a slain guardsman. Well, she also knew what it was like to live with the ghost of a dead soldier.

She looked up at the man next to her. He was huge. Big as a door. Six foot four, she estimated. Five inches on Michael. She sighed. It would be difficult going back to the pub. They'd been regular visitors when her husband was on leave. But it had to be done. She gave Sorrenson a friendly nudge. 'Come on, but I warn you, if you're afraid of ghosts you're in for a shock. The place we're going to is haunted.'

They walked past the Lanesborough Hotel, where doormen in top hats and white gloves scrambled as a Bentley pulled up outside. A young man with a neat beard and close-cropped hair decanted himself from the vast car while a female companion exited from its other side. Immediately the pair were surrounded by doormen. Deference filtered on the breeze. Kate couldn't help but stare at the couple. They didn't seem to belong together but it was clear that, to the doormen, they were the most important individuals in London that night. That was why people worshipped money, she thought. It wasn't about what you could buy with it. It was about the power it conferred. Money made everything possible. That was why bankers were the most powerful gods in town.

Faisal Bin Taleed Sin Abdullah greeted the doormen as if they were old school acquaintances. There was mutual recognition but no warmth between the young prince and the hotel's employees. It was a typical, everyday interaction for him, one in which he found himself at the centre of the attention and yet somehow removed from what was happening. From his earliest years he'd felt like an outsider. He'd not been popular at Harrow, which rankled even now he was in his late twenties. They'd been unwelcoming, his fellow pupils. His request to keep falcons had been denied by the school. He'd not enjoyed the rugby, the cross-country or the compulsory drills with the Combined Cadet Force. And the decadent drug-taking and alcohol had not been to his liking at all. Not with hindsight, anyway. His father had done nothing when he'd demanded that he should be allowed to leave. He'd felt betrayed, abandoned.

The sense of insecurity had scarred him. It had festered. Ever since, he'd had an acute need to protect himself, surround himself with his own modern-day militia wherever he went. He was a regular visitor to the Lanesborough and his arrival was always preceded by a flurry of security activity as his bodyguards swept his suite for bugs and put anti-listening devices in unobtrusive locations.

The sweeps were necessary. The prince wasn't paranoid. His team had found evidence that he was being monitored on numerous visits to hotels. Faisal regularly wondered whether the bugging had been carried out by the security services or commercial rivals. Both, probably. His hedge fund, Quest Partners LLC, was responsible for managing more than $300 billion on behalf of the world's richest clients. Its investment strategies moved markets. Even the merest hint that Quest was going long or short on a stock could send it soaring or crashing to earth. Certain countries' currencies were equally vulnerable to Quest's mood.

Understandably, the hedge fund was as secretive as a serial killer. A leak could undo weeks of carefully calibrated planning.

Ostensibly, Quest was based in Mayfair, although it really existed in Faisal's BlackBerry. The Mayfair office was chiefly for showing off his vast art collection, facsimiles of the real things that were secured in vaults in Geneva. Faisal's taste in art was eclectic. There were Freuds, Van Goghs, Monets and Manets. A giant Henry Moore greeted visitors in the office's atrium, replete with a sizeable saline aquarium that boasted nurse sharks and three types of ray. Faisal liked to joke that several of his rivals in the hedge fund world had ended up in the tank. He made the joke regularly when Quest held glitzy bashes for the elite of London society.

The truth was that Faisal came to London only to be seen. His expensive PR team ensured that photographs of him with some of the world's most eligible women found their way into the papers. It was good publicity, he felt. The more he was seen with actresses and models, the higher Quest's profile. And the higher the profile, the more people wanted to invest with Quest.

Rumours were now circulating that the heir to one of the biggest fortunes in the world was about to take a wife. Bookmakers regularly quoted odds on the chances of Faisal going down the aisle with a particular celebrity. His current companion, the woman sharing the Bentley's back seat, was a famous Bollywood star, worshipped by millions. The bookmakers had her pencilled in at 5–1, the tightest odds they'd offered so far, Faisal had read with interest.

Privately, though, he didn't fancy the Bollywood star's chances. She was a delightful woman, he thought. Clever and, like him, a lover of horses. But, no, she was simply camera fodder.

Faisal and his glamorous companion entered the hotel accompanied by the flash of cameras and a phalanx of security personnel.

Carlyle was waiting for him in the foyer. 'Your father sends his regards.'

Faisal inclined his head. 'He is well, I trust?'

'As well as can be expected.'

Faisal paused. He often forgot his father was dying. 'Yes. He is an example to us all.'

'Indeed. Shall we . . . ?'

Faisal bowed slightly to his companion. 'I will see you later,' he said to her, 'after I have attended to one or two things with my friend here.'

The two men watched the departing actress with varying degrees of interest.

'A remarkable woman,' Faisal said.

'Quite.'

'Now, to business,' the prince said, ushering Carlyle towards a private booth in one of the hotel's anterooms, just off the foyer. A concierge unhooked a velvet rope and beckoned them through. The rope was replaced and the concierge clicked his fingers, summoning a platoon of waiters, waitresses, flunkeys and administrators to attend to the two men. Two bodyguards stood outside the booth, wires running down their backs from their earpieces.

'Here are various documents you need to read,' Carlyle said, thrusting a fat manila envelope across the low-slung mahogany table that separated the two men. 'Nothing to get too excited about. Various complaint letters from wildlife groups about the impending expansion of the airport. The usual frightening stuff about the risks of flying planes into areas heavy with birdlife . . .' Carlyle let the words hang for several seconds.

Faisal nodded.

His fixer continued with his debriefing. 'Confirmation from the structural engineers that the runway will be reinforced and extended within the two-month time frame you have agreed, invitations to various auctions and charity dinners, an invitation to your school reunion. Shall I?'

'Yes.'

Carlyle ripped up the invitation. 'This is probably the most interesting thing you need to see. Bit of intel from Droll. Could be a concern.'

Faisal clapped his hands together. 'At last. What's the point of having the City's biggest gumshoe on retainer if they never cough up anything?'

'Quite,' Carlyle said. It was his favourite word, 'quite'. Curt, anodyne, it could be inserted unobtrusively into any conversation.

Faisal scanned the document as a waiter poured Cristal. He raised his eyebrows. 'Are we sure about this?'

'Quite.'

'You married?'

Sorrenson shook his head. 'Engaged once. But, well, it was a bit of a rush job. I was barely out of university. Then she lost the baby and it didn't seem so urgent. She was a copper, too. Would have been a nightmare.' He sipped his Guinness and looked around the pub approvingly. There was a lot of pewter on display. On the cramped wooden bar a small hotplate warmed a metal tin containing sausages. Long candles burned in candelabras. Imposing, heavily moustached men in bearskins frowned down from paintings on the walls.

'I always said I'd never marry someone in my field,' Kate said. 'Tricky, though, doing our job. It's good to be able to talk things through with someone who understands. Like someone who has security clearance. For the first few months of any relationship I was told to tell people I was a cartographer as cover. Only I'm terrible with maps.'

Sorrenson laughed. 'Probably just as well you ended up with Five and not Six, then.'

'That's what my husband says.'

Sorrenson cursed inwardly.

Kate choked up. She couldn't even get the tenses right. She corrected herself. 'That's what my husband used to say.' She sipped her wine, waited for the inevitable question.

Sorrenson had grasped from her tone that she wasn't divorced. 'I'm sorry. How did he . . . ?'

'Die? That's the terrible thing. I don't know. I mean, I know a bit. I know he was shot dead in Baghdad. Single bullet.'

'When?'

'Just over four years ago.'

'When did you stop wearing the ring?'

'A couple of years ago.' When I started fucking other men, she thought.

'What did the inquest say?'

'There hasn't been one yet. Still waiting. Average wait is six years, so still some way to go. Cutbacks et cetera. But I'm not sure it will yield much. Michael was special forces. They

81

don't really get inquests. Not useful ones, anyway. MoD don't want the glare of publicity shone on specialist operations. They claim it poses a security risk.'

'Single bullet, you say?'

'From what little they told me he was killed by a sniper as he was entering a house to meet members of some militant brigade. It looks like someone was waiting for him, a tip-off. He died almost instantly. A good shot. If there can be such a thing.'

'Christ.'

'So that's two men I've lost to war. Well, that's how I see it. My father died in a car crash in Belfast during the Troubles. He was in the security service, too. He was the director of a front company that provided cover for him and several other agents. If it hadn't been for the Troubles, he wouldn't have been in Belfast. And if he hadn't been in Belfast, he wouldn't have been killed in a car crash. And he would maybe still be alive to look after my dying mother. Who knows?'

'That why you ended up in the security service? You wanted to follow in your father's footsteps?'

She smiled. 'No, not that clichéd, thank God. And, remember, I'm only seconded to the security service. I worked for what used to be called the Serious and Organized Crime Agency as a financial analyst. Then I went to the Treasury and worked in risk management. I was the person they brought in to trace money through tax havens. I'm good with balance sheets, modelling financial risk, following paper trails. Fascinating stuff like that.'

Sorrenson laughed. 'So how come you ended up at Five?'

'Money. Or the lack of it. These days they need financial analysts much more than they need agents. It's all about snipping the purse strings. Cut off the money supply and you can kill the monster. But all the clever guys and girls go and work at mega banks and earn millions. Five can't afford to pay them that sort of cash. So they have to work with what they've got. Or who they can borrow. Hence me. PPE from Oxford. Looks impressive on the CV, so they tapped me up. Never bothered to do it when I was at university. I was about the only person they didn't approach, apparently. I was quite indignant.'

The barman rang the bell, called time.

'One more?' Sorrenson realized he sounded mildly desperate.

She looked at him thoughtfully, held his gaze for three seconds. 'All right.'

Sorrenson approached the bar and brought back more drinks.

'Thanks.'

'I was just thinking while I was getting the drinks that terrorism doesn't cost much,' Sorrenson said. 'Nine/Eleven was done for peanuts. It doesn't cost much to commit an atrocity if you've got fanatics involved. Suicide cults come cheap.'

She shook her head. 'True, but it's the infrastructure around those guys. You want to brainwash them into believing seventy-two virgins are waiting for them in Heaven, you'll need a lot of education. You need *madrasah*s, you need clerics, you need recruiters to get them out of their country of origin and into the hot places where they can be turned into human bombs. It all costs money. So you need to follow the money, where it's coming from, where it's going to. You need to examine the *hawala*, the informal financial systems they use in the Middle East.'

'You make terrorism sound like an extension of banking.'

'That's because it is. It's not faith that drives people to terrorism. It's money. The lack of it, the lure of it, the love of it, the loathing of it. One way or another, it's money that builds the bombs.'

'You sound like you're driven by some sort of faith, too. You're pretty evangelical about what you're doing.'

Her eyes burned. 'I am. I'm just so sick of people blaming religions for such murderous lunacy. It just perpetuates the cycle of violence. Psychopaths will use any excuse for their actions. Religion is just convenient to blame. It gives people a cause. Makes them feel their actions are noble. The number of devout Muslims we've got working for Five shows that not many buy into such rubbish.'

'Well, I come from a long line of Lutherans so I'll agree with you about matters of faith and leave it at that.'

'Sorrenson. Scandinavian name, right?'

'Yeah. My mother is English, Dad was Norwegian. Worked on the rigs. Met my mother when he came over on leave.'

'You ever go back?'

'To Norway? Sometimes. I reckon there must be something in me, something genetic, that makes me miss the cold in a place I've never lived – it's like I miss the snow or the absence of long-dead ancestors or something. Sometimes I kid myself that's why I ended up on the coast. It reminds me of a sort of previous home that I knew in a former life. Sounds mad, I suppose. But sometimes, when the wind blows across the North Sea from Scandinavia, you can pretend you're no longer in England. I've got this house . . .'

Sorrenson stopped. He was giving far too much away.

'Go on.' She cupped her chin in her hand, gazing up at him. Her pose unsettled him. He felt like a piece of art she was studying.

'Well, it looks out onto the sea. Big glass and wood construction, like the sort you get in Norway. It's got a deck, and if I was any good at fishing I could cast from it into the sea. Reminds me of school holidays when I'd go back to Norway to see my father's family and they'd take me out fishing on the fjords. He had four brothers, my father. They spoilt me. Gave me the taste for the outdoor life. That's why I run. It makes me feel free.'

She sipped her wine, pushed a beer mat around the table. 'It's funny,' she said, 'but some runners don't seem to be very free at all. They're chained to their jobs. It's almost as if running gives them their only taste of freedom.'

'Like Holahon, you mean.'

'Yeah. I did a bit more research on him. Can't really call it investigating because it's not relevant, but I was curious. He really was into running. I mean *really* into running. He ran the Badwater Ultramarathon – that's a hundred-and-thirty-five miles through California's Death Valley. And he recently did the Wall. That's sixty-nine miles along Hadrian's Wall. There's no way I could run that far in one go. I'd love to know what his time was. But that's bankers for you – they're driven. Or maybe so trapped in their jobs they need that merciful release. Running is a drug. They become addicted.'

'His results are probably on the net. You should check

them out,' Sorrenson said. 'Set yourself a target, maybe. Something to aim for when you hit your fifties.'

'I'd planned on having problem teenagers by then. Look how that one worked out, hey?' She winced. She was revealing too much of herself. It was the wine talking. She would make a terrible agent, far too ready to divulge.

Sorrenson saw the flash of red in her face, read her shame. 'I'll tell you what I don't understand,' he said, quickly trying to change the subject.

'What's that?'

'Well, if he was such a running fanatic, what was with all the coke and alcohol in his bloodstream? Maybe performance-enhancing drugs I could understand, but not the sort of stuff that would stop you running.'

'That's been puzzling me, too. I might ask to see the pathology report again. Maybe get a second opinion. We asked around. He had some distant family in the States and his ex-partner, of course, and colleagues at the bank. They were approached. They all said he wasn't a drinker. Pretty much said he was teetotal, according to the Met guys who made enquiries on our behalf. A few people in his running club have hinted otherwise to me but I'm not sure they would repeat the claim to you. But something else has been troubling me as well.'

'Go on.'

She slid the beermat between her hands. The action gave her confidence, made her feel like a magician working with cards. For a few seconds she stared at it, wondering whether to proceed. She remembered what McLure had told her. It wasn't her job to investigate murders. She was wasting time thinking about Holahon, time she should be spending checking out leads on Higgs and other potential sources of terrorist financing.

'Well,' she said, 'don't you think it was a bit strange to find a headless and handless body with a tattoo that clearly allowed it to be identified? OK, you have to check missing-persons records and that sort of stuff, but it doesn't take long. We had his name within a couple of days of the body turning up. We've never found the rest of him. Presumably dumped somewhere in the sea. Why not dump all of him? And why leave the arm with the tattoo? Why leave bits of him behind?'

Sorrenson nursed the cool, wet Guinness glass between his hands. So dark, the drink, he thought. Just like the conversation. It had been a grisly end for Holahon, true, but lots of people ended up dead for the most perfunctory reasons. One day an ex-lover would confess or it might turn out to be a business rival. The motive would be boringly logical one way or another. He sipped his drink, savoured its bitterness. 'I suppose it could have been a very stupid murderer,' he said. 'A lot of them are.'

She shook her head.

Sorrenson watched her curls dance in the candlelight. A party of four sitting nearby stood up and left the bar. He saw that he and Kate were the only ones left drinking.

'No, I don't buy that,' she said. 'You have to be pretty intelligent to kill someone, cut off their body parts and drop them on a beach without anyone seeing you. You'd be bright enough to spot the tattoo. You'd know it would lead to the body being identified in time.'

'Right. I agree. But something else doesn't make sense.

We've pretty much established that bodies, or anything else for that matter, don't wash up at Traitor's Point. And yet . . .'

She nodded. The pathology report had recorded that the cause of Holahon's death was drowning. That would indicate that the body had washed up on the shore after being dismembered at sea. And yet she felt the sighting of the van was too much of a coincidence to be discounted. Police vans didn't speed along deserted coastal roads for no reason. A dead, headless, handless Holahon had been in that van, she was sure. Someone, she felt, had wanted Holahon placed where the police would find him. Someone had had a point to make. Someone had thought Holahon was a traitor. There was a grievance, a motive. That was useful. You could trace motives back to murderers. But who would want to murder a leading banker? She flipped the question around in her mind: who wouldn't?

The barman ordered them to drink up. She bit her lip, tilted her head to one side and looked at Sorrenson. She held his gaze for eight seconds.

Chapter 6

'So, how can we help?'

It sounded innocent enough but to McLure the question was loaded. He felt as if he was staring down the barrel of a gun. He gazed at the two men in front of him. He'd expected to meet only Carey. They had spoken on the phone and exchanged emails. Now he was thrown by the appearance of Brandeis, Carey's ultimate boss.

Brandeis was legendary in spook circles. Leaked US embassy cables suggested he'd been implicated in numerous plots to destabilize regimes in South America. His position as head of the National Security Agency's Financial Intelligence Unit was seen as a cosy sinecure, a reward for all of the havoc he had caused down south. But McLure didn't have Brandeis down as a money man. For a start he didn't have the right hairstyle: Brandeis sported a buzz-cut. Behind the desk he looked like a recently demobbed soldier. No, McLure decided, whatever the FIU was up to, it was a lot more interesting than it liked to make out. He was just asking questions about one specific bank, that was all, and yet the FIU seemed to have gone into full-on defensive mode. Interesting.

'Thanks for seeing me at such short notice,' McLure said. There was no response from the two men opposite. They were really trying to shut down their body language, he could tell. Even more interesting. They hadn't begun and already the Americans were stonewalling him. And they were rolling out the big guns, too. Heavy artillery. Something wasn't right.

'I'd like to talk to you about Higgs,' McLure said. 'As you know, we've been interested in it for some time. There's been some intelligence we've received that indicates it's facilitating money laundering on a large scale. Some of that intelligence has come from data sucked up by our GCHQ. Mainly banking instructions between London and Frankfurt relayed across the Tat 42 submarine cable coming out of Land's End. Nothing that your NSA won't have seen, of course. But it's a handful of Higgs's clients who are potentially interesting to us. We would be grateful to learn if you know them and, indeed, if any are working for you. As you will appreciate, a senior member of the bank based in London, Brad Holahon, was murdered recently. We've been told that he once worked for you. We don't want to stumble into something that could have . . . implications.'

McLure folded his arms and studied the two Americans. He had played his hand. It was time to see what they had.

Carey pressed his fingers together as if in prayer. Brandeis stood up and moved to the window. 'That's real good of you to let us know, Tony,' he said quietly. 'Appreciate it. Good of you to come all that way to tell us that in private. Some conversations have to be had face to face.'

McLure remained silent. The onus was on the Americans

to offer up some information, he felt. They had to give him something for his journey.

'Thing is,' Brandeis continued, 'we know nothing about Holahon. He hasn't worked for us for quite a few years. We understand he had some interesting clients—'

'Like Prince Aldud,' McLure interjected.

'Like Prince Aldud,' Brandeis agreed, 'but, from what we understand, there's no suggestion Holahon's death was connected with his job or the intelligence community. Maybe he was working for someone else and became too hot for them – or not hot enough, if you get me. You wouldn't have to look too far. The FSB pay well. We've got fucking Chinese agents hiding in every major bank over here. Doubt your banks are any different. States will pay for intel. There are hedge funds that would probably like to know what he knew.'

Brandeis was looking down on the old Ground Zero site. He turned to Carey. He seemed almost to have forgotten that McLure was in the room. 'You remember the fliers after Nine/Eleven?'

Carey nodded. 'The ones pinned up to the notice-boards running down the streets in the days after?'

'Yeah. People desperately seeking their loved ones. Thousands of 'em. Saddest thing I ever saw. Just photos on top of photos. One big album of grief.'

Brandeis turned to McLure. His eyes flashed anger. McLure felt the air turn hostile.

'Told myself that was it,' Brandeis said. 'Told myself it could never happen again. We would do whatever it took to ensure the American people were protected. Whatever it took.' Brandeis had repeated the last three words slowly, deliberately, like he was spelling something out. 'That is our only aim,' he added. 'To protect American citizens. Everything else is secondary. Nothing else is of interest to us.'

'Including helping allied agencies seeking intelligence on suspected terrorist financing?' McLure felt himself getting angry. The two Americans said nothing. He glanced at his watch. The meeting was barely five minutes old. 'We're trying not to make things difficult for you,' McLure said. 'We've seen enough going on in Higgs to launch a major operation that could see it closed down. But we don't want to do that if we're threatening some bigger plan of yours.'

Carey was staring at the desk.

Brandeis was gazing out of the window again, admiring the April sunset over Manhattan. On a night like tonight, he thought, you didn't want to be in any other city in the world. He ran his fingers across the glass. 'No plan,' he said quietly. 'Higgs ain't ours. Never has been. Despite those mad rumours you keep hearing.'

'Oh, come on!' McLure exploded. The stonewalling he could cope with. The obvious lies were impossible to swallow. 'Everyone in intelligence knows Higgs is yours,' he said. 'The spook bank, they call it. You built it. It's your baby.'

Brandeis shrugged. 'Everyone's wrong. Dead wrong. We really can't help you. We know less than you do.'

'So,' McLure said, 'I've had a wasted trip.'

No one spoke for several seconds.

Then Carey said, 'I wouldn't say that. There's this new brasserie that's opened on 48th and Madison. The snails are the best you'll try outside Paris. Go there. I promise you, you won't regret it.'

McLure stood up and left the office, with a curt nod.

Fucking Americans. He remembered what he'd told Kate. 'They lie, they lie, they lie,' he'd said. He shouldn't have been surprised by their reaction. And if they weren't going to trade any intel on Higgs, he couldn't be blamed if the British security service were soon trampling all over it. The two of them were clearly hiding stuff, lots of it. Everything surfaced in the end. Higgs was toxic, McLure thought. You could hide that stuff for only so long. He struggled to curb his anger. The way they'd looked at him. The obvious disdain. It was a joke, the special relationship. They were supposed to be on the same side. Christ, they had enough military bases in the UK to launch a substantial European war. And yet they treated the British security service like it was an enemy state. He took several deep breaths. He reminded himself that he had a meeting with the Higgs chairman the next day. Maybe that would yield something.

The two Americans heard the lift ping, signalling McLure's descent.

'Went about as expected,' Brandeis said. 'Fucking Brits. Always expecting something for nothing.'

'Yeah. You gonna phone Parker?'

'Too right. He's meeting McLure tomorrow. He knows the drill. But a pep-talk can't hurt. If nothing else, tomorrow will give him a chance to earn his massive fucking salary. Remind me, how much are we paying him?'

Carey thought for a moment. 'Something like eleven million a year.'

'Jesus fucking Christ. Not bad for someone who was a pretty lousy general.'

'True,' said Carey. 'And he was a better soldier than he is a banker.'

'That's what worries me.'

Gary Carlton had the best job in the world, as he told anybody who would listen. 'I get to work outdoors, among nature, in one of the most beautiful places in London,' he would say. 'And I get my own company car.'

The mention of the car was his attempt at a joke. The long-base bottle-green Land Rover supplied by the London Parks Authority, his employer, was to be used only for traversing Hampstead Heath. Despite regular requests, the twenty-four-year-old was forbidden to take the vehicle home at weekends. Still, he got to drive it most days. And it made working the odd Saturday more bearable knowing that 'the Beast', as he called it, was available.

He could have done without working Easter Saturday, though. He had mates going up to the Peak District. They'd hired a cottage. He was jealous. Paint-balling. Chance for them to play soldiers, they'd explained.

He opened the Land Rover's rear door and pulled out a chainsaw. He had to clear a copse of several trees, brought down in strong winds the previous week. He loved using the chainsaw almost as much as driving the Beast. He placed the saw on a tree stump, evidence of his work the previous day, felt in his pocket for his chewing gum and realized he'd left it in the glove compartment.

As he turned to go back for it, something on the ground caught his eye. For a second, he couldn't tell what it was. The object was little more than a shadow. It seemed incongruous in the mud of the Heath. Black rubber and glass. He bent down and picked the watch up. Expensive. He peered at the screen. Blank. He pressed the buttons on either side of the face. No response. It was dead.

He put the device in his pocket and returned to the saw. He would hand the watch in at the ranger's office later in the day. Not that it was any use to anyone now. He fired up the saw, shattering the quiet of the copse. God, he thought, I really love that sound. It was the sound of things crashing to earth.

The prince sat in his orangery looking out over his perfectly manicured lawns. He watched a team of gardeners at work on his two croquet lawns. Another group was busy with topiary, turning box hedges into ornate animal shapes. The prince didn't normally approve of ostentation but he was soon to throw a garden party for some distinguished guests, and his team of advisers had suggested that such measures would raise a smile among the VIPs. The prince had merely nodded. He didn't understand Western sensibilities. The English and their obsession with gardens was equally perplexing. Almost as strange as their fascination with tall buildings. Each year London seemed higher. Were its inhabitants trying to build stairs to God? Skyscrapers were an insult to Him, the prince thought. Nothing should dwarf minarets.

Around him, architects and engineers were unfurling the final plans for the airport. They included the construction of a major new terminal, car parks, a hotel and shopping village.

But the prince was focused only on the runway, nothing else. In particular, he was interested in its length. It needed to be long and resilient, capable of taking serious punishment. Faisal could worry about the commercial side of things, bringing in airlines that would one day ferry millions of people to sunspots in Europe and beyond, when the prince had finished using the runway for his own purposes. The team in front of him were his mercenaries, effectively. They were going to war. A just war.

Carlyle appeared at his side. 'May I remind you, gentlemen, that you have signed non-disclosure clauses. Nothing that is said in this room may be repeated outside. What is said in here stays in here.'

There was a general muttering of agreement from the group.

'His Highness is interested only in the answer to one specific question,' Carlyle said. 'And that is, can the runway support his programme?'

All eyes turned to Gibson, a sandy-haired former US naval engineer, who was the project's manager. He handed Carlyle a fat folder. 'The short answer is yes. It's all in here. We need to extend the runway three-hundred more metres. And it needs to be completely resurfaced. It's going to take a lot of pounding. But yeah.'

The prince smiled. He rarely displayed emotion but he couldn't stop himself. He was close to delivering his legacy. The runway would be his gift to the world. People would remember him.

'You should have the snails. Everyone says so.'

'Not for me,' McLure said. 'I'll have the club sandwich. Don't like to eat too much before flying.'

'You going back tonight?' Parker was surprised. He'd thought McLure would hang around longer. Brandeis had briefed that the Brit would be in New York for several days.

'I've changed my plans,' McLure said. 'Got to get back.'

It was the truth. McLure had cancelled his extended weekend in New York. His experience with Brandeis and Carey had made him so angry that he wanted to put as much ocean as possible between himself and Americans. He looked around the brasserie. Waiters in black waistcoats ferried silver trays of entrecôte and fries through constantly slamming doors. Definitely a brasserie. A French-themed American brasserie. It was only a matter of time, McLure reflected, before a branch opened in London. Everything in the US was exported to the UK eventually. Even crises. 'When Wall Street sneezes, London catches a cold,' went the adage. Well, if what he was starting to suspect was correct, it wouldn't be a cold that the City was going to catch. It would be a full-blown flesh-eating virus.

'Well, that's a pity,' Parker said. 'New York's a fun city at Easter. Some good parades.'

'Another time.'

'I hope so, Tony. Come at Christmas. Higgs throws one helluva party.'

'I'll make a note of it.'

'You do that. So, anyway, you want to talk about Higgs, I take it?'

'I want to talk to you about some of your bank's accounts.'

A waiter materialized at the table. Parker ordered the clam chowder and the club for McLure. So bland, British agents, he thought. They looked like accountants. The man in front of him didn't seem to pose much of threat. He couldn't even interrogate a menu properly. Parker sipped a root beer and leaned forward across the table. 'How can I be of help?'

McLure took a sheet of paper from his jacket pocket and slipped it across the linen. 'Here are the names we're interested in. I must stress we're interested in them for reasons of national security. We wouldn't be asking for your help otherwise.'

Parker glanced down at the list. He had perfected the poker face. You couldn't become a general in the US military by revealing your emotions. Inscrutability was a shield. He ran his eyes over the names. 'I'll see what I can do. You're taking the lead on this, right? It's your baby? You're the go-to man?' There was sarcasm in his tone.

'Right,' McLure said. Parker was immaculately suited despite it being a Saturday. You want the world to think you're a banker, McLure thought, but you're always going to be a retired general. You're always going to be fighting old wars even when they're long over. He felt as if they were separated by a card table. The old general was dealing him a rigged pack, he knew. Just like Brandeis and Carey. He hadn't expected anything else. But at least he'd learned something from his trip. The Americans were going to a lot of trouble to look as if they didn't know anything about Higgs.

Sorrenson allowed himself a deep draught of ozone, a reward for his exertions. He was nine miles into his run and comfortable with the pace. Four more miles and he would call it quits. He ran between two skeletal yawls, beached high on the shingle. The sun bounced off the waves. It was a Tuesday morning in April but it felt like June. There was real heat in the day already. Sorrenson felt glad to be alive on his day off, as if he was running back the years.

He wondered what Kate was doing. He pictured her out running. The image made him smile. The morning after hadn't been as awkward as he'd feared. There had been coffee, brought up by the hotel's room service, and then he'd gone. It had been efficient, almost clinical. A perfunctory exchange of gifts. But he could tell that that was what she'd wanted. No small-talk. No intimacy. He wondered if he would see her again. Probably not, unless there was some major development in the Holahon murder. And that seemed unlikely. There were no new leads. He'd lost count of the number of times he'd studied the CCTV footage outside Holahon's Holland Park apartment from the night he'd gone missing. It showed the banker leaving his house in his running gear and jogging down the street. And that was basically it, the last moments of Holahon. They'd trailed him to a towpath near Regent's Park using CCTV footage and then he'd disappeared.

Sorrenson's chat with the locum pathologist who'd conducted the autopsy hadn't helped either. He'd visibly bristled when Sorrenson had asked whether there would be any benefit in seeking a second autopsy.

'Do you know how much our budgets have been slashed?' the pathologist had said. 'You want to waste resources on getting someone else to tell you what I already told you? Cause of death: drowning. It appears he was held down, whether intentionally or accidentally I can't determine. But I'm not sure how much he would have felt anyway. He was so whacked on drugs and drink that he was probably unconscious.'

And then the pathologist had said something that had completely thrown Sorrenson, sent everything spinning.

'He drowned in fresh water.'

Sorrenson was incredulous. 'He was found on a beach.'

'Well, that's as maybe, but he drowned in a canal, a river or a lake. Not the sea.'

'How come you're only telling me this now?'

The pathologist shrugged. 'Half of the forensic service is outsourced. The results got lost in the post. The preliminary report gave the cause of death as drowning. It was only when the full follow-up report arrived that we found out what sort of water was in his lungs.'

Sorrenson was furious. It was a vital piece of evidence and they'd come close to losing it.

'Don't blame us,' the locum said. 'I'm covering three people's work here. Your usual guy is off on stress-related sick leave and we now have to use all these outside agencies to do what we used to do in-house. It's chaos.'

The test results confirmed the hunch that Holahon's body had been placed at the scene deliberately. Maybe it gave more credibility to the sighting of the police van too, Sorrenson thought. He tried to imagine what Holahon had done to make someone want to turn him into such a gruesome example, someone so dehumanized that they were barely recognizable as a dead person.

The banking world was a pretty vicious place, he thought. When big sums of money were involved anything could happen. But, still, it didn't seem to hang together. Why not have him murdered discreetly? There was no shortage of people who could arrange it for the right price.

He felt the lactic acid burning in his calves as he ran along the remote final spit of peninsula. It was as good a place as any to build a nuclear power station. The plant sat back on the shingle, glowering at the sky, like a giant Easter Island statue.

He ran onto a salt-bleached road that shimmered in the heat. Wild flowers poked up through the scrub, scattered slashes of yellow, red and blue across the near lunar landscape. The sea was dazzling. It was close to a perfect moment.

Sorrenson's iPhone, cradled in a pouch on his arm, vibrated.

It was Hughes.

'Yes?' Sorrenson shouted into the microphone hanging next to his mouth.

'We may have something on the Holahon murder,' Hughes said. 'May be nothing, but . . .'

Sorrenson broke into a sprint. A new lead would give him an excuse to see her again. 'I'll come in.'

'It can wait until tomorrow.'

'I'm coming in now.'

McLure hadn't felt the ligature around his neck. He was too busy having a heart attack. They'd rushed him as soon as he'd walked into his hotel room, three of them, all wearing paper suits. The first hit him in the chest with an electric prod to induce a heart attack. McLure's body jerked back against the wall and flopped to the floor. The second bent over him and dropped the ligature over his head, pulling it tight and holding it until he'd stopped breathing. The third kept lookout by the door.

In his last moments McLure tasted blood in his mouth and saw only blackness. He could hear his death but not see it. He was conscious of the enormous pain in his chest – his ribs were going to shatter. He felt the terror of having run out of options. He was incapable of movement. His last thoughts were of his ex-wife and eleven-year-old daughter, Alice. He pictured Alice walking down the aisle on her own at her wedding. He tried to resist the thought, conscious it would be his last. But it was too powerful. A sea of sadness drowned him.

They got me, he thought. They got me.

It was all over in under two minutes. An onlooker would have had the impression that the men had performed similar murders before. They were so efficient, so composed. It had almost been graceful, the killing.

The three men removed their paper suits and gloves to reveal janitor overalls. They pulled baseball caps firmly down over their faces to protect themselves from the CCTV cameras in the hotel's hallways. They shut the door behind them with a soft click.

McLure's body was left supine on the floor, staring up at the ceiling. Anger lingered in his eyes.

Chapter 7

Gary Carlton was enjoying the attention. For a man who still lived with his parents, the appearance of the two detectives was a high point of his week – his month, even. He would have preferred them to look like detectives, instead of school teachers. Especially the younger one with the faded leather jacket and the curly hair. He looked like he taught geography. But, still, their attention made him feel important. He didn't quite understand why the two men were so interested in what he had to say, but they were really keen to know where he'd found the watch.

The three of them stood in the copse near the top of the Heath where he'd been felling trees.

'So you found it here?' Hughes gestured at the ground.

The park ranger nodded. 'Right there.'

'Just under those brambles?' Sorrenson said, pointing.

'Yeah. It could have been there for some time. This a quiet part of the Heath. Not many people make it up here.'

'Mmm,' Hughes said. 'I can see that. And after you found the watch, you handed it in at the ranger's office, right?'

'Yes. There was no name or anything on it. I thought it didn't even work. The screen was blank.'

'You have to charge it up,' Sorrenson said. 'It's got a GPS system that tracks a satellite so you can monitor your runs.'

'Brian, the head ranger, must have done it,' Gary said. 'Next thing I know he's telling me you guys want to speak to me about it. What's with the interest? It's just a watch.'

'We believe the owner of the watch was murdered,' Hughes said. 'Your head ranger discovered who owned it after he powered it up. He took it down to the running club at the bottom of the Heath to borrow a charger, hooked it up to the internet and it told him who owned it. Then he called the parks police, who called us. So now you know about as much as we do.'

Gary Carlton had a flash of inspiration. 'Belonged to that banker, right? Brad Holahon? I saw it reported in the papers. He was a member of the running club. It was him, yeah?'

'Clever,' Hughes said. 'You're in the wrong line of work.'

Gary was thrilled. He rarely received praise. And he'd always fancied himself as some sort of maverick cop, someone who wasn't afraid of being at the sharp end of things. Yeah, that sounded good: a risk-taker.

Hughes looked around the copse. 'Tell me, there any lakes up here?'

Gary laughed. 'Nope.'

Hughes shrugged. Another spent lead.

'No, no lakes,' the ranger said. 'Plenty of ponds, though.' He was delighted to see the eyes of the two men lock onto his face.

'Where?' Hughes gestured around the copse.

Gary pointed through a wall of trees. 'Mixed bathing pond's through there. The men's and the women's are further down the Heath.'

'Show us,' Sorrenson said.

Gary beamed. It was turning into an interesting day. 'Happy to oblige,' he said. 'We'll take the Beast.'

Callow poked his head around Kate's office door. She glanced up from her screen and felt sick. She'd been braced for bad news for several days. Callow's face confirmed it. 'McLure?'

Callow grunted something vaguely affirmative. 'Webster wants to see you. Now.'

She followed him down the corridor and took the lift up to the top floor. The office had a stunning view of the Thames, stretching from the Oxo Tower down towards Vauxhall Bridge. After a guaranteed knighthood and a posting as master of an Oxbridge college, the view was the third-best perk that came from being the head of MI5. Callow ushered her though the door. 'Tell him what you know,' he said. 'Don't hold back.'

Idiotic advice, she thought. Jesus, Callow could be patronizing. No wonder the agency had problems recruiting more women with a man like him as Webster's deputy.

'Pendragon, thanks for coming,' Webster said. 'I won't get up.'

She attempted a smile. It was Webster's little joke. He'd been in a wheelchair for most of his adult life. A motorbike accident had paralysed him when he was in his thirties, after he'd returned from a long stint in Northern Ireland. Couldn't have kids. He had made the security service his life, to fill the void. At least, that was what the newspaper profiles intimated.

He gestured for her to sit down. A thin file lay on the desk in front of him. He glanced down and closed it, a little too hurriedly for her liking.

'McLure's dead.'

She resisted the urge to cry. McLure dead. It didn't seem likely. He'd been about the only constant in her life since she'd been seconded to the service. She swallowed hard as she struggled to keep her composure. 'I take it that, as you've called me up here to tell me this, he didn't die of natural causes.'

'Sort of.'

'Meaning?'

'He actually died of a heart attack in his hotel room. Though there were ligature marks around his neck. We think some sort of device was used to stun him, to stop his heart.'

'So . . .' The words wouldn't come.

'So, not some robbery that went wrong, no,' Webster said. 'It was a very professional job. Very quick. He was clearly targeted.'

'Oh, God, no.' She struggled to reconcile the living McLure with the dead one. Suddenly the enormity of what she was doing hit her. She had told people her job was boring and she'd believed it, been grateful for it, even. But, actually, it wasn't so pedestrian after all. She felt scared. Scared and alone and fearful. What had McLure found? As head of Five's financial intelligence division he'd been overseeing multiple investigations. But she knew of nothing that would have made him the target of a professional hit. She thought about his attempts to hire a skip, his divorce and their clumsy affair. It was the everyday stuff that went on in humdrum offices up and down the country. Only MI5's work got its operatives killed.

Her mind drifted to the knock on the door four winters ago. She had been at her mother's house in Sussex. She'd known as soon as she'd opened it. The soldier's uniform had told her Michael was dead. The shoes were so polished. The cap's peak gleamed under the porch light. You only make that sort of effort for bad news, she'd thought immediately.

But McLure's death was different. Soldiers got shot. It happened. But it was unusual for agents to die in the field. It was even more unusual when they were largely desk-bound and focused on unpicking prosaic banking transactions.

'When did you find out?'

'We've known for a few days,' Webster said. 'We have some basic facts to go on. Three men dressed as janitors, we think. We've checked CCTV cameras but they hid their faces well. They seemed to know where the cameras were in the hotel. The Americans say they've swept the room for clues. We've got people from the embassy investigating, but it doesn't look like the killers left any traces.'

'Do you have any theories?'

Webster rocked back in his wheelchair. 'We were hoping you might know something.'

'He'd asked me to look into Higgs Bank. He was becoming slightly obsessed with it, in my opinion. I'd been monitoring it for some time at his request. We'd picked up chatter that it might be helping finance terrorism. Vague rumblings in the City. Bit of traffic from GCHQ. Nothing much. But then one of its bankers, Holahon, turned up dead and we wondered if there was some link between his murder and the rumours about Higgs. We checked out some of

Holahon's clients. They're interesting, although we're not sure how interesting. It seems to be organized crime, not national security stuff.'

Webster pressed a button on his desk. 'Jane, could we have two coffees, please?' He looked at Kate. 'Well, he must have found something.'

'I'll have another look at the Higgs file,' she said. 'See if I can find anything. There's a lot of stuff I haven't yet got to grips with. A lot of accounts linked to Higgs based offshore in tax havens. They might yield something. I'll check them out.'

'Do. We've got very little else to go on.'

The coffee arrived. Webster waited for his secretary to leave the room. 'We have yet to tell his family,' he said meaningfully. 'Although, of course, they must have their fears.'

Oh, God, please, no, she thought.

'We were rather hoping you could visit them. Give them a sanitized version of what happened.'

She felt as if she was struggling to breathe. How sanitized a version could it be? And wasn't she the most inappropriate person in Five to deliver it? Not, of course, that she could admit it. There were forms you were supposed to fill in if you were in a relationship with another member of the service. It was a ludicrous form of bureaucracy that everyone ignored. Far from increasing transparency, it just made everyone even more secretive. She swallowed hard. 'I'd rather . . .'

'You knew him better than anyone,' Webster said soothingly. 'Far more appropriate that it comes from you, a trusted friend.'

'But—'

'He was divorced, wasn't he?'

She stared at the floor. 'I believe so.'

Sorrenson rolled his chair back from his desk and massaged his neck. He'd been staring at his computer screen for too long and he was drained by all the information he'd been absorbing.

On the screen a plethora of electronic maps was linked to dates and tables of information. Each table recorded the average speed of Holahon's run, his fastest pace, the total distance travelled, the elevation, the estimated calories burned. Most of the maps showed fairly similar routes that he had taken across Hampstead Heath.

'What's that one?' Hughes pointed at the screen.

Sorrenson moved closer to the screen and gave a low whistle. 'Badwater Ultra. Fuck, this guy really was tough.'

'And that one?'

Sorrenson paused. Something was puzzling him. 'Well, I think it was the Wall, the sixty-nine-miler along Hadrian's Wall. But he won the veteran's category in that race. Did it in twelve hours thirty-eight minutes. I know because I looked it up on the website. But his watch data suggests he did it in just over six hours. That's not possible. He'd have had to be running at almost Olympic marathon pace for the entire race. No one in the world could do that.'

Hughes slipped a cigarette between his lips, scratched his head. 'I'm going out for a smoke. All this running talk is way too healthy.' He pointed at the screen. 'I guess the satellite signal got fucked up or something.'

Sorrenson rolled his hand across the computer's mouse and navigated the arrow on the screen so that it hovered over the map of the Wall. He left-clicked on the mouse and the map disappeared, replaced by a line graph showing Holahon's speed throughout the race. Sorrenson stared at the graph. He traced along it using the arrow, studied the numbers scrolling on the screen as he followed the line. For a second or two he struggled to understand what the data was telling him. Maths had never been his strong point. But, as he stared, his doubts about what he was reading vanished. It had seemed implausible, but now he understood. The data wasn't lying. The watch had been telling the truth. Only the truth was so fantastical, so outlandish, that it couldn't be true — at least, not in the way Holahon had portrayed it.

Sorrenson burst out laughing. 'Sly, sly old fox,' he whispered. 'You nearly got away with it. You made them all believe you. And if you hadn't died, no one would have known. You were a fraud, Mr Holahon. One big fraud.'

She walked through the Plaza Mayor, Madrid's main square, and felt as if she'd landed in another time, another place. Kate knew Madrid well. Michael had taken her there for weekend breaks, cramming in trips to museums and art galleries around the bullfighting. 'Very Hemingway,' she'd tell him.

'Exactly,' he would reply.

She'd known then that Michael wasn't the sort to choose a quiet life. His ridiculous love of bullfighting wasn't an affectation. He was a man who enjoyed the novelty of acute danger. It was inevitable, then, that he would end up in special forces, that he would put himself in harm's way. Ever since they'd walked out of Islington town hall as husband and wife on a grey Saturday in May, she'd been half expecting the knock on the door, the one that would tell her that her husband was dead. She felt she'd been living under a death sentence all her married life. The fear had been hardwired into her. When it came, with the awful news, it was almost a relief, the closing of a book in which the ending had been all too predictable.

The four years since then had seen her running on autopilot, avoiding his friends, the places they used to go. It wasn't so much that she was trying to avoid the pain of being reminded of him, which never left her, it was more that she didn't have the energy to deal with the emotions, the time she needed to convalesce after they attacked her. Better to throw herself into her work, running, other, more shameful, distractions . . .

Only on this occasion she'd had to visit Madrid. She'd had no choice but to confront her past. Webster's orders. Payback for past sins. It was exhausting, guilt.

She walked towards the restaurant in the corner of the square, picking her way through the human statues and the beggars. She'd never seen so many beggars in a major European capital before. Scores of them, many with placards around their necks explaining how they'd lost everything during the banking crisis. There was a melancholy about Madrid that she didn't recognize. The city seemed to have lost its grandeur, its swagger. The machismo, the exuberance were gone. Not very Hemingway now, she thought. Madrid seemed half derelict, as if it had been the victim of riots. It was true: money, the absence of money, could do far more damage than terrorism would ever achieve. If you wanted to make a statement, you took out a building. If you wanted to cripple a country, you took out its banking system. It wasn't that hard to do. Economies were built on confidence. People were built on confidence. Once confidence evaporated there was nothing left to sustain the necessary illusion that everything was normal.

She looked at the woman sitting at a table outside the restaurant reading the *International Herald Tribune*. Her hair was grey, cut short, almost like a boy's. She wore designer black spectacles and a cream blouse. She looked what she was: a lawyer taking her lunch hour.

'Marion?'

The woman looked up. She ran her eyes over Kate's near-six-foot frame. 'You're taller than I expected.'

Kate didn't say anything. There was nothing she could say.

'I mean, Anthony had a thing for short women, I always thought. Well, women shorter than himself, and he was only, what, five foot nine, five foot ten on a good day? I suppose it made little difference once he was lying down.'

Kate was relieved that the woman was using the past tense. It was clear that she suspected her former husband was dead. 'I have bad news,' she said, sitting down and ordering an espresso from a passing waiter.

The woman gave a short, bitter laugh. 'Well, I didn't think this was some sort of social call. I mean, if you were taking the time to fly out here . . .' Her voice trailed off. There were tears in her eyes.

'Right,' Kate said.

Marion dabbed her eyes with a tissue. 'And you of all people. I take it you're the Kate he sent the texts to.'

'Yes.'

'You're far too attractive for him. Jesus, you must have issues if you were his mistress. You must have very little confidence.'

Kate bit her lip. 'Mistress' was a ludicrous word. It had been just a handful of times, and a mistake, a huge mistake. They had both regretted it. They had both moved on. It happened everywhere. But, still, to argue back would be unkind and unnecessary. Now was not the time to get trapped in some semantic debate about the nature of betrayal. She had a message to deliver. 'I'm sorry to tell you that Tony, Anthony, is dead.'

She waited for a response but the woman simply eyed her dully.

'We believe he was murdered. He was in New York and it seems he was the target of a professional assassination.'

Marion began to sob quietly. 'New York. He'd always wanted to go back there. It was where we . . . Oh, never mind. What am I going to tell Alice? Oh, Anthony, what on earth did you get yourself involved in?' Then she quietened and frowned. 'He wasn't the sort to get involved in that side of things. He used to joke about it with me. He called himself a desk warrior. Alice bought into it, saying she wanted to be a desk warrior when she grew up.'

The espresso arrived. Kate sipped it, grateful for the distraction. 'Tell Alice whatever you feel is necessary. That her father was a good man who tried to make the world a better place.'

'Do you know who did it? Do you have a theory, even?'

Kate remembered what she'd been authorized to say. Or, rather, what she'd been banned from divulging. Well, tough. She would tell Marion something. That would be her

113

apology. That was all she could do as a form of penance. 'We believe it may have had something to do with terrorist financing. We think he may have identified how a particular bank was helping facilitate Islamist terrorism although, I stress, this is still speculation. It had become something of an obsession with him, this bank. I was helping him on certain bits of the investigation. There were some targets I'd identified for further inspection. But it seems he knew a lot more. It will be my job to go into this now and prepare a full case report. From there we'll try to piece together who might have wanted your former husband dead. We're liaising with the American authorities and relevant agencies and we're studying CCTV footage, that sort of thing. We're pursuing a number of lines of enquiry.'

She was careful with her terminology. They had lines of enquiry, not leads. They basically had nothing to go on. She was talking to the IT team because she wanted McLure's computer decrypted so that she could read his files. There might be something in them, but the reality was that his death was a mystery. It would probably remain a mystery, too. There wasn't much closure in their world. She saw the concern on Marion's face.

'Money. Anthony paid Alice's school fees. She's doing well over here at her new international school. We might have to—'

'That will be taken care of,' Kate interrupted gently. 'Someone will be in touch. All agents have comprehensive life insurance. There aren't many perks when you work for the security service, but that is one of them.' She winced. Stupid thing to say. It was hardly the time for making jokes. But Marion seemed lost in her own thoughts.

'He was always so worried about money. I think that was what drove us apart in the end. No offence, but you were a symptom, not the cause. All of you were. You weren't the only one – I do hope you know that. We argued about money a lot towards the end. I think I pushed him too much. I wanted him to get a job in the private sector because the money was so much better. Advising some energy company or bank on security issues. But he didn't seem keen. Wasn't that ambitious. But I think it ate away at him, how poorly he was paid. He kept saying if he had it all again he wouldn't have joined the service. "I got seduced by the glamour of the job," he would often say. "But that was just a marketing ploy to suck me in." Well, look where the glamour got him in the end, hey?'

Kate felt mildly shocked by what she was hearing. She hadn't had McLure down as someone who'd been so money-motivated. But it made sense, given some of the things he'd said to her. She sighed. It was trivial and un-important, but the service's rules said such intelligence had to be reported up the chain. Money problems were a poten-tial sign that an agent could be compromised. But not McLure, she thought. He wasn't the type.

Her phone vibrated. A text. She glanced down, aware that it was poor protocol to check messages when delivering bad news. Still, it might be relevant. The message was from Sorrenson. She looked at Marion. 'I really am sorry,' she said. 'About everything.'

Marion attempted a smile. 'Don't be. In many ways for me Anthony died a long time ago. This is just some sort of horrible confirmation. I'm enjoying my life here. It's allowed me to dust off my old qualifications and start afresh.'

'What do you do?'

'I'm a corporate lawyer, a receiver, basically. I'm paid to go in and act on behalf of the creditors when things go wrong.' She gestured across the square. 'There's plenty of work here, unfortunately. My firm tells me they've never been so busy. We're one of the few to be doing well on the back of the banking crisis. Business is booming.'

Chapter 8

Prince Faisal Bin Taleed Sin Abdullah, eldest son of Prince Aldud Bin Taleed Sin Abdullah, looked out of the boardroom of his Mayfair office and onto Hyde Park. But he wasn't interested in the grand vista commanded by his piece of prime London office space. He was too distracted. He kept turning to the large screen at the end of the room. An observer would have been curious as to the cause of the prince's fascination with it. It showed a jumble of letters and numbers. They were impenetrable and made no sense.

Schwartz, the chief operating officer of the prince's Quest hedge fund, pressed a button on a device in his hand. He gestured at the screen as the letters and numbers changed. 'So, as you can see, if this particular scenario, our plan A, unfolded, there would be urgent contagion that would place great stress on the entire banking system. Most banks, those using high-frequency trading platforms at least, would suffer catastrophic damage. According to our modelling, the majority would not be able to survive given their current reserves. Meaning—'

'Their governments would have to bail them out.' The prince clapped his hands with delight.

'Correct, but—'

'They're too stretched to do it. They're so indebted they can't do any more.'

'Correct.' Schwartz hesitated. Was the prince going to interject again? He liked to show he understood complex financial modelling but Schwartz was dubious about whether he truly appreciated what he was being told. You really needed a degree in astrophysics or access to mind-expanding drugs to fully comprehend the genius of the plan. Schwartz knew that Prince Faisal's interruptions were his way of proving that he was following what was being said. But they were a bluff, really. The prince was keen on bluffing. Gamesmanship was everything to him.

Schwartz cleared his throat to allow the prince time to say something more, but his employer remained silent, content to nod with quiet approval.

'Under this scenario,' Schwartz said, pressing the button and changing the screen, 'every major government would be sucked into the ensuing chaos. They would quickly realize the hopelessness of their situation. Quite simply, if they try to prop up their banks, they won't be able to do it. They haven't the firepower to deal with something on this scale.'

'And if they don't try to bail out their banks?'

'There will be anarchy. There will be a run on the banks as people try to get their money out. We predict widespread looting, the rise of vigilantism, the deployment of the army. And that is just within the first few days.'

'Go on.'

'Well, the next thing that will happen is that the food and fuel distribution chain shuts down. Schools shut, hospitals shut. If you can't pay people, they won't work. Supermarkets, shops, wholesalers, distributors will be ransacked of every-thing. Within a week there will be nothing left for people to eat. There will be acute shortages everywhere.' Schwartz allowed himself a smile. 'MI5 always says that Britain is only three missed meals away from anarchy. Well, this scenario would reveal whether or not they're correct. It would sub-ject countries to the ultimate stress test and show how they coped when their citizens couldn't get their ready meals.'

The prince pointed at the screen. 'How long before they would be able to assess the true damage, if the scenario actually happened?'

Schwartz thought for several seconds. 'Well, according to our sources in nuclear security, between five and eight days. This was what happened in Japan after the earthquake. Took them a couple of days to recover, get specialist radiation teams on site. Then they had to test for radioactivity, make sure everything was properly shut down. We're looking at a minimum of six days before they can confirm whether their worst fears have been realized.'

'And you think this . . .' the prince chose his word care-fully '. . . incident would generate so much terror in the financial system that it would do real damage to Western governments?'

Schwartz looked at the giant screen. 'From our analysis of their still extremely weakened financial situations, I would say yes, unequivocally. They've been left very damaged by the banking crisis. True, they are repairing their balance sheets, cutting spending, but they're still at the edge of the abyss, psychologically speaking. Obviously, this scenario has never happened before, but all the modelling indicates that it would have a tumultuous impact on the world's financial systems.'

The prince smiled. 'Well, then, it would indeed be very interesting if that unfortunate scenario ever unfolded. Many Western governments must hope that it remains the stuff of nightmares.'

Schwartz nodded. 'Yes.'

'But fortunately, Schwartz, we are experts at modelling risk, are we not? If that scenario was ever to unfold, we would be protected? We would have hedged ourselves against the apocalypse?'

'Correct. Better than protected, you could say. We'd be the only ones to stay dry when everyone else was drowning.'

The idea had come out of nowhere. Schwartz had built an elite team within Quest whose job was to model financial risk. They'd experimented with wildly different scenarios as they sought to mimic the effects of natural disasters on global markets. The idea had been to create a suite of products that they could offer clients as a form of insurance against worst-case scenarios.

But then, seizing an opportunity to impress the prince, one of the Quest team, a former NASA engineer named Westinghouse, had wondered aloud what would happen if their risk modelling was applied not only to natural disasters, but also to man-made ones.

There had been silence in the room when the suggestion was made. The five-strong team overseen by Schwartz had collectively held its breath awaiting the prince's response. His reaction, after several minutes of uncomfortable silence, had surprised them. He had barked into a mobile phone, calling up security to ensure the room was swept for bugs. When the team had gone he had been encouraging. 'That is a most interesting suggestion, Mr Westinghouse. Although I'm at a loss to understand what you mean. No one can just create disasters. No man can play God. Not even me.'

Westinghouse's face betrayed little emotion. 'Hypothetically speaking, of course, but say you were categorically aware of some terrorism-related event looming on the horizon. We've seen what happens to the markets after a major incident, how they go into free-fall. If we happened to know that one was coming, we could prepare for it. We could take positions. And they'd be risk-free. Because we'd know what the outcome was going to be.'

'And what positions would those be, Mr Westinghouse?' The prince sounded playful, like a teacher with a favourite pupil.

'Basically, we'd do what everyone does in times of acute turmoil. We'd buy gold and sell oil futures just before the world plunged into the next Great Depression.'

'Interesting, Mr Westinghouse,' the prince had said. 'Very interesting. But I foresee a major flaw in your plan, one, I would suggest, that owes much to your fascination with numbers rather than people.'

Westinghouse had seemed nonplussed.

'I think what Prince Faisal fears,' Schwartz interjected, 'is that the problem with Great Depressions is that they are both great and depressions. If the world was to be tipped into another, the whole financial system would be devastated. And, while we might clean up in the short term, in the longer term no one benefits. Everything would grind to a halt. Saudi oil, Russian gas, Chinese manufacturing, India's nuclear-power programme, civilization, everything. We'd have a lot of money and very little to invest it in.'

There had been a short silence. Then Westinghouse spoke in the dispassionate tone of someone who couldn't understand the footling problems being presented to him. 'But what if it was all an illusion? What if the fear was invented? What if it lasted just a few days, enough for us to clean up financially, to blow away some of the bloated, indebted banks, humble a few governments, and then everything went back to normal, albeit with a lot of people out of work, maybe the odd president or prime minister ousted and a heap of dumb investors out of pocket?'

Schwartz couldn't suppress his laughter. 'So you're a magician now, not a financial genius, Westinghouse? You're going to make the Pyramids disappear next, right?'

Westinghouse was impervious to Schwartz's sarcasm. His mind was elsewhere, scrolling through a million potential nightmare scenarios. It was as if his brain was some sort of super-computer, the sort they rolled out to take on chess grandmasters. Colours flashed in his mind, forming complex patterns. His mind alighted on a particularly vivid crimson: he focused on it, felt himself walking through it, as if it was a door. Numbers raced through his mind, huge numbers. He stood up and went to the window. He watched a flock of Canada geese descend on the Serpentine. Big birds. Yeah, he thought, that would work. Those birds could do real damage if they hit something. Something . . .

He turned back to the prince and the Quest team.

'Chance of a bird-strike on a plane, one in ten thousand. Chance of a bird-strike that brings a plane down on a nuclear power station, one in three million by my rough estimates. But what if you cut the odds out altogether? What if you blamed a bird-strike for bringing a plane down on a nuclear reactor, when the reality was that you had made it happen, something that made Chernobyl look like a picnic? That would trigger a global panic. That would create carnage in the markets, carnage we could take advantage of. You'd do a lot more damage than Enron and Lehman Brothers rolled into one.'

It was Schwartz who added the sobering corrective. 'Great plan. We'll just advertise for some suicidal pilot and then we're good to go.'

Westinghouse shrugged. 'You could, I guess. But it would be easy to do it using remote control. That's what they do when they're trying to assess the impact of a crash on a jet. They just fly it into the ground in the desert, using remote systems. The beauty of this plan is that no one dies. Well, maybe quite a few banks, but that's it. Sure, some radiation may seep out. Maybe we'll get some three-headed sheep one day. But the authorities will clean it up in time. Fukushima, Chernobyl, they'll get cleaned up in the end. Life will go on. You could say it's a victimless crime. We're only doing what really needs to happen if some of the toxic, debt-laden parts of the financial system are to be cleansed properly anyway. Hell, you could say we're basically doing the world a favour, sweeping away the dead wood. I'm not sure the markets have really learned the lessons from the crash. The world needs to improve the security of its nuclear plants, too. This could be a wake-up call. It would be Darwinian. It's just evolution speeded up, really.'

It was a powerful speech but the word 'crime' hung in the air, like a suspended exclamation mark. The four other members of Schwartz's team were acutely conscious that their group-think was in danger of morphing them into different beings. In one sense they could see little that was wrong with the plan. After all, it was, as Westinghouse suggested, merely an extension of what they were doing already. Hedge funds manipulated markets all the time. If they made money it showed that their bets were right, their hunches had been correct. They had little fear of regulators. Some of the tricks they'd performed confirmed just how little oversight there was of their activities. But, still, they would be going completely through the looking glass in initiating a plane crash. All eyes had turned to the prince.

'A bird-strike, right,' the prince murmured. 'But where would we find a runway near to a large bird population and a nuclear power station? We'd need to own the runway if we were going to do this. We wouldn't want people watching us too closely. Kitting out a plane with remote control would set alarm bells ringing. It would be unfortunate to put so much effort into something, only for us to be subjected to such unwelcome attention. And what of the absence of a body and the remains of the remote-control device? Surely that would show the whole thing had been manufactured.'

'No,' Westinghouse said. 'You could make sure the cockpit was obliterated upon impact so there was nothing left.'

There was another long silence.

'I'll do some checking,' Schwartz said. 'The world isn't short of runways. And, given the state of the economy, there must be quite a few whose owners are keen to sell.'

The prince and his father had bought the runway in Kent a month later, from receivers selling off the assets of a bombed-out Irish bank.

'Under two miles to my mansion,' the prince had told his son. 'Most convenient. The Gulfstreams will no longer have to use Gatwick. Using that airport is a horrible experience. I don't understand why anyone flies when they have to put up with such horrors.'

It was shortly after the airport had been acquired that Schwartz had presented the prince with an alternative plan. Westinghouse was on to something, he acknowledged. But there was still risk involved. Flying a plane into a nuclear power station would open a Pandora's box. For all of their combined genius, they didn't know what the consequences would be. No one had ever done something like it before. It was a useful default position, Westinghouse's plan, one they could stress-test, bounce ideas off, but what if they explored a different scenario?

'Like what?' the prince had asked.

'Markets are powered by fear,' Schwartz had explained. 'Fear lies in its anticipation, not in its delivery. What if you could monetize that fear?'

She checked her reflection in the bar mirror. She was due to visit her mother later in the evening but had agreed to see Sorrenson for a drink. He had texted to say he was running late. Copper bandits had stolen half the cabling on the railway line and all trains were delayed. She was annoyed. She'd wanted to spend longer with him than they were going to have.

She was curious about her actions. She didn't usually spend too much time peering at herself in mirrors. She knew that she was attractive enough to get looks from most men, and usually, for her purposes, their appearance rarely mattered. They were there to do a job. They were there to shut out the pain, make her forget her dead husband and her dead father and her near-dead poisonous mother for just a few hours. And then they could be dispensed with.

It was a fine *quid pro quo*. Most were grateful for her attention. Only Sorrenson had complicated things. Still, she told herself, one drink and she would leave. She was interested to learn more about his investigation, but not professionally. Holahon's death was one giant red herring when it came to Higgs, she felt. It had nothing to do with terrorism, nothing to do with McLure and nothing to do with her. She needed to focus on what she was paid to do. And yet the investigator in her was still interested in what Sorrenson had to say. At least, that was what she told herself. It was his information she was interested in, not him. Yes, his information. That was it.

She saw him walk through the door and glance around the unfamiliar bar. He was looking good, she thought. Alive, alert. He must have been hitting the trails heavily since she'd last seen him.

'Hey.'

She stood up, let him kiss her cheek. She poured him a glass of wine from a bottle on the table. 'Côte du Rhône, right?'

'Right. Sorry I'm late. The train, well, you know . . .'

'No worries. You look well.'

'Thanks, so do you. You look great. I mean . . .' Sorrenson gulped his wine.

She smiled, patted his hand. She was pleased that he was embarrassed. It made him seem vulnerable, more normal.

126

'Cheers. It's good to see you. I'm not just saying that. I'm sorry if the other time . . . Unprofessional, I know.'

Sorrenson laughed. 'Don't apologize. Made my year.' His face burned red. 'I mean . . . Anyway,' he said quickly, aware that he was behaving like an out-of-control satellite, space junk, flying around her orbit, 'about our friend.'

'I'm all ears.'

'Well, it's more a case of being all eyes, really.' He pulled a laptop out of its case, unfolded it and revealed a screen of electronic maps.

'Your running routes. Fascinating stuff. It used to be etchings us girls were invited to view.'

'Good one. No, these aren't mine, they're Holahon's. His watch was found on Hampstead Heath and handed in to us. It reveals a mine of data. Tracks his runs going back years.'

'OK. I see that.'

She couldn't understand why Sorrenson sounded so excited. It was just a dead man's running record. It wasn't even his banking transactions. Following money could reveal the truth of things. But not old races. Not distances over time. Her thoughts turned to McLure's computer. IT had decrypted it. She would examine it tomorrow.

'Look here.' Sorrenson pointed at one of the maps on the screen.

She peered at it, sipped her wine. 'Mmm. Long one. The Wall. Oh, yeah, that was the sixty-nine-miler he did, wasn't it? Didn't he come first in the veterans' category?'

'Right. Now look at the time it took him to do the race, the time recorded by his watch.'

Kate studied the screen. 'That's just not possible. I mean, not even a world-class athlete could do it in that time. His watch says he did it around six hours faster than his actual winning time.'

'Correct, and that's what I thought,' Sorrenson said. 'But if I click on the screen, we can monitor his speed over the course. There's this great stretch here, some thirty-odd miles, which he apparently did in barely more than a couple of hours. And then look – his watch suggests he waited here at the end for several hours before he started jogging again.'

'So?'

'So it looks to me like he was waiting to rejoin the race after having ensured he was going to win. That thirty-mile stretch I was just talking about runs close to a quiet road. I checked using satellite photos. I'll bet he made that journey on a bike or something, then hid for a while to make his time seem realistic.'

She flashed him a smile that he wanted to own. God, he was pleased to see her.

'Well, Holmes, good work. We'll book him with faking his running times. It's a shame he's not alive. He'd be going down for a long stretch.'

Sorrenson grinned. 'I suppose you guys only get interested when the words "national security" enter the frame. Fair enough. But it's curious, isn't it? If he lied about that, did he lie about anything else? And if you took risks like that in your private life, does that mean you'd take risks in your professional life? Did he push something or someone too far?'

She looked at her watch. She really needed to get to her mother. She had cancelled the previous visit because of work. There could be no more excuses. 'Maybe,' she said doubtfully. 'But I've never been convinced his death had anything to do with his work. I can't tell you too much, but we've been monitoring his bank for some time and I don't see any link between what it's getting up to and Holahon's murder. Some of my colleagues have been going crazy trying to prove a link. They're desperate to find a connection, but I don't think it's there.'

'You're probably right. Look where an obsession with running gets you.'

She was going to reply when something made her hold back. She had the same watch. It was vulcanized rubber and once it was strapped to your wrist it was almost impossible to remove it without some effort. It was not the sort of thing to fall off a wrist accidentally. She examined the screen for several seconds, sipping her wine. 'You looked at all of the runs?'

'Most of them.'

'The last one?'

Sorrenson was confused. There were so many, he couldn't be sure. 'Don't know. Why?'

'Hang on. Let me have a play with this.' She pulled the laptop towards her and clicked a couple of buttons on the keyboard. She dragged the cursor around the screen, used it to scroll through a series of tables. After a few seconds a thin smile hovered on her lips. 'Hmm.'

'What?' Sorrenson watched her work with undisguised fascination. She was something else.

'According to his watch, this is his last recorded run.'

'Right.'

'Now, I can't be sure – you'd need to check the records – but I think this run here, his last recorded on the watch, was on the night he went missing. You told me CCTV cameras captured him leaving his apartment in Holland Park and heading east. Look at the map. It tracks the probable route. And look where he ends up.'

Sorrenson peered at the map. 'The Heath. Jesus. Look at where the run ends. Right there at the top of the Heath. That's the spot where the watch was found.'

'Interesting. Where exactly was it found?'

Sorrenson thought for a few seconds. 'Under a bush in a copse.'

'So, not in some open space where a passer-by would be likely to find it easily?'

'No.'

'Well, maybe he chucked it into the bushes. Maybe as he was attacked he tore it off and threw it into the bushes as some sort of clue. He didn't have much time and he needed to leave some trace. Have you checked the surrounding area?'

'We're thinking about trawling the ponds but it's difficult to get authorization for the operation. It's expensive and the chief constable couldn't see how it might be justified. But if our man was on the Heath the night he disappeared, I imagine that would change everything.'

He saw her glance at her watch. She smiled at him apologetically and stood up. She really had to go. 'Well, it sounds like your job's far more interesting than mine,' she said. 'I'm sorry but I really have to leave. My mother . . . Well, I told you about her. I'm sorry we didn't have more time.' She bent down and kissed his cheek.

Sorrenson wanted to say something but she was already halfway out of the pub. He watched her weave through the throng. The image of her departing would stay with him for ever, he thought.

★　★　★

Brockman handed the lap-dancer a stash of Rhino dollars, the plastic chips used to pay for the grinding dances that took place in the darkest environs of the club. There must have been a thousand pounds' worth of chips, Ennis calculated. 'Here, Kayleigh, these chips are for you. Cash 'em in – you've worn me out. Now make yourself scarce for a while but, be a darling, come back after my friend here has dined with me.' He gave her a big, leery Texan grin.

'Oh, babe, you're always so generous. I'll save a dance for you later, you can be sure of that.' She blew him a kiss, pulled on her red thong and bra and sauntered off to the other side of the club.

Ennis watched her walk away. 'Why does my wife never wear heels like that?'

'Because if she did, young girls like the lovely Kayleigh would be out of a job,' Brockman said. They watched the next girl take to the pole in the centre of the club. 'We don't want our wives to be lap-dancers and we don't want our lap-dancers to be our wives,' Brockman murmured. 'It's the madonna-whore thing. That's why we pay them the Rhino dollars. Money helps us delineate. It gives us choices. But, the way things are going, those chips are going to be more valuable than the real thing pretty soon.'

'That bad, hey? Fuck.'

Brockman nodded in the gloom. 'Higgs is one step away from the abyss, I'm sure of it. It's basically me who's stopping it from falling off. Thank fuck for the towel-head. It's his cash pile that's propping us up. His father's been taking billions out of Higgs, but the son is still doing a lot of business with us.'

'Jesus.' Ennis sipped his bottle of beer. He turned his head forty-five degrees to study the face of the near upside-down dancer. 'You need good muscles to pull that move off.'

'Bet she works out,' Brockman said. 'You eating? The surf and turf here is very good. Reminds me of the big grill-houses we have back in Texas.'

Ennis shook his head. 'Nah. Got a race coming up. Need to watch what I eat. Even the odd beer puts me on a guilt trip.' He waved his bottle regretfully.

'Tell me about it. I'm in the same boat. This is my last blow-out before Berlin. I really need that personal best. If I can't do it there I'm never going to. I'm so close I can taste it.' Brockman lowered his voice as the dancer finished and the music died down. 'So, how you keeping? You robust, sport?'

Ennis scratched his nose. 'I'm holding up all right. You?'

'Can't complain.'

'You know the police were around Higgs the other day, checking the CCTV footage again?' Ennis said.

'They did that weeks ago. They got nothing. Most of it will have been wiped by now anyway. Relax.' Brockman leaned back in his chair and gave Ennis a thin smile. 'They ain't ever going to find anything. Don't you worry.'

'They're dredging the ponds on the Heath.'

'I heard. So maybe they find something in the water. Who knows? They may get lucky. But what's it going prove if they do?'

Ennis shrugged, swigged his beer. 'Yeah.' He turned to Brockman. 'There any CCTV cameras on the Heath?'

Brockman sipped his Merlot. 'Maybe, but it strikes me it's a bit of mystery, poor old Brad Holahon's death. Can't see it ever being solved. How's business by the way? Hear you're leading on the Interdata IPO. Big float. You got to have big *cojones* for that. One of my client Prince Faisal's big investments, Interdata. He's very keen to get it to market soon. He seems to be a man in a rush. I want to help him in it. Long as I got the prince I'm impregnable. That's why I told you not to worry. Higgs looks after its employees who look after its star clients. Can't afford to kill the fatted calf. You know that. Well, you should. The bank knows it needs to offer its staff security, to protect them.' He grinned at Ennis. 'The linguini is good here. You really need to start carb-loading.'

Sorrenson stood outside Higgs Bank and tried not to fall in love. It was beautiful, a supermodel in building terms. A 1930s art-deco glass construction with smooth, wavy lines fronted by an impressive revolving door. In the fading spring evening, the bank assumed an ebony façade that reflected passing traffic, which made the building itself seem to be rushing past stationary cars. It sat squat in the middle of Fleet Street, surrounded by buildings hundreds of years older. But none had its presence. The bank was in a different league.

He looked up and down the street, his eyes trained on the first floor of the buildings, checking for the all-seeing eyes. Sorrenson counted six sets of CCTV cameras within the first hundred metres of the bank. Useful. More helpful than the Higgs security team anyway. They'd searched through the footage captured on their CCTV cameras but everything from the night of Holahon's disappearance and his death had been erased. Sorrenson accepted the line grudgingly. It was standard procedure to erase footage after a while, he knew from countless previous investigations. But, still, it was all a little neat. He gestured at Hughes. 'Come on. I'll buy you a pint. It's gone eight. Anything?'

Hughes pointed across the road. 'Two sets there, and another four further down. You can't move here for cameras. Shame there's hardly any around the Heath.'

'No one wants to blow up the Heath, that's why. This place is one massive target. No wonder everyone walking around here looks so wired. It's one big conflict zone.'

Hughes glanced around and lit a cigarette. 'We going to inform the Met that we're requesting the footage from the Corporation of London?'

Sorrenson grimaced as Hughes exhaled smoke in his direction. 'Maybe. I'm still not sure if this is in any way useful. It's probably more a City of London Police thing. Perhaps we'll keep it to ourselves for a bit. So many of the big private security firms have got police on retainer that things might leak out and then we'll be having to explain why we're spending valuable man hours on a murder that was, in all likelihood, committed in the capital. Doesn't look good, given the constrained budgets. The chief constable is already insisting we scale back on this. It's not as if we're under pressure to get a result here. No one seems to be missing Mr Holahon very much. Maybe a few people in the City but that's about it.'

'Right.' Hughes inhaled deeply. 'Now, about that drink.'

Sorrenson's phone bleeped. He pulled it out of his pocket. There was nothing cryptic about her messages. Jesus, she could be direct. The language was very Anglo-Saxon. His heart started to race. 'Something's come up. Apologies. I have to go.'

Hughes shook his head. 'I just hope she's worth it,' he muttered.

Chapter 9

Mozart filled the late spring air as a string quartet comprising four perfectly made-up women wearing figure-hugging black dresses enthusiastically caressed their instruments as if they were new-born babies.

The peacock was in imperious form, its feathers fanned out in such a gloriously ostentatious way that it was almost as if it knew the importance of the occasion. A small army of waiters and waitresses ferried canapés and Champagne across the prince's lawns. Ice sculptures glistened in the sun. Animals carved from hedges cast long shapes across the vivid green grass.

Carlyle appraised the view from the vantage-point of the rose garden above the lawns. They'd been lucky with the weather, he thought. The brilliant English sunshine was made for garden parties. He watched Prince Aldud talking to the Prince of Wales, the next in line to the throne cutting an awkward figure in the middle of the pastel throng. The two royals were old friends and regular shooting companions. They shared a common love of classical architecture and a grave suspicion of GM food.

The prince's fixer turned his attention to the handful of carefully screened journalists congregating at the edge of the party. They were sipping Champagne and swapping small-talk, every now and then breaking off to point to a well-known figure strolling across the lawn. It was the perfect venue for celebrity spotting. The prince's helicopters had been kept busy ferrying in the great and the good from London. As one diarist had remarked in a newspaper column that Saturday morning, the event promised to be 'one of the most talked-about parties of the year'.

He almost smiled, remembering the comment. It would certainly be that, he thought. He pictured the journalists pulling out their mobile phones and dialling in their stories. They thought they were attending something akin to Royal Ascot without the horses. They would be surprised when the prince gave his speech. Very surprised. He was preparing a political ambush. Its effects would be felt around the world. There would be tremors across every continent.

Carlyle recognized the cracking sound immediately. He'd spent enough time dealing in guns to know what high-powered rifles sounded like. He watched the Prince of Wales recoil in horror as his host's brain splattered over his linen suit. The sound of screaming filled the air as scores of security goons came storming through the gardens, screaming at people to lie down. The peacock, alarmed by the mêlée, flew up into a low-hanging branch.

The fixer turned to the trees behind him for the tell-tale glint of the rifle. But he could see nothing. The sniper must have been more than five hundred metres away, he estimated. An expert shot. Weariness overcame him. He surveyed the carnage and popped a mint into his mouth. So, there would be no speech. The prince's legacy would be unrealized. This is how it ends, Carlyle thought. This is how it was probably always going to end. He descended the marble steps from the rose garden and walked towards the chaos of his own uncertain future.

Kate looked at Sorrenson and felt a small, unexpected stab of guilt. How many times could she use him? He seemed happy to be used but that didn't offer her an excuse, a way out. In the long run, it wasn't fair.

And, besides, by sleeping with him again she'd broken her golden rule. She operated a one-strike-and-you're-out policy when it came to men. Anything else seemed a betrayal of Michael.

But it had been difficult, she conceded. Her mother had been in scabrous form. The drugs were really eating away at her now. Her old kind self had almost completely disappeared. All that was left was bile and rage. A heady brew.

The last visit, Kate had brought out the family album again only for her mother to comprehensively destroy the past. 'Your father,' she had practically spat, 'loved his work more than me, more than us.'

Kate had tried to gently remonstrate, pointing out how happy the pair of them had been. But her mother wasn't having any of it. It was almost as if she wanted to hate her past so much that letting go of it, closing it all down, saying goodbye to everything she had held dear, would make its passing bearable. Kate hadn't been prepared to allow her mother that reinterpretation. It would have been a betrayal of them all, she felt. She owed it to Maggie to stand up to her hate-filled self, even if it made her last weeks difficult, confusing, ugly.

But her mother had seemed to grow more vengeful as the minutes ticked by. Her face was so twisted by anger that Kate barely recognized her. Her sentences became confused, accusatory, wild.

'Heading to the Causeway. What was he doing going that way, hey? Nowhere near Belfast. A girl, hey? Where was his girl?'

She had been shocked by her mother's words. She no longer knew the woman who'd given birth to her. The pain must be intense, she thought. Her mother was so warped by the cancer that she could distance herself from it only by lashing out at everything she loved. It was horrible and almost hypnotic, she thought, watching her mother's disintegration. It was like watching the production of a painting in reverse, something beautiful being stripped down to just the base elements, something reduced to the abstract, made only half recognizable.

It had proved too much to take. She had needed escape. Hence the text. Direct, to the point. He had been grateful to receive it, she was sure. But losing herself in someone else was unhealthy, she knew. It didn't address what drove her to take such actions. It didn't answer why she felt it so necessary to lose herself. She remembered what an alcoholic friend had told her about his addiction. 'They call it a God-shaped hole, the space in my life I'm trying to fill with drink,' he'd told her. Well, she had a Michael-shaped hole. She carried his absence with her everywhere.

She eased herself out of the hotel bed and padded into the bathroom. It had had to be a hotel. There was no way she would have taken him back to hers. That would have been far too much disclosure, too much de-robing. She stared at herself in the unflattering mirror. The windowless bathroom made the lighting harsh and unforgiving. She was getting old. Crow's feet, and her blue eyes looked duller than they used to. Soon she'd have to start dyeing her hair. But, still, for forty she looked OK. Better than OK, she conceded, examining her naked self.

'Jesus.' Sorrenson's voice from the bedroom. She walked out of the bathroom. He had the television on. She was surprised to see that the clock in the corner of the screen was showing it was gone one o'clock. They'd slept late.

'What's up?' She stood before him naked, unembarrassed.

Sorrenson looked at her, then checked himself. He was momentarily lost for words. He pointed at the screen. 'Looks like someone your end is going to have their work cut out this weekend. Maybe my end too, come to that.'

A rolling-news channel was reporting that a Saudi prince had been assassinated at his stately home.

'They said his name yet?'

Sorrenson shook his head, held her gaze for several seconds and gently whistled. 'No,' he said finally. 'But it was in the south-east. Can't be too many. Oligarchs, yes. Saudi princes less so.' He pointed to the screen. A map was showing the location of the house.

Kate sat down on the bed. She felt a need to start making connections, sifting through her mental files for names, bank accounts, information. 'You know that airport down your way?'

'Yeah, the one owned by the . . .' Recognition flashed in Sorrenson's face.

'Saudi prince, right?' Kate said. 'The billionaire who wants to extend the runway. Well, I'm betting he's the deceased. And I've got a really bad feeling that somehow this is going to get linked back to Holahon's death. There's going to be a massive effort to connect the two deaths now. The press will be all over this. There'll be a huge rush to join the dots, make sense of it all. What a mess.'

Sorrenson rolled out of bed, located his jeans on the floor. 'And what do you think?'

Her eyes were focused on the television screen. 'I don't know. But a link isn't established just because two people who were connected by a bank are now dead. All I'm saying is that people are going to rush into thinking that it is. Intelligence likes clean patterns. But this feels messy and complicated.'

'Still, you've got to admit, it looks more than just coincidence.'

She turned from the screen and contemplated him. 'You're dressed?'

'Nothing gets past you.'

She pointed at the bed. 'We were supposed to check out an hour ago. Now that we're going to be charged for an extra day we may as well make it worthwhile.'

The diner was one of Reynolds's favourites. It did the best fried potatoes in New York and the coffee was decent and plentiful. The waitresses hardly seemed to change either. He liked that, the continuity. But his main reason for choosing the diner was that it was quiet in the early hours of the morning. Lying just off Wall Street, it only started to get busy when the traders came in around six thirty. At five Reynolds had the place virtually to himself. He sat in a leather-backed booth and sipped coffee, pretended to read his *New York Times*, pretended that he was free of worry. You could do anything if you exhibited confidence. Life was about gamesmanship, ultimately. Wall Street was full of people well practised in faking it. The sound of footsteps made him look up. The two men nodded at each other. Reynolds gestured for Carey to sit down.

'How long you been coming here?' Carey said.

Reynolds thought for a few seconds. 'Maybe ten, possibly eleven years.'

'I figured. This place is like your second office.'

'I feel comfortable here.'

Carey laughed. 'Not like Higgs.'

'Right.'

Carey studied the breakfast menu. 'You know, Dick, you could always come back to the Agency if babysitting Higgs is not to your liking any more. Someone else can run your bit of the FIU. Let someone else worry about the bank. Ask yourself, do you need the grief? At your age too.'

Reynolds massaged his temples with his right hand. It was going to be a long day. 'You make it sound like an ultimatum.'

'No, I'm just saying that if you want out you've got it. Brandeis will buy it. He's sympathetic. He understands the pressure you're under. He's hearing the rumours. You've been there a long time. It's bound to drag on you.'

Reynolds pushed some potato across his plate with a fork and eyed it contemptuously. He'd lost his appetite. He stared at his rejected breakfast. 'I guess you're telling me it would be convenient if I was moved. That it might be a good idea to put some distance between me and Higgs.'

Carey sat back in the booth, let his head sink against the seatback. Then he picked up a paper napkin and tore it into strips.

Reynolds watched, fascinated. He felt like a child at confession. Maybe, he thought, some truths wouldn't hurt. Maybe it was time for Carey to be handed the bomb. Bring him into his circle of confidence. See how he liked the truth.

'Maybe you're right,' Reynolds said slowly. 'I mean, all that Holahon stuff, there's bound to be blowback from it. Eventually. One way or another. People are crawling all over Higgs now. The dead prince isn't helping either. The bank is under a massive spotlight. It can't stay in the shadows any longer. People are going to start making links to the Agency.'

Carey looked at Reynolds. His face was a series of frowns. 'Something you're not telling me, Dick? Are we not getting the full picture here?' He continued ripping the napkin into ever-smaller pieces, taking satisfaction from his puny act of destruction.

Reynolds watched the tissue fall like confetti. There was a time when he had wanted Carey's job, a stepping stone to Brandeis's position. But no longer. Reynolds couldn't cope with more responsibility. What he already had was close to destroying him.

'But now, well, I'm concerned,' Carey said, in the laconic voice of a late-night radio presenter. 'Maybe we're not clean. It seems like maybe you're trying to tell me something. Maybe you know things.'

Reynolds held Carey's gaze. A blur of flashing lights outside the diner signalled garbage-men were at work. The sound of banging bins indicated that New York was getting busy. The bankers would be descending on the diner soon. They always followed the trash, he knew from experience. And one day, not long from now, Reynolds thought, one of those bankers would take a good long look at Higgs. They would do a proper forensic audit. They would see its huge debts, realize it was teetering on the edge and push it off the cliff. Something that seemed so mighty, so permanent, so vast, would implode in just seconds.

The weapon would probably be a humble analyst's note questioning the bank's cash reserves. Hardly a bomb. But it would do its devastating job nevertheless. It would send tremors across the Hudson that would end up washing over every shore. Dangerous tremors. That could not be allowed to happen, Reynolds thought. Whatever it took, he had to prevent that scenario unfolding.

The confessional was over before it really started. There would be no disclosure to Carey. Fuck Carey and Brandeis and everyone else in the Agency, Reynolds thought. Those pricks could remain in the dark. He tried to smile at Carey and took a sip of his coffee. 'No, I'm not trying to tell you anything,' he said quietly. 'Everything's in hand. Higgs is sound.'

'Good, cos if we have a problem we need to know about it. Higgs is still your baby. You call the shots. It's still giving us valuable intel. And, remember, closing it all down would be more difficult than allowing it to live in many ways. We can't just make it disappear overnight. So you make sure Higgs has no problems. You hear me? I'm telling you to sort things, OK? We don't want blowback on this.'

Reynolds poured some more sugar into his coffee and stirred. He watched the black liquid spinning, lapping at the edges. The coffee continued to swirl in the mug, the circles acquiring a momentum of their own. It was almost hypnotic, Reynolds thought, the momentum of something you had started but over which you no longer had control.

There were so many files. Too many. Hundreds, she thought. It was apparent that McLure had been wading through oceans of information. It was far too much for one person. Whatever the service had been paying him, it hadn't been enough.

She scanned the file names in the hope that she would recognize some. A lot were related to offshore trusts and companies hidden in tax havens. So much effort had gone into hiding entire companies. It was one thing for IT to have decrypted McLure's computer, but the huge volumes of information it contained made her hunt almost impossible. It was going to take time, lots of it, before anything became clear. She wasn't sure she had a lot of time to play with. She looked up at her whiteboard. Dotted lines connected the names of Holahon, the prince and McLure. In the centre she'd written 'Higgs Bank'. It was hardly revelatory. The newspapers were running similar diagrams, albeit with McLure's name absent. So far the news of his murder hadn't leaked. You had to hand it to the Americans, she thought. They could close down bad news really quickly. When it came to information suppression, they were in a league of their own.

She found the electronic file containing the Higgs accounts that she'd earmarked for McLure's attention. She clicked on the prince's file and read the notes she'd made for McLure. She'd written an extensive memo on Holahon's involvement in setting up the prince's accounts, in London and in several tax havens. It was clear that McLure had read it several times because he'd typed his own additions to the memo. She scanned McLure's electronic jottings. All basic box-ticking stuff. There was nothing. She was about to shut the file down when a name jumped out at her. At the bottom of the memo McLure had added 'Brockman' and a question mark.

A coincidence, she thought. Weird, but just a coincidence. Surely. She recalled the Texan with the same name that she'd run with on the Heath. He'd known Holahon. And he was a banker, too. She typed 'Higgs and Brockman' into Google and within a nanosecond had learned that the Texan was head of private client relationships for the bank's London branch. Interesting. Why had McLure been looking at him? A quick search suggested that he didn't manage any of the accounts she'd drawn to McLure's attention. Still, McLure had thought he was worthy of further interest.

She stood up, added Brockman's name to the whiteboard. Probably nothing, she told herself, but it filled some space. The action gave her confidence: she was making progress.

She returned to McLure's files. Something about the late prince's file bothered her. Vast quantities of money – billions and billions of pounds – had been consolidated into one account. It was almost as if he'd been doing some house-keeping, tidying up his finances. She thought of the mess her father had left behind after his untimely death. It had taken months for her mother to go through it and sort it out.

She looked at the accounts again. Yes, they seemed to suggest someone was clearing things up. The sort of exercise performed by someone who knew they didn't have long to do it. A form of probate. She noticed a large portion of the prince's equity portfolio had been converted into cash, too. Large amounts of money had been transferred out of the accounts to an investment vehicle in the Turks and Caicos Islands, called 'Relief 1'.

She sat back and sighed. It was gone ten in the evening. The automatic lights in the corridor had switched themselves off. Everyone had left. She really needed to go home. She walked over to the water dispenser and filled a plastic cup. The cool water refreshed her, brought clarity.

She returned to her chair and idly scanned McLure's files. She was fishing, she knew. There was no method in her actions. It was random, uncoordinated delving. And yet she felt she was close to learning something. She was using her intuition, the sort of thing Webster or Callow would laugh at.

But it was worth pushing – she just knew it. One file caught her eye. At first she thought she was mistaken or that she'd already read it. She clicked it open, scanned the documents inside. They related to the Quest hedge fund run by the prince's son, his anointed heir, Prince Faisal. The playboy, she recalled from what she'd read in the newspapers, the one who dated only actresses. At first the documents made little sense. They were just codes, a bewildering array of numbers and letters. Dense and impenetrable, they seemed to have been written by a computer.

Gradually she realized what she was looking at. She examined the documents three times, to make sure she wasn't seeing things. She felt short of breath.

She was looking at a massacre. Or, rather, something that had been designed to take advantage of a massacre. It was almost beautiful, what she could see, with its perfect symmetry. There was a geometry to it, a coherent, cogent pattern.

Rows upon rows of electronic orders instructed a battalion of computer networks to buy vast amounts of gold and other precious metals. The value of the transactions possibly amounted to hundreds of billions of pounds. The money to fund the gargantuan buying spree flowed in from a separate account. She scanned the linked account. Rows and rows of instructions to liquidate shareholdings in major companies – banks, airlines, aerospace manufacturers, nuclear power conglomerates – and turn them into cash to fund the metal purchases.

The high-frequency trades, carried out by super-computers at near to light speed, were extremely high risk but brutally simple. Get them wrong and it could backfire spectacularly. But bet the house, get it right, and the rewards would be huge. It was a testosterone-loaded blatant display of machismo. It lacked nuance, subtlety, any sense of caution or ambivalence.

She checked the date of the forthcoming trade: 8 September. Some thirteen weeks' time.

She looked back at the files. It could be a gigantic modelling exercise, she thought. A hedge fund stress-testing a hypothetical business model. But that was unlikely. Why go to so much effort if you weren't going to do it? No. It seemed clear that somebody was enthusiastically preparing for very bad news. Quest was looking to plough everything it had into gold and other precious metals, the classic default position of the risk-averse investor, someone battening down the hatches before the storm hit. She was looking at an enormous flight to safety, a one-way bet on the imminent arrival of Doomsday that would be activated nanoseconds before any of the other banks had a chance to act.

She glanced at her online diary. There was nothing in the global calendar to suggest that devastating news was on its way. No major economic figures, no geo-political summits, no trade talks, no Supreme Court judgements. It was quiet. Ghostville.

She swallowed. McLure had clearly seen the files. He would have understood their importance. It was unmistakable what they were saying. They could hardly be more obvious. And yet he'd said nothing to her. In fact, he'd said the opposite of nothing. He'd deliberately withheld material that was relevant to what he'd asked her to investigate. McLure had charged her with examining Higgs's sprawling empire, encouraged her to delve into its complex, hermetically sealed accounts, when he must have known that one of its biggest clients was preparing for the global economy's equivalent of Judgement Day.

She felt cold. She hadn't known McLure at all. What could explain his silence? She groaned as she remembered her conversation in Madrid. Marion had told her he had money worries. She'd meant to pass the information up the chain as it was potentially relevant. Only, in the end, she'd decided to withhold it, believing it amounted to a betrayal and that it was unimportant. But now, well, probably not. McLure could have made a killing with the sort of information he'd been privy to. Jesus, it was all getting dark.

She opened a drawer and pulled out a request sheet. She was going to ask for permission to examine McLure's personal bank accounts. Her hand shook as she signed her name. Her mouth felt dry. What she'd found could have major consequences for the security service. There was the very real possibility that a rogue agent had been operating in its midst, an agent who'd been treating top-secret information, gleaned on behalf of his country, as a commodity, chips for the roulette table.

She played with the thought. McLure's trip to New York suddenly took on a whole new complexion. Had he gone there to sell what he knew? Any number of banks or hedge funds would quite literally kill to have intel on Quest's trading strategy.

There were far, far too many questions. And there was no one to ask, no one she felt she could trust. She couldn't share her concerns with Webster. She didn't have enough to desecrate a dead man's reputation but she had too many suspicions to leave him untainted. It was a total mess.

She looked around her office and out through the frosted window into the dark corridor beyond. She heard Big Ben strike eleven. She had a horrible, dizzying memory of a familiar sensation, the one that had ripped into her when she'd answered the door on a winter night and learned that her husband was dead. She felt completely lost. She had no anchors and she was listing badly. There were no safe havens. Her head sank into her hands and she concentrated on the sound of her breathing. The rhythm was calming. After several minutes she sat up and shut her computer down.

She picked up her mobile phone and punched out a text. Tomorrow was Saturday. She needed space. She needed lots and lots of space.

The two smaller men were not that small. Both were around six feet two and weighed in at more than sixteen stone. But they were dwarfed by the larger man whom they had skilfully lifted into the air, only to flip him over and drop him onto his head. The gruesome assault was almost balletic in its grace, its brutal co-ordination.

The larger man, all six feet seven inches and nineteen stone of him, lay lifeless in front of his two assailants, who were doing their best to look blameless. They chatted between themselves, ignoring everyone around them. But they were fooling no one. The 70,000-strong Twickenham crowd had seen the assault in almost forensic detail, the multitude of spectators groaning as the two centres had spear-tackled the flanker only to smash him into the ground in a blatant and illegal action caught on multiple cameras and replayed on the ground's huge screens.

The two men in the private box overlooking the rugby pitch's halfway line studied the looping horror show intently.

'Both of them will walk. Red cards definitely,' Carlyle said, pointing at the two assailants. 'It could end up being a police matter in time. Lunacy. Sheer lunacy. What they did was borderline criminal. And it's not as if they can hide the evidence. Cameras don't lie.' He indicated the screens. 'It's all there. You can't hide that.' He took a sip of his Champagne and skewered an olive with a cocktail stick.

His companion swigged from a bottle of beer. 'Pretty brutal, this game. Don't understand why your guys don't wear
pads and helmets, like our footballers. They just rushed him.
He never stood a chance, the big man. That was an ambush.
It was all-out assault.'

Carlyle allowed himself a half-smile. 'We do things differently here. We play by different rules.'

Reynolds laughed. '"We", you say. You're about as British
as I am. And you don't do things that differently, it strikes me.
I think it's fair to say that recently we've been playing the
same game. We've been on the same side. Got the same goal.
Mutual interest.'

The crowd roared as the referee held up two red cards
and the centres were directed off the pitch. A small crowd
of paramedics hoisted the prostrate body of the giant unconscious flanker onto a stretcher as the crowd clapped in mass
consolation. Carlyle was still watching the giant screens.

'Those two guys didn't stand a chance with those
cameras,' he said pointedly. 'They recorded everything.'

Reynolds nodded. 'But if they could just take care of the
cameras they'd be in the clear.'

Carlyle sipped more Champagne. 'Right. The problem is
you can't kill them all.'

A substitute, a tree of a man, ran onto the pitch. The
referee blew his whistle and the game resumed.

'I think most cameras were taken care of,' Reynolds said.
'You know that I personally oversaw things. Very difficult to
trace anything back to Higgs now. You did the right thing,
alerting me. There could have been, uh, complications.'

'Yes,' Carlyle said. 'It would have generated unwelcome
interest at a sensitive time. There might have been difficulties

if the authorities had started examining what was going on at Higgs. The prince's plans might have been . . . disrupted. I'm sure he will be generous in his gratitude. He will continue to reward Higgs for its excellent client services. He will build on the relationship his late father had with the bank. I'm sure those behind Higgs will be relieved to hear that. It wouldn't do to lose such a big customer. People might get edgy.'

The two men nodded at each other. Some things were better unspoken.

'That's good to know,' Reynolds said. 'Things are cool. No one's going to finger Brockman now. Your prince's point man inside the bank is safe. He's protected. More than can be said for the prince's father, hey? You got any intel on that?'

'A terrible business,' Carlyle murmured. 'You talk about protection but it's clear no one is truly safe. You become too much of a risk factor in someone's plans, well . . .' He looked at Reynolds but his guest was swigging beer, his face expressionless. 'Well, the insurance policy kicks in,' he continued. 'They have to deal with the risk. I heard about an unfortunate incident in a hotel in New York recently.'

'Mmm,' Reynolds said, throwing peanuts down his throat. 'It's a city that's got a low crime rate, but it can still be one violent place. I heard about it, too. Grisly business. Looks like an accomplished job. Our agencies are stumped as to who was behind it. Think that the Brit agent might have stumbled across stuff that someone didn't want him to stumble across. Dangerous thing, information. It can kill you.'

Carlyle ran a finger and thumb down his nose. 'Quite. London's a grisly place, too, it seems to me. If anything, it appears to be growing more violent. Maybe something to do with the economy. The worse things get, the more it affects people. There's a real menace in this city now. Going to get ugly here in the next few years. Just look at poor old Holahon . . .'

A whistle blew amid the roar of the crowd. A try had been scored.

Reynolds pointed around the private box. 'This has been swept, I take it?'

'Yes,' Carlyle said. 'It's clean.'

'Don't go worrying about Holahon,' Reynolds said. 'What's done is done.'

Carlyle shook his head. 'I've seen some things down the years, seen people do some bad stuff for strange, trivial reasons, but . . .' He trailed off. Another cry from the crowd indicated that the conversion had gone over.

'Seven–nil,' Reynolds said. 'That a high score?'

Carlyle laughed. 'We're only ten minutes in. There'll be a lot more to come. It promises to be quite a final. Thirteen men playing fifteen. It's game over before it's really got going. No one would bet on the thirteen. It'll be a blood-bath. Prince Faisal will be happy. It's his team that have fifteen on the pitch. The silverware will look good in Quest's boardroom. Listen to that crowd – they know it's all over. If you'd bet on the team with thirteen players you'd be feeling pretty foolish now.'

Reynolds shrugged. 'Maybe the two who walked were in on it from the start. Get themselves sent off, hand the game to the other side. They collect. Everyone's happy. You could easily rig something like that. You can rig anything. You just need to control the situation.'

There was another exchange of nods. The sharing of more unspoken truths.

'Then again, there are some things you can't control,' Carlyle said. 'Psychopathic bankers with grudges, for example.'

Reynolds guffawed, glugged beer. 'Oh, lighten up. We took care of the van, you know that? Cleaned it out. Not that we were too worried. Done that sort of thing a thousand times. The body bag was sealed tight. Nothing gets out of those. We returned the vehicle a few hours later, before anyone noticed it was missing. It was very smooth as an operation. Good of Droll to get us the van, too. Helpful. They have good contacts your gumshoes. That's private security for you – good connections to the criminal world who know people who owe them a favour. Useful interface. Symbiotic.'

'Right,' Carlyle said.

'You were probably wondering why we did what we did with the body,' Reynolds said, grinning.

He seemed to be enjoying the conversation. Carlyle was seeing a new side to him. He'd been more reserved, sober, on the previous times they'd met clandestinely. But now Reynolds had a swagger about him that bordered on recklessness. At some stage soon, Carlyle thought, he was going to have to shed his relationship with Reynolds and his American employers. Peel it off like dead skin. They thought he owed them for all their help down the years, for building him up. Well, they were wrong. He was his own man, who knew his value to his employers and the intelligence agencies. He realized that Reynolds was staring at him, his grin wider than before.

'I said, you must have been wondering why we did what we did with the body,' Reynolds repeated.

'It had crossed my mind,' Carlyle murmured.

'Well, to be honest, we thought it was probably the most ... helpful thing. Removing the head and hands helped complicate things. Made it look like some premeditated act of vengeance. Someone meting out their own form of justice. We hit on the idea of putting the body down at an old place where they used to hang traitors. That would set the hares running, we figured. Police would think maybe it was some sort of banking feud, payback for a deal that went sour. We reckoned the more we muddied stuff, the more untraceable it all became. We couldn't just make him disappear. The absence of a body would have triggered more questions than its presence. Someone like him anyway. His absence would leave a big hole. Now, that really would have put Higgs under the spotlight. And we agree we can't afford for Higgs to become immersed in some major investigation right now. Both of us got skin in this game.'

Carlyle nodded. 'A lot of that sort of thing went down in Bosnia at the end of the war. Body parts were strewn all over the place to complicate things, put UN investigators off the scent. No one had a clue what was going on by the end. There were a lot of dead people who could never be put back together. Real Humpty Dumpty stuff.'

Another roar signalled that a second try had been scored. Reynolds glanced around the private box, as if he was assessing it for threats. The mention of Carlyle's past had made him remember his task. Carlyle had been a CIA intelligence asset for more than two decades, but sometimes he didn't seem to be with the programme. The Agency had helped

157

him become a major arms dealer, then a well-connected fixer for several prominent Saudi families. They'd built him from the bottom up, taken a two-bit entrepreneur who ran pizza parlours, laundering money for East European Mafia, and catapulted him into the big-time. But the Agency had never been entirely sure whether he was playing them, keeping some stuff back. It was risky, running assets who might be playing for more than one side.

Reynolds stood up, opened another bottle of beer and selected a sandwich from a silver salver on a nearby table. 'Some stage something'll have to be done about Brockman and Ennis,' he said. 'They're fucking liabilities now. The idiots. Brockman thinks he's untouchable because he runs your man Faisal's private banking operations. And Ennis is stupid enough to believe him. But they're both expendable. They're just not bright enough to know it. They don't have that fear. Well, they should. They really should understand the consequences of their actions. I just don't think they appreciate risk.'

Carlyle poured himself another glass of Champagne. It wasn't even as if he liked the stuff, but the conversation with Reynolds was boring him.

'Yeah,' Reynolds said, 'we all need the fear. We need to hear that voice. It's what keeps us in check.'

'Quite,' Carlyle said. 'And if they're not fearful they're more likely to be loose-lipped, those two. And that makes them very dangerous. It's one thing to cover up for them in the short term. Quite another to do it indefinitely.'

'Right,' Reynolds said. 'We agree on that.'

The whistle signalled half-time. A team of cheerleaders took to the pitch. Carlyle gestured at the barely dressed women. 'See? Our sports are going the same way as yours. We owe you that. You never used to see cheerleaders at rugby matches. Thank you for the vulgarity. Where you lead, we follow. As in so many things. Sport, leisure, finance, politics, crime, you name it, the US is our weathervane.'

'Don't forget national security,' Reynolds murmured. 'You guys will be rendering bad sorts soon. You'll build your own Guantánamo. Ha, you'll build a Higgs, too.'

Carlyle shook his head. 'No,' he muttered. 'We've got enough problems with our bombed-out banking system as it is.'

The cheerleaders departed and the two teams returned to the field. The May sunshine streamed down. Carlyle shifted in his leather chair. He was becoming quite drowsy. He needed to wake up. The Champagne was getting to him. He felt increasingly loose-lipped, as if he didn't own his mouth any longer. 'Tell me, did you do the prince?' he said quietly.

'Nothing to do with us. We wanted him alive. We were sponsoring his pet project. His goddamn legacy was as important to us as him. A global Islamic relief network that could dispatch plane loads of medicines, food, supplies to the world's troubled hotspots would have been a perfect counter to the Islamists. Sure, it would have gotten corrupted pretty soon, the terrorists would have infiltrated it, but it would have challenged Islamic State for hearts and minds on the ground for a year or two. It would have been a force for good. And we could've been part of it. We've used aid to win over enemies in the past tons of times. Just another way of mitigating risk. Bags of rice speak louder than bombs. Sometimes.'

Carlyle felt his vision blurring. 'Maybe,' he murmured. It was becoming difficult to speak. Shadows were appearing in the corners of his eyes.

'You want to know who terminated the prince?' he heard Reynolds saying. 'Look to Mossad or maybe some jealous Saudi rival.' His companion's voice was becoming more and more indistinct, as if he was talking inside a drum or something.

With a sigh Carlyle realized what was happening. He was dying. He should have known. It was always how it was going to end one day. That was the problem for people like him, the go-betweens. They were expendable. Poison. Carlyle's head slumped to one side. He looked at Reynolds but was unable to speak. He managed to raise an eyebrow. His mouth twisted into a smile.

''Fraid so,' Reynolds said.

A whistle signalled another try had been scored.

'Turning into quite a rout,' Reynolds said, pointing to the pitch. 'Hey, do you think the cheerleaders will be coming back on? They were kind of hot.'

Carlyle said nothing. His heart had stopped. He was a corpse, an immaculately dressed corpse in a Savile Row suit. A farmer's son from Iowa who'd allowed himself to be manipulated by too many people and had reached the end of a game he'd played skilfully with a limited hand. But he wasn't a big enough player to stay in the game for ever. He wasn't a whale.

Reynolds surveyed his dead host. He'd unwittingly dressed himself for his own funeral, he thought. 'Been real interesting,' Reynolds said. 'Thanks for the invite. Enjoyed it. My first rugger match. That what you guys call it, hey, rugger? Guess I'll be seeing you.' He stood up, carefully placed the Champagne bottle and Carlyle's glass in a bag. The poison had taken longer to work than he'd anticipated. There had been a lot of small-talk, almost more than he was capable of in his exhausted condition. He took a final look at Carlyle, an asset who had come to know far too much about Higgs. We built you, Reynolds thought, so we were always going to unbuild you.

Chapter 10

They stood outside an old artist's shack, a converted fisherman's hut made of tar-black wooden planks surrounded by a garden of driftwood sculptures and rusting metal totems reclaimed from the sea. There was an isolated, defiant sense of beauty and space about it that soothed her. A sense of calm had been building inside her while they'd walked along the peninsula. It had grown as she'd watched thousands of birds from the nearby nature reserve take to the sky in formations as thick as rainclouds. It had deepened as she'd followed the railway tracks of the steam train that ran along the shore, past the dead, discarded hulks of the yawls and smacks, past a beaten-up old smokehouse and through the undulating dunes of shingle.

In the early evening sun of a late May Saturday the shoreline seemed to stretch for ever. There was something infinite about the place. Kate realized she was in love. She had fallen in love with a peninsula. Makes sense, she thought. Aloof, distant, secret, haunted by its past: yes, if the peninsula was a person, it would be her. She slugged water from the plastic bottle that she normally carried on her running belt, then offered it to Sorrenson.

'Thanks. I need to get one of those.' Sorrenson took it.

'They're useful. But you can overdo it, you know.'

'All the gear, no idea?'

She nodded. 'Holahon had the latest GPS watch but it was all for show. He was faking it. If his watch could talk it would tell us some interesting stories.'

Sorrenson ran a hand across his lips. 'Just a shame his killer didn't wear a similar watch. We'd have no trouble tracking him down.'

'Killers.'

'Huh?'

'Killers. At least two people were in on it. You'd need two people to hold him down, dismember the body. And, well, the drink and drugs thing . . .'

She was so smart, Sorrenson thought. She clearly wasn't going to let it go. She'd obviously been thinking about it a lot – more than he had. 'Go on.'

'Well, we agree it doesn't make any sense, Holahon's murder. Basically, from what we've learned, he was a narcissist. They're not the type to drink an entire bottle of whisky and snort up a mule's worth of coke. They want to look good, not a total mess. So my theory, for what it's worth, is that he was forced to consume that shit. Someone made him pollute himself before they killed him. I spoke to the pathologist. He thought it was plausible.'

'That's quite fucked-up.'

'It's a fucked-up world. At least, it is in the City. Any place where men and money mix is dangerous. Not here, maybe. This place, I've never been anywhere like it.' She waved down the beach. 'It just gets under your skin. I'll find it hard to rub it off. It's really haunting. There's a bleak beauty about this peninsula. I feel almost like I've lived here.'

'They looked out to sea. The first wisps of cloud in an otherwise perfect blue sky were skimming in from across the Channel. Sorrenson felt calm, rested, alive. He felt whole. He hadn't felt so content in a long while. He examined the gamble forming in his mind. It was worth the risk. 'You could stay. Tonight, I mean. Stay down here. My place isn't far. We could get some fish from Bill Henry's smokehouse just down from here.' He gestured towards a shack in the distance. 'He'll probably have some crabs, too. They're good, so I'm told. But only if you're not doing anything. You've probably got plans.'

She smiled. 'No plans. So thanks. I'd like to. Anything that keeps me down here is fine by me.'

They walked towards the shack, the evening sun on their backs. Smoke could be seen pouring from its chimney, a grey stain on a near perfect blue canvas.

Sorrenson ran a hand through his hair. He'd swum earlier in the day and could almost feel the salt in it. He turned his head towards her. 'The thing with your theory, the forced drink and drugs, well, it seems to make sense. But to do that to someone, well, you've really got to want them to suffer. It's not a case of just eliminating someone who got in the way. There's real hatred there.'

'That thought had occurred to me, too. The more I look at it, the more I think Holahon's murder has nothing to do with Higgs. Someone had a real grudge against the man. It was personal, not professional. If it had been professional he would have been quietly bumped off. In some ways I guess that's good news for you.'

'How do you mean?'

'Well, it suggests to me whoever did in Holahon knew him – knew him well. Cast your net around those closest to him, you'll find your killers.'

'Ha, you're in the wrong job. We should do a swap.'

She shook her head. 'You couldn't cope with the boredom mine involves. It's all about numbers. Numbers aren't interesting. People are.'

'The problem is Holahon himself doesn't seem to have been that interesting,' Sorrenson said. 'He kept himself to himself. No partner for several years. No close family. He was a real loner. Maybe that was why he liked running. It's pretty solitary. Ha, his running club was probably the closest thing he had to family.'

'Mmm,' she said. Something was eating away at her. She remembered her whiteboard. 'Did you ever interview a colleague of Holahon's called Brockman? He was also a member of the same running club. I've known him a bit for a few years, although not that he worked for Higgs until recently. Texan, I think. Big ego. Given he worked with Holahon and ran with him, he might know something.'

They approached the shack. The smell of smoke from the chimney filled the air.

'Higgs really haven't played ball,' Sorrenson replied. 'We requested all internal emails, CCTV, all that stuff. But we got fragments. They claim it was all deleted automatically. Standard procedure apparently. Their systems do it every few days unless told otherwise. Seems a bit lame as an excuse, but . . .'

'Let me guess. Resources. To go after those emails would involve trips to server farms in India or somewhere. Maybe

I could call in favours from the NSA, although they're loath to give us anything now because of the heat they're getting. Still, needs must. Tell me, how did it go at the ponds?'

'We're going to send divers in on Monday. We might get lucky. We're still studying video footage near the bank from the night Holahon disappeared. That might throw up something, too.'

They shared an innate professional optimism, she realized. They thought that what they were doing was important, could make a difference, even though they were competing against enemies with deeper pockets and darker motives than they could ever realistically hope to confront or expose. But you had to be optimistic to do the jobs they were doing or you'd go mad. Their jobs could only ever throw them the odd quick win. There would never be a final victory. There would always be murders, assassinations, bombings, dismemberings, drownings. There would always be the ebb and flow of violence, just like there would always be the sea.

The sound of Van Morrison singing 'Madame George' was filtering out from the shack. It filled the evening air.

'Bit of a music nut, Bill,' Sorrenson murmured.

'A favourite of mine,' she said. 'We had it at our . . .' There were tears in her eyes. 'Sorry.'

'I think my Vandal blood still makes me think I'm a punk,' Sorrenson said. 'Most coppers my age were punks. I'm sure psychologists would have a field day with that if they cottoned on to it. All the suppressed rage that's been bubbling under the surface for decades. It's a powder keg just waiting to explode. But I don't think the sound of the Ramones or the Clash works so well down here. It's out of kilter in a place without people. The anger doesn't fit. Like I told you, it's Ghostville.'

'Maybe that's why I like it so much. It's like one long mood, this peninsula. A place of memories. I'll just get my stuff out of my car. I could do with putting a top on.'

'I'll find Bill,' Sorrenson said. He watched her walk back up to the peninsula road. She looked as good from behind as from the front.

Sorrenson didn't have to look far for the fisherman. He was in his shack, sitting in an old office swivel chair, an eighties affair of plastic and chrome that looked incongruous in the gloomy wooden interior. He was facing the clock on the wall of the smokehouse. Sorrenson seemed to remember that it hadn't worked for years. It was always fixed at ten thirty-four.

'It's not going to start working again if you keep looking at it, Bill,' Sorrenson said. 'You can't bring it back to life.'

The man in the chair said nothing, his back to the detective. 'Madame George' finished and 'Cyprus Avenue' came on. The music filled the hut.

Stoned probably, Sorrenson thought. He tried again. 'You got much fish, Bill? Need some smoked mackerel, crabs too. Maybe some prawns.'

Still nothing. Sorrenson shook his head. Prickly sort. Understandable, though, given the grief Bill Henry sometimes got from the police. But, well, what could he expect? He was the king of the red-diesel thieves.

'Hey, Bill.' Sorrenson put his hand on the man's shoulder and sprang back as if he'd burned himself. Bill Henry's head slumped forwards.

Sorrenson was not a medical man. But he didn't need to be. As he moved around the swivel chair he could see what was wrong with Bill. He was dead. The thick red line across his throat told the story in vivid detail. Bill's eyes bulged open in shock. He looked like a just-landed fish, stunned by his fate. Sorrenson pulled his phone from his pocket and dialled his station. He turned to see Kate in the doorway. 'Don't come in,' he said quietly.

She remained in the doorway, her silhouette blocking out the fading evening light. She cocked her head to one side, intrigued by the command. 'Why's that?'

He wondered whether their worlds were colliding or fragmenting. Things, people, places seemed connected, yet he couldn't see the link, couldn't decode the information that would make sense of everything. He felt he was seeing shadows of the truth only for it to disappear when he tried to focus.

'Crime scene,' Sorrenson said, surveying what was left of Bill. 'We need to protect a crime scene. Jesus, Bill, what on earth did you get yourself into?'

Reynolds had wondered if he would have the balls to blow his brains out. Very Hemingway, he'd thought, whenever the idea crossed his mind. It would take guts, machismo, real bloodlust. The ultimate risk-based challenge. Whiskey and a revolver. Better than jumping. Too many spectators. Death should be done privately, Reynolds thought. Like banking or murder.

For a second or two he found himself jealous of Carlyle. It had been pretty quick, his termination. One of the quickest dispatches of a used asset he'd ever performed. If he'd been doing it on behalf of his employers it would have been something to boast about. But, no, he'd been operating in a private capacity. He'd become quite entrepreneurial when it came to killing people. Just not when it came to himself, it seemed. He had his answer on the whiskey and gun question. He wasn't Hemingway. His brain wouldn't decorate the wall in the attic at the top of his house that he used as a private office. There would be no horror show for his second wife to find. His children wouldn't be traumatized. There was no need for the notes he'd intended to leave behind, explaining in almost forensic detail the imminent ruination of Higgs.

Reynolds placed the Glock back in its metal box and turned the key in the lock. He put the ammunition in a separate box, turned another key, and placed the equipment by which he had sought to solve a dozen personal problems back in his safe.

He sipped his whiskey. It wasn't even a special bourbon. Hardly a fitting drink to end his life with. Perhaps he'd always known that he wasn't going to kill himself. He'd just been going through the motions, vicariously experiencing the joy of his own non-existence.

In the eight minutes Reynolds had held the loaded pistol to the roof of his mouth – while the sound of Williamsburg's early evening traffic told of soccer moms returning with their children from post-school practice – he'd been filled with hope. He'd allowed his mind to roam unchecked. In Reynolds's fantasy world Higgs no longer existed. The stinking, fetid, selfish, gruesome monster of an organism that he had helped to create had never been. And if there was no Higgs, there was no hidden debt. So much debt.

How much debt, Reynolds still couldn't fully fathom. He'd stopped asking questions when the truth had threatened to emerge. He remembered the conversation well.

'So we've got SPV1 and SPV2. As their name implies they're special-purpose vehicles, used to, erm, contain debt,' the head of Higgs's compliance team had told him. 'They're effectively tax havens that we have created. SPV1 and SPV2 are barges located in the Niger delta. Quite neat when you think about it. They are literally offshore vehicles, only we're treating them as floating piles of debt. Hidden debt.'

Reynolds had known where the conversation was heading. It was quietly taking him to the brink of sanity. It would let him stand there awhile, contemplating the drop, and then it would bring him back, knowing that he would be in a state of a paralysis, too scared by the enormity of what was happening to do anything about it. He'd looked at the head of compliance, wondered if he could be trusted to keep secrets buried.

'How much debt are these fucking freak shows holding? What's our exposure?'

'Well, it sort of fluctuates.'

'Right. But ballpark?'

'Ballpark figure, if you ponied up our realized debt and the potential debt, we're talking maybe five hundred.'

'Five-hundred-million pounds. Jesus, that's almost a quarter of our annual profit in a good year.'

Feltzer, the head of compliance, had remained silent. He was one of the very few within the bank to know its true relationship with the CIA, the FIU, the NSA and every other arm of the US intelligence network. He stared at Reynolds, waiting for him to decode his silence.

Reynolds groaned. 'We're not talking millions, right? You mean billions?'

Feltzer nodded. 'But I stress that's worst case. A lot of our potential debt may never be realized.'

'You don't say.' Reynolds hated himself for sounding sarcastic. It wasn't the time. It was way too late for that sort of thing. But, honestly, how could a bank worth around fifty-billion dollars end up with debts so far beyond what it was worth? How was that possible? Who'd let it happen and how?

'Yeah,' Feltzer said, reading Reynolds's mind. 'We were lending way too much. It got so complicated nobody questioned who we were lending too. The answer is we were lending to trailer trash, people who were never going to pay us back. We chopped up all the debt and spread it around, thinking that would smooth out the risk. But all it meant was that we had no idea who were the good debtors and who were the bad. So even our good loans may be compromised. As a result we just don't really know how fucked we are. But some of the stuff we think is toxic may escape. If the markets bounce back, well, anything's possible. We could still get lucky. We might live.'

'You see that happening?' Reynolds tried to hide the desperation in his voice.

Feltzer shrugged. 'There's hope. But we've got to work out what we tell the agency. See if they can get Congress to arrange some sort of bailout on the quiet.'

'We'll never get a bailout that size through without the whole thing coming out,' Reynolds snapped. 'And then, fuck,

I don't know what happens. No one's gonna understand how something got so out of control because we were trying to protect our nation's security. Jesus, how much of this do Brandeis and Carey know?' Feltzer had shaken his head. 'Not much. They've heard the rumours like everyone else. But for now, this is pretty much our problem. It remains sealed within these four walls.'

As he recalled the conversation, Reynolds looked out of the window of his attic, ran his hands through his thinning hair and took another slug of whiskey. He was properly drunk. His wife and kids would be back soon. It would be difficult to explain his inebriated state to them. He'd need to pop some sleeping pills, have an early night. The conversation with Feltzer had taken place four months ago, but it felt as if only four minutes had elapsed since he'd been told the apocalyptic news. Since then he'd felt like he'd been running, sprinting at full, lung-bursting tilt, simply to stand still.

He remembered the last thing Feltzer had told him that day: 'You gotta make sure no one gets nervy. You can't afford for people to take their money out of Higgs. It'll unwind quicker than a cobra. Keep the big clients, the ones with billions in the bank, on board. Do whatever it takes. And keep up the act. Don't let anyone in the intelligence community catch the scent that tells them Higgs is in trouble. If bankers sense it there'll be a bloodbath. Banking is all about confidence. Loads of people are looking at Higgs right now. Don't blink.'

Reynolds poured himself another glass of whiskey. The next day would be a write-off. He should have been a carpenter, he told himself. Or, at the very least, he should have stayed within the boring old world of intelligence, the one where people assassinated politicians or tortured terrorists in other countries. But, no, he'd been seduced by the un-glamorous, quiet ambition of Higgs. It had promised so much. It had had the potential, to use Carey's phrase, of being a game-changer. True in so many ways.

And now it was such a mess.

Through a whiskey haze, Reynolds contemplated his options or, rather, the lack of them. There really was only one option left, now he'd gone cold on the idea of self-negation. He thought of Carlyle. The man had been a liability. He'd known far too much about the agency's rela-tionship with Higgs. Sorting out the aftermath from the Holahon killing had meant he'd had no choice but to close Carlyle down. He couldn't have someone knowing just how desperate he was to save Higgs from scrutiny. That sort of knowledge made them dangerous. Gave them leverage. Reynolds had had enough of leverage.

But Higgs's relationship with the Saudis had given him an idea. For years he'd been forensically monitoring Carlyle's conversations and emails with the younger prince. And he knew what the prince's hedge fund was planning. He'd been surprised how easily he'd learned Quest's plan. Their emails and phone conversations were hidden behind encryption systems but they hadn't been that difficult to pierce. Bit by bit he had pieced it all together, some of it with Carlyle's help, so that, finally, he understood the plan in its full audacious glory. Reynolds could see the apocalypse on the horizon and the weird thing was that he wasn't scared. Most people would be terrified by what was coming. But for Reynolds it offered a glimmer of hope. The only glimmer of hope. The end would be a new beginning for Higgs. Out of the ashes of a nuclear power station something could flourish again. Wild flowers in the scorched black scrub.

Reynolds figured that all Higgs needed to do was mirror the giant set of trades that Quest was soon to activate and it, too, could ride off into the sunset while everything around it imploded.

It was a massive gamble, of course, but it was the last card he had to play. The question was whether he would play it. Well, he knew the answer. If he wasn't going to kill himself then he had no option. He was a desperate man who'd been thrown a lifebelt. Everyone else would have done the same. Given the choice between flailing and drowning you would choose to flail. You would thrash about, flounder in the waves, pray that you could stay afloat long enough for someone to rescue you.

Others, of course, would have to drown if Higgs was going to be saved. And there was no guarantee Higgs wouldn't be exposed before it could make the play. There were eleven weeks left to go. Eleven long, boring, nerve-shredding weeks. And then Reynolds would know. He would know if Higgs had been saved. There would be a lot of whiskey in the weeks to come.

'A carpenter,' Reynolds murmured woozily. 'Should have been a carpenter.' He pressed his hands into the sockets of his eyes, as if he was trying to block out all light, all illumination. He stayed in his self-imposed darkness for some time.

'Save it. We don't have time.'

Hughes glared at the solicitor. She shrank back in her chair. The junior detective's anger bounced off the walls of the interview room. Sorrenson poured himself a glass of water, offered one to Davey Stone.

'I apologize for my colleague's outburst,' Sorrenson said to the solicitor. 'What he is trying to say is that we all understand that Davey is here to help us with our enquiries. He is not under suspicion, far from it. We're grateful to him for coming in and we don't need you to remind us that he has not been arrested and has come to the station voluntarily. Again.'

Sorrenson allowed himself a big exhalation. Jesus, Hughes could be hot-headed. At some stage they would have to have it out. If Hughes wanted to keep his job he was going the wrong way about it. He'd watched too much *Sweeney* or something when he was a kid.

'It's fine,' Stone said. 'I'm keen to help. Terrible, terrible business.'

'Yeah,' Hughes said, continuing to glare at the man in front of him. 'Terrible.'

Stone returned Hughes's glare for several seconds. 'But at least you got the man,' Stone said. 'I read in the paper you'd arrested someone. A great result for our upstanding Kent police force.'

Sorrenson exchanged looks with Hughes. It was clear from the way he had spoken that Stone didn't believe the arrested man was Bill Henry's killer.

'Yeah,' Hughes said. 'We're getting the drinks in.'

Sorrenson sighed. There was no point in dodging the issue. 'You know as well as us, Davey, that Jim Pickard didn't kill Bill. Sure, the pair hated each other's guts. But, well, there was good reason for Jim to make those threats. Bill shouldn't have tried to compete with him on the cannabis front. Jim was doing good work with the Vietnamese gangs. Bill should have known better.'

'And he shouldn't have done Jim's wife, either,' Hughes growled. He was in a fierce mood. He had pre-season rugby training in the evening. There would be blood on the tackle bags before the night was out.

'So you're telling me stuff I know,' Stone said. 'I take it you've let Pickard go?'

Sorrenson nodded.

'So you're back to square one,' Stone said, with a grin directed at Hughes. 'And you're left asking yourselves who would want to kill one of the coast's biggest smugglers. A man who was responsible for half of the south-east's illicit trade in knocked-off fags. A man who stole more red diesel than everyone else put together. Well, how long have you got?'

'Come on,' Sorrenson said. 'He was a crook, but he wasn't bad. And he did a good line in at least pretending to be a fisherman.'

Stone laughed. 'Ha. That's right. He was a giant fucking fake. He hadn't been to sea properly for years. All his fish was knocked off from the trawlers coming in down the coast. Half of his smoked mackerel was stolen to order by a cousin who worked at the local supermarket. That fisherman act was just so he could bring in the knocked-off fags from the supertankers in the Channel. No one suspected nothing.'

'OK, we get it,' Hughes rasped. 'He wasn't Snow White. Now fucking tell us. Who fucking killed him?'

Jesus, Sorrenson thought. Hughes was going to ruin everything if he continued. Stone would shut up like a clam. 'Davey, we need your help,' he said firmly. 'There's just an outside chance that Bill's murder may be connected to other stuff. Big stuff.'

Stone scratched his head. 'Connected in what way? Like to the body of that banker at Traitor's?'

'Yeah, that,' Hughes said.

'You found the van yet?' Stone grinned at Hughes.

'No,' Hughes said, glowering back. 'No traces of one being stolen from the police anywhere in the country. If it ever really existed it was probably an old one kept by some collector or something.'

'Or something.'

Hughes stared angrily at Stone. The rugby training couldn't come soon enough. He was going to explode. Sorrenson was such an idiot to give Stone so much respect. He was vermin. Hughes wondered what damage his thirty-two-year-old body was capable of inflicting on Stone. It would be interesting as Stone was twice his age. Hardly a fair fight. Good. 'Or something,' Hughes said. 'What's that supposed to mean?'

Stone switched his focus to Sorrenson. They had a better understanding. He couldn't deal with the psychopath. He'd stick with the semi-Viking. 'Well, ask yourself something,' Stone said. 'Why's it need to be stolen? Why couldn't it have been borrowed?'

'What the fuck are you insinuating?' Hughes banged the table with a hand.

'There really is no need—'

'I know, I know, I apologize,' Hughes snarled at Davey's solicitor.

'Insinuating. That's a long word,' Stone said. 'Never had

the education. Neither did Bill. But that didn't stop him thinking.'

Sorrenson sensed Davey Stone was ready to cough. 'Go on.'

'Well, if you're going to move a body no-questions-asked, get the people you don't want to ask the questions to do the moving. No one's going to stop a van being driven by a copper. Seems to me that you're looking for a bent copper.' Stone grinned again. 'Seemed that way to Bill, too, more importantly,' he continued. 'He asked around, you know. Talked to some of the Kent gangs who had coppers on their payroll. Asked them if they knew anyone who might fit the spec. Someone from the thin blue line who was prepared to borrow a van, ship a body to the coast, no questions asked. Came back with a list as long as your arm. Seems that in these straitened times everyone's on the make or take. Criminal, what you guys get paid, these days. And now I read they're after your pensions. All because the nasty banks have lost the money. Scandalous.'

Hughes gripped the table tight, as if he was trying to shatter it.

'Yeah, interesting,' Stone said, holding Hughes's gaze. 'The names that came back. I reckon someone in that lot might be able to help you with your enquiries. They might know a bit more. Shed some light on it. But the problem is, gents, you need those names.'

'Did he tell you them?' Sorrenson was conscious that Hughes had stopped talking.

Stone stared straight at Hughes, almost as if he was looking through him. 'No, he didn't. If he found anything it went with him to the grave, poor sod. Maybe it was asking around that got him done in. High risk. Those gangs talk. Coppers talk, especially bent ones. That sort of information filters out. People get jumpy.'

Stone's smile was so wide that Sorrenson could see a gold tooth at the back of his mouth, a light at the end of a dark, dark tunnel. He turned to Hughes. 'You have any other questions?' Hughes shook his head, threw a stick of chewing gum in his mouth, chewed it frantically. 'Thanks, Davey, been useful,' Sorrenson said. 'Good of you to come in. As always.' He stood up, showed Stone and his solicitor to the door. His mobile vibrated. 'Yes?'

'DCI Sorrenson?'

'Right.'

'DCI Summerskill, Met.'

'Uh-huh.'

'You requested we send divers into the ponds at Hampstead Heath.'

Sorrenson gripped the phone tight.

'Well,' the voice at the other end of the phone said, 'we've found a bag, the contents of which we believe could be germane to your investigation.'

Sorrenson's attempt at restraint failed him. 'Cut the plodspeak and get to the point. What the fuck have you found?'

'A head,' the voice said matter-of-factly. 'And some hands.'

Chapter 11

Webster spun back and forth in his wheelchair, its hard rubber tyres rolling smoothly across the polished wooden floor of his office. The constant movement, a clear sign that he was anxious, didn't escape Callow. Years of watching Webster progress through the ranks had made him a good judge of his boss. A non-wheeling Webster was a rarity, these days, Callow reflected. He was always pushing himself back and forth, as if he was never comfortable with his position.

It was seven o'clock in the morning and few people were in the service's headquarters. In that respect it was like any other office at that time of the day, Callow thought. Come to think of it, it was just like any other office. Only, in other offices, if things went wrong, people might be fired or a company close down or the chief executive forced to resign.

But Five's failures were recorded in fatalities. And it wasn't past fatalities that haunted the service: they were spent — there could be no come-back on those. It was the future deaths, the unknowns that lay ahead, that spooked the spooks. They could take any form, the unrealized dead. You couldn't see where or how they'd emerge. All you could do was try to picture how they would be extinguished, explore the myriad scenarios that would conclude with people dying and hope, pray, plead, connive against them. It was a relentless, hopeless game that the service could never win. And the more time you spent in it, the more fearful you became about the odds, the more you understood just how everything was stacked against you. It became apparent that it was a case of fragmenting, multiplying threats versus a shrinking, exhausted security apparatus whose best days were long, long gone. No wonder Webster was wheeling, Callow thought.

He decided that there was no point in delaying the ruination of his boss's day. 'Pendragon says she has found evidence that just over a million pounds made in three payments were transferred into a secret account set up by McLure in the Isle of Man. It seems someone was paying him a lot of money to tell them what the security service knew.'

Webster nodded. 'Yes, as we suspected.'

'We know from what Pendragon said that McLure appeared to have money worries.'

Webster snorted. 'Him and half the fucking country. But they don't go round betraying their nation. Jesus, what a fucking mess. I'm not sure we're going to be able to contain this. There's bound to be some horrible inquiry.'

'We will,' Callow said soothingly. 'It's all in hand. Pendragon won't talk. It's in no one's interests for this to come out. News of McLure's termination hasn't leaked. No reason it will now.'

Webster said nothing. Callow saw his boss's fingers blanch as they gripped the wheels of his chair.

Webster sighed. 'Have we got any idea who was paying him?'

'Pendragon's preparing a report now. The list should be

pretty thin. He was, after all, working in a specialist department following hot money. I'm not sure many foreign states
would pay for that info. Most of them know more than we
do. Doubt it's the Chinese. They could probably hack the
information if they wanted to. Which means—'

'Some private company or individual. Maybe. We checked
his traffic?'

'His emails and phone records are clean. Nothing indicating he was talking to anyone. Whoever he was in contact
with, it must have been done in person. He would know
there was a risk his traffic would be sucked up by the NSA
or GCHQ.'

'What does Pendragon think?'

Webster's voice sounded like it might snap at any minute,
Callow thought. He hesitated before replying. No, he needed
to say it. The information needed to come out. The clock
was ticking. Ultimately Webster would have to make a call.
'She's focused on something else at the moment,' Callow
said.

'What the fuck could be more important than establish-
ing who bent one of our agents?' Webster's voice had
become a bellow.

'You know all the chatter we're picking up about some
major threat coming down the line?'

Webster nodded.

'It may be related to that. She's picking up signs that some
people have been forewarned.'

'Signs?'

'Right. A hedge fund called Quest, linked to the Saudis,
is taking massive defensive positions on the stock market. It
seems to confirm something ugly is going to happen.

Remember the bets that were made on the stock market before Nine/Eleven?'

Webster gave up rolling his wheelchair back and forth. He massaged his temples with his right hand. 'Pendragon does know that's she paid to examine bank accounts, not issue threat assessments?'

Callow took a fortifying sip of coffee and grimaced. It was stone cold. Even the vending machines seemed to be conspiring against him. Probably some sort of sinister Chinese plot to bring the service to its knees. They would stop at nothing, foreign intelligence agencies.

'Yeah, she knows. But she thinks something's definitely up. Maybe she's too immersed in all of this. McLure asked her to conduct an audit of Higgs Bank's London operations. He gave her a list of names and accounts suspected of being connected to certain terrorist factions. Seems Quest's name turned up.'

Webster removed his spectacles and rubbed his eyelids. 'Higgs,' he said. 'I keep hearing that name everywhere.'

'Well, you know it's got close links to the CIA,' Callow said. 'They've used it to fund covert ops in the past.'

'The same is true for loads of banks, most probably.'

'Well, if she's right, whatever is coming is going to happen soon,' Callow said. 'We need to make a call on Pendragon's credibility. We need to work out how much we should back her. If we should back her, even.'

Webster thought for a few seconds. Callow knew what was going through his mind. Webster was conducting his own risk assessment. If they backed Pendragon it would mean informing Number 10. Cobra, the emergency committee that dealt with threats to national security and infrastructure, would have to be activated. The National Security Council would have to be informed. The national terrorist threat assessment would possibly have to be raised to maximum. The Joint Intelligence Assessment Committee would have to be alerted. The Met's counter-terrorism division would need to know. In short, within hours, something that only three people knew would be familiar to scores, and the number was bound to increase exponentially. They wouldn't be able to contain it. And, while they could be vague on the nature of the threat, take steps to mask it, news that an attack was coming would leak almost immediately. The fear, Callow knew, was that if nothing happened the service would be accused of setting a hare running.

And that was the best scenario. The nightmare scenario was that it became apparent that the service had failed to act, had tried to keep the fear to itself, had locked it down. And then if something happened, well, there was no protection against that. The service would be flamed. Callow pitied Webster. It was an impossible situation. You couldn't insure yourself against those kind of risks.

'I need to see Pendragon,' Webster said, after what seemed like several minutes had passed. 'I need to work her out. How long has she been with us? She came on secondment, right?'

'Yeah. She worked for various banking regulators, then SOCA, then was loaned to us from the Treasury and the FSA. Been with us almost three years. Expert on money laundering. She's sharp, but she's not service. She knows nothing about terrorism. She's just good at following money. That's her real speciality.'

'Significant other?'

'Husband was special forces. Killed in Iraq. Four years ago. No one of interest since then, apparently.'

'Hmm,' Webster said, rolling back and forth once again in his chair. 'Do a bit of checking around, then. We can't take any risks with this. All we seem to know is that she's a bit of a loner, like most who work here.'

'Something like that. Running freak, apparently.'

'Wasn't the dead banker, Holahon, a running freak?'

'So I read. She's got a theory on his murder, too. She reckons it was personal not professional.'

Webster wheeled himself back and forth furiously. 'Well, she's got a theory for everything, then,' he muttered. He looked at Callow. 'Are we getting any help from over the Pond on this?'

'Even less than normal. I guess it's to be expected. Can't see the Agency wanting us to get too close to its stooge bank. You know it's rumoured the Agency actually built Higgs?'

'Stranger things have happened,' Webster replied. 'We set up loads of front companies in Northern Ireland. Some of them became quite successful for a while. They had bigger incomes than some of our intelligence units.'

'That wouldn't be difficult, these days.'

'Right,' Webster agreed. 'Hang on. Pendragon. Quite an unusual name. Her father wasn't in the service, was he? There was a Pendragon who died in a car accident near Belfast. Outdoors freak. Climber. Skier. Marathon runner, I believe. Women threw themselves at him, I seem to remember.'

'I believe it was him, yes.'

Webster rubbed his hands together several times. 'Terrible business,' he said, as if talking to himself. 'It looked like an accident. But that was the problem with it, ultimately. Too perfect. He was a risk-taker, Pendragon's father, made him something of an easy target. Well, like father like daughter, hey? Send her up.'

Callow walked out of Webster's office. If he'd turned round he would have seen his boss biting his thumbnail hard, his face twisted in concentration. Webster wore the expression of a man who'd bumped into his ex-wife at a party. He looked trapped and nervous and guilty and fearful. He began wheeling back and forth in his chair.

The small jet sped down the runway, its engine screaming. The plane was little more than a black blur some three metres off the ground. It was clearly going too fast and it rolled heavily in mid-air, as if its pilot was uncertain of its direction.

Then, suddenly, as it approached the end of the runway, near to the hangar where a fire engine was housed, it speeded up. With a final lurch it flew upwards and then, just as it seemed to be clear of the hangar, it clipped its roof and quickly spiralled downwards, in a series of hopeless pirouettes, smashed into the runway and shattered into a thousand pieces.

Prince Faisal clapped his hands with the sheer joy of witnessing deliberate destruction. 'Excellent,' he said to the small group of men who'd been watching the display. 'We are making good progress. Very good. But it's one thing to fly a model plane remotely, something else altogether to do it with a Gulfstream jet. But then, as my dear father often told me, you must aim high. Ha. Very funny, don't you think? We must all reach for the sky. We must have ambition.'

The Quest team attempted a communal laugh but it was difficult. Normally such things would have been left to Carlyle, the human bridge between them and the prince, to orchestrate. They would have followed his lead. But since Carlyle had disappeared without explanation, they had grown nervous. No one wanted to articulate their fears, but it was becoming uncomfortably apparent that his absence confirmed the stakes had increased dramatically.

The Quest team were used to dealing with algorithms and faceless, humanless equations. But now Carlyle was missing and they'd become very scared. Even the preternaturally sanguine Schwartz seemed edgy. The prince had tried to quell their fears. Each of the Quest team had been given his own private security contingent, but that served only to heighten their anxiety, remind them of their vulnerability.

It had dawned on them that what had started as a daring attempt at market manipulation had turned into something that now seemed to carry huge personal risk. But there was too much risk in quitting, too. The team feared the consequences. They'd noted that the prince appeared to have taken the news of Carlyle's unexpected departure well. Too well. He appeared unconcerned about the loss of his lieutenant, almost dismissive. His attitude had prompted several to question whether he had sanctioned Carlyle's murder. An ugly sense of paranoia had swept through them. All wished they'd never signed up to Project Apocalypse, as the prince insisted on calling it. They might get paid millions, they conceded, but they might also end up dead.

A shrill buzzing filled the air as a second model plane made its way down the runway. The group watched its progress dispassionately. The prince clapped his hands and beamed. He continued smiling as the second plane hit the hangar and shattered into pieces.

'Good,' the prince said to the engineer flying it. 'But, remember, you only get one chance with a Gulfstream jet. You won't be able to have another go if you fail to hit the target.'

He looked about for Carlyle, expecting him to materialize at any minute. He'd half forgotten that Carlyle was dead. It hadn't exactly been unexpected, his lieutenant's demise, given what the prince knew of Carlyle, his years of double-dealing. That was what happened to traitors. They were made examples of. They paid with the only thing they hadn't stolen: their lives.

But it was still difficult without Carlyle, the prince felt. Living with a spy had been reassuring. If you wanted something distributed to others – intelligence, say, on a major attempt to rig the world's banking system – then it was good to have Carlyle around. Everything he did, every conversation he had, text he sent, email he exchanged, was monitored by the NSA and shared with his handlers. It was like having your own CIA agent in the room with you at all times. That sort of intrusion was invaluable, the prince had thought.

Yes, he really would miss Carlyle. More so than his father, if he was being honest. Patricide was such an ugly word. It made a son's killing of his father sound unnatural, unjust even. It masked a million motives. Was murdering a dying man even murder? Or was it some sort of mercy killing, one that, admittedly, had stopped his father squandering billions on his ridiculous legacy. There were better ways of leaving your mark, the prince had decided. He stroked his beard, then twisted the bristles on his chin into a sharp point, like a dagger. He recalled his father had performed a similar ritual when he'd been thinking.

The prince watched a third plane hit the hangar and tried to suppress a smile. An expensive business, spreading fear. But such destruction was necessary. It would be noticed. Cameras, satellites, phones, computers: they would all be watching. And there was all that financial data, millions of putative trades flowing out from Quest across telecom networks ready to be activated, being sucked up by an eager, dumb NSA, desperate to see fear wherever it looked. They would see the trades and the intelligence agencies would be able to draw only one conclusion. Doomsday was coming. It was the only scenario they could see. The only risk. Well, he wasn't going to disappoint them. Not until the last minute, anyway. They wanted fear, well, the prince would give them fear.

He looked up at the sky, as if he could see the myriad lenses being trained down on him by the satellites silently monitoring the grainy images of prototype destruction he was witnessing before him. Aim high, he thought. Yes, that really was good advice. Perhaps the best thing he'd inherited from his father. Maybe the only thing. You had to aim high, especially in games of bluff. There was just no point, otherwise.

Sorrenson clicked his mouse and slowed the footage on his computer screen. 'So,' he said. 'Tell me, what am I missing?'

'Do you see anything?'

He continued looking at the screen. 'Some fat men in suits. Some attractive women in short skirts and high heels. Typical central London scene. You called me off a murder investigation to show me this? I mean, it's great to see you but . . .'

Kate silenced him with a pout and a shake of her head. 'Come on, look again.' She took the mouse from his hand and dragged it across her desk.

Sorrenson studied the screen. It was just CCTV footage, miles of the stuff, it seemed, spliced together from different cameras along a particular route that ran along Fleet Street, then up Kingsway to Euston and King's Cross before completing a three-mile journey up York Way to Tufnell Park and Hampstead Heath.

'Let me make things even more obvious for you.' She pointed at the screen. Two joggers could be seen leaving through the revolving door of a building – a building that Sorrenson was in love with: Higgs Bank. 'Blink and you'd miss them. Got our tech team to do this. I decided I could get it done quicker for counter-terrorism reasons than you could for a murder hunt.'

'Yeah, figures,' Sorrenson said. 'Terror commands bigger pay cheques than murder.'

She clicked her mouse again. 'Now watch carefully. Our jogger friends are seen here, here, here, here and here.' The screen split into smaller screens, each showing a grainy freeze frame capturing the blurred appearance of two men in running vests.

Sorrenson nodded. 'OK. I'm with you. We've found some

joggers from Higgs. I expected you'd have a bigger office, by the way.'

She tutted. 'It's not all about size, you know.' She smiled at him. 'So?' She frowned in frustration at his obstinacy. It really was so obvious.

'So, if I'm following this correctly, on the probable night of Holahon's murder we've got a pair of joggers who leave Higgs Bank and run up to the Heath,' Sorrenson said. 'And that's it.'

'Jesus. Are you being deliberately obtuse?'

'All right, sorry. OK, so we've got two people who are presumably known to Holahon making their way to the probable murder scene. Can't make out their faces too well, though.'

'True, but you don't need to.'

'How so?'

She laughed. 'It's funny, but I would have missed this if I hadn't accidentally pressed fast-forward on the footage. It speeded them up and sort of dramatized their actions. It brought out their gait, how they run. I realized I recognized it. Everyone has a running style, you know that. It's as individual as a fingerprint. I know who these two are. Their gait betrayed them. Meet Ennis and Brockman.'

Sorrenson nodded thoughtfully. 'I'm looking forward already to arresting them. Can't wait to explain to them why we've picked them up. Arrested for having a guilty gait. It's an open and shut case.'

'That'll be what passes for Scandinavian wit?'

'Or deep hopelessness. There's not a lot of difference in my experience.'

'Whatever. But you can just ask them in for questioning, to help with your enquiries. You don't have to arrest them under caution. You might rattle something out of them. Coffee?'

'Ta.'

She disappeared into the corridor. Sorrenson continued looking at the screen. He double-clicked on one image and enlarged it. He craned forwards. Could she be right? Was it too much to hope? There were shadows on the men's wrists, he noticed. But, of course, they weren't shadows. They were watches. It was fanciful but, well, bankers were a strange lot. They might just have been egotistical enough to wear their watches on the night in question. It made sense. After all, why put them on if they weren't going to use them?

She returned with the coffee. 'Apologies. These are luke-warm. The machine's on the blink. We have devices for tracing radioactive isotopes across the country but not a working coffee machine. Welcome to my world.'

Sorrenson pointed at the men's wrists.

'Interesting,' Kate said. 'Good spot. Unlikely—'

'That they had them switched on, I know, but it's got to be worth a shout. How on earth do you get your hands on their data, though?'

'We have people who can do that. We pool them with Six because of the cutbacks. They're paid to hack into Iranian intelligence, China, the usual targets. We swap a lot of what we find with the NSA. A lot goes to Australia and New Zealand. They look at it and tell us if anything is useful. That way we're cut out of the loop, should any politicians get too interested in how much data we're sucking up in our own country. Welcome to the great covert world of espionage outsourcing. For our friends Down Under it should be a couple of minutes' work hacking into some sat-nav company in California or wherever the data is stored.'

'Cheers. Appreciate it.'

'Well, I'm an interested party in this. Sorting out Holahon's murder may help make things clearer regarding Higgs. I've still got lots of unanswered questions about what's been going on.'

'You and me both.'

Sorrenson's words hung in the air. She looked at the floor, bit her lip.

'I mean about our investigation,' Sorrenson added hurriedly.

She was conscious that her cheeks were reddening. It wasn't a good place or a good time to be opening that door.

'How's it going on those fronts then?' She tried to make her voice sound light, measured. It creaked under the strain.

Sorrenson sipped his coffee and winced. 'Wow! That really is grim. You secret-agent types are a tough breed.'

'Yeah, it's part of the induction process. You should try to drink the stuff they give the agents in the field. Anyway, you were saying?'

He shrugged, scratched his stubble. 'Well, the head and the hands didn't throw up that much. It just seems to confirm that he was killed on or near the Heath and dismembered up there. We found an almost empty whisky bottle in the bag with the body parts. There was a small plastic pouch, too, which could have contained the coke. If true, it would suggest it was all carefully premeditated. Somebody took that stuff up there. Don't see your joggers clutching a whisky bottle and some marching powder as they make their way up to the Heath.'

'Oh, come on. They could have hidden it beforehand, then jogged up there knowing he was going to turn up and wham! The perfect crime.'

'You've been reading too many detective novels.'

'Sounds like you haven't been reading enough. Come on, meet me halfway here. At least admit my theory cannot be refuted by anything you've seen so far.'

'OK. I'll give you that. Providing you have dinner with me.'

'When?'

'Tonight is good.'

'Can't. Sorry. Have to see my mother.'

Sorrenson looked at her.

Sentences collided in her mind. 'It's not an excuse,' she blurted out. 'I really do have to see her. Honestly. We don't have much time left. She'll be gone soon. In many ways she's gone already. I'm sorry, you don't need to hear any of this. But, well, it's the truth. After Michael and my father she's all I've got left. When she goes . . .' She didn't finish her sentence. To have completed it would have been to face up to the future, to focus on herself. She was ready for neither. Her life at that precise moment needed to be one extended distraction. She stared into Sorrenson's dark brown eyes. Michael had had similar eyes. She had always thought they were too gentle for what he did. A distraction. Yes, that was it. She wanted to lose herself.

'Maybe you could pick me up after.' She hated herself for sounding needy.

Sorrenson placed a hand on hers. He felt awkward sitting in the small, strange office with the tall, strange woman who was so strong and yet was barely holding it together. He felt uncomfortable yet uncharacteristically optimistic. He smiled at her. 'After. I'd like that. I'd really like that.'

Webster studied the report in front of him and groaned. 'Seriously?'

Callow gave a curt nod, examined his nicotine-stained fingers.

'How long?'

'Not that long. Just a few months. Over before it began, really.'

'But still.'

'But still, yes, it doesn't look good.'

'We're sure about this?'

'We interviewed McLure's ex-wife. She told us about the text messages he sent to Pendragon. He had a separate phone that we'd missed. There's no doubt there was a relationship. Not serious, though.'

'She sets the standard pretty low if she grants someone like McLure that sort of access.'

'True enough,' Callow said. Typical Webster, he thought. He saw an affair as some sort of simple technical process, like the opening of a door.

'What a mess,' Webster muttered. 'As if it wasn't messy enough before all of this.' He wondered if he had the energy to propel his wheelchair out of the window of his office. He imagined himself smashing into the ground, the blessed release of oblivion. All his problems would be negated in a fantastic collision of metal and concrete. The thought briefly thrilled him. If the Joint Intelligence Assessment Committee ever got to hear about it, he would be a laughing stock. Two of his agents had been having an affair and the surviving one seemed hell bent on trashing the dead one. It was the stuff of soap opera, not national security. The one thing, given his years of devotion to the service, that Webster couldn't abide was the thought that he would be reduced to an object of ridicule. Hated, yes. Laughed at, no.

'Well, this certainly puts things in perspective,' he said sourly. He ran a hand over the knot in his tie, feeling its tightness. If he could just pull it a bit tighter . . .

'It doesn't mean her suspicions about McLure are invalid,' Callow murmured. 'There's no suggestion that she's operating out of spite. And the near million pounds in McLure's offshore account needs to be explained.'

'Oh, come on!' Webster exploded. 'Most people like McLure have a million pounds lying around, these days. It's just wealth passed down the generations. His parents die and, hey presto, he's left a million-pound house. The service would collapse if it wasn't for that sort of munificence. Half of our agents couldn't afford to work for us otherwise, all those ex-public schoolboys. The moneyed classes are effectively subsidizing our intelligence service. They should get some sort of fucking rebate from the Treasury.'

It was a weakness, Callow knew, Webster's inability to empathize. Understandable, really, given what had happened to him, how he'd channelled all his pain, all his rage into the service. But it meant he didn't do relationships. He didn't really understand humans. It was a flaw, a massive flaw, recognized by the regular psychometric testing he underwent.

Ideologies, codes, patterns, networks, structures, threats: he was good with the abstract. Just not with people. He'd never married.

'Where is she at the moment?' Webster snapped. 'I haven't seen her for days.'

'Compassionate leave. She's taken some time off. Her mother died.'

'Jesus.' Webster snorted. 'How inconvenient. Well, we need to see her urgently. This is what happens when you bring in outsiders on secondment. No comprehension of the agency's culture. I despair. I really do.'

Callow didn't say anything. Webster would calm down given time. He always did. But Callow also knew that he was going to have to fill in the blanks in the interim. The clock was ticking. He would have to make his own calls. The perils of being a deputy. Get it right and the boss took credit. Get it wrong and you were ruined. Callow cleared his throat. 'Today's the funeral, I believe.'

'Find yourself a black tie and turn up to pay our respects. And before you go, what's this?' Webster held up a piece of paper.

Callow pretended to study it, but he already knew what it was. 'Surveillance request form.'

'I can see that. But why is she making it?'

'She thinks we need to increase our monitoring of the target.'

'This Saudi prince?'

'Yes.'

'Christ, I hope the Saudis don't get to hear of it. It'll be just horrible if they find out we've put one of their royal family under surveillance. There'll be a diplomatic firefight.

They'll stop sharing stuff from their listening stations. Oh, Christ—'

'It's not just him we're targeting,' Callow interrupted. 'It's the whole team that work for his hedge fund, Quest. We're picking up all sorts of chatter now, coming out of the City and Wall Street. The Treasury is talking to the US Financial Intelligence Unit. They've got super-computers that seem to be detecting some potentially strange trading positions that have yet to be activated. There is some evidence that someone somewhere is taking a huge position on an imminent terrorist threat. Like I said to you the other day, remember what happened before Nine/Eleven. Certain investors in the stock market saw it coming. Now everyone's getting scared.'

Webster groaned again. 'Well, you're right about that. I for one am permanently scared. Does she not know how many operatives we've got on surveillance duty right at this moment? We're tracking more than two thousand in this country alone. It's relentless, this game of chase. And you're talking to me about super-computers and trading patterns?'

Callow looked at his boss. He would never want to be in his position. The happy prospect of retirement loomed large in his mind. Three more years to go. Then a *mas* in Provence beckoned. The former silk farm he'd bought was a ruin, but it would be a project for him and his wife. There were olive trees and vineyards nearby. Some days he just wanted to fast-forward through his life to the sun-dappled future. He nodded at Webster. There was only so much he could do to shore up Pendragon, he felt. There was only so far that he could stick his neck out for her. He didn't have an appetite for unfettered risk.

'Jesus,' Webster muttered. He lowered his voice yet further. 'Jesus,' he repeated venomously. He grimaced as he swallowed cold coffee. 'It was so much easier during the Troubles. People took terrorism seriously back then. But these days it's losing out in the pecking order. All this global warming and these bird-flu epidemics, the prospect of a second Great Depression, the chance of the earth being hit by a meteorite, for fuck's sake – we're having to compete with all that shit. We're way down the list of what gives people nightmares. Terrorists don't need to perpetrate acts of terrorism to make us terrified. The world's managing pretty well by itself. It's farming fear on an industrial scale. Which is fucking bad news for us every time those upstairs make a budget decision. Some massive terrorist event might be just what we need to get the wheels rolling again. Give everyone a wake-up call.'

Webster's voice had become almost a murmur. Ten years he'd been in the top job. And in ten years everything had changed. The world had become infinitely more complex and dangerous while the service had become ever more limited, sclerotic, restricted. The tilting of the playing field would have grave repercussions, he knew. There would be blowback. No wonder they were resorting to using supercomputers to spot threats. The world in which they lived, the risks it was facing, was getting beyond the understanding of humans.

He glanced out of his window to the Thames and the concrete theatres of the South Bank baking in the early summer heat. Crowds of people wearing shorts and summer dresses snaked along the riverbank. He could almost sense their joy at being alive. He envied them their ignorance.

Chapter 12

Superintendent Steven Cassidy stood behind the desk in the foyer of Victoria police station and tried not to hate the two desk clerks loitering beside him. Cassidy had twenty years' service under his belt and thought he had seen most things. But the introduction of non-police service personnel into police stations was an unwelcome novelty, one that, even months later, was no easier to deal with no matter how familiar his two assistants had become to him.

It just didn't look right, Cassidy thought, the public walking into a cop shop and being met by civilians. It sent out the wrong signals, suggested that the police, uniforms, the rule of law, were no longer important. But it was the way things were going, Cassidy recognized. More and more of the police service was being outsourced to anonymous unaccountable private companies that promised they could do things cheaper, faster, shinier. How long, Cassidy wondered, staring at the two twenty-somethings texting furtively on their mobile phones, before they outsourced detecting and counter-terrorism operations, riot control and everything else? How long before the private dicks gave orders to their public brethren? He was struck by a depressing thought. How long before they started using computers to replace certain police roles? Not long probably. Luckily, he'd be out of the service before that happened. But it would be a close-run thing. He would barely escape before everything came crashing down. It was all about targets and economies and shrinkage, these days. He should have seen the warning signs when the police had stopped being a force and become a service. It was as if they were supposed to act like a hotel chain or something preposterous like that.

Cassidy looked up from his desk as he heard the sound of footsteps. A sweating, pale-faced man in a suit lurched towards him. It was just gone three o'clock on a boiling Thursday afternoon in late July. It was clear from the man's flushed face that he'd been drinking heavily.

Cassidy waited. He wondered what the man wanted. To report a stolen wallet, most probably. That would figure. There were many like him around Victoria station. Their numbers increased in proportion to the heat. Lunchtime drinkers were easy targets for pickpockets. They were oblivious to the thieves, too focused on filling their warm livers with cold white wine.

The man approached the desk. Cassidy gestured at the clerks to let him deal with this. He could smell alcohol on the man's breath. He could see beads of sweat, alcohol sweat, on the man's forehead. Cassidy attempted a reassuring smile. 'How can I help you, sir?'

The drunk stared at Cassidy, seemingly astonished by the question. Cassidy could tell his suit was expensive. The shoes, too. He wasn't the normal drunk they got in Victoria. Maybe he'd been on his way to the races or something. The man gripped the counter for support. He took a deep breath.

'I want to report a murder.'

Cassidy's heart sank. The man was clearly unhinged. He would be wrapped up for hours sorting out the fellow's problems. There were no hostels to take him. And all the psychiatric institutions in the borough were full, he knew from exhausted experience. He couldn't remember when or why or how mental-health problems had effectively been outsourced to the thin blue line, but they had. Most days Cassidy felt more like a social worker. He'd like to see the private dicks assume that role. Or a computer. 'I see,' he said at last.

'Only it's not . . . wasn't a murder,' the drunk mumbled. 'It became a murder. Sort of. But that was never the intention. You've got to believe me on that point.'

Cassidy popped nicotine gum into his mouth and instantly felt calmer. He picked up a pen and grabbed a notepad. 'OK.'

The man looked alarmed. 'I don't think you're taking my complaint, sorry, I mean my story, my statement, seriously. You don't know how much courage it has taken for me to come in here and explain what went wrong.' He looked like he was about to cry.

Dutch courage more like, Cassidy thought. He opened a ledger on the desk in front of him. 'I apologize, sir. So, let's start at the beginning. You want to report a murder that was never meant to be a murder.'

'That's right,' the drunk said, with almost childish enthusiasm. 'You got it.' His face broke into a smile.

'And your name?'

'Ennis,' the man slurred. 'Scott Ennis.'

★   ★   ★

Kate stood at the door of the church and shook hands with the departing mourners, a stream of black and grey coats that had no place in the summer sunshine. She remembered Michael's funeral, when half of those paying their respects had been in uniform, their brightly coloured medal ribbons clashing with the solemnity of the occasion. Her mother's funeral had been very different. Everyone was old. Everyone had been prepared for her death. Indeed, they had all half been hoping for it, a blessed release to end the big C. So there had been few tears. No proper sobbing at all. It had been about as perfunctory as a funeral service could be.

As she traded empty hugs and kisses with the last of the crowd, the young vicar nervously beside her, worried that his garbled sermon had failed to do justice to an expended life, she realized that she would never again be the centre of such attention. No one was going to pity her again, she thought. Never again would hundreds of faces be trained on her own. The thought gave her strength. There would be no more outpourings of mass grief or mass love directed at her. All her loved ones were dead. She would never remarry. She would never have children and watch them be baptized, graduate or marry. There would be no more big ceremonies in her life. The future, her future, was going to be uniform and quiet and solitary. She really was alone.

She noticed that Callow had held back, a lurking presence some twenty metres away from her mother's grave, half hidden behind ornate Victorian monuments commemorating the supremely wealthy dead, the hedge-fund managers and investment bankers of their day. The inscriptions on their stones talked of philanthropy and epic deeds. But they were fooling no one, she thought. Their wealth had been built on exploitation, on casualties. You couldn't become wealthy without leaving a trail of damage. No amount of good deeds would hide that reality.

Callow approached only when the last mourner had gone, bringing to an end the anxious minutes she had spent squinting in the bright sunshine, trying to read his face from afar. He was clearly not there to pay his respects.

'The service has come to support me in my time of grief,' she said. 'That's nice.'

Callow didn't say anything. He examined the wreaths left by the church door, read the cards nestling among the flowers. 'Good ceremony?'

'Great. The best.' She checked herself. 'Sorry, no need for the sarcasm. I'm just a bit wired. Haven't slept much and I'm still not sure if I gave her what she would have wanted.' She turned away from the gravestones to Callow. He was scrutinizing the cemetery, as if he was picking his own final resting place. 'You spend all your life knowing someone and when it comes to summing them up, to doing them justice right at the end, you can't help feeling that you've failed them,' she said. 'Just how would they want to be remembered? What would they want their legacy to be? And the really bad thing is you're not sure whether it matters in the grand scheme of things because they're dead and, well, that's it. They're gone. You don't have to worry about them any more. There's no risk of letting them down. And that's a terrible feeling. Like you've been given a licence to stop caring. It's horrible.'

Of all the people to open up to, Callow was possibly the worst person she could have picked, she thought. Imperious, impossible, impenetrable: he was an embodiment of the

205

service. There was a dourness about him that seemed to emanate from every male agent in MI5. It was like they'd been groomed to be aloof. Callow was the sort of man who seemed to belong at funerals.

The cemetery was a small, calm city of stones, a peaceful place bisected by neat paths, well-trimmed grass verges and rose gardens. There was a sense of order, of proportion. The dead knew how to live better than the living, she thought. The living were being dragged down by chaos. She looked at Callow. 'So?'

Callow seemed uncomfortable. 'Webster wants to know about you and McLure. He needs you to explain yourself.'

She struggled to suppress her laughter. She was surprised at how long it had taken them to find out. They were fucking spies, after all. But, God, their timing was truly fucking terrible. Remorseless. Bastards. 'You realize what day it is today, don't you? The clues are all there. All those people wearing black.'

'Yes, I'm sorry, truly sorry, but he was adamant. He needs to work out how much credence he should give your hunch. You know what he's like. Not great when it comes to managing people. He gets anxious when the personal and the public collide. He just starts imagining the headlines in the papers and what it'll mean for the reputation of the service. In an ideal world I think Webster would like us all to be drones.'

She almost did a double-take. It was as if a stranger had assaulted her in the street. 'Credence? Jesus. Does he think I'm punting this to boost my promotion chances? Credence. He makes me sound like some third-rate intelligence asset.

We're on the same side, remember? Or am I missing something here?'

The sound of heavy footsteps made them look up. The gravediggers were arriving. The final act of concealment, she thought. The final cover-up. And then she would be left with no one.

'It's just that Webster's a bit jumpy,' Callow said. 'Well, more than a bit jumpy. He knows you want more surveillance of the targets and he needs to make a call on how much manpower we devote to this. You know we're stretched.'

She glared at him. 'And what? That I fucked someone in the service has a bearing on this? You're honestly telling me that you're not going to back me on it because of my personal life? That's insane. You're putting people's lives at risk by not trusting me, you know that, don't you?'

Callow attempted to put an arm round her shoulders. He felt clumsy. Old, clumsy, uncertain, protective. They were not emotions he enjoyed. He studied her face for several seconds, then gave up trying to reach out to her. He lit a cigarette and sucked smoke into grateful lungs. 'If you're wrong, we've devoted resources to a big mistake and that means something else might slip through. And then there'll be hell to pay. Webster's simply trying to get his ducks in a line before he pulls the trigger.'

He sounded like a tax lawyer advising a big client on his options, she thought. She nodded to herself and looked at him fiercely. She almost spat her words out. 'Tell Webster to go fuck himself.'

Callow chewed his lip, watching the soil being piled on the coffin. The action scared him. He was going to be cremated when he went, he'd decided. He wasn't taking any risks. The fear of being buried alive was almost overpowering. He suppressed a shudder. He'd spent most of his life covering things up, hiding things. He didn't want his dead years to be spent the same way.

'Look,' he said finally. His voice was gentle, conversational. She was surprised. She looked at him suspiciously. 'Today is the worst day to be having this conversation. But Webster's on your side. He was a fan of your father, you know.'

She recoiled, thrown by the unexpected reference to her father. 'What?'

'They worked together. In Belfast. He wants to talk to you about it some time. But, well, he's got more pressing things on his mind right now.'

It made sense that Webster had known her father. But it still felt strange. Once again her personal life was intruding on the professional. There were strange synergies at work. Things were fusing. She wished she could separate the two worlds. She needed to switch off. She needed to run. 'Tell him I'll be in tomorrow.'

'You sure? You haven't even begun grieving.'

'I've been grieving for my mother for a long time. I lost her months ago. Like we agreed, the clock is ticking. We need to get moving.'

Callow smiled through a wreath of smoke, alarming her. She'd never really seen his teeth before.

'I'm glad to hear you say that,' he said. 'That's why I've initiated surveillance of the targets already.'

'Interesting, Callow. Webster know?'

'Not yet. He will. Later today.'

She nodded to herself. 'Hmm. Maybe I've got you wrong. Maybe you're not such a service robot after all.'

'I doubt that. I've been indoctrinated for way too long. But, for what it's worth, you'd better see this.' He handed her a manila envelope stuffed with black-and-white long-range photographs.

'What the . . .?'

'It's a puzzle. Maybe he's got a new hobby.'

'Flying radio-controlled model planes?'

'Not just flying them. Crashing them. They must have smashed up at least a dozen so far. These were given to us by our friends over the Pond. They were taken at the prince's private runway down on the coast. It's been resurfaced recently. It can take jets now, big jets weighing seventy tons fully laden. His father was going to use it for some pet project, we think. Flying medicines and aid to the world's trouble spots in Airbus A380s. Apparently he wanted to do some huge humanitarian relief initiative funded out of his oil billions. He was obsessed with his legacy, how he'd be remembered. But God knows what his son wants to use it for. To perpetuate his state of arrested development, perhaps. He really seems to enjoy smashing things up.'

She allowed herself a half-smile. 'Thanks.'

'What for?'

'You know what for.'

Callow remained inscrutable. 'You needed an ally.' He turned to go, paused for a second and turned back to her. 'And I really am sorry about your loss. I never knew my mother. She died when I was two. Biggest regret of my life, not knowing her.'

She smiled at him, properly this time. It figured. The service was full of the motherless and the fatherless. Orphans made the best agents. They'd known little in the way of love so they made the service their parents. It made them strong and vulnerable. They were the perfect people to bend. They were perfect people to bend others, too.

She watched Callow make his way through the rose garden. She had more in common with him than she'd thought. She pulled her BlackBerry out of her bag and switched it on. The act of reconnecting with the world felt like a betrayal of her mother. Her coffin hadn't even been covered over, yet her daughter was already switching back into service-think. She checked her messages. Sorrenson had texted to say something major had come up in the Holahon investigation. She checked her emails. Scores of them. So much information. Too much information. It was hard to know what she should read and what should be discarded.

At first she didn't see it. It was as if her mind had screened it out, given that it was an impossibility. It was only when she scrolled through the emails a second time that it registered. A small explosion rocked the inside of her head. McLure. There was an email from McLure. An email from a man whose funeral she'd attended just weeks before. She found herself struggling for breath. She checked her inbox to make sure she wasn't mistaken. Yes, it had definitely been sent by McLure. It had come from within the service's intranet system. She kept staring at her inbox, willing the email to disappear. She noticed that the gravediggers had almost finished their task. Her mother was no longer of the earth but underneath it. The separation of mother and daughter was nearly complete.

She swallowed hard, clicked on McLure's email. It felt like she was prising open a coffin lid, like she was bringing the dead back to life. She stood trembling among the gravestones bathed in summer sunshine. She felt lost and frightened and alone.

'I think he must have had some sort of breakdown. It's not uncommon in our field. Very stressful, investment banking.'

The sentence was delivered in a laconic Texan drawl, as if the man delivering it was discussing the ailment of a family pet. Brockman smiled at the two detectives sitting across from him. He knew they had nothing. It was why he'd agreed to present himself at Margate police station in response to their request for his help with their enquiries. It was such a civil way of not helping the police, Brockman thought, arranging a time and place to be interviewed. Quaint. Very English. Thank God British cops had yet to copy the methods employed by their American counterparts. The latter were so much more uncouth, so gung-ho.

Ennis could go round saying whatever but he couldn't make any of it stick, Brockman knew. There was no evidence to link him to the murder. Even the detectives had admitted Ennis seemed to be on the cusp of some sort of meltdown. And you couldn't rely on the testimony of the mad. Otherwise the jails would be full of bankers incriminated by their burned-out colleagues.

Brockman glanced down at his watch. He'd been questioned for just over an hour and they'd landed no blows. They were just shadow-boxing, really. He would be out in a few hours. Probably take himself out for a meal to make up for such a spectacularly wasted day. He fancied surf and turf. Again. He was going to spend a lot of Rhino dollars, he promised himself.

Sorrenson produced a series of CCTV images, pushed them across the table. Brockman's solicitor leaned forward to view them. Brockman nodded at him. The last time the two men had been in the same room, Brockman was being grilled by the Serious Fraud Office about paying massive kickbacks to a Saudi sheikh in return for a major weapons contract that made billions for his client, an arms manufacturer owned by a US venture-capital firm. Nothing had stuck that time either. Nothing ever stuck if the scales of justice were weighted in your favour. Money really was very heavy. Saudi money especially. That had been his epiphany.

Brockman stifled a yawn. No, they were just trying it on, the hick detectives. They were just doing their job but, boy, they really sucked at it. Inevitable, really, Brockman figured. If you paid peanuts . . . No one with even half a brain would enter the police. There was just no money in it. Absolutely none. How could the police hope to solve any complex crimes with their limited talents and resources?

He almost felt sorry for them. Almost. Still, that was capitalism. That was freedom in action. It didn't bode well for the future, admittedly. The world would become increasingly lawless. The cops just weren't up to the job, couldn't cope with the enormity of what they were up against. People were going to have to start paying for their own private police forces if they wanted some semblance of law and order. The status quo wasn't going to hold much longer. It was an increasingly wild world out there.

Sorrenson pointed at the images on the table. He turned them around so that Brockman could see the photographs the right way up. 'We believe these are images of you and your colleague, Scott Ennis, running up to Hampstead Heath on the night of Holahon's murder.'

Brockman peered at the images and gave up trying to stifle a yawn. His mouth gaped open. He took a sip of water from a paper cup. 'I run all the time.'

'You ever run with Holahon?'

Brockman turned his attention to the questioner: Hughes, the shorter one with the glaring eyes, who was almost incandescent with anger. Or was it anger? Brockman wondered. Maybe it was something else. Yes, maybe. He knew fear when he smelt it. That was what made him a good banker, the ability to sniff out someone's vulnerability, exploit their anxieties, play to their fears. Strange, though, that the younger detective looked so ill at ease. 'We were members of the same club, yes.'

'You run the same races?'

'Sometimes.'

'He was better than you, right?'

Brockman frowned. 'I'll let our records speak for themselves. You gunning for a job with ESPN or something? I guess sports commentators earn more than police. Wise move, Sherlock.'

Hughes unwrapped a toffee and placed it in his mouth. He wasn't going to let the banker rile him. He really needed to stay calm. He had to play the role that Sorrenson expected of him. They'd had words. He pointed at Brockman. 'So, you're saying the night of Holahon's murder you weren't on the Heath?'

'No, I'm just saying I can't remember.'

'Convenient.'

'If you like. But it's also the truth. Can you remember where you were the night of Holahon's murder?'

Hughes opened his mouth to respond but Sorrenson held up a hand, gesturing for his colleague to remain silent. Hughes had become familiar with the action. It annoyed him intensely.

'We would like you to look at these images,' Sorrenson said quietly. He pushed them closer to Brockman. 'Now, then, tell me, do you think there's a possibility they're of you? It's clearly someone from Higgs. We can see them leaving through the bank's revolving doors. The footage is admittedly grainy, but it certainly looks like you and Ennis.'

Brockman shrugged. 'Impossible to tell, I'm afraid.'

Sorrenson stared at him. 'You've got a particular running style, you know. Distinctive. You really pump those arms, so I'm told by people who've seen you run. Same as this guy in the photo.' He pointed to the character in the image.

Brockman started laughing. 'So charge me. First-degree homicide. Show this to the jury. You've got a watertight case, hotshot. It's crystal clear I murdered Holahon because of the way I run. Jesus, is that really all you got? Do I have to stay here any longer?' Brockman looked at his lawyer for confirmation, then made an ostentatious display of checking his watch.

Sorrenson indicated the device. 'You had that long?'

'The watch? A couple of years.'

'Nice. Nice model.'

'Yeah, real nice. Present to myself when the bonuses were being handed out.'

Sorrenson smiled at him. 'Satellite link-up with heart monitor, right? Comes with an alarm button you can activate that will have a helicopter dispatched to you in an emergency. What's the annual subscription for that service? Thirty thousand dollars, isn't it? But useful, if you get into trouble. Useful if you need bailing out of an avalanche. Money can buy you a lot of insurance. We can't all afford that sort of protection.'

The words hung in the air.

'Yeah,' Brockman said. 'It also tells the time.'

'I've got one myself,' Sorrenson said. His voice was calm, subdued even, as if he was working through a problem aloud. 'Not top-of-the-range like yours, obviously, but the entry-range product. I couldn't run without it now. Many runners feel the same, I'm told. They need to track those runs. Every run. They want to measure themselves so they need all of that data. You've just got to wear it at all times because you never know when you might hit your PB. That's why the data is useful. It tells you what you're capable of. Allows you to build algorithms that will let you learn just how far you can go. Just how far to push things. The risks you can take. Everything comes down to how you analyse the data.'

'I can relate to that,' Brockman said. 'We have super-computers crunching stuff for Higgs every nanosecond. We know all about risk. Movements in the market? We spot them. We know everything that's happening because we suck up all the information available. We can insure ourselves against any contingency. Makes us bomb-proof.'

He was puzzled. The stupid detective seemed intent on running down the clock discussing his watch. They were even dumber than he'd first thought.

'Ennis told us what happened,' Sorrenson said. 'A jury would be sympathetic.'

'Ennis has gone cuckoo.'

'He told us how you rumbled Holahon. You worked out he'd faked some of his times. The time he ran that ultra – the Wall, wasn't it? He used a mountain bike for part of the race, then hid at the end, so he could win the veterans' category.'

Brockman said nothing.

'You obviously had your suspicions,' Sorrenson said. 'Ennis said it drove the two of you mad, trying to work out how he was doing it. Even when you confronted him he didn't confess.'

Brockman stared at the table.

'So you held a gun to his head and made him drink a bottle of whisky and snort some lines,' Hughes said. 'Only he still didn't admit it. So you held his head under water. Your version of water-boarding, Ennis said.'

Sorrenson cut in: 'And then, well, we know what happened then. He confessed and laughed at you and you got mad and held him under water for a few minutes too long. The next thing you know, he's dead and your attempt to bring him to justice has gone badly, very badly wrong. You started out with the best intentions, to right a wrong, bring a man to account, and suddenly it all goes very black. Something petty becomes something else altogether. You're facing a long jail sentence if you get done for manslaughter, even longer if the jury buy a charge of murder. There was clearly a premeditated element to the attack.'

Brockman examined his fingernails. They would have charged him if they'd had the evidence. They were fishing. The detectives were desperate. He couldn't incriminate

216

himself if he remained silent. He just had to sweat it out. Poker-face time.

'I notice you're not saying anything,' Sorrenson said. 'Fair enough. That's your prerogative. The thing I don't get is what happened next. After you killed Holahon, I mean. What's with the dismembering? Who dumps the body down the coast? Not you or Ennis, that's for sure. You've got cast-iron alibis for the night in question. You're both picking up banking awards in the City. Remind me what they were for. Best client integrity managers, wasn't it? So it looks like someone else cleaned up your mess. But – I'll level with you here – I don't know why. What's so important about you that makes you worth protecting? Who was looking out for you? Hey, tell us about the van.'

Sorrenson noticed Hughes flinch. He looked at his colleague curiously. Recently he'd been acting so strangely. Something was clearly up.

Brockman continued examining his cuticles. He would need a manicure soon. He'd have one tomorrow, maybe even that evening, just as soon as he got back to London. It was unlikely that Margate had the sort of salon he was after. Brockman wasn't even sure the town was a place where people actually lived. It seemed to be little more than a dead amusement park. No banker in his right mind would pay it a visit. It was a total hole. The sooner London declared independence and let the rest of the lousy poverty-stricken British Isles sink below the waves, the better, Brockman thought. London was the only part of the UK that the US was interested in. Maybe the US should just get it over and done with and buy it outright, there were so many Americans in the capital.

'May I?' Sorrenson gestured at Brockman's watch.

Brockman frowned, unstrapped the chunky black device and handed it to the detective.

'Thanks,' Sorrenson said. 'It's a beauty. These things cost over five grand if you buy them with a heart monitor. And, of course, the helicopter option carries that hefty subscription fee. Never thought I'd get to hold one of these.'

He turned the watch over in his hand. He smiled. 'And look. You've got it engraved with your name on the inside. Classy. You ever lend it to anyone?'

'Course not. Why would I do that?'

'Just curious.' Sorrenson rummaged in a bag under his desk, pulled out a white adapter and lead and connected it to a laptop. He played with the buttons on the watch, hit keys on the computer, all the while staring at the screen, as if it was the only thing in the room that interested him. 'So, I guess at this moment you're making some calculations,' Sorrenson said matter-of-factly. 'Here's where I think you are in your mind. You know Ennis is borderline delusional. You know the testimony of someone who's had a breakdown isn't going to stick. You know there's nothing to connect you to the body. No DNA, no CCTV really, no eyewitness testimony, no nothing. So you're thinking, Play it out for a few hours more and then it's home time. Well . . .'

Sorrenson pressed a button on the keyboard. A map appeared on the laptop screen. 'Check the date.'

At first Brockman didn't know what he was looking at. Then he realized he didn't want to know what he was looking at. He started to tremble gently. He pulled out a handkerchief and dabbed his lips, swallowing hard several times. His sun-bed tan seemed to fade a fraction.

'For the purposes of the tape, we are showing Mr Brockman the data recorded by his satellite watch,' Hughes said. 'It shows a route run by whoever was wearing the watch from the London headquarters of Higgs Bank up to the top of Hampstead Heath. The journey ends at the exact location where Mr Holahon's satellite watch was found. We believe the data provides convincing evidence that Mr Brockman was in the same place at the same time as Mr Holahon when Mr Holahon was killed. The times on both watches indicate as much. Mr Brockman has testified that he has never lent his watch to another person. We have presented this evidence to the Crown Prosecution Service along with testimony from Mr Ennis and CCTV footage corroborating his journey in the direction of the Heath. The CPS advises us that we have a strong case for prosecution.'

Brockman's body shook violently. He tried to grab the watch but Sorrenson pulled it out of his reach. Brockman turned to his lawyer for support.

'My client has nothing to say on this matter,' the lawyer said. 'I suggest you either charge him or release him with immediate effect.'

'Good idea,' Sorrenson said. 'Jonathan Julius Brockman, I'm charging you with the manslaughter of Bradley Francis Holahon on the third of February of this year. We are making the same charge against Scott David Ennis. You do not have to say anything but anything you do say may be used in evidence against you . . .'

Brockman continued to shake. In his mind he could see a huge steak and a lobster tail being delivered to him on a silver platter by a small army of bejewelled, smiling

219

lap-dancers. The vision seemed so real, so attainable, and then it dissolved, leaving him staring at the bleak white wall of the interview room. A blank expanse drained of all colour, all possibilities.

Chapter 13

From: McLuretx14ygh9@xeromail.com
To: PendragonKate@ssfive.gsi.gov.uk
Subject: Surprise!

So, naturally you have questions. I guess the first would be: why are you receiving an email from a dead man? I take it I'm dead, right? The only way you would be reading this is if I am dead. So damn. I'm dead, you're reading this, and things look pretty fucked up.

I set up a special email account and put a timer on it to release this email if I didn't instruct it otherwise. A voice from beyond the grave, hey? Pretty creepy, right?

OK, that's the attempt at the light-hearted intro done. Take a few deep breaths to pull yourself together. While you're doing that I'll try and clear a few things up for you. First, I imagine you've found the money. The Isle of Man account. You're smart, Kate, so I'm guessing you've seen it. Almost a million, hey? You think I'm bent, don't you? Fair enough. I may be. I can't convince you otherwise. After all, none of this stuff makes any sense at the moment for you, I'm sure. You're not even sure if this is really me. Well, I could write some intimate stuff but that would be embarrassing and I'm guessing the service will be reading this at some stage, so all I'll say is that when I come back I'm going into skip hire and hope that this will convince you I am who I say am.

Now, about the cash. It came from our dear friend Holahon. He believed he was paying me for intel on what the service knew about Higgs. He knew there was so much hot money flowing through the London branch of the bank that it was only a matter of time before it got raided. Holahon just needed to know how much time they had so he could bury the bodies. He, in turn, helped us fill in some of the blanks. I'll explain those later. Taking the money was a good way of building up a relationship with him. It allowed him to think he owned me. Bankers love that feeling.

I know. I should have told you. But you would have been high risk. The fewer people who knew I was running Holahon as an asset the better. Not that I don't trust you. It's more that I trusted you too much. If you knew Holahon was ours you would have gone into full-on Charge of the Light Brigade mode, smashing through the doors, and I didn't want that. We need to be careful before we take on Higgs. It's a behemoth. We need to know what's really going on. Hence my asking you to check those accounts. We need to rely on our own evidence, not just stuff from assets with axes to grind. And it's risky, going after Higgs without nailing it all down. There may be people in the service who would, for political reasons, chiefly our relationship with our friends across the Atlantic, prefer it if we didn't smash up a Yank bank that is essentially an annexe of the CIA, if the rumours are true – and I'm sure they are. I've certainly seen enough to know the bank had a symbiotic relationship with the agency in the past. I strongly suspect the CIA actually built it but now it's out of control and the agency is struggling to rein it in. Hence my trip to New York. I needed to give the Americans the opportunity to tell us to back off if we threatened their operational capabilities by going after Higgs.

When Holahon was killed I believed it was because he had been rumbled. Someone knew we were gaming him and vice versa. I still believe that. Or, rather, I did before I died (you have no idea how horrible it is to write this). But you need to follow that line of enquiry through for yourself. Maybe my theory is just too neat.

I guess, too, that whoever terminated me (again, you have no idea how horrible it is to write this) had suspicions about my relationship with Holahon. Somebody became very nervous about that, about what he could end up feeding back to me. He had some interesting clients, of course, so they might have motives. More likely it was someone at Higgs, though. Maybe across the Pond. They can't have British agents poking about in the bank. They can't have someone in the bank leaking. It's a basket-case, Higgs, dripping in debt. I'm convinced of it. It could blow up at any minute. Check all the offshore stuff. There's got to be something there. Given what I've seen, and I guess what you're finding, the last thing Higgs needs is anyone exposing just how fucked it is. With me and Holahon out of the picture, that's two threats extinguished. Pretty smart, really. Someone doesn't want the cage rattled too hard.

Holahon was desperate to know what the intelligence community knows about some of Higgs's clients. I would have thought that as an ex-CIA agent he would have had good access to that sort of intel, but he insisted he was no longer in the loop on any of that sort of stuff. For what it's worth, I believed him. He, too, thought Higgs was some sort of quasi-CIA play, but he seemed to genuinely have no idea how far the Agency had penetrated it. I've tried to gauge that myself. That's why I went to New York. I figured they might share something with me face to face. Now that I'm dead I have no idea whether I was successful. Maybe I never did even when I was alive.

Please understand one thing. At all times I've acted out of the interests of national security. Hard to believe, I know, and to be honest, now that I'm dead, I don't really care, but if I was really bent I would have taken the money and quit.

I'm really sorry to lay all of this on you. But there really is no one else. Did I have a good funeral? Did they play Elgar's 'Nimrod'? A cliché, I know, but I thought it would be a fitting send-off. Take good care of yourself. Trust no one. It can be a leaky ship, the service.

Tony

Kate read McLure's email four times. Each time, his voice grew louder in her head. In many ways it helped her little. It was dated, of historical interest only. But she was reassured by it. She was sure it had been sent by McLure. It had his voice, a curious mix of humdrum building-society-manager-speak and informed spook. She found herself smiling as she remembered her former colleague. The Holahon stuff was interesting. It made complicated things even more compli-cated. It certainly suggested her hunch about Holahon's murder had been wrong all along. He had been disposed of because someone knew he was leaking stuff about Higgs to the service. She thought about her whiteboard at work. It would need a few dotted lines adding to it, but McLure had clearly seen a pattern. Everything was linked together. It was all to do with Higgs.

She put away her BlackBerry and stood looking at her mother's grave. It would be months before the soil had settled and she could put a stone on it. She'd been surprised that her mother had chosen not to be buried with her father in the quiet cemetery in his native Suffolk. It was strange what death revealed about people, she thought. After all, it was only now that he was dead that she felt she knew McLure. She understood his legacy, his lasting imprint. Holahon, too, was becoming far more interesting as a corpse than he had been, from what she knew of him, when he was alive. It was almost as if death had some great liberating effect, made the deceased more truthful, more loquacious.

For several minutes she stood in front of the mound of earth while the sound of Twickenham traffic competed with birdsong. It was going to be a scorching July afternoon. The world around her seemed alive and vital. It was a day that refused to recognize death. It was hard, she thought, to imagine anything ending on such a day. The thought heightened her sense of grief, of loss, of loneliness. It was not a good day to be alone. She stood stock still for several seconds, thinking. Then she texted Sorrenson.

The smaller, older man knelt on the ground, blood pouring from his mouth. He combed the dusty yard for his lost false teeth, jettisoned, spectacularly, by a punch that seemed to have taken months to arrive on his jawbone. He'd witnessed his assault in spectacular high-definition slow-motion. It had made the attack all the more ugly, squalid.

The much younger, taller man stood over him, shaking with anger. He felt he'd been robbed of inflicting unilateral and unrelenting violence. One punch was all he'd delivered. A waste, really. He'd hoped his victim would at least have had the courage to stand on his feet for a while longer. But no, straight down. Cowardly.

It was quiet behind the pub. There was the sound of the odd car crawling along the sea front a hundred or so yards away and the intermittent cawing of the gulls warming their wings in the afternoon sun. From the far distance came the sound of bleeps and whistles and synthesized arpeggios. Margate's numerous slot arcades were doing brisk business.

But in the yard, where smokers lurked among piles of brown plastic beer crates stacked like mini skyscrapers, there was the sound only of gasping as the older man tried to regain his breath.

Davey Stone located his teeth and wiped them on his trousers. Hughes thought about punching him again while he was on the ground. Make him swallow the stupid dentures, he thought. That would teach him. That would learn him not to go round spreading shit.

'You done?' Stone looked up at Hughes. His mouth was awash with blood. Hughes had really done a job on him, the fuck. His jawbone felt like it would crumble to nothing at any minute.

'Not sure,' Hughes said quietly. His voice was thick with suppressed rage. 'Depends.'

'On?'

'Well, you gonna stop trashing me? The Richards gang . . .'

Stone stumbled to his feet. 'The Richards gang can go fuck themselves. I've said nothing to anyone about you. Never have. You're not that big a deal around here, Hughes, believe it or not.'

'Not what Ben Richards or his brother Charlie says. Or their father, Keith, for that matter. They say you've been going round telling half of Margate I borrowed a police van.'

'So what if you did? Nothing to do with me,' Stone said, dabbing the inside of his mouth with a tissue. 'Perk of the job, maybe. Like a company car or something.'

Hughes walked over to him.

The older man shrank back against the pub wall. He'd been in many fights but he was too old for a beating now, especially one that he felt was unmerited. Hughes was bent. Everyone said so. If people were talking about him, he deserved it. Stone held up his hands to protest his innocence, cowered before Hughes. 'I was just saying it's got nothing to do with me, that's all. I'm not saying you borrowed no van or anything.'

'Well, that's not what I've been hearing. Most of the firms in Kent think I'm on the take, thanks to you. Difficult to do my job when that sort of rumour gets out.'

'Honest, not me. Dunno where they got that from,' Stone spluttered. He licked the inside of his dentures. He could taste grit from the yard. Raw Margate tasted terrible. He looked up at Hughes and held out his hands imploringly, like a centre forward seeking adulation from the crowd. 'I guess everyone's been trying to make sense of things after Bill Henry's murder,' he said, spitting out some grit. 'People gossip. You know how people talk in this town. There's fuck-all else for them to do half the time.'

'Spare me that crap,' Hughes said. 'People have always talked down here. Even when the town had money. Nothing's changed. So much for the big regeneration project, hey? No matter how many art galleries like the Turner they put in down here, there's still going to be scum like you and the Richardses around, hey, Stone? We'll really know Margate's made it when the likes of you have disappeared.'

Stone said nothing. The way Hughes was acting, anything he said would rile him. He didn't want another punch.

'Tell me something,' Hughes said. 'Where were you the day of Bill's murder?'

'Drinking in the George, like I do every Saturday.'

'You can prove it?'

'I could find thirty people who'll say I was there. What – you suggesting I did one of my best mates? Bladed him? Fucking ridiculous.'

'Stranger things have happened, Stone. There's not a lot of loyalty down this coast. There's too much criminal competition. And, let's face it, you were muscling in on Bill's red-diesel racket. The fags, too, if I'm hearing right.'

Stone groaned. 'Fuck you, Hughes. You're just talking crap. He was a good mate, Bill. He was trying to help you lot, too. Same as I was. And this is how you repay us. One of us ends up dead and I end up picking my teeth out of the ground. Tell me something, does Sorrenson know you're here?'

It was Hughes's turn to go silent.

'Ah,' said Stone, after a pause. 'I see. Interesting that you decided not to tell him you were coming to see me. I wonder why that was, eh? Worried he might ask you what you wanted to ask me? You shouldn't sneak around like you're doing, Hughes. You're shit at it. You're too big. Someone's going to see you. Someone's going to ask questions. You know it wouldn't look right if Sorrenson found out you'd paid me a visit on your own.'

Hughes watched in admiration as his left fist connected with Stone's nose. There was the thrilling sound of bone and cartilage crumpling and an almost bestial wail from Stone, as a torrent of blood poured from his nostrils onto the ground. Hughes watched the crimson rain down, pleased with his work. That was more like it, he thought. That was a much better way of holding someone to account. The spilling of blood solved a lot of things. It was an efficient reckoning system, tried and tested down the millennia.

Stone whimpered as he collapsed onto the ground. He curled up in a foetal position, both hands clasped around his nose, trying to protect its smashed remains. He was gurgling blood in his throat. This is how death tastes, he realized. Through his pain came a thought of immense clarity: Hughes would pay one day. Hughes would be held to account for what he'd done to him. He turned onto his back and looked up at the perfect blue sky. It was like something out of a travel brochure. The feeling of the sun on his face made him smile.

Hughes read the look and sneered. He felt the familiar anger that came whenever he thought he was being cheated. He was almost permanently angry, these days. 'You want some more?'

Stone shook his head. 'No, no more. We're done.'

'Good,' Hughes snarled. 'I don't want to have to spend another moment fucking you over. I really don't. You make

229

sure people know I had nothing to do with that van, right?
You get that message out. Or next time you'll really be in
trouble. I'll break you into so many pieces they'll be able to
feed you through the slot machines. You hear me? And don't
breathe a word of this to Sorrenson or anyone else, right?
I'll know if you do and I'll come looking.'

Hughes walked back into the pub. Stone lay staring up at
the sky. One day even the sun would disappear, he thought.
Everything, even bent cops, would disappear. Everything
would be washed away by darkness. The thought gave him
comfort.

Chapter 14

Reynolds sighed the sigh of a man whose life had just become immeasurably more difficult. Not that it had been easy before. Shoring up Higgs from imminent collapse was exhausting. It would do for him one way or another. He'd noticed that his hands were trembling almost all the time. He was struggling to hold it together and the effort was causing contagion: his body was suffering collateral damage. His eyes were bloodshot. His skin almost grey. He was developing a paunch from all the drinking. Yes, he was exhausted, all right.

And now the Brits had started raking over the bank forensically, like a coroner conducting an inquest. He had thought their interest might die down after he'd had the Brit agent terminated, the one asking all the questions, but everything was in play again. Everyone wanted answers from Higgs. Thank God the bank had puppet directors who did as they were told, he thought. If any of them had had a spine and been prepared to ask awkward questions he'd have been truly screwed.

He read McLure's email again. Clever move sending it after he'd died, Reynolds conceded. He hadn't gamed that particular scenario among the millions of others that his whiskey-soaked mind had fretted about in the small hours. So, then, now he was fighting corpses. It was tricky, dealing with the dead. They had a lot less to lose than the living. Speaking out wasn't so risky for them.

He punched several letters on his laptop's keyboard and poured himself another drink. His attic had become his own private speakeasy. He'd started to spend so much time in it that it was becoming the only place he felt even vaguely comfortable. He remembered sitting on the bleachers in Central Park with Carey. Christ, he couldn't cope with that sort of public exposure any more. He needed to be alone. Alone and hidden away, like some sort of hermit. His attic room was his only sanctuary.

He was cracking up, he knew. Properly cracking up. And the worrying thing was that he was only half interested in the outcome. It was almost as if he'd become detached from himself, as if he was watching someone else experience a car crash. Maybe it was his way of coping, seeing himself as somebody else. That made everything less intense, like he was watching a film. A film that would have an ugly ending, that was for sure.

If only he was as reliable as the NSA's surveillance apparatus, Reynolds thought, rereading McLure's email. It was amazing what they could do, the NSA. They'd infiltrated firewalls and placed what they had told him were zombie programs on the computer servers that directed traffic to and from McLure's personal email account. Nobody knew they were there. Tests wouldn't reveal them. And yet there they were, lurking, allowing Reynolds unfettered access. Technically he needed approval from higher up the chain, but he wasn't in the mood to talk to Carey or Brandeis. He couldn't tell them why he was hacking an MI5 agent's personal email: that would have triggered way too many questions about Higgs. He was on his own. He was Higgs's last chance of survival. Come to that, he was the intelligence community's last chance of survival. He was its remaining firewall. The blowback if Higgs went down was just too enormous to comprehend. Reynolds didn't want to comprehend. He slugged more whiskey.

His fractured mind tried to sift the evidence swimming in front of him. He needed a plan. He needed to take action. The female colleague McLure had contacted clearly had her own suspicions about Higgs. And, Jesus, now she knew that Holahon had been trying to buy intel from British intelligence, the dumb fuck, she'd be crawling all over Higgs. That particular posthumous revelation had been an eye-opener for both of them. You couldn't trust anyone in banking, Reynolds thought angrily. Everyone was out for themselves or serving several masters, which made things messy. Just look at Carlyle . . .

He glugged three fingers of whiskey. He'd never felt so alone. There was no one he could confide in. Teri, his wife, was shunning him because of his permanently angry state. Not that he could really talk to her about the situation anyway.

He was aware that in his heightened sense of isolation he was making poor decisions. His judgement was becoming impaired. His terror was having the opposite of paralysis. He was becoming too loose in his actions, too urgent in desiring results, closure, no matter the cost. Calling in a hit on the Brit agent from his old contacts in the Serbian underworld confirmed that he was losing it. It had made sense at the time, but now, well, it was clear that he was becoming desperate. And in some ways the killings were closing things down, restricting his options, not liberating him. They were just drawing attention to everything, leaving a trail of mayhem that could be traced all the way back to Higgs.

Three more fingers of whiskey. Then three more in quick succession. He should eat something. But, God, he was so damn tired. And now it was clear that he was going to have to fly to London the next day to sort out a few loose ends. He was going to be exhausted when he arrived. There was a danger he would be too exhausted even to arrange another killing. That wouldn't be good. Higgs was just one giant heart attack waiting to explode. Yes, it would definitely do for him. His colleagues wouldn't miss him. His wife wouldn't miss him, the way things were going. His children . . . He took another slug of whiskey.

From outside in the evening dusk came the sound of a buzz-saw. Fucking carpenters, Reynolds thought. They had it so easy. They were never going to get corrupted by their trade. They could just do an honest day's work and knock off for a few beers when dusk fell, then start again the next morning, clear-headed, content.

But there was no starting afresh for him. Every day was another battle with a cancer that was threatening to devour him, devour everyone. Even if he pulled it off, he would have to live with the terrible knowledge of the price he'd paid. That would be the legacy of saving Higgs, Reynolds knew: the complete and utter destruction of his personal morality.

He played with a few keys on his laptop, pulled open the file of emails and texts received and sent by McLure's colleague. She seemed a good person, Reynolds thought, studying the correspondence with a flicker of his old professional interest. Bright, thoughtful, seemed to be involved with some detective. Seemed to have had something with McLure, too. Quite the woman, Reynolds thought. Three fingers. Four fingers more. The bottle was nearly empty. There were others hidden in the wardrobe, out of sight of his children's prying eyes. He would be a mess in the morning but at least oblivion was coming his way in a short while. He slumped forward on his desk, cradling his head in his crossed arms. The woman was getting too close, he thought. Everyone was getting too close. He would need to take out yet more insurance. He felt alarmed by the perfunctory nature of his thinking. It neither excited nor repelled him. It was a banking transaction, murder. Killing had become a form of problem-solving, a way of hedging himself against risk. He had, Reynolds realized, been afflicted by a disorder common to many bankers. He had become a psychopath.

'I knew your father. A great man. Huge charisma. Gave inferior people like me a complex. He was born to work for the service. Like it was programmed into him or something. Such a great, great loss.' Webster shook his head several times.

It wasn't how she'd imagined her debriefing would start. The mention of her father so soon after she'd buried her mother set Kate reeling. Two types of grief were knotting together inside her. Far too much pain to be dealing with. She was in danger of losing clarity.

Still, she supposed Webster was trying his best to reach out to her. She should be grateful, but she felt uncomfortable.

She hated the personal mixing with the professional. It never worked out well. But it was so difficult to separate when the professional was basically all you had left. Just look at Webster. Service all his life. He'd be lost when he retired, she thought. There would be some private consultancy work for a bank or oil giant probably, but then he would become a memory, a fossil, of what he'd once been. He'd leave few footprints. She noticed he was eyeing her closely, waiting for her to respond.

'Thank you,' she said, accepting Webster's gesture for her to take the seat in front of his desk. 'I understand you were in Northern Ireland at the same time as he was.'

'Sort of. I'd fly in every now and then to, erm, take care of certain things. Pay people, arm people on occasions. Swap intel. It was very cloak-and-dagger. Exciting stuff. I was supposedly the director of a small engineering firm that specialized in repairing ship's hulls. It was a good cover. Meant I could fly in and out without too many people asking questions. But your father, well, he was the real deal. Spent months in the field undercover. Immensely brave man. Several of his colleagues were identified and tortured to death. It will be decades yet before their true heroics become common knowledge and people know the sacrifices they made. Some of the stuff can't be disclosed for the next half-century. A terrible pity, really. Then people would appreciate just how important the service has been down the years. Stop taking it for granted so much.'

She said nothing, looked around Webster's office. There was a series of line graphs on one wall.

Webster saw her staring at them. 'The nought to sixty charts we call them.'

'Sorry?'

'How many years, months, weeks and days it's taken for various suicide bombers and would-be suicide bombers to go from being radicalized to turning themselves into a deadly weapon. We used to be talking years. Now we're talk-ing months. Soon, I fear, it will be weeks or even, madness I know, days. Everything is speeding up in this game. Even terrorists seem to be moving at near to light speed now. It's a constant struggle to keep up. Times like these, we really could do with someone like your old man around. He had such a quick mind. Such a waste . . .' Webster trailed off. He rocked back and forth in his wheelchair.

'You believe that? It was a waste, an accident? There had been rumours.' It seemed bizarre to Kate that she was even asking the question, especially to the head of Five. There were more pressing concerns than a decades-old traffic acci-dent, she felt. But there was something about Webster's demeanour, an air of penance almost, that seemed to invite the question.

'Well, we did look closely at it,' Webster said quietly. 'I guess if it happened today we'd be able to do a better job, forensically speaking, but it did have all the hallmarks of a car accident. Funny though it was . . .' Webster shrugged and looked at Kate apologetically.

Kate felt herself go cold. 'Funny?'

Webster ran a hand over his forehead. It was 1 August and his office's air-conditioning wasn't really up to the job. Little beads of sweat were forming under his hairline, Kate could see. But she felt as if she was sitting in a fridge. A chill had consumed her. Webster murmured something to himself, as if weighing up his next move. He managed the thinnest of smiles.

'Well, I shouldn't be saying this, but as you're pretty much one of the family, so to speak, for what it's worth, and I was very much in the minority over this, I always felt the problem with it, your father's death, I mean, was that it looked like a car accident. By that I mean it looked too much like a car accident. It was too perfect, too neat. It was a sunny day when it happened. No traffic around.'

She nodded several times, too stunned to take it all in. Was her suspicion correct? Was Webster hinting at something? Did he know more? Suddenly her father felt far more alive to her than her mother. She'd buried her mother, seen the ground cover the woman who'd delivered her into the world. But her father, well, the soil was shifting above his grave. He wasn't enjoying his sleep. Too many questions were emerging from the ground and multiplying like weeds. She tried to shut out of her mind the pictures of the crash she'd seen in the local paper. A tree, skid-marks, police crime tape, all in grainy black-and-white. The image was indelibly scored into her brain. She would often shut her eyes to find it there, lurking, alongside the picture of her dead husband that was placed on his coffin the day of his funeral. Death, Kate felt, seemed to account for around 50 per cent of her current identity. She was formed from the endings of others. Their legacy was her pain. She dragged her mind from the past to the present. There would be time soon enough to delve into her father's past. There were more urgent concerns.

'Thank you for being so candid, sir,' she said. 'It means a lot. But, right now, I need to brief you on the Higgs stuff. There've been quite a few developments.'

Webster frowned. 'I thought that was all resolved?'

'Sir?'

Webster pressed his hands together to form an arch. He examined the gap between the opposing fingers with great interest. 'The murder of the banker. Grisly business, for sure. But from what the police seem to be saying it was down to a grudge between some running rivals. Bizarre case, but it seems like a petty feud ended up with the unfortunate, erm, dispatch of Mr Holahon. Two of his colleagues have been charged, I believe. So, case closed, as they say in the more vulgar American movies. We can go back to more important things now. Bankers with grudges don't get a look in.' Webster pointed at the graphs on the wall.

'Well, yes, I can see that must be a pressing concern, but I don't think solving Holahon's murder or manslaughter or whatever it was has got much to do with Higgs Bank. I think other stuff is happening there. That's what we need to focus on right now.'

Webster continued to examine the arch of his fingers.

Kate tried again. 'I mean what McLure was claiming, that needs—'

Webster interrupted. His voice had turned icy. 'I think the less said about Anthony McLure the better, don't you?'

She struggled to hide her shock. Jesus, it was like being at school or something. People talking about you behind your back, insinuating, implying when they didn't know the facts, and even if they did, it had nothing to do with them, nothing to do with anything. 'I really don't think—'

Webster interrupted again. 'You don't think. I know, I know. It has nothing to do with this but, come on, look at it from my point of view. You're compromised when it comes to McLure. And there does seem substantial evidence that he was on the make and take, as they say. He admitted to being paid by the late Mr Holahon, who was also, need I remind you, until recently a senior member of Higgs Bank, according to a now infamous email dispatched from beyond the grave. How would that fact, an agent in thrall to a bent banker, look if we had some security committee poring all over it? Do we really need or want to rake all of this up?'

Webster glanced at the graphs again. He felt reassured by their shape, their sober analysis of an individual's path to destruction.

She felt herself trembling with anger. She couldn't believe that Webster could be so dismissive. 'Sir, I appreciate the service must be alert to the threat of an urgent atrocity, but I do, strongly, feel that something is about to happen that will help fund a thousand atrocities in the not too distant future. I think there is overwhelming circumstantial evidence that we need to be targeting Higgs Bank. I really feel that we don't have much time.'

'Spare me the dramatics, Pendragon. All this stuff about Higgs. What's wrong – the real story not big enough for you? We've got suspected terrorist sleeper cells in every major city in this country – groups of angry young men blinded by warped clerics who want to take us back to the era of the Crusades, and you're worried about the state of a US bank?'

Webster started wheeling himself back and forth. He was staring at Kate as if he was appraising her. It was almost as if he saw her as a threat, she thought. She tried another tack. 'Prince Aldud's assassination is still not explained. He was a big Higgs client. Maybe—'

'Aldud was murdered by a hit team contracted by big oil interests,' Webster murmured. 'I think, given what he was up to, he was always a dead man walking.'

'Sorry?'

'He was dying. He wanted to leave his mark. He was setting up a massive aid mission to fly urgent medicines and relief teams all around the world from his private airport down in Kent, I believe. That would have taken billions of pounds of his money. The Americans were keen on helping with it, using it to sprinkle aid across deprived places where terrorism thrives. But his main legacy, so to speak, was information. He was going to tell the world just how much oil was left in the Ghawar Field.'

She was dumbfounded. The idea that a Saudi prince would reveal just how much black gold was left in the world's largest oil reserve seemed outlandish. What could be the possible benefit? The effects of such a disclosure would be seismic. If he wanted to be remembered, it was certainly the way to go about it. 'OPEC would collapse if that information got out,' she said. 'If there's loads of oil left in the Ghawar Field then prices fall and a lot of Middle Eastern sheikhs are seriously out of pocket. If there's very little left, then it will speed up the path to alternative energy technologies and reveal Saudi as a busted flush. OPEC would become obsolete within a few years. Either way, that information seeping out would be toxic. I'm not saying it's untrue but, I mean, it's so out there. It seems so . . .'

Webster's eyes flashed anger. 'I appreciate your input and what you have to say about Higgs. But you've become too close to this. This is a core agency matter, not one for you.'

Jesus, the service was closing ranks on her. They just didn't want to know. Inside she was seething. Webster ran a finger under his eyes, as if he was trying to rub the bags away. 'I'm sorry, Pendragon, but the service doesn't share your concerns about Higgs. It's understandable that you have them because you've focused on it as McLure asked you to. And you, erm, clearly shared some of his obsession. But maybe you should take some time off. The last few weeks can't have been easy.'

For several seconds she contemplated what it would be like to assault a disabled person. She wondered if hitting Webster would feel like gross cowardice or brave, quixotic, an action that would bring some sense of release. She swallowed hard and attempted one last effort to convince him.

'If I'm wrong, I'll take the hit, but I'm really worried that I may be right about this.'

'But you won't take the hit, will you?' Webster snapped. 'You're not the one who will have to explain to the next set of victims' families that you were too focused on some inexplicable, fantastic financial fraud to spot the next suicide bomber. You're not the one who faces the music, Pendragon. I am. I live with that every day. Think about that, why don't you? Now, please, consider what I said about taking some holiday. Get some rest. Come back to us refreshed and let's see what use we can put you to then. What about it?'

She walked with great care towards the door. Each step was a temptation. She wanted to run, run faster than she'd ever run before. She wanted to keep running until she hit the coast and then she wanted to keep running to the horizon, to the point where endings and beginnings fused. Under huge skies truths emerged. It was only at the point where land met sea that clarity truly existed. Cities corrupted

people, corrupted the truth. They politicized their inhabitants, turned them into players, made them frightened
hustlers who were always watching their backs, always fear-
ing that their weaknesses would be exposed by the relentless,
mad savagery of crowds. Space provided perspective. Webster
was right. It was time to take some holiday.

Chapter 15

Ghent stood in the doorway of Reynolds's office, unsure whether to enter. His boss's temper had become volcanic in recent weeks and he didn't relish the response to the briefing he was about to deliver. One more nudge and the man would fall off the edge. Reynolds seemed to have flipped out over the summer and now, with autumn on the horizon, he was turning into someone else again, someone darker, brooding, a man prone to astonishing rages that lasted days. He'd gone from being the grounded Agency veteran with the long memory, clear ideals and affable persona to a clenched, angry ball of spite, ready to lash out at colleagues without warning. He was clearly under a lot of pressure. Ghent really didn't want to add to it but, as head of Reynolds's elite team tasked with detecting strange permutations in stock-market trading patterns, it was his duty to brief his boss.

He allowed Reynolds time to pop some alarmingly large pills and take a long, weary slug from a bottle of water, then coughed conspicuously. Reynolds looked up. A scowl immediately formed on his face. 'What you got?'

Ghent said nothing. He walked towards Reynolds, de-posited a sheaf of papers on his desk. Reynolds looked at the papers, then at Ghent. 'So?'

'So maybe we've just found the reason why we exist. We've detected some unusual potential trades about to be made by the Quest hedge fund.'

Reynolds hesitated. 'That Prince Faisal's mob?'

'Yep. Third-biggest fund in the world after the Chinese and Qatari sovereign funds. All Saudi money. It can move mountains, Quest.'

'Right,' Reynolds muttered.

Ghent was taken aback by his boss's apparent lack of inter-est. It had become more conspicuous as the summer had worn on. At first he had just seemed aloof, absorbed in a personal problem, maybe. But he had become more and more removed from his team, a satellite that had broken free of its orbit. Something would have to be done, Ghent knew. They couldn't see the year out with Reynolds in his current state. It was just too risky. They'd spent years looking for pat-terns, signs of unusual activity in the world's stock markets, and now for the first time they seemed to have something. If Ghent and the team were reading the runes correctly, something very, very bad was about to happen in six days' time: 3 September. And yet Reynolds seemed out of the game, unready, unwilling to absorb urgent information. It was as if intelligence no longer interested him. Ghent pressed on. 'It appears, from the encrypted Quest trading positions that the NSA has been sucking up from the transatlantic submarine cables, that the hedge fund is preparing to liquid-ate all of its stock-market investments. I mean everything. It's all going into gold. Well, mainly. A bit into platinum, a bit

246

into copper and tin, a fraction into silver. But mainly gold. We are talking about the best part of a hundred billion dollars exiting the stock market and buying into precious metals. It's seismic, unprecedented and, to be honest, pretty scary. Quest is spooked. It thinks something bad is going to happen. The question is: what does it know?'

Reynolds eyed Ghent dully. 'The markets are listing,' he murmured. 'Maybe Quest figures they've still got some way left to slide and it's time to get out. Find a safe haven and hunker down for a few years. Pretty sensible if you ask me.'

The old Reynolds, Ghent thought, would at least have been curious. He would have been open-minded about the prospect of Armageddon. He would have had questions.

'True,' Ghent said. 'But why now? Markets have been spooked for a long time. Things are picking up. Oil price is ticking up, stock markets ticking up, China's GDP, India's GDP – they're all ticking up. US unemployment figures are falling. Factory payrolls are rising. All the signs are turning good. There's reams and reams of positive data sloshing around. People are betting on a global recovery. It's a strange time to go cold, don't you think? Strange time for a hedge fund especially. It makes absolutely no sense. Unless, well, they have inside information. This is what we've been wait-ing for. It justifies everything we've been doing. Think about it. This will get Congress to write us fat cheques.' Ghent realized his voice had lifted a couple of octaves in his excitement. Years of nothing and now a possible lead. Yet Reynolds looked like a man whose doctor had just given him bad news.

'Hmm, well, let's keep it to ourselves for now, shall we?' Reynolds said flatly. 'Don't want to be responsible for a massive run on the markets if this gets out, hey? Pretty ugly if it was sourced back to us. Risky.'

'But it's in six days' time,' Ghent said, struggling to suppress his frustration. 'And Quest – well, you must know about Prince Faisal and his sympathies. We know who he's been linked with in the past. He's funnelled money to Islamic militant front groups. If he knows something bad is going to happen, something devastating, you've got to think there's a chance it's terrorism-related. That's the most likely intel he would have access to.'

Reynolds needed to play for time. He just had to keep stalling Ghent and his team. Get through to 3 September and then it would be payday. Higgs would collect big-time as pretty much every other bank was going under. In the ensuing chaos he would personally save Higgs, his creation. He would save the Agency, too. And then he would retire. With immediate effect. Nobody would know just how close Higgs had come to destroying the Agency or him. Yes, he really just needed to play for time, he kept reminding himself. He scowled again at Ghent. His colleague was in danger of ruining everything, with his stupid fucking diligence. An enthusiastic employee was another risk factor he could do without. He sighed deeply and pointed a shaking finger at Ghent. 'OK, leave this with me for now, you hear? You understand me? I'm leaving for a few days. Got something urgent we need to take care of. But, er, keep in contact with me. Don't share this intel with anyone outside our group, you hear? Right? Keep this classified.'

Ghent stared at Reynolds. His boss was almost skeletal.

There had been rumours about his drinking. And just when they seemed to have the breakthrough they'd spent years waiting for, searching for, hoping for, he was preparing to go AWOL. Reynolds's understanding of risk was completely shot, Ghent thought. 'Right,' he said. 'Whatever you say.'

Sorrenson sat with his legs dangling over the sea wall and looked out onto the familiar fat stretch of sand. Behind him amusement arcades and empty shops competed for the attention of the few people enjoying Margate's sea front before the town had woken up.

It was eight on a Monday morning but a hot sun was already licking at the beach, turning yellow sand golden. It was going to be a baking, arid day. The sea air had been sucked dry of all moisture and the sky was assuming a rich, intense blue. It felt more like Morocco than Margate, Sorrenson thought.

He looked out beyond the beach and across to the old bathing pool built into the sea. At high tide it was invisible but at low tide it resembled a fortress, a stone square that protected its charges within. Kept them safe from the tides. To the south-east the hulking white cuboid presence of the Turner Gallery dominated the harbour. To the north-west sat the old red-brick hospital where Victorian health tourists had stayed when they'd come to Margate to take its waters, in the belief that they had rejuvenating powers.

He drank in the scene. He never got tired of it. It didn't have a great reputation, Margate, but Sorrenson loved it. It made him think of Hopper paintings. There was a sense of hopefulness about the town, hopefulness in the despair.

When the light caught it in a certain way, illuminated its old stucco-fronted buildings, casting their long shadows across the pavements and the perfect crescent of the beach, the town acquired a grandeur, a reconnection with its former Victorian self. It had known glories. It was in possession of sun-bleached memories. Its old self resurfaced, came back from the dead. It lived on.

Sorrenson studied the impossibly blue sky. There would be a fierce sunset later. He understood why Turner had been such a regular visitor. Its skies were just one huge canvas.

He sipped coffee from a Styrofoam cup and watched Hughes approach, a bullock of a man, clumsy and strong. His colleague was dangerous, he thought. Hughes would end up doing great damage if he wasn't careful. He really needed to calm down.

He had played the impending scene over in his head many times. He needed to be calm and restrained. Hughes needed to be given space. Back him into a corner and he would just charge. He raised a hand in welcome.

'So, look at you,' Hughes muttered, as he sat down next to Sorrenson. He took his brown leather jacket off and ran a hand through his stubble. He turned to Sorrenson, who was in jeans and a polo shirt. 'You're dressed like a tourist.'

'Feel like one sometimes,' Sorrenson said. 'Most times I come down here, in fact. I only live a few miles further along the coast but it's a different world here. Cosmopolitan. You get all sorts. Eclectic. Makes for an interesting place. Lot of stories. Some good. Some bad.' Sorrenson eyed Hughes closely. He hoped that his colleague understood him. He was giving him a clear warning that the conversation could carry consequences.

'Yeah, true,' Hughes muttered.

Sorrenson sipped his coffee, watched a mother chase a toddler across the beach. The sound of their laughter filtered across the sand.

'So, I heard about you and Davey Stone,' Sorrenson said. 'And, before you say anything, it wasn't him who told me.'

'He had it coming.'

'Maybe.'

'You know what he was saying about me?'

'About the van?'

'Yeah.'

'I don't think it was him who was talking,' Sorrenson said quietly. 'Not what the Richards brothers tell me, anyway. Seems a lot of people have it in for you, Hughes. Why's that, do you suppose?'

Hughes shrugged. 'I'm putting too many people's noses out of joint. I'm just doing my job, that's all.'

'Perhaps. Strange, though, that people fingered you for the van. Of all the things to pin on you, that was the one they chose.'

A seagull approached the two detectives, on the prowl for discarded chip wrappers. The two men watched it suspiciously. The bird glared back at them. Hughes waved a fist at the bird, which took to the air with an angry squawk. 'Seems even the gulls have a grudge against me,' Hughes said.

'They'd better join the queue,' Sorrenson replied. 'Now, this is a conversation we're not having, understood? I don't want it to end up becoming an official reprimand, OK? We can't deal with the paperwork for a start. But listen to me. You've got to stop fighting the world, right? It's all aggression with you, these days. Just calm down, OK? You've watched too many US cop shows. If he wanted, Davey Stone could prise you out of your job. You know that pub's got CCTV cameras in its yard, yeah?'

'No.'

'They've had a lot of break-ins, apparently.'

'Fuck, who'd want to break into that hole? The beer's piss. Most of its regulars are criminals.'

Sorrenson sighed. 'Just drop the attitude. Save it for the rugby pitch. We've got too many things going on right now. We've got an unsolved murder in the Bill Henry case, an assassinated prince and we still don't know who transported a headless body down here days after its owner was killed and dumped in bushes on Hampstead Heath, if the rantings of a bombed-out banker are to be believed. We've got plenty of work. Let's not make any more.'

Sorrenson looked at Hughes intently, waited for his reaction. His colleague said nothing. 'This is Margate, not Miami,' Sorrenson said. 'This sort of stuff isn't supposed to happen down here but it is happening and we've got to deal with it. Now, I'm going to ask you straight out, and this is the only time I'm going to ask it. Did you have anything to do with the van?'

The younger man shook his head vigorously. 'Fuck, no. There never was a fucking police van. That's just Davey Stone's bullshit. He's trying to smear me because he knows I can do him for tons of stuff.'

'If that's what you want to believe, fine,' Sorrenson said.

Hughes glared at his senior colleague. 'Will you stop looking at me like that?' He jumped to his feet, pulled his jacket round his shoulders.

'Like what?' Sorrenson's voice was quiet, studious.

'Like I'm a suspect. Ask yourself what the fuck I'd be doing driving a police van with a headless body in the back.'

Sorrenson took another sip of his coffee. 'Plenty of bent coppers out there,' he said thoughtfully. 'Maybe you're not so different. Maybe you were just doing a favour for someone.'

Hughes twisted round and brought his left fist down on Sorrenson's jaw. The coffee spilled onto the ground. Sorrenson fell backwards against the pavement, giving Hughes the chance to stand up and drill a series of kicks into his ribcage. He tried to stagger to his feet, but he was out of breath and the effort was beyond him. He managed to assume a kneeling position, the ideal height for Hughes to train three sharp blows onto his face. Cuts instantly materialized on his right eyebrow and left cheekbone. He could taste blood in his mouth and his vision was obscured by small black stars. He collapsed and vomited. He lay still for several seconds, conscious that Hughes was walking away. Should have given him more space, Sorrenson thought. He ran a finger gingerly along his bruised jawbone, looked at the mother and her child playing on the beach. They were the only people around. His assault hadn't been witnessed. It was pretty much the only positive to draw from the morning. That and the fact that Hughes had effectively confessed.

'Jesus.'

'Yeah.'

She jumped up, ran across the deck behind Sorrenson's house. 'What about the other man?'

'Didn't get a blow in,' Sorrenson said apologetically.

'I mean, Jesus.'

'You said that already.'

'You got a first-aid box?'

'In the kitchen, below the sink.'

'Right,' Kate said. 'Wait here. Try not to get into another fight while I'm gone.' She left him sitting on the deck facing the sea. She'd been grateful for his invitation to come and stay for a few days. His shack of a home, with its woodburner, rough timber floors and sea views from most windows, felt about as far away from city living as possible. Only now she seemed to have become not so much a guest as a nurse. She found some TCP and bandages and returned to the deck.

Sorrenson attempted a grin.

'So?' she said.

'So, not much to say. Professional disagreement. That's all.'

'Hughes?'

'Yeah, good guess. I told you about him, right? Good detective but a bit of a liability.'

'Clearly. You asked him about the van, right?'

'Mmm.' Sorrenson winced as the TCP was applied to his cuts.

'What did he say?'

'Not very much. He let his fists do the talking.'

'Evidently.'

'Seems he may have played a part, but difficult to tell what or why exactly. He wasn't particularly forthcoming.'

'Right.'

'I'll take the matter up with him again.'

'Maybe do it somewhere public next time. Your face can't afford a rematch.'

'I'll be ready next time.'

'You keep telling yourself that, champ. Honestly, I'm quite shocked. I just didn't think anyone over thirty got into fights, these days. Everyone our age is too exhausted to get violent. Too ground down, too worried about money or their job or a million other reasons. But I was wrong. You men, you never lose it, do you? The urge to fight.'

She finished patching him up. He was a mess and clearly in pain. The thought distressed her. Careful, she thought, careful.

'Thanks,' he said. 'Almost made getting beaten up worthwhile.'

'Well, don't make a habit of it.'

They stared out to sea, listening to the waves dragging the shingle back and forth. Supertankers cruised across the horizon. So much effort went into transporting things from A to B, she thought. Cars, oil, guns, bodies . . . 'Finding that van would be good,' she said. 'Helpful.'

'Might allow me to prosecute a colleague, if nothing else. He's holding something back.'

'It's more than that, though.'

'How do you mean?'

'Well, it would provide answers.'

'Like who wanted to protect Brockman so much that they were prepared to move a body for him?'

'Right. But it's not so much the who that interests me, it's the why. Why is Brockman so crucial in all of this? Who valued him so highly that they were prepared to break the law for him, to help him cover up the fact that he killed Holahon? What's so special about Brockman?'

'We could ask him. It's not as if he's too busy at the moment. He's in HMP Wandsworth, I believe.'

'What about Ennis?'

Sorrenson shook his head. 'On suicide watch. He's in a real state. Doubt whether he would be of much use to us.'

'Pity.'

Sorrenson felt his jaw. 'Remind me again. Who were Brockman's clients?'

'His main one was Prince Faisal,' she said. 'That was all he needed, really.'

'Figures. You have a billionaire client and I guess the cheques write themselves.'

She shook her head. 'He's a real enigma, Brockman's star client. You should see the file. A hidden homosexuality that conflicts with his apparent devout religious beliefs. In the past he's been an enthusiastic donor to a number of front companies linked to Islamist terror groups. Runs a massive hedge fund bigger than most countries' economies but claims to have little time for money. Some suggestion he was being monitored very closely by the CIA, who had an asset working for him. Yet he doesn't seem to be a credible threat. If anything he seems a bit immature. He spends a lot of time flying radio-controlled planes on his private runway. Seems to have crashed most of them, too. Strange way of spending your time.'

Sorrenson thought for a moment. 'Yes, that is strange. He must know he's being watched closely. People like him always are.'

'Right. He would know that what he's doing is going to be captured by half the world's intelligence agencies. So . . .'

'So what? Do you think he wants to be seen?' Sorrenson said. 'He's playing to the cameras? That makes no sense. Why draw attention to yourself?' He felt the cuts on his face. The day he'd first met the tall woman with the long black curly hair now sitting beside him seemed to belong to another era. So much had happened since Holahon's body had turned up on the beach. A single murder had been transformed into an issue of national security. The personal had become the political. A local problem had become an international one. His sliver of the coast was immersed in something so big that it was hard to see where it all started and ended. Why was it happening here? Why not somewhere else? There was nothing special about the peninsula, nothing that those who didn't live on it would understand, anyway. Except . . . 'The runway,' he murmured. 'It's next to a nuclear power station.'

She felt something twist inside her. 'Go on.'

Sorrenson shrugged. 'Toxic mix,' he said. 'I mean, Christ. A plane, a nuclear plant. It's the stuff of nightmares. It would be like Nine/Eleven only with even more horrific conse-quences. I mean, that's a truly terrifying prospect. He'd be turning the coast into one giant dirty bomb.'

'Why advertise it, though? What could possibly be gained by people knowing what you were about to do?'

The sound of dragging shingle answered her question. She remembered when she'd first heard the sound, a frosty day months before, when McLure had dispatched her to the coast. McLure and his obsession with what was going on inside Higgs. It had seemed almost comic at the start. It wasn't now, though. She thought about his posthumous email to her, sharing his suspicions about Higgs and the CIA. Higgs. Higgs, Higgs, Higgs. It all came down to Higgs one way or another. Maybe not in any sort of neat way but, nevertheless, Higgs appeared to be like a spider in a web, spinning ever more complex strands to trap everything that came near it.

She stared hard out to sea. In her mind she was no longer by the coast. She was back in Webster's office. She remembered their last conversation. She remembered what he'd said about her father's death. *Almost too perfect, too neat.*

She thought of the perfect rows of trades Quest had prepared, all of them ready to be executed in a single electronic moment by a super-computer that could function almost at the speed of light and which cost more than the GDP of many small nations. She thought about the precision that had gone into creating them, the clean symmetries of moving vast amounts of money out of the world's stock markets and into precious metals. It was the sort of massive defensive play that you'd employ if you thought something terrible was going to happen, something that would send the markets into free-fall. Something terrible like a nuclear catastrophe.

Only, what if . . .

She reached into her bag and pulled out a laptop. She hit keys urgently, as if she was trying to destroy her computer. Multiple screens bounced into life. She negotiated a series of them, each one taking her further into the labyrinth of her Higgs files. Deeper and deeper she went, all the time nodding to herself, reassuring herself that she was right. Or, if not right, at least not wrong. Nothing she saw disproved her theory. Nothing. 'We've got to talk to Brockman,' she said, jumping to her feet.

'What – now?' Sorrenson didn't fancy the drive into south-west London. He wanted to feel salt water on his torn skin.

'Now,' she said.

'Food's not bad, thanks for asking. A choice of four meals. Vegan, halal and vegetarian options, plus a meat alternative. If you behave you can get cable TV, too. It's useful as it allows me to follow the market reports. Keeps me up to date.'

'You'll get fat,' Kate said. 'Sitting around, eating, watching TV, doing nothing all day.'

Brockman's face soured. 'Well, it's no fucking wonder, lady. Access to the gym is almost impossible. They've got five treadmills, which are never used and I can't get near them. This place is terribly run, you know. The sooner it's taken over by a private company the better. We need more market forces when it comes to incarceration. Your prison system could learn a lot from Texas. When I get out in a few weeks' time I'm going into the captivity business.'

'It must be tough, not running,' Sorrenson said. 'For someone like you, who loves running so much, it must be very difficult.'

Brockman looked round the prison's communal meeting room and said nothing. There were three other prisoners with visitors. A prison officer was stationed at the far wall. Nearby, two prisoners were cleaning the floor, earning their wages.

'We might be able to help,' Kate said. 'Get you access to the gym, I mean. You'll presumably want to keep in shape for the trial.'

'Too right,' Brockman snapped. 'When I walk free I want to be in peak condition. Not going to let you fucks ruin my physique. This isn't going to set me back.'

She smiled. 'Good for you. Stay positive.'

Brockman glowered at her. He really wanted to return to his cell. Even sharing a ten-by-eight room with a chain-smoking armed robber was better than talking to the dumb detective and his colleague. At least, Brockman guessed the tall, athletically built woman was the detective's colleague. She hadn't really been introduced. He studied her more closely. She didn't seem like a detective. She didn't have the aura. More like some kind of analyst or consultant. Then Brockman groaned inwardly. He'd met her before, up on Hampstead Heath, when she'd told him she was an account-ant. A lie so dull he'd swallowed it unquestioningly. He felt cold. He knew he had to be wary. She was dangerous, a man-trap. But he was interested. She was pushing his buttons. Her confidence was attractive. He wondered what she looked like naked. 'How could you get me access to the gym?'

Got you, she thought. 'We could talk to the governor here. My employer could make a recommendation. I think it would have influence.'

Brockman snorted. 'Lady, I don't want to sound offensive but I don't think a provincial police force based in a dead town by a part of the coast that no one ever visits carries too much weight around here or anywhere else for that matter.'

'Mmm,' she said, pushing her card across the table.

Brockman picked it up. 'Financial Intelligence Unit, MI5. I'm honoured. Sure beats accounting.'

'You should be. Honoured, I mean. I don't make offers to help usually. But you're a special case, Mr Brockman. Very special. I'm clearly not the only one who thinks so. Lots of people seem to value your talents. People who have tried to protect you.'

Brockman clenched his fists. He felt anxious. The woman seemed to know more than she was letting on. He felt an ugly power asymmetry opening up between them. It was a rare, almost unprecedented sensation, Brockman realized. Pretty much a first in his experience with women. 'Well, I'm not that special.'

'We disagree,' Sorrenson said.

'Yes,' Kate said. 'We really do. Not many people have been personal bankers to Prince Faisal, for example. His Quest fund is a behemoth. That thing can move markets.'

'Don't use the past tense,' Brockman barked. 'The prince hasn't dropped me. Far from it. He's helping put together my legal team. That's how much he values me.'

'How lucky you are,' Sorrenson said. 'You're going to get access to the best justice that money can buy, then. That's got to shuffle the cards in your favour, having that sort of legal firepower.'

Brockman stroked his chin, said nothing. Idiot British detectives, he thought.

'It's the least the prince can do for you, though, isn't it?' Kate said. 'After everything you've done for him at Higgs. Your client–relationship skills must be impressive. Tell me something, have you heard the rumours flying around? It seems Quest believes there is some very bad news on the way. People better take care. Batten down the hatches. A big storm's blowing in.'

Sorrenson noticed Brockman's shoulders tense. The Texan looked ready to shatter at any second.

'Rather worrying for everyone else who didn't take a similar position,' she continued. 'They'd be washed away in the flood.'

Brockman stared back at her. 'No crime in mitigating risk. Especially in these difficult times. That's what good banking is all about.'

'No crime whatsoever,' she said. 'But tell me something. You've got all these Quest trades, all being run through Higgs. But I've looked hard at them and something is puzzling me.'

'You don't say,' Brockman growled. 'So shoot. Be careful with that trigger, though. You could hit anyone.'

She gazed at him, unperturbed. 'Yeah, anyway, the thing is—'

'What?'

'The thing is they're really neat, the transactions. Perfect, really. Rows upon rows of high-frequency trades all waiting for some super-computer to flick the switch and activate them. They telegraph disaster. They positively scream it. If I was at Higgs and I'd seen that, I'd be seriously worried. I'd wonder what Quest knew. I'd be looking to take out some insurance against the apocalypse arriving.'

'Clarity is kind of useful in the banking world,' Brockman said slowly, a teacher talking to a dumb pupil. 'It helps keep things simple. Stops people making costly mistakes.'

'Mmm,' Kate murmured. 'I suppose it does. So tell me about the offshore account you run for Quest. The one set up by you. The one in the BVI. Not so much clarity there. That's kind of hidden, I'd argue.'

Brockman folded his arms. His heart was racing, like he was sprinting. How had she found it? She really was dangerous. Toxic. 'So what about it? Most of our larger clients take advantage of their legal right to operate entities in low-tax locations.'

'That's not what interests me. What interests me is that it's been set up to take mirror positions on the exact trades Quest is looking to make through Higgs. I'm asking myself, why do that? Why create a second set of trades? What on earth could their purpose be? Why have one set running through Higgs and the other offshore, hidden?'

Suddenly Brockman felt sick with fear. The woman had worked out too much. He thought about the prince and how he'd react if the plan was exposed. All their subterfuge would have been for nothing. The great hypnotic lie that Quest had spent months selling the intelligence agencies, selling Higgs, would be exposed. He would be blamed, he knew. If he hadn't done for Holahon, the security services wouldn't have been crawling all over Higgs. He'd thought that Carlyle had taken care, sorting out the movement of the body and all the other gruesome stuff to put the cops off the scent. But it was painfully evident to Brockman that he'd lit a fire that couldn't be contained and now threatened to torch the whole project. Prison would be the least of his problems if Quest's plan went up in flames.

For the first time since entering Wandsworth he felt truly trapped. He considered his limited options. He took a series of deep breaths and tried to calm himself. He needed to make some calls. Yes, that was what he needed to do. He'd discovered it wasn't difficult to get hold of a mobile phone in prison. Exercise time, yes. Guns, drugs, booze, phones, they

were dead easy to come by. He knew that the chance of anyone pulling strings to get him released would evaporate if
the Quest plan collapsed. He was under no illusions. He was
powerful because of who he worked for, what he did for
them. Lose the prince, and he would be facing at least a
decade behind bars, with nothing waiting for him when he
got out, if he got out. Bad things happened in prison. Plenty
of inmates would be happy to serve more years for his
manslaughter in return for a fat cheque when they got out.
Yes, he knew where his loyalties lay. He didn't owe the cops
anything. They couldn't protect him. And he didn't owe his
employer anything either. Higgs was on life support. He'd
worked that much out months ago. It was weak and it was
going to die soon and no one would miss it. Quest was simply putting it out of its misery. It was going to be a mercy
killing. He needed to stay on the side of the killer.

Brockman looked back at the woman sitting in front of
him, his face blank. He no longer imagined her naked. 'I
don't know what you're talking about,' he said. 'I'm sorry,
lady, I really can't help you.'

Chapter 16

Reynolds negotiated his way through Heathrow's immigration control, pulling his sour mood behind him like stubborn luggage. He'd been trying to restrain his drinking on the flight over and he felt jumpy and irritable as a result of the sudden withdrawal from alcohol. He could have killed for a drink but there was not long to go until the main event. He needed to stay in control. Or, at least, as close to being in control as possible.

Suddenly he found himself laughing. The main event, he thought. Yes, that was one way of putting it. He thought about Quest's plan for rigging the market, by far the most invaluable intelligence he'd gleaned from that snake Carlyle. It was simple. It was outlandish. And it was going to work, Reynolds just knew. Crash a plane into a nuclear power station and blame it on a bird-strike. He'd thought that it had sounded insane when Carlyle had leaked the plan to him, made him suspect, not for the first time, that he was being fed a line by his asset, but he'd come to learn that such an event was not uncommon. There had been the plane that came down on the Potomac, for a start. And it was clear from what Carlyle had told him that Quest had done its homework. The runway it planned to use, some place south-east of London, was next to the largest number of bird species in Europe so, statistically speaking, the collision of a jet engine and a flock of Canada geese was not unlikely. It was just that no one really knew what would happen in the event of the impact. No one knew what its legacy would be.

Reynolds had wondered why they'd bothered blaming the catastrophe on a simple, natural event. Why not just blame some fucking towel-heads? he'd asked Carlyle. His late asset had simply shrugged.

'Something to do with the way the prince thinks,' Carlyle had said. 'It appeals to the way he looks at the world. He's making a point. Just one simple action, the collision of a bird and a plane, will bring Higgs and the CIA to its knees. That's how fragile American hegemony really is. Pretty humiliating when you think about it.'

It was ingenious, Reynolds conceded. Quest was going to unleash beautiful, lucrative chaos. In the period that followed the strike, when a terrified world tried to gauge whether it had a full nuclear meltdown on its hands and countries panicked over which way the radioactive wind was blowing, the financial markets would go into meltdown. The flight to safety, as terrified investors rushed to get into the safe havens of gold and other precious metals, would be unprecedented. The mass stampede to escape the plunging stock market would be equally dramatic. Except Quest's super-computers would have got there first and cleaned up, bolting the door behind them. The hedge fund would have arrived nano-seconds before everyone else. It didn't seem like much but in the hyper-connected world of banking it was the difference between being in the lifeboat and drowning. And Higgs would be saved, too. By copying Quest's dense pattern of trades, Higgs's debt mountain would be wiped out. Thank fuck he'd sorted out the Holahon fiasco. If the prince had got nervous and taken his money elsewhere, Higgs would be six feet under. But now it had prospects. It was practically alchemy, what Higgs was about to achieve, forging gold in the ruins of a dead nuclear plant. And if Higgs was saved, the Agency was saved. Too bad a hedge fund linked to Islamic terrorism would clean up. But, as Reynolds told himself, there would be time enough to deal with Quest once he'd saved the CIA. Thank God for the market, he thought. You couldn't argue with the market. It was the most efficient system in the world. He thought of a quote he'd read somewhere: it isn't enough to win, somebody has to lose. Exactly. There were people who made a killing and people who were killed. That was how it was. That was how it would always be.

Fear made money, Reynolds had come to understand. Frightened markets were the future of banking. Money only moved when people were scared.

'You've got to talk to him. You've got to tell Webster we're all being played. Quest isn't trying to blow up a nuclear plant; it's trying to blow up a bank.'

Callow sighed heavily. 'You know that you're a lone voice on this, Pendragon. We're picking up all sorts of chatter that some kind of spectacular is on the cards. A really major spectacular. Loads of stuff coming out of our listening stations in Saudi. Talk of some sort of nuclear incident. It'll be made to look like an accident, apparently, but terrorism will be the beneficiary. The markets will go into free-fall. Lot of investors in the Middle East betting on Armageddon happening soon, lot of people who aren't too friendly with the West. We're talking huge sums being wagered on this. That sort of money could buy their terrorist friends a lot of bombs. It could recruit them an entire army.'

'Exactly. That's what Quest want you to believe. It's a lie, the opposite of the truth. They're just trickling stuff out there. Furtive phone calls, cryptic emails, encoded financial trades – they know it's all being sucked up by the NSA and GCHQ, giving the impression that something massive is about to happen. We've seen the satellite photos of what's going on down at the airport near the nuclear plant. So has the CIA and God knows who else. We know from intelligence sources in the aviation industry that a Gulfstream jet is going to be fitted with a remote-control device. I agree, it all seems to point to a catastrophic attack on a nuclear installation. But I tell you, nothing is going to happen. It's just an illusion.'

Callow lit a cigarette, sucked smoke into his lungs as if his life depended on it. 'Come on, you remember what happened before Nine/Eleven? Saudi-based investors were selling airline stocks. That should have put everyone on a state of red alert. One massive fucking sign that everyone missed. No intelligence agency wants to be caught out a second time. MI5, the CIA, they probably wouldn't survive if it got out that they were aware there were signals that something major was about to go down and they'd failed to act.'

Kate almost groaned with frustration. They were being duped. Couldn't they see that? Their obsession with terror meant that they saw only terror. They were blind to the real threat. 'You listened to the tape?'

'The tape of Brockman phoning Quest from prison? You get a warrant for that intercept?'

'Yeah,' she said hurriedly. She didn't want to dwell on the warrant issue. 'Home sec signed it off within minutes of us visiting Brockman in Wandsworth. The tape is proof I'm calling this right. You can hear how desperate Brockman is. He's really straining to keep control of his voice. He talks pretty cryptically but it's clear he's trying to send Quest a warning. He wants them to know we're on to them. He tells them they need to consider all their options. He tells them to take out insurance.'

'Quest seemed pretty unimpressed by what he was saying,' Callow muttered.

'They know people are likely to be listening. And they're hedge-fund managers, not cheerleaders. They're not prone to big displays of emotion. But they'll have understood what he was saying and they'll be rattled. Brockman is a man who understands people's fears and exploits them. That's what makes him tick. But if he's scared, they're going to be scared.'

Callow shook his head.

'Ask yourself something,' she said. 'Don't you think it's strange that Quest uses Higgs? Of all the banks in the world, it chooses the one that screams "CIA front". We know that the Agency has run black ops out of Higgs. We know McLure believed the CIA actually built Higgs but that it then lost control of the monster it created. We know McLure suspected that Higgs has got massive amounts of debt hidden away, that it's close to imploding.'

'So?'

'So why would Quest use Higgs? Because it wants Higgs to see what it's doing. Quest has actively encouraged surveillance because it needs to sell Higgs a lie. It's dangling the bait. I suspect it wants Higgs to believe that Armageddon is coming because it knows the bank will copy its trading positions, as it's drowning in debt. But if Higgs makes that bet it's going to be destroyed when there is no nuclear catastrophe. That will have massive blowback for the CIA. If you really want to make the world a safer place, start worrying about a catastrophe that isn't going to happen.'

Callow stood up, strode to his office door, closed it quietly. He turned back to her. 'I hear what you're saying but you're supposed to be on holiday, Kate. Don't think you need a proper rest? We deal in threats. Not the absence of threats. All the signs are there. We know Quest has been preparing for this moment. Like I said, we're getting a lot of stuff back from the NSA and GCHQ telling us that this moment is imminent. We've got the runway under close scrutiny. We have planes ready to be scrambled, army on standby. If this is going to happen, we'll be ready. We're not now going to pick up the phone and tell the Americans we think a CIA bank is about to bet the farm on a nuclear catastrophe that isn't going to happen.'

She swallowed hard and concentrated on slowing her breathing. She was in danger of screaming. But she knew that her one chance to convince Callow would be blown if that happened. She tried again. 'This could set the West back decades. It will create great swaths of poverty. And you know that terrorism feeds on poverty. Someone has got to signal to Higgs that it mustn't buy into Quest's lie. Someone's got to stop them before they fall off a cliff. All these high-frequency trades Higgs has prepared are designed to go off nanoseconds before the supposed strike. When that doesn't happen Higgs will implode. It will lose billions and billions of pounds betting the wrong way against a market that will follow Quest because all the other banks' super-computers will almost instantly copy its real trades. That's how high-frequency trading works. It encourages a pack mentality. One phone call, that's all I'm asking. One fucking phone call. Ring the Federal Reserve. Tell them what we suspect.'

Callow said nothing, continued dragging on his cigarette. She was getting to him, she could tell.

'If Higgs goes down, the entire psychology of the market is completely spooked. Everyone goes into panic mode. It'll be like Lehmans all over again, only a lot worse because everyone's stamina, everyone's confidence, is completely shot to bits right now. They can't cope with any more bad news. Most of the banks are extremely fragile. If investors start pulling money out of them, it could send the entire global economy into free-fall. And you know what happens when people don't have jobs, don't have hope that things will improve. They become vulnerable to extremists who seem to offer them all the answers. That's the real terrorist threat in all this. It's toxic banks, not terrorist bombs that you should really fear. They're going to do a whole lot more damage in the long run.'

Callow ran a hand over his icy forehead. His entire body felt ready for the morgue.

'Look,' she said, detecting a flicker of uncertainty in his body language, 'think about what is at stake for the Americans here, too. Faisal knows that Higgs is the CIA's bank and that everything he does is being monitored. He knows exactly what he's doing. He's launching the economy's equivalent of Nine/Eleven. And he's using the CIA's own debt-laden bank to do it. Pretty neat, you have to admit.'

Callow blinked several times. He reminded himself that he was going to be retiring in three years. He refused to have a heart attack until then. 'So where does Aldud fit into all of this? I mean, presumably, his assassination has got to be linked to all of this?'

She shrugged. 'I don't know. Maybe it's unrelated. Maybe your intel is right and he was going to reveal how much oil was left in the Ghawar Field. Pretty unlikely but I've learned cancer does strange things to people. But, think about it, if that was true, that sort of information would ruin Quest's plan. Everything is so finely calibrated that a shock of that sort to the system would take years to bed down before you could again make the giant bet that Quest is about to place.'

'Oh, come,' Callow said angrily. 'Are you suggesting he would murder his own father? That's preposterous.'

'I know it's thin and I wouldn't be pushing this if we had more time. But all it needs to close this down is some urgent communication. I'm not asking you to send in tanks.'

Big Ben chimed eleven.

'There is no protocol for this,' Callow murmured. 'This is way off the scale.'

'You guys share intel all the time.'

'Yes, but about third parties, rogue states, security initiatives. We would effectively be telling the CIA that we suspect their bank is playing casino capitalism using a major terrorist incident as gambling chips and it's about to lose. It would create a diplomatic crisis of the utmost severity. All co-operation between the agencies would dry up. As for access to their satellite, telecoms and drone data, all collected by the NSA, well, we can forget that immediately. We don't tell the Americans what to do. It's the other way round, remember? They're the ones with all the power, with all the money. Britain's entire security strategy is based on keeping the Americans onside.'

'One phone call,' she said. 'Just one phone call.'

Callow shook his head. 'I'm sorry.'

'One phone call.'

'Sorry. I'm really sorry.'

The prince examined the photographs of his new Gulfstream jet with the enthusiasm of a father admiring his firstborn. The plane was beautiful, as graceful as a falcon; similar colours, too.

'She will land this afternoon?'

His assistant nodded. 'Yes, shortly after three.'

'Good,' the prince muttered. 'Very good. The latest visitor to our new, extended runway. It is the size of a whale, is it not?'

The assistant was about to reply when Schwartz material-ized in the Quest boardroom. The prince raised his eyebrows expectantly. The two men waited for the assistant to leave the room.

'The remote-control system has arrived,' Schwartz said. 'It will be fitted this afternoon. I'm sure our watching friends will be very interested.'

The prince smiled. 'Then we are good to go?'

'We are good to go,' Schwartz replied.

'The phone call from Mr Brockman?'

'There's no sign that anything has leaked into the market,' Schwartz said. 'Brockman's maybe losing it a bit. Perhaps he is starting to feel guilty about his part in Higgs's impending demise. But it would be wise to take out insurance.'

'Good. We have it?'

'Insurance?' Schwartz said. 'A contingency plan? Yes, of course. But we don't need it. As I said, nothing's leaked.'

'Excellent,' the prince said. 'I cannot tell you how much I enjoy the idea that we are about to destroy the Central Intelligence Agency by doing nothing more than selling them a simple lie. Tell me, our fake trades predicting Armageddon will be deactivated when?'

Schwartz shrugged. 'Maybe five, perhaps six hundredths of a second before the real ones run out. The switch will spook the market. A lot of computer systems are going to start flashing red when it happens. But it will be too late for Higgs. The bank will have started selling off billions of dollars' worth of shares, shares it bought using borrowed money, in the blink of an eye. And, approximately eight nanoseconds after they sell, it will emerge that we're the lucky buyer. Higgs is not going to know what's hit it. All the other banks will follow us as their super-computers kick into life and activate programs mirroring our trades. It's going to drive the prices of the assets that Higgs is left holding through the floor. We're talking massive trading volumes. Thank a benevolent God for the genius technology that is high-frequency trading. It makes market manipulation so much easier. When things happen at light speed there's just no chance for anyone to question what is happening.

There's no time for anyone to take evasive action. It's like, boom, the plane has crashed before the pilot has signalled an emergency.'

The prince laughed. 'I would guess that the late Mr Carlyle's friend Mr Reynolds is a very nervous man right now. He is gambling on the end of the world. He will be mortified when that doesn't happen. What a shame for him that terror is not as ubiquitous as he'd feared. A shame for the other banks, too, when they feel the impact of Higgs's collapse in the coming days and weeks. Collateral damage, you could call it.'

He gestured out of the boardroom window. 'People will look back on tomorrow and say that it was the day when US hegemony ended. It was when the American Dream finally died. It's all too perfect for words.' He started whistling 'Somewhere Over the Rainbow'. 'We are not in Kansas any more, hey, Schwartz? No, we are not in Kansas any more.'

Chapter 17

A click, click, click of stilettos on a polished marble floor. It was early. The Mexican cleaners had only just finished making Quest's offices gleam like a Porsche showroom. The sun was filtering through smoked-glass windows. The place had the feel of a mausoleum. Sepulchral. Cold. Moneyed.

The security guard looked up from his newspaper and frowned. It was far too early for anyone to be entering the building. He examined the woman walking towards him, saw her heels, her short skirt, her heavily made-up face. Yes, he thought, it was far too early. Unless, he thought, maybe . . . No, no one from the hedge fund's executive board was in. Mayfair's high-class escorts would be having to look elsewhere for business today. Quest's executives were all out of the office. They had given strict instructions that they were not to be contacted.

The woman arrived at the security desk several seconds behind her perfume. Expensive scent, the security guard thought. Expensive sunglasses, too. She studied him from behind her shades, offered up a broad smile of perfect white teeth. 'Hi. I'm Angela Warwick. From the Icarus Consultancy. We do crisis PR for Quest.'

The security guard nodded. 'Right.'

'I have a meeting with the Quest board in ten minutes.'

'Not today, madam. No one here.'

The woman frowned, made a show of dragging her BlackBerry out of her handbag. She studied the device, frowned some more. 'No, it's definitely today.'

'No,' the guard said, 'it isn't.'

The woman muttered something under her breath. 'Well, I'll just phone the prince and see what's happening.'

'You do that, madam.'

She swore quietly. 'My phone's just died on me. May I?' She pointed at a phone on the reception desk. The guard thought for a couple of seconds, then agreed. They'd had some anti-capitalism protesters try to storm Quest recently and he was wary of strangers. But the woman was one big designer label. She clearly loved money. She was no threat.

The woman flipped open a small notebook, flashed another smile, read a number out loud as she typed it into the phone. As she did so, she drank in the huge expanse of Quest's reception, then smiled up at the security cameras located in four places. 'Pretty tight security you've got here,' she said to the guard. 'So many monitors. They must see everything.'

The guard said nothing. The woman smiled again. It was clear someone at the other end had picked up but the guard couldn't hear the conversation as the woman had lowered her voice almost to a whisper.

'Mr Ambassador, I'm sorry to bother you at this time in the morning. I'm a whistle-blower calling from Quest, the Saudi hedge fund . . . Yes, I appreciate your mobile number is hard to find but I thought you should be made aware of a grave and urgent threat to the United States. You will appreciate that, as a whistle-blower, I need to protect my identity but if you check with your NSA I'm sure they will confirm that this call is being made from within Quest's London headquarters, a mile or so from your embassy. I believe the NSA has been monitoring Quest for some time . . . No, I can't explain how I know that. But you should also understand that Quest is aware it's being monitored. Now listen, I need to talk to you about Higgs Bank and the threat it poses to the Central Intelligence Agency. I appreciate that, as with all your calls, this conversation is being recorded. That kind of monitoring is useful. It keeps a record of things. I'm certainly recording this call myself. I would hate for it to emerge that you'd had this conversation and then not acted upon it. Things have a habit of getting into newspapers . . .'

'Unusual location. Very unusual time.'

'Yeah, I'm sorry. I wouldn't have rung if it wasn't supremely urgent.'

The smaller, older man scratched his salt-and-pepper beard. 'Supremely urgent,' Brandeis said. 'That's what I figured.'

Carey gestured at the empty bleachers, their white wooden slats partially illuminated by the creeping dawn. 'It's easiest to talk here,' he said. 'What I'm about to say cannot be said inside the FIU, or the Agency, for that matter. It goes no further. We need to seal this off.'

'Uh-huh.'

'We have a situation.'

Brandeis sighed, continued to fiddle with his beard. 'Looks like it. Otherwise I wouldn't be sitting in the middle of Central Park at five in the morning. I take it it's Higgs.'

'That's right,' Carey said. 'Higgs. Higgs, Higgs, Higgs, Higgs. It's always been Higgs. I fucking wish we'd never built Higgs. But, anyway, we've received some intel we think came from our friends over the water. I won't bore you right now with how we know this but they believe Higgs is about to place a catastrophic bet, using huge amounts of money borrowed from other banks. They think Higgs is being manipulated.'

'Ballsy claim,' Brandeis said. 'Not something they usually do. They're normally very cautious in doling out risk analysis. Could backfire spectacularly if they call it wrong. Does it check out?'

'It seems to. We've got people going over it all right now.' Carey lowered his voice until it was barely a whisper. 'You know that it checks out. This is what we've feared for a long, long time. You can't build something like Higgs and expect to control it. It assumes a life of its own. It's Frankenstein's monster and the Death Star all rolled into one.'

'Where's Reynolds?' Brandeis said.

'London, Ghent says.'

'Ghent?'

'He's an asset we have inside Reynolds's team. Useful insurance.'

Brandeis gave a low whistle. 'How long we had him in there spying on our man?'

'Some time. He's been feeding us worrying intel on Reynolds recently. He thinks Reynolds has gone rogue. His drinking is off the chain, apparently.'

'Likely,' Brandeis said. 'He's clearly under a lot of stress. His creation's bombed out and he's running out of options. What's he doing in London?'

'Don't know, but my guess is he's trying to clear up some of the mess. Or at least prevent further fallout. I've prepared a briefing. The Brits seem to have called this one right. Higgs is seriously in debt. We should have spotted it earlier but it's taken steps to hide a lot of its exposure. And now it's about to go for broke on a single event that it believes will send the global markets into chaos.'

'Jesus,' Brandeis said. 'The event being?'

'From what the Brits tell us, it appears that Higgs believes a plane is going to collide with a nuclear reactor. It will look like a bird-strike has brought the jet down but it's all going to be done remotely. The Agency know about it. They've been informed. It's pretty elaborate. MI5 have been conducting a major surveillance programme. They've picked up a lot of chatter, got some audio that seems to confirm something of the kind. Saudi listening stations are reporting similar things to MI6. We've got some satellite intel of our own. NSA sucked up a lot of comms suggesting something big is going to happen. A lot of encrypted financial trades are due to be made via the Frankfurt bourse, according to stuff we've intercepted from the transatlantic submarine cables. All the signs are there.'

Brandeis sighed. 'I sense a "but" coming, right? Am I right? A big but?'

'Right,' Carey nodded. 'The Brits reckon it could all be hokum, according to our ambassador over there, who claims to have been personally briefed on this. He's got real excited about it. He's going to have a stroke if he continues the way he's going. He's been asking how long the NSA has been monitoring Quest. Wants to know what kind of monitoring we've put on Higgs. What kind of capital ratios it's got. I really didn't want to answer that one. Anyway, the Brits think Higgs is being spun, the banks are being spun, we're all being spun. Like I said, it's all in here.' Carey waved a sheaf of papers in the air.

'Right,' Brandeis said quietly. 'So what do we think?'

'Certainly it appears that Higgs has taken some very extreme positions, which are going to kick in imminently. Unless it unwinds those positions, if the Brits are right, it will implode. It has leveraged itself up – borrowed billions and billions from other banks, effectively – to buy those positions. If Higgs has bet wrong, well, you'll hear the explosion in space. The Agency wouldn't survive the fallout. There'll be debris strewn everywhere.'

Brandeis scanned the papers, angling them so that he could use the light from a nearby street lamp. He bit his knuckle, whether in concentration or rage it was hard for Carey to tell in the gloom. 'Difficult for Reynolds to take care of anything on foreign soil,' Brandeis said.

'True.'

'He must be desperate.'

'Yeah,' Carey said. 'So?'

'So we are where we are. We clearly can't continue like this.'

'Endgame?'

'Endgame.' Brandeis shook his head. 'Didn't think I'd see this happen on my watch.'

'Right. For sure. Parker?'

'Yeah, Parker,' Brandeis murmured. 'I'll brief him. Time for the chairman to earn his massive salary. Shame, though. Feels wrong, flicking the switch. Gonna get messy.'

'Agreed,' Carey said. 'But it's better this way. If the other banks end up following Higgs, we're talking major wipe-out and we're the cause. The CIA would be blamed for triggering the second Great Depression. I just hope Parker doesn't flake. That would be unfortunate. His performance is going to be crucial to what happens in the next twenty-four hours.'

'He won't flake,' Brandeis said. 'Parker's a general. He'll see this as the ultimate sacrifice. He'll do it for the Agency. This is his Alamo.'

She pulled on white ankle socks and the flimsiest running shoes Sorrenson had ever seen. They were built for speed, he thought. His trainers were built for endurance. They were designed to take a beating. 'So, how did it go?' he asked.

She looked at him. His face still told of a lost fight. Its ugly collage of red welts and purple bruising was out of place in her sparse loft, like spilled wine. Suddenly there was too much colour confronting the apartment's white walls and engineered oak floors. But, then, the face of any man would look out of place in her home, Kate conceded. Sorrenson was the first to have made it over the threshold. 'It went OK, I think. Glad to get out of those clothes. I think my vamping days are behind me. Good to get these on.' She pointed at her running shoes.

'You're going for a run?'

She shrugged. 'Nothing I can do now. Running will help. Make me feel in control.'

'But, still . . .'

'Still.'

'You could . . .'

'What?'

'I don't know,' Sorrenson said.

'I know. You mean I could do something more. Well, I have. I've taken out insurance. I emailed copies of all Higgs's imminent trades to the CIA, the Fed, the NSA and several members of the Senate Security Committee. All anonymous and sent from an encrypted drop box so that it can't be traced back to me. People are crawling all over Higgs. That's the great thing about surveillance. There's just so much of it. There's a lot of people out there who won't be able to say they weren't warned that Higgs was about to hit the wall.'

She laced up her trainers, pulled on her GPS watch.

'What do you reckon is going to happen?' Sorrenson said.

She strapped a heart-rate monitor under her running vest. 'I think they're in listening mode. I've just been studying Higgs's positions. Looks like they're being unwound. Someone is sweeping clean at Higgs. It won't be enough to save it – it's got way too much debt for that. It will go under but later rather than sooner. It will die a dignified death, kept alive in some banking equivalent of palliative care while bits of it are probably sold off to other banks. No one will ever know how toxic it really was.'

Sorrenson searched the floor for his trainers. 'I'll come with you. Give me a second to find my kit.'

'Fine.'

'What if you're wrong?' Sorrenson's voice echoed from the bedroom. 'I mean, what if something devastating really is on the cards and you've made the wrong call?' He could see the strain showing on her face. It was clear the same thought was close to enveloping her.

'Well, first, they're still monitoring the runway so if I'm wrong and anything does happen, they can take action. Second, I trust my instincts. People lie but money doesn't. Intelligence agencies have known that for years. You study where people are moving their cash and you can read their minds. There's not going to be any catastrophe – at least, not tomorrow. I just hope the security services can cope with that. They're not great at understanding it's the things that don't happen that are the most dangerous in the long run. Seize a suicide bomber and they think they've got a result. Drinks all round. But what about the guys who don't show up on their grids, the dull ones who don't do anything for years, decades even? The ones in the background who keep clean but send the recruits out to the extremist *madrasah*s to be indoctrinated, to be turned into killing machines, hey? In the long run they're far more dangerous. But I'm not sure the intelligence community is capable of thinking along those lines. It needs action, urgent action. All that machismo washing around in those places is dangerous. It's blinding them to the real risks out there.'

Sorrenson pulled on a running vest. 'Rant over?'

'Rant over.'

'The Heath?'

'The Heath.'

They ran along the streets of Clerkenwell, which were as quiet as a disused film set, its entire population decamped to City law firms, banks and consultancies. They ran through a leafy, well-groomed square where Marx had railed against the injustices of capitalism. They ran past cafés with crisp white linen on their tables, digital branding agencies and bespoke stockbrokers. They ran north above the subterranean river Fleet, its powerful flow once harnessed by the capital's flour mills. They ran past a new King's Cross rising out of the rubble of the old one. They ran past once-derelict canal warehouses that were now homes to anyone with a million pounds to spare. They ran through a city that was sculpted by money.

They didn't notice the van.

Chapter 18

Hughes, sweat burning in his eyes, viewed his mode of transport dispassionately. It wasn't much of a boat, he thought, barely large enough for two people. Its blue paint was peeling badly and it looked like it would take on water at any minute. But he was glad that he wasn't stealing a better vessel, one that someone would miss. He'd done enough damage.

He dragged the boat down the shingled shore, surprised at its reluctance to be returned to the sea. It was almost as if it knew what was about to happen, that it was determined to thwart Hughes, frustrate his hopes, just like everything and everyone else.

Once the boat was being buffeted gently by the waves, Hughes walked back up the beach and retrieved a pair of wooden oars. He made another journey and dragged a black bag down over the shingle, struggling, briefly, to lift it into the vessel. He looked up at the blue sky. The warm weather seemed to have inhabited the coast for months. For the first time he could truly understand Sorrenson's attraction to it.

He dragged himself away from sky-gazing. There was urgent work to be done. He opened the bag and pulled out a bottle, waves drenching the bottom third of his jeans. There was no one on the shore, just him, some derelict huts and a million dead organisms captured in stone. But he wasn't interested in fossils. He wasn't interested in preserving the past or even the present. It was too late for saving anything now.

Hughes took a long swig from the bottle. He felt drowsy. The near lethal combination of alcohol and painkillers made concentration almost impossible. It was so warm, he thought. He felt the sun burn into his face. His throat was dry from the bottle-and-a-half of vodka he had gulped before the dawn had broken, before he had achieved his hard-won drunken clarity. Maybe should have drunk some water, he thought. It would at least take the stinging out of this throat. It didn't really matter, though. Nothing really mattered any more.

He peered up at the sky, at the fearless sun, then glanced at his digital watch. It was coming up to two in the afternoon. He was astonished by the date on its display: 2 September. It was his birthday, he remembered. He suppressed a laugh. Well, there was a symmetry to it, if nothing else.

Wearily he pushed the boat through the waves, grateful that the sea was calm. Gulls rode the winds above him, watching his progress.

When he was beyond the waves and the sea was above his waist, Hughes pulled himself up into the boat. The exertion surprised him. He felt even wearier. He was so very tired, not just by his efforts but everything: life. He was still wearing his leather jacket. It had become like a second skin, a form of protection, in recent days, something that he would pull around him no matter how warm the weather.

He sat up in the boat and grabbed the oars. As he rowed

he watched the shoreline diminish. The change in perspective reassured him. He was leaving the land behind, his problems behind, and everything was becoming smaller to the point of insignificance. He watched the power station shrink from view until suddenly it didn't look man-made any longer. Rather it resembled a vast shadow, the opening of a tunnel to another world.

Things changed so quickly. Time brought a multitude of new perspectives. Hughes thought about the body, how it hadn't looked human the day he'd dumped it on the beach. Jesus, if only he'd known then what he knew now. He had thought it was just a corpse, some rival that the Harrison gang had wanted disposed of in return for wiping his slate clean. Gambling debts. Poker. Hughes had never thought of himself as a gambler. Until it was too late. Far too late. By then he owed hundreds of thousands to a variety of syndicates, and his card was marked across London and the south-east. Maybe that was his problem with Margate, he thought. The town's ubiquitous slot machines reminded him of his abject failure, his recklessness.

The Harrison gang had offered to consolidate his debts. 'Just like the banks do,' Jonno Harrison, the septuagenarian leader of the firm, had promised. 'Then we'll work out an easy repayment programme, like they mention in those ads on the telly. You're not the first copper we've done this for. Far from it, in fact. Must be something in your DNA makes you prone to gambling. Everyone makes bad bets in their lifetime, but we're giving you the chance to be free of them. What do you say?'

No, he hadn't thought of the body as human, as flesh and blood, as something that had been loved or pitied, hated or desired. And he certainly hadn't thought it would come with so much baggage. He hadn't thought a dead body could be so powerful.

If Holahon hadn't been a banker, things would have worked out differently, Hughes had come to understand. He wouldn't have been so interesting, so important to the living. Questions wouldn't have been asked. So many questions. A thread would not have been unpicked. A thread that seemed to span half the world, connecting everything. Without the body Sorrenson wouldn't have got involved. That woman, too, the one with the strange job that Sorrenson never mentioned. The Harrisons, Davey Stone, no one would have known. Bill Henry should have stuck to smuggling counterfeit fags and stealing fish, Hughes thought, with bitterness at the injustice of it all. He could still see Bill's eyes: the shock in them, the way they seemed to burn through the gloom of the shack.

And all because Hughes had moved something. He had taken something from A to B, an activity that millions of people did every day. But something so simple, so seemingly risk-free, had brought the entire house crashing down around him. He still couldn't see how it was all joined together, how the structure was made complete. But he knew that he had started it. Fucking bankers. Why couldn't Holahon have been an asylum seeker? No one gave a fuck about them. No one asked questions when they disappeared.

Hughes rowed on, conscious his arms were struggling to work the oars. His eyes were constantly burning. He couldn't tell whether it was sweat or tears. It had been years since he'd cried. There was so much to apologize for, he thought. So many mistakes. So many bad bets, bad decisions. Well, it was time to take responsibility, to atone. The letter he'd written would be his fossil, he told himself. They would read it when they examined his car parked up on the beach. It would be proof of his existence, something that would survive his spent self.

The shoreline was barely visible now. The sky really was a perfect blue, Hughes thought. He pulled the oars into the boat, leaned forwards, unzipped the bag, drank more from the bottle. He had so nearly got away with it. He had returned the police van and no one had noticed. Someone, Hughes never found out who the Harrisons had used, had wiped the CCTV footage on the day he had borrowed the van so there was no record of its disappearance. They should have just burned the body, Hughes thought. Or weighed it down with rocks and sent it to the bottom of the sea. The thought made him uncomfortable.

But, no, others had chosen to complicate things, turned what remained of Holahon into a symbol, something cryptic, in a bid to confuse people. And that was when the problems had started, Hughes realized. When people had started to over-engineer things. The more you added layers to stuff, the more complex everything became, until you could no longer see what you were supposed to be doing in the first place.

He thought back to his first days at police training college. It had been so simple then. He had wanted a job that kept him fit, with good promotion chances and a healthy pension. He wasn't really interested in law and order or whether his profession would help others. It had been for selfish reasons that he had joined the thin blue line.

All those reasons for signing up had evaporated.

Paperwork had seen him pile on the pounds. His promotion hopes had plateaued as he had watched lesser colleagues rise through the ranks. The government was cutting his pension, too. He should have been a banker, Hughes thought. It was a similar job to the police. Both relied on the pretence of order being maintained. Both, falsely, insisted on the most stringent forms of probity for their members. Both had rules and laws and codes and ethics and did seemingly simple things that had become so much more complex. Yeah, a banker. That would have suited him better. But he had backed the wrong horse. Another bad bet. At least he wasn't alone. Everyone had made bad bets. Even the bankers. Just like Jonno Harrison had said.

Hughes could no longer see the shore, although he could sense its presence. It was there in front of him, a sea mon- ster that would attack him if he approached. Got to get away from it, he thought. It knows I'm out here. It will be merci- less. Dark shadows crept around his eyes. His brain seemed to throb in his skull. God, he was thirsty.

He drifted in the boat. It was a pleasant sensation, almost dream-like. The odd screech of a gull above broke the silence. He felt as if he was floating a few inches above the sea, as if the boat was hovering. Light jumped out of the waves, like darting silver fish. A jet engine rumbled far above. Hughes watched its grudging journey through the sky. It seemed to be going so slowly. All those people on board, he thought. All those people with their hopes, their unchecked optimism that the plane would land and everything would be fine.

Only it turned out that everything came crashing down in the end, Hughes had learned. It was just a question of time, a question of luck. One day the darkness would engulf you. There was no escape. He swigged from the bottle and found with dismay that it was empty. There was nothing left. All the anaesthetic was gone. He threw it over the side of the boat, laughing as he heard it land with a fat splash in the sea. He took a deep breath, tried to ignore the stinging in his throat. He folded his leather jacket neatly, placed it beside him. He pulled the bag towards him and thrust his left arm inside. His right hand sought out the handcuff inside the bag, clasped it around his left wrist. He stood up uncertainly, the action sending the boat rocking from side to side. He bent down and, with a struggle, picked up the black bag containing his weights, chained to the other end of the handcuffs. He examined the bag, rocked it gently, as if it was a baby he was nursing to sleep.

Hughes took a last look at where the shoreline had been. He thought about taking another deep breath but that would just delay things. With a groan he threw the bag over the side of the boat and felt a strange thrill as his body followed it. He tasted salt, felt it burning his throat. He really should have drunk some water.

Suddenly he felt an overwhelming urge to live, to fight. But it was too late. The light blue water above him was getting darker as he sank rapidly. He desperately needed to breathe, to gain air. He opened his mouth to suck in the oxygen he so desperately craved. But there was only salt water.

Webster sat staring out of his office window. He didn't see the throngs of people snaking along the Thames. He saw only ghosts. He saw a crashed car and an ambulance crew. He saw fire engines and police cars and the flash of cameras. He saw skid-marks and a stretcher. He watched the scene play out in his mind for several minutes, studying it, as if he was examining the brushwork of a painting.

If Pendragon hadn't died he might have ended up running Five, Webster thought uncomfortably. He felt almost exhausted by guilt. He was ashamed, too. They were uncommon emotions, which he'd thought he'd blocked out years before. It was all too late. There was nothing that could be done about the past, nothing useful at any rate. Some legacies were never neat.

Webster sighed, took his Belfast memories, their fragments and shards, and put them back in a sealed box to be deposited in the furthest recess of his mind, a place of shadows and unspoken truths. He slowly wheeled himself back and forth in his chair.

A knock, and Callow entered his office. 'You may want to watch the television. I believe CNN are carrying it live.' He picked up a remote control and turned it on. A large man, whose suit seemed to be struggling to contain him, was seated behind a desk, taking questions from reporters. Words flashed up at the bottom of the screen: 'Breaking news: Higgs bank alerts federal prosecutors to systemic fraud, non-compliance and abject breach of banking covenants. Requests emergency bailout and federal help in restructuring. US Treasury suggests initial risk assessment indicates contagion will be contained to Higgs.'

Callow and Webster watched Parker's performance in silence. It was clear to both men that the bank's chairman had been preparing for his moment in front of the cameras throughout most of his civilian life. He took the questions soberly and calmly. There was none of the flamboyance for which the general had once been famous. Callow thought he looked like a football coach explaining his side's failure to win the Super Bowl. Pride shone in Parker's eyes but the sense of failure was almost palpable. The big man knew he was making the last public speech of his life. He was about to become a Wiki footnote.

'Turn the sound up a bit.' Webster gestured at the screen.

Callow picked up the remote and turned up the volume. Parker's voice boomed, 'Our internal audit and compliance team has detected large-scale money-laundering across Higgs's numerous international divisions. The bank appears to have been engaged in illegal transactions on behalf of the Iranian government, Mexican drug cartels, the Russian and Latvian Mafia, Hezbollah, FARC and several al-Qaeda franchises. That this was allowed to happen on my watch is clearly inexcusable and a source of deep regret. I will be resigning as chairman with immediate effect but will seek to help prosecutors, external auditors and investigators as much as I can. As a result of this clear and profound scandal, we have requested, and have been granted, the immediate freezing of all Higgs's transactions. In short, Higgs is in lockdown until further notice. No transactions, none, can be processed through its accounts.'

There was a clamour from the reporters as Parker stood up to leave. He turned to face the press pack. 'It would be clearly inappropriate to say more with the very real prospect of criminal prosecution now on the cards. I appreciate you have a million more questions but there is nothing I can add at the moment.'

Parker departed. The picture flashed to a studio and a stunned-looking news anchor.

Callow switched off the television. 'Clever,' he said, 'blaming Higgs's problems on money-laundering. Finger the Iranians, the Mexicans and all the other obvious suspects and no one thinks to delve any further. Buys the Americans time to terminate Higgs in their own fashion.'

'Yes,' Webster said. 'They do like to control how things end.'

'"Now I am become Death,"' Callow murmured, '"the destroyer of worlds."'

Webster looked at his colleague. 'Oppenheimer?'

'Yes. After he tested the first nuclear bomb.' Callow pointed at the blank television screen. 'I take it you made the call?'

Webster nodded. 'Yes, but it seemed they knew already. I think I just helped remind them that they couldn't hope to ride this one out. They knew we knew. They knew they had to act. It's impressive, really, the way they're dismantling Higgs so quickly. Reminds me of Enron. Blink and it was gone. Nothing left. Extraordinary.'

'So Pendragon was right. Higgs had swallowed a lie. Fears of a plane crashing into a nuclear power station were just that: fears.'

'Yes,' Webster said doubtfully. 'It doesn't really matter. It was enough for the Americans to know that we were aware Higgs was a basket case. They knew they had to kill it then. But there will be another Higgs soon enough. It's not a game-changer, closing Higgs. There is no such thing as a game-changer in this game. The game is bigger than us now.

It's out of control. Terror, financial systems, everything. We don't play the game. The game plays us.'

'Still, her father . . .' Callow said.

'Her father would be proud,' Webster said, agreeing with Callow's unfinished observation.

'We'll need to talk to the Americans,' Callow said.

'Yes. Can't see it being the most enlightening of debriefings, though. They must be pretty embarrassed by all of this. They're not going to be very keen on a full confession. Don't bank on full disclosure.'

'We should talk to Pendragon, too,' Callow said.

'In time. She's on leave, yes?'

'Yes.'

Webster wheeled back and forth. 'We should try to have her secondment to the service made permanent.'

'We should,' Callow agreed. 'We need more people like her, more Pendragons.'

Webster frowned. 'People like her?'

'People who understand complexity, I mean.'

Webster thought for a while. 'Yes,' he said finally. 'Yes, we do.' He gestured out of the window, turned to Callow. 'Want to know my favourite Oppenheimer quote?'

Callow nodded.

'"The optimist thinks that this is the best of all possible worlds. The pessimist fears that this is true."'

'And which are you?' Callow asked quietly.

Webster looked back out of the window. Sunlight dappled leaves that were turning brown and crisp. The Thames glittered. 'I don't know any more,' Webster said. 'I really don't know.'

★ ★ ★

Schwartz's screams could be heard down the long, darkly lit corridors of Quest's Mayfair HQ. They bounced off its living wall, off its bombproof glass windows, off its Rothkos and de Koonings. They bounced off everything. Aural shrapnel.

Schwartz's colleagues ran into the Quest boardroom, searching for the source of the screaming, the stunned witness to the bomb blast. They found him staring up at the huge trading screen that dominated one end of the boardroom. He was shaking gently, tears rolling down his face.

His colleagues had no need to ask why they'd been summoned back to Quest so urgently. Suddenly they understood. It was all there on the screen. The impossible nightmare scenario, the one they'd thought couldn't come true had come true. They stood collectively motionless, as if they were petrified. Above them numbers and letters flashed red and, occasionally, black. To an outsider the numbers were unfathomable, a jumble that could not be decoded. But to the Quest team the information flashing above them was all too obvious.

'Somebody leaked,' Schwartz said, pointing at the screen.

'Fucking Brockman,' one of the team muttered. 'What a flake.'

'Maybe,' Schwartz said. He looked at his colleagues suspiciously. 'Maybe not.'

They continued staring at the screen, half believing that the very act of witnessing the gargantuan transaction taking place before them could undo it. Higgs was unwinding all of its positions, an event that was being witnessed and emulated by every super-computer in every bank. The herd had taken fright. Quest was on its own. It was betting against the market. It was betting against the collective wisdom of every other financial institution, investor and Treasury department. It had sold the world a lie and at the final, crucial moment, the world had sold it back.

'We're going to have to tell the prince,' someone said.

They all looked at Schwartz.

Chapter 19

Sorrenson focused on her disappearing calves. They were the most beautiful he'd ever seen. Smooth, lightly tanned, they were taut and curved, like the breast of a bird. Her trainers seemed to hover above the ground, bothering to strike the earth only rarely and then for barely a nanosecond. She didn't run so much as glide, he thought.

He pounded on behind her. The ascent up the Heath to Kenwood had nearly done for him. His lungs had failed him, deserters in his time of need. He saw tiny black stars burst in front of his eyes. Sweat poured down his face. Veins in his arms throbbed as if they were going to burst. His legs felt leaden, unwieldy, as if he was drunk. He tried to get angry, use its power to spur him on. He thought of Hughes, of the beating his younger colleague had inflicted upon him, and was grateful when his legs delivered a small surge of power. But, still, it was heavy going. She was too quick. A mountain goat to his ox.

He felt a stab of relief when he saw that she'd stopped up ahead to give directions to a family. He picked up the pace, determined to catch her. The heat engulfed him. The Heath felt as if it was never going to let go of summer. Dust trailed behind him. The paths were so dry that the mud had cracked, forming little fissures. It hadn't rained for weeks and the sloping lawn in front of the mansion was the colour of straw. Even the weeds seemed to have given up the battle to stay green.

He was about ten metres from her, running parallel to the long wall of transparent plastic sheeting protecting the stately home during its renovation, when he saw something glitter up ahead. At first he thought one of the family had pulled out a camera or an iPhone, some sort of shiny device that had caught the sun. But then panic ran through his body, sent adrenalin pumping through his system, so that he almost flew the last few metres towards her. It was as if some deeper part of him had worked out what was happening long before his brain. It had seen the knife; it had sensed the threat.

With a roar Sorrenson piled into the three men. Even though it was a warm day, the men had hoods pulled over their heads and wore scarves around their mouths. One of the men grabbed Kate as the smallest sought to thrust a knife into her side. She twisted and screamed as the blade missed with the first lunge but caught her on the second. Her head sprang back, smacked into the face of one man, causing him to scream and clutch his nose.

There was no third time. Sorrenson barrelled into the smaller man, smashed him into the ground. They fell down together, Sorrenson gripping the man by the throat, choking him. She staggered a few metres away from the group and dropped to her knees, a hand pressed to her side, feeling her wound, her body shaking.

Sorrenson brought his head down on his opponent's nose, felt the crumple of cartilage on impact. The man cursed, in a language that Sorrenson guessed had travelled from some-where in Eastern Europe, and curled up into a ball in pain. But Sorrenson's satisfaction was short-lived. The two taller men rushed him, both flashing blades. In desperation he tried to kick the kneecap of one but his legs were so heavy from all the running that the action carried little power. He saw that Kate was on her knees crawling through the dust, trailing a line of crimson petals behind her. He turned back to his attackers as their blades pierced his sternum. He felt his breast plate shatter and the hot intrusion of metal run deep inside him.

'Run,' Sorrenson rasped, blood in his mouth. 'Run,' he repeated. He grabbed the two attackers in a bloody embrace, pulled them into him. They fell back against the transparent sheeting, the action leaving red smears on the polythene. A small group of startled walkers, who'd come running when they'd heard screams, held back, terrified.

Sorrenson slid down the sheeting, his eyes struggling to focus. Blood poured from his mouth. He wore a stunned look. He saw with dismay that the attackers had turned back to Kate, their knives raised. He attempted to reach out to them, implored them to attack him again, but he fell awk-wardly to his side, his cheek grazing the dust.

One man turned back and advanced towards him, his knife held aloft. Sorrenson braced himself. He had no words left. He closed his eyes.

The bellow of a straining diesel engine filled the air. A bottle-green Land Rover sped up the grassy bank in front of Kenwood, its four-wheel drive straining to make the forty-five-degree incline. The vehicle seemed to bounce off the lip of the bank and, for a second, it hung in the air before crashing back down and piling into the man closest to Sorrenson. There was the muffled sound of bones crumpling and of screaming. His two associates staggered back towards him and dragged him with them down the bank and towards a wood.

'Call the cops,' Gary Carlton shouted to the walkers, a phrase that he'd wanted to utter most of his adult life. The man on the ground was clearly in a bad state. He was losing a lot of blood. The park ranger thought for a couple of seconds. He wasn't first-aid trained but he did have an emergency kit in the Beast.

It was highly likely that he was about to lose his job anyway, he thought. In the grand scheme of things, administering first aid without training was the least of the manifold breaches of the Park Ranger's Code that he'd just committed in the last four minutes. And it would be one to tell the paintballing crowd. They didn't get to experience real blood when they went off shooting each other in a national park. He had to act. He needed to stem the blood.

He reached into the back of the Beast for his first-aid kit. He bent over the seriously injured man and started winding bandages around his wounds to staunch the blood. He'd seen them do it on numerous survival shows. There was nothing to it, really, providing you could cope with the sight of other people's blood. It was all about confidence. He was surprised to recognize the injured man as one of the two detectives who'd interviewed him about the watch. A thrill rippled through him. He, Gary Carlton, was starring in his own real-life cop show. Yes, it beat paintballing any day.

Black clouds rushed Sorrenson's vision. He felt himself struggling for breath. He saw waves roiling in the winter sun.

He sensed he was hundreds of miles away, somewhere across the North Sea. He could make out small, brightly painted wooden shacks hugging a shore riven by inlets. He saw gulls circling above and a small fishing boat sailing to a makeshift pier. His head lolled to one side. His left eye closed, then the right.

'You keep listening to me,' Gary Carlton said, recalling the advice from one of his favourite survival shows. 'So long as you can hear my voice you're going to be fine. I've stopped the blood loss, an ambulance will be here in minutes. You've just got to hang on until then. Keep listening to me, Detective. Keep listening.'

Sorrenson's laboured breathing slowed until it was barely perceptible. He didn't see the arrival of the police car, its uniformed passengers surrounding him as the wild-eyed park ranger continued to shout at him, urged him to hold on. He didn't see the ambulance arrive or the application of gaudy yellow tape around the spot where he'd fallen. He didn't see the arrival of the reporters with their notebooks and blank, bored faces, inured to the narrative of city stabbings. He didn't see any of this. Sorrenson had slipped into the darkness. His last image before he lost consciousness was of a bird's wing. Smooth and taut, it skimmed across a dark green sea, before making its way out towards the horizon, to where all things begin and all things end.

Tears burned her eyes. Focus. She needed to focus. She couldn't think straight. She was trembling. Words tumbled out of her mouth but they made no sense. She needed comfort. She needed the familiar. She ran on and on until she reached Parliament Hill, where she looked down on the London she knew well through a prism of salt water. In the distance, miles in front of her, she could see the Shard and then, to the east, the multiple towers of Canary Wharf, the sprawling, gleaming city within a city. A citadel.

Her breathing came in angry gulps. She felt numbed by the murderous intentions of men. It had been so random, so unexpected, the attack. And yet, as her left hand explored the wet wound, a new mouth ripped into the flesh above her right hip, she knew it must have been premeditated. That sort of damage, that fake mugging, needed planning. Executions took a lot of executing. The thought terrified her. She was shaking violently, as if she had hypothermia. Focus. She needed to focus.

She thought of Sorrenson, of the young man kneeling over him. He was going to be OK, she told herself. He was going to be OK. But, still, she couldn't think straight. She needed to put distance between herself and the violence. That was her only thought. She needed to keep running. She could see things only when she was totally isolated, and for that she needed to keep in motion. She was a machine. If she stopped moving she would stop functioning. If she was moving she wasn't vulnerable. She had to keep running. Focus. She needed to focus.

She ran down past the ladies' bathing pond, conscious that she had no idea what she was doing. She couldn't think of anything but the recent, brutal past. Each metre further from the scene felt like an abject act of betrayal. Her mind kept looping back to the horror of only minutes before, when Sorrenson had sunk back against the sheeting. Just what had she felt at that precise moment? Fear? Terror? Yes. But other emotions too, emotions that seemed to have no place among the violence.

Still she couldn't stop running. Movement was the only thing that made sense. And she was too scared to think ahead, to face the consequences of the future, to face what would happen once she stopped moving.

A crouching horror, lurking in the bushes edging the trail, suddenly leaped out at her. She had cost someone tens, possibly hundreds of billions of pounds. That was a heavy bounty to have on your head. You could never be safe with that sort of price hanging over you. She'd learned that much. You couldn't run from money. It created its own links, its own chains. It trapped everyone, one way or another. It would find her.

She needed to ring Five, ring the police, but in her terrified state she doubted her allies. Somehow someone had worked out that she was a threat. She had no idea who they were or how they'd done it but she was suddenly supremely aware of just how vulnerable she had made herself, just how alone she was. She remembered what McLure had said: trust no one.

She saw the horror in the eyes of passers-by as they were confronted by a bleeding, sobbing, sweating woman whose face was racked with pain, despair and anger. She had been dehumanized by trauma. She was no longer a person. She was something dragged from a nightmare into sunlight.

Just what had she been thinking? To have exposed that sort of manipulation, that sort of abject, expertly woven lie was always going to have consequences. She'd been oblivious to the risks she'd been taking, risks that had damaged others. She'd become like McLure. Too obsessed with Higgs to see the threats.

She was almost at the edge of the Heath that morphed into Gospel Oak. She had been barely aware that she had been running. The noise of traffic reassured her. She was grateful for it. Grateful that the isolation she'd thought she craved was not an option.

Still she ran on. Through increasingly thick crowds of people she ran down towards Kentish Town, calmed by the familiarity that came with running, the sense of control it offered. Her mind became clearer. Each stride seemed to bring greater clarity. Focus. She needed to focus. On she ran, her brain screaming under an assault of long-buried information. She dredged it all to the surface, the act of recovery an act of defiance. Her movement, her thoughts, were a form of political protest. She refused to be cowed by the destructiveness of men. She wouldn't give them that option. She understood that she was traumatized and that there was no point running from it. The trauma was embedded. She'd been running from it for the last four years. And it had got her nowhere. It was time to stop running. She slowed, almost to walking pace, her head drooping. She looked down at the pavement, clutched the wound in her side. She came to an abrupt stop, stood at the side of a bus lane, panting and sobbing. No, she thought. No more. She turned round and started running back towards the Heath.

Thoughts continued to drip-feed through her mind until they became as constant as the brush of her feet on tarmac. The attack had been planned; someone wanted her dead; it stood to reason it was because of what she'd discovered; she'd ruined someone's plan. The thoughts kept repeating themselves until she seemed incapable of absorbing any-thing else.

And then, just when the thoughts had combined to form a mantra, another came crashing in, one that made her almost stop dead. She remembered Brockman's warning to Quest. He'd urged the hedge fund to take out insurance. She'd disrupted a plan, a carefully constructed, meticulously assembled plan that had taken years to form. Huge vested interests were at stake. Of course people who made such plans would take out insurance. It was obvious. They would have a plan B if plan A failed.

And that plan B would work only if it was the opposite of what the market expected. It couldn't work otherwise. So if the market wasn't expecting a nuclear incident . . .

The thought came close to paralysing her. Was Quest that desperate? Probably. No, definitely. There was just too much money at stake not to go through with it. Quest had the alternative trades ready to go — she'd seen them. The hedge fund just needed to activate a different super-computer pro-gram and it would still clean up. It would make the killing it had always intended. Just so long as Armageddon arrived.

She was almost back at her apartment block. She'd refused to go to hospital. She'd dealt with the police but she'd delib-erately sanitized the information. There just wasn't time to answer their questions. To the police, the attack seemed like some sort of random mugging. They would have to wait for the truth. There were more urgent matters.

It was five in the afternoon and the markets were just closing. But in little more than twelve hours they would open again and she was fairly certain that she knew what would happen. She'd exposed a giant lie and the only way for Quest to make the lie work now was to turn it into the truth. She thought of Sorrenson. There was nothing she could do on that front. He was in a liminal place, somewhere between dead and alive. He was unconscious, wired to machines that would determine his future, whether there would even be a future.

She was in the communal entrance, about to climb the stairs leading up to her apartment, when she checked herself. In the last three hours of her life she'd become far more risk aware. She was no longer taking her own personal security for granted. No one could protect her but herself.

She felt the zipped pouch in the back of her running shorts. Her fingers made out the contours of her mobile phone and a bunch of keys on a ring. Carefully she slid the keys out of the pouch and into her shaking hand. She stared at the jumble of metal, her mind working through her options. No one would believe her, she knew. She'd burned through all of that capital. Higgs was being put on life support. The intelligence agencies, the financial authorities, they all believed it was over. There were only so many times you could cry wolf. Even if you were right. And, she had to admit, there was a chance she might be calling it wrong. She was working on a hunch, that was all. But she would rather be wrong than live with the consequences of her inaction. She stared at the keys. So, then, she was on her own. She made for another door and descended some stairs to the underground car-park, holding her keys in front of her like a knife.

She hadn't driven the rusting 2CV for months but it started first time, a rarity. Michael had laughed at her when she'd bought it. 'It's almost an antique,' he had told her. 'Buy a proper car, one with a working heater.' But the car had been her private joke. It was dented, impractical, ponderous and as far as anyone could get from the low-slung, testosterone-fuelled gleaming alternatives that filled London's stuffed streets. A man would never drive it. That was why she'd fallen in love with it.

She rummaged in the glove box and found some tissues. She stuffed several under her vest, refusing to look at her wound. She eased the 2CV out of the car park and drove towards East London, then the A12. She drove slowly, her red tin can of a car incapable of exceeding sixty miles an hour, all the time checking her mirrors, fearful that she was being pursued, astonished that such fear was warranted.

As she made her way out of London and into Kent, her breathing slowed. She felt calmer. She pushed the accelerator to the floor but she knew now that she was in no rush. There was plenty of time. She knew where she was going, if not what she was going to do when she arrived. She could reach a decision during the journey.

She pulled out her phone and laid it on the ripped leather seat beside her. Maybe there was one person she could phone. It was a gamble whether he'd believe her. But everything had come down to this, a final gamble. She might be wrong, spectacularly wrong, about what was going to happen. But she had to trust her hunches. She had to back herself. After all, no one else would.

Chapter 20

'My father found peace here.'

Schwartz nodded. 'I can see why.'

Prince Faisal turned his gaze away from the impressive topiary that dominated the gardens of his late father's stately home and regarded his ashen-faced hedge-fund manager. The setting sun burned green leaves red. There was a drowsy stillness about the place that made Schwartz think of cemeteries. 'Yes,' the prince said, more to himself than to Schwartz. 'Perhaps this garden will be his true legacy. I rather think he cared more for it than for his children. Certain things he did towards the end of his life, certain plans he had for his money, they were . . .' He shook his head and looked at Schwartz. 'I wonder how he will be remembered. What will be his legacy, hey? And what will be mine?'

So, Schwartz thought, the prince knew that the plan had been exposed, either by accident or by intention. It didn't matter. All that mattered was that the plan was dead.

'Well, then,' the prince said, 'we have a problem. A very big problem, it seems.' He smiled, which unnerved Schwartz. He glanced behind him and saw a young man sitting on a bench. The prince's favourite consort. For a second Schwartz

313

was glad of the prince's romantic longings for young men. It suggested that his employer was not a complete sociopath.

'Yes,' the prince repeated. 'A very big problem indeed.'

Schwartz said nothing. He knew from experience that it was best to let the prince ease himself out of his reverie and play for time. He watched the young man rise to his feet and saunter into the orangery at the back of the mansion. There was something unhurried, almost cat-like, about his actions. Schwartz was jealous. The man was clearly untroubled.

The prince nodded approvingly, then turned back to Schwartz. The smile had disappeared. 'So,' the prince said again. 'What to do, hmm? What can be salvaged from this mess?'

'We have options,' Schwartz said.

'Options?'

Schwartz checked himself. 'An option.'

'Ha, yes. To activate Mr Brockman's insurance recommendation. The famous plan B we discussed all those months ago. It is good to plan for contingency, is it not? We should be ready for a rainy day, even if it seems the summer is here for ever.' The prince gestured at the manicured, perfectly irrigated lawns. 'Yes, we must plan for a rainy day. That is good insurance, yes?'

'Yes.'

'We have come a long way since we first discussed plan A, Project Apocalypse,' the prince murmured.

'A long way,' Schwartz agreed.

'It would be a shame to fall at the last hurdle, to use a sporting metaphor.'

'Indeed it would.'

There was a pause. The prince stroked his beard, rolled the hairs on his chin into tight coils. 'I don't know,' he said. 'Plan B is not without risk. We could fly a plane into a nuclear reactor. We could make it look as though a bird-strike brought it down. It can all be done remotely – we proved that with our models. But we cannot guarantee the collision will not trigger a radioactive leak. High risk indeed.'

'There is risk in everything,' Schwartz agreed. 'The world thrives on risk. And, besides, some leaks are worse than others. Everything leaks in the end. Reactors, people, plans. The nuclear plant is already leaking, apparently. The government just won't admit it, that's all.'

'Hmm,' the prince said. 'But, still, it is an old reactor. Surveys suggest it was never stress-tested for a plane crash.'

'It is risky,' Schwartz agreed. 'There is no doubting that.'

'We saw what happened in Fukushima,' the prince said. 'And Chernobyl before that. All along we only ever wanted to create an illusion of catastrophe, not the real thing, Schwartz. But now, here we are, discussing ways that may end up doing that very thing. Plan B.'

'We can't eliminate risk completely,' Schwartz said. 'No one can.'

'No,' the prince said quietly. 'We cannot.'

'But, well . . .'

'Well?'

'Even if it goes wrong, the contamination will be quite localized. And we'll be rich. Even richer. Think about it. We will have bet against the markets and we will have won. All those banks, those American banks, will lose out. It will push some, the most over-exposed, off the cliff. It will be the same result that we wanted. Only . . .'

'Only there will be consequences,' the prince said. 'There would be victims if there was a radiation leak.'

'Collateral damage,' Schwartz said. 'There is always collateral damage in any war. And you have always seen this as a war.'

The prince sighed. 'Indeed. That is the nature of wars. But such damage can be justified if the war is just. And this is a just war. We are taking the long view. We need to beat the West at its own game. We dictate what happens.'

'Well, this will do it,' Schwartz said. 'We can still win. We just need to deal ourselves a new hand, raise the stakes.'

The prince smiled approval. 'Raise the stakes. A good metaphor. Yes, indeed. There have already been . . . sacrifices along the way. To stop now would be a waste. A criminal waste. But our friends will be watching us.' The prince pointed to the sky.

Schwartz looked upwards, as if he could see the satellites. 'We'll be nowhere near it and it's going to be almost impossible for them to prove it had anything to do with us. The cockpit will be destroyed on impact. We've taken steps to ensure everything inside it will be devastated. And, besides, you'll be back in Saudi when it happens. They can't get you there. You'll be safe. You'll be protected.'

The prince nodded. 'So, then,' he said quietly. 'We commence Plan B. B for Bird-strike. We have moved from A to B.'

'I'll activate the insurance,' Schwartz said.

She sat on the deck behind Sorrenson's house and looked out to sea. She sensed that dawn was not far off but the sky gave no hint of illumination. She sat cross-legged, an old fleece, found in her car's boot, pulled tight around her. In front of her she'd assembled a picnic, culled from the chiller cabinets of a local petrol station: hummus and pitta bread, Greek salad, bananas, orange juice and several energy drinks. She set them out in front of her, like votive offerings.

It had been a macabre decision to take refuge in her lover's house, but it was the only place where she felt half safe. She took a slug of energy drink, grimaced at its taste, and looked out to sea, at the dark liquid field stretching out into the heavy blackness of the night. She felt exhausted and was almost overcome by her urgent desire to sleep.

She checked the time on her phone: three fifty-eight. She scrolled through her messages, but she knew already that there was nothing she'd missed. It was clear to her that Callow didn't want to return her text, didn't want to engage with her outlandish, lunatic claims. No matter. It was enough that she had sent it. They could track her via her phone. That was the point. It was her beacon, a private distress signal.

She reached forward to grab some pitta bread. The action made her wince. The wound in her side continued to throb malevolently. She popped a couple of painkillers and reluctantly felt the gauze covering the gash. The memory of applying TCP in a lay-by a few hours before still made her retch. But at least the wound was no longer leaking. She had made a good job of patching herself up. She remembered the last time she'd tended a wound. She found herself sobbing.

A gust of wind whipped across the shoreline. It was cold and whispered of autumn. It must have blown down from

Scandinavia. She pulled the fleece tighter. There were only a few hours left and she had no idea what to do next. She thought of her mother, her father and her husband. She thought of the children she would never have. She felt full of loss and was gripped by the quiet terror that came from contemplating a future alone.

She stood up unsteadily, wincing as the wound rubbed against the gauze. She took several deep breaths and forced herself to have another pull on the energy drink. The first flicker of dawn was discernible now on the horizon. She scooped her makeshift picnic into a plastic bag and headed towards her car. She had a plan. Of sorts.

'Mr Andrews needs no introduction,' Callow said, pointing to the home secretary. 'His permanent secretary, Mr Chilcot, is the gentleman to his right. For the purposes of the official minutes, subject, need I remind you, to the Official Secrets Act, I am Phil Callow, deputy director of MI5. With me we have Robert Kitson, head of counter-terrorism operations at Scotland Yard. Next to him is Susan Urquhart, director of resilience at the Home Office, and next to her, Lord Ouseley, head of the Joint Intelligence Assessment Committee. Beside him we have Martha Townsend, head of external liaison, the Foreign Office. Cobra meeting convened at 0:42 a.m., Wednesday, the third of September.'

Callow sank back in his chair. He'd had no sleep, and playing host to Cobra, the government's emergency response committee, in a barren room deep in the bowels of MI5's headquarters was draining what little energy he had. He wondered again if he'd gone mad. Convening the meeting based on the strength of a text message was unhinged. He didn't recognize himself. He was taking extraordinary decisions at huge personal and professional risk. The home secretary was unlikely to be in a benevolent mood if he'd made the wrong call. The prospects of alienating the Saudis and their elaborate informant network was potentially disastrous. He knew he had nowhere to hide if Kate Pendragon's claims were bogus. Well, he'd placed his bet. It was a long way for them to fall. There would be little left of their bodies after impact.

Chilcot coughed and sipped a glass of water. He pointed to the photographs Callow had pinned to the wall. 'These are?'

Callow gestured at the grainy images. 'Long-range surveillance pics of Prince Faisal's private airport next to Osford nuclear power plant in Kent.'

'They appear to be of model planes,' Chilcot said coldly.

'Most are,' Callow replied. He was struggling to remain polite. Career civil servants like Chilcot didn't live with risk. They had no conception of the pressure others were under. Theirs was a life free of turbulence.

Callow stood up and walked towards the photographs. He took another out of a suitcase and thrust it across the table. 'This was taken yesterday,' he said. 'It shows the arrival of a Gulfstream jet touching down at Osford. In the background you will also see several Airbus A380s.'

'Impossible,' Andrews said. 'I was Transport before Home Office, remember. I know you can't land planes that size down there.'

'The runway was recently extended,' Callow said. 'The prince's late father intended to use it to fly A380s on mercy missions around the world. His eldest son now appears to have developed an alternative vision for the runway.' Callow pointed at the photographs pinned to the wall. 'We believe there is an immediate and urgent terrorist threat to the power station. We believe there is a plan to crash the Gulfstream into it imminently.'

'Really?' Kitson shot back. 'It's only a few hours since we were informed that such a threat had been discounted. How imminently?'

'A few hours,' Callow said.

'Can you be more specific?' Kitson again.

'It will be timed to have maximum publicity so my guess, for what it's worth, would be early afternoon, when the east coast of the US has woken up. So maybe nine hours from now.'

Kitson nodded. 'That figures,' he said. 'Like Nine/Eleven.'

'Right,' Callow said, grateful that the policeman was proving an ally.

'You say you believe,' Chilcot said acidly. 'What is the basis of your belief? On what grounds has Cobra been activated?'

Callow took a deep breath. He had rehearsed the speech in his head but there was no denying that he was about to serve up some thin gruel. Chilcot was clearly a man used to banquets. 'We have an agent who has uncovered evidence of unusual trading patterns on the stock market that indicate some sort of major event is about to take place. We believe the trades are being made by a Saudi hedge fund run by a known donor to Islamist terrorist groups. Our surveillance teams have collected evidence indicating that the target has been experimenting with remote-control models as he prepares for the real thing. We believe the intention is to fly the Gulfstream into the nuclear plant remotely.'

'So it really is like Nine/Eleven,' Kitson muttered.

Callow shrugged. 'Except they don't need suicidal pilots this time. We're not sure whether this is intended to be seen as an act of terrorism. Primarily it appears to be an attempt at market manipulation. They might seek to pass it off as some sort of accident.'

'Like what?' Chilcot asked, shaking his head. It was clear he didn't believe what he was hearing.

'Engine failure,' Callow said. 'Maybe a bird-strike.'

Silence filled the small, bombproof office. Even Kitson looked uneasy. Callow decided to play his trump card. There was very little time left for playing it safe. 'The CIA shares our belief that the unusual trading patterns indicate something is about to happen,' he said. It wasn't exactly the truth but he knew that even the vague mention of the Americans would impress the committee. The intelligence community still genuflected before Langley, before America Washington, New York, they still called the shots. Be grateful for small mercies, Callow told himself.

'Well, that is a comfort,' Chilcot said, unsmiling. 'So, to be clear, on the strength of some strange trading patterns we are about to launch a major counter-terrorism operation having discounted said operation only a few hours ago. Have I understood that right?'

'Yes,' Callow said firmly. 'You have.'

'Well,' Chilcot said, 'that is helpful to know. There are no doubts about who is responsible, then. There is no doubt about who has provided the evidence base for this strategy.'

The bland management-speak hung in the air, like fading piano chords.

'No doubts,' Callow said. 'It's our responsibility, our call. You will know who to blame. The service.'

Chilcot stared at Callow. 'Fine,' he said.

The committee members looked at the photographs, then back at Callow. Andrews drummed his fingers on the table. 'So what do you propose?' he asked.

Callow thought for a couple of seconds. He didn't really have an answer. 'Well, we know this is time-sensitive,' he said. 'The plane crash is intended to move the market one way so that the hedge fund can take advantage of the panic. If we can prevent the crash, we prevent the market moving and we stop the fund cleaning up. It's highly likely that in doing so we'll stop a number of banks going to the wall.'

'I can see the logic of the argument,' Andrews snapped, 'but what do we do about preventing the plane crash in the first place? Quite frankly, the markets can fend for themselves. I'm talking about trying to stop a nuclear disaster.'

Callow cursed himself. He was so tired. He wasn't thinking straight.

'I would argue that intervention is an essential action,' Kitson said. 'It is true that Prince Faisal has been cited in numerous intelligence reports as a major funder of Islamist groups. He may not plant the bombs but he provides the infrastructure for those who do.'

Callow nodded. 'He's ruthless, too. There are claims within Saudi dissident groups that he had his father assassinated.' It wasn't a lie, but it was barely an approximation of the truth. The intel came from a single source, a Saudi cleric who had fallen out with the regime and had been wrong before.

Callow prayed the committee wouldn't ask him too many questions. It was necessary to paint in abstract. Detail would destroy the picture.

'Could it be a bluff?' Andrews's voice was hoarse with fatigue.

'Quite possibly,' Callow conceded. 'It might be one giant hoax, but our analysis suggests not. It might be that the aim is to fly the plane into the reactor without triggering a nuclear leak. But, I must stress, we just don't know what will happen. No one has done this before. The scenario has been gamed many times. There have been risk assessments but—'

'But?' Andrews's voice had acquired a new urgency.

'But they're relatively old,' Callow said. 'Four or five years old. And no one knows how quickly these nuclear plants are crumbling. One report suggests Osford is already in trouble even before someone flies a plane into it. There have been several low-level radioactive leaks, which have so far failed to make it into the public domain.'

All eyes turned to Urquhart.

'Could be true of any of our nuclear plants,' she said. 'All these reactors were built in the sixties and are now being mothballed. There isn't the money to maintain them to the standards we would like. Those are the risks you take with nuclear power. It's either that or buy more gas from the Russians.'

'Spare me the hard-luck story,' Andrews barked. 'It seems to me the bottom line is this: based on the flimsiest of evidence, we believe there is a chance a hedge fund linked to one of the world's most prominent Saudi businessmen is preparing to fly a plane into one of our nuclear reactors.'

'Correct,' Callow said.

'What does Webster think?' Andrews asked.

'He's put me in charge of this,' Callow replied. Typical Webster, he thought. Ever the politician, he was distancing himself from the decision-making process. He could learn a thing or two from his boss, Callow mused. Like how to survive.

'Interesting,' Chilcot said. 'Very interesting.'

Callow pressed his fists into his eye sockets in an attempt to massage out the exhaustion.

'This could damage our relationship with the Saudis for years,' Townsend said. 'If this is the wrong call, no amount of diplomacy will heal the scar. It will leave a gaping wound. You understand? It will be decades before there can be any form of reconciliation.'

'I get it,' Callow said.

'Yet you're telling us we need to ring Hereford and get a team down to the south-east coast right now,' Chilcot interjected.

'Maybe it's more a job for the SBS rather than the SAS,' Kitson murmured. 'This plant is practically in the sea.'

'Well, that's the home secretary's call,' said Chilcot, smirking.

They looked at Andrews. Andrews looked at the photographs pinned to the wall.

'It's not a lot to go on, is it?' Andrews murmured. 'It's high risk. Very high risk. The consequences—'

'We've invaded countries on less,' Callow snarled, no longer able to keep his reserve. The clock was ticking. It was time to call the game one way or another. People needed to make choices.

'A good point,' Chilcot said. 'And look where that got us,

hey? Maybe it indicates we need to be more cautious in the future. Think a bit more about the risks we're taking before we go in all guns blazing.'

Out of the corner of his eye, Callow caught Andrews nodding at Chilcot. He had a sinking feeling. His poker face had slipped at the last moment. He had revealed himself, exposed his urgent desire to convince Andrews of the need to act. That rashness would cost him.

But, then, his hand had always been weak and Andrews had known it. You couldn't blame a politician for playing things safe. Callow looked at the clock. It was gone five. He looked back at Andrews, who had given up bothering to hide his yawns. The room felt very still, almost devoid of life. It was as if the Cobra members had been turned to stone, he thought. Fear of making the wrong call had petrified them. They were human fossils, shells on display in a dimly lit glass box somewhere in the bowels of a faceless London building. It was pitiful. Pitiful and predictable.

Chapter 21

She watched the thin grey line fatten on the horizon. It started as a gossamer thread that spoke of light and hope, then thickened until the sky had assumed a metallic quality. The dawn promised a day of rain. Dark clouds had whipped in across the sea. A strong wind had blown up. Summer had been banished.

For hours she sat motionless, staring out at the autumn sky, listening, listening, listening. As midday approached she broke open another energy drink and peeled a banana. Rain pattered on the canvas roof of the 2CV. She watched, half fascinated, half bored, as a trickle of water sneaked its way through a hole and dripped onto the passenger seat. The rhythm of the droplets felt reassuring. She watched them fall, counted a hundred of them, then turned on the battered radio. The dying strains of Elgar's 'Nimrod' filtered through the car's tinny speakers. She struggled to suppress a laugh as she thought of McLure. His murder seemed so long ago, another age. She had been a different person back then, someone who thought they understood how the world functioned, someone confident of their place within it.

But now, well, she understood it all perfectly and not at all. She could see how everything was connected, how everyone was part of one giant machine that dictated the terms of how they should live, their life chances, their fate, even. There were expert, complex systems at work over which no one had any control. But that only made it harder for a person to understand their place in it, their own autonomy.

The last stirring chords faded, leaving the percussive pouring rain as a soundtrack. Yes, she thought, you couldn't beat systems. That was the point of them. They were bigger than individuals. They controlled markets, continents, the world. They were monsters that couldn't be slain.

She looked through the car's chipped windscreen at the bank of conifers on the other side of the road. To her left stretched the sea. The shoreline seemed like a film-set created to simulate the D-Day landings. Rusty barbed wire and discarded oil drums were littered across sand and scrub. A fading yellow sign declared 'No Trespassing'.

She knew what lay beyond the conifers. She had downloaded the satellite images on her mobile phone, enlarged them so that she could inspect the site forensically.

She watched the rain slide down the windscreen. The continuity announcer on the radio said they were heading for the news at noon. She stared at the trees, as if she could see through them. But the trees were decades old and formed a thick fortress that guarded the runway, held its secrets. It was no matter. She would know if her hunch was correct. She would know because she would hear it. She would hear the engines. She would hear them roar.

★　★　★

The door of the hotel room clicked shut. The burqa-clad figure stepped into the corridor and walked calmly to the lifts. CCTV cameras tracked the individual's progress through the foyer and out onto the Strand. It was just after midday and the porters on duty paid the figure little attention. They knew from experience that the burqa brigade didn't need a cab summoned for them. They had their own cars, their own bodyguards.

Once burqas had been quite exotic. But no longer. The Savoy was the hotel of choice for the Saudis. As the oil price continued to tick up so, too, did the visits from the wives of the billionaire sheikhs visiting the capital to buy up property, turn black gold into bricks and mortar, take out insurance against their precious resource drying up.

No one noticed the figure in the burqa step into the dark-blue Bentley that then sped down the Strand towards Trafalgar Square. No one noticed the figure remove the burqa to reveal a well-built, short man in a white vest and black jeans. No one noticed the Bentley sweep through Mayfair and turn back towards Grosvenor Square. No one noticed the gates of the US embassy slide back to allow the car to enter. No one saw the gates slide shut behind it.

Reynolds's body wasn't found until the maid entered his suite the following day. He was slumped in the bath. His throat had been cut. A coroner later recorded that he had been unconscious when he had been murdered. A combination of pills and alcohol had combined to form a powerful sedative. The coroner recorded a narrative verdict, in which he considered whether Reynolds might have been trying to end his life before he was murdered. One could only speculate, the coroner said. No note was left.

Chapter 22

She switched off the radio, halting the newsreader in mid-flow. The bored-sounding woman filtering through the 2CV's speakers had been explaining that governments around the world were taking steps to freeze Higgs accounts and that plans were being drawn up to ring-fence its massive debts so that somehow someone somewhere could work out a way for them not to drag down the entire banking system. Such international co-operation was unprecedented, the newsreader explained, confirming fears that Higgs's collapse might have had dire consequences for the world's banks if the contagion had spread.

The newsreader spoke of the fragility in the financial system, of a deep anxiety among bankers. An expert interviewed for the bulletin opined that the banking world had once again come close to sliding over the precipice. One more shock and anything could happen, she'd suggested. 'We have little to go on now but blind faith in the financial system,' she'd added. 'Another shock and all remaining confidence would evaporate. It would be like Lehmans, only to the power of ten.'

The sudden roar of jet engines drowned the expert's final comments. It was then that Kate knew her hunch was real. An insurance policy was kicking in. Something truly terrible was about to happen. She checked her mirrors. No signs of reinforcements.

She felt only slightly betrayed. She hadn't really expected to be believed. She didn't blame Callow or anyone else. It was in no one's interests to back her, a rogue agent with what must have seemed a gimcrack theory. The risk of humiliation for her potential backers had been just too high. Perhaps they knew something she didn't. That would be one explanation for the no-show. Perhaps she was still wrong. Perhaps there was another explanation . . .

For a second or two she doubted herself. She wasn't thinking clearly. She was in a state of deep shock. She had escaped London, fled a city of danger, but it seemed that the trauma, the terror, had made her even hungrier for risk.

There was no time left. She needed to make her call. The noise of the jet's engines had become a howl. It was clear that the plane was being prepared for take-off. She checked her phone a final time. No messages. She had an urgent need to scroll through the photographs stored on the device. She smiled when she saw the ones of her late husband. He'd been so handsome. She tried to picture him as if he were still alive. He wouldn't have changed much, she felt. Same big grin. Same fearlessness. He would have been a good man to have around now.

She placed the phone on the seat beside her and turned the key in the ignition. The windscreen wipers kicked into life and brought new clarity. She depressed the clutch and put the car into first gear. It started trundling towards the conifers, then speeded up as she slipped it into second. As she shifted into third, the 2CV shook with the effort of acceleration. The sound of smashing and ripping accompanied its journey though the five-metre wide thicket of conifers, and then the darkness was left behind as the 2CV exited the trees and trundled across open land.

A thin wire fence was all that now stood between the car and the runway. Kate put her foot further down on the accelerator and heard the car's engine scream as it tried to obey her command. The 2CV hit the fence and charged through, dragging flailing strips of metal behind it.

Ahead of her she could see the runway, and at the far end she made out the gleaming Gulfstream jet. It looked sinister head-on, like an advancing bird of prey.

She slipped the car into its fourth and final gear, felt the drop in vibrations as it eased onto the runway. She estimated the plane was some four-hundred metres from her. In the distance, to her right, she could make out an SUV and two figures standing beside it.

She turned the knob on the radio and was rewarded with the strains of Barber's *Adagio for Strings*. The plane was only three-hundred metres away. The two men were gesturing at her as they ran up the runway. A third man jumped out of the SUV and joined them.

The plane was two-hundred metres away. Kate could see there was no pilot in the cockpit. Its speed was constant: it was trundling up the runway, ready to turn for take-off. There were seconds left to make a decision. To delay would be to abandon options, to give up all control. It had to be now.

She pulled hard on the steering wheel and the 2CV lurched to its left and into the path of the oncoming plane.

From thirty-metres away the jet's wheels looked enormous, easily capable of flattening the car into a thin tin line.

Twenty metres. The plane attempted to steer around the car but she pulled hard on the wheel again and ensured the 2CV and the Gulfstream remained on a collision course. Ten metres to go and the noise was deafening. She made out the hydraulics on the wheels, the blurred markings under the wings. Five metres. She thought of her mother, her father and her husband. Three metres. She thought of McLure. Two metres. She thought of Sorrenson. One metre. She pulled gently on the wheel, twisting the 2CV away a fraction and thwarting a full-on impact with the plane's front wheel. Jet and car brushed against each other as she screamed with fear, with rage, with hope, and with a hundred other emotions that could surface only now there was no time remaining.

The left-hand corner of the 2CV seemed to evaporate as it glanced against the plane's front wheel. There was the sound of shattering glass and a muffled explosion as the windscreen and then the canvas roof took the force of the impact. The car's left front tyre shot out across the tarmac and bounced into the grass at the edge of the runway. She was conscious of the sky pouring through the gaping roof, of air rushing in and the terrifying screaming of rotating turbines above her. The rear-view mirror shot off the windscreen and struck her left cheekbone forcefully. She felt as if she'd been pistol-whipped; her head shot back and smashed into the upright behind her seat. Sparks seemed to fill the car, fill her mind. The presence of dark shadows suggested she was going to lose consciousness imminently. She felt intense fear. She was going to die with too many things unknown. She would never know the consequences of her actions. She would never know what had really happened to her father. She would never learn the full details of how her husband had died. Sorrenson. She was leaving with too many questions unanswered. There would be no one left to ask them, to perform a reckoning.

Adagio for Strings continued to blare as what was left of the 2CV spun round from the force of the collision. The car was facing up the runway just as the jet's left wing passed over what remained of its roof. Instinctively she ducked as shards of metal flew across the inside of the vehicle, smashing the rear windows. She felt blood seep down her face. There was the sound of hissing and of something grinding and then came a stunned sort of silence, an urgent absence where once there had been uncomfortable noise. The Gulfstream had stopped its journey across the tarmac.

The black shadows that had been on the periphery of her vision seemed to envelop her. She vomited and suddenly her mouth was awash with the taste of energy drink and bananas. Her head slumped forward.

It had happened in seconds, but it seemed to have stretched across many minutes. She tried to look at her watch but she could hardly see. Her face was wet with vomit, tears and blood. She was conscious that half of her car was missing. She could smell fresh rain on tarmac.

She thought about crawling out of the 2CV but it seemed like far too much effort. She was paralysed by exhaustion. And, besides, even if she could make it out she wouldn't get far. Her legs were gone. She could feel blood seeping down one of her calves. She could command her legs to run but they wouldn't obey the instruction. She had no control, no power.

She sensed that the three men were only a few metres away. She wondered whether she would pass out before they reached her. One had a gun and was waving it furiously above his head. She hoped unconsciousness would arrive before them. The reprisals would be ugly. She thought of Sorrenson's face twisted in pain as the knives had plunged in.

She willed the blackness to come but instead she found that things were becoming a little clearer. Her vision was blurred but she could still make out her surroundings. A flock of geese took to the air at the edge of the runway.

The driver's door was wrenched open and she found herself being dragged from her car. The three men, she noticed, all had buzz-cuts and olive complexions. They slammed her onto the ground and screamed at her. She studied their faces with interest. She could see them but she couldn't hear them. *Adagio for Strings* seemed to be drowning everything out. It made for a strange soundtrack, half soothing, half terrifying.

The men were very angry, she could see, but they also appeared confused, as if they were waiting for orders. This was what vast amounts of wealth got you, she thought, looking up at them. You could buy your own soldiers. You could declare war on whoever you wanted to. Money was the ultimate weapon.

She saw one of the men pull out a mobile phone and bark into it. He looked down at her and nodded frantically, then shouted to his gun-wielding colleague, who frowned, then gestured at the third man to stand away from her prostrate body. The man with the gun shuffled towards her, his left hand clasped around the weapon trained on her head.

She noticed that he was wearing an earpiece, pressing it into his ear as he seemed to be receiving instructions.

So this is how it ends, she thought. This is my exit. Covered with blood, tears and sick. It was perhaps not so different from how she'd come into the world. She grinned up at her murderer's pockmarked face. It was a cruel face, Kate thought. Or, rather, a face that had been made cruel by his job. He was clearly no stranger to violence.

She wouldn't allow him to see her frightened. She wouldn't give him that. She wasn't running. A gun was a totem, a sign of weakness, not strength. Anyone could be powerful with a gun in their hand.

'Do it,' she whispered. 'Do it. Do it now.'

Her executioner closed one eye. He crouched over her. The action made her think of a priest dispensing the last rites over a dying soldier. She saw that her murderer was momentarily distracted. For a second she felt hopeful that her execution was to be commuted. A flurry of activity to the side of the runway had caught her killer's eye. But, no, it was just the geese coming back in to land. The man pointed to the birds, said something to his colleagues, then adjusted his position.

It was then that she knew the end had arrived. She had seconds left of her life to live. It was a strange, horrible feeling, a rare experience. Most people were unconscious before they died, she appreciated, even in her terrified state. Few were ever aware that they had reached their final moment.

But it was all too obvious what was happening to her. Someone was about to switch off the lights and then the show would stop. Presumably they would dispose of her body somehow, somewhere. They wouldn't have to travel too far if their plan was to use the sea.

She thought of the coast, its strength, its permanence. She found comfort in the physical. The cliffs, the seas, the shores will outlive us, she thought.

'Do it,' she said again, but this time her voice was stern, commanding. She was giving her murderer an order. She was ensuring he had no option but to obey.

The executioner loomed over her. She watched, half fascinated, half horrified, as his hand started to squeeze the trigger. Her eyes became pools. The taste of salt filled her mouth.

The geese scrambled angrily into the air as the shot rang out. The fat birds were indignant at being disturbed.

Blood was spattered up one side of the 2CV. There were crimson rivulets in the dents of the car door.

Chapter 23

'I can do it.'

Callow looked at his boss doubtfully.

'I've been in this chair longer than you've been in the service, pretty much,' Webster snapped. 'I can push myself.'

'Fine,' Callow said. They were like a bickering husband and wife, he thought. He really did need to retire. He stopped pushing Webster's wheelchair and the two men remained at the edge of the cemetery, bit-part players in a much larger set-piece. The deputy head of MI5 lit a cigarette and surveyed the black-clad crowd spilling into the church. The dark colours somehow seemed inappropriate for what was supposed to be a memorial service, he thought. They were meant to be celebrating someone's life, their work, their public service, not giving them a second funeral.

But, still, the nature of the death meant there was little room for joy, Callow conceded. It had been a life ruthlessly cut short. He looked through the church's porch and admired a Christmas tree towering over a nativity scene. It was a long time since he'd been in a church. The only weddings he went to were second weddings and they rarely involved God. Baptisms had been an age ago and he was still a few years from hitting the thick funeral seam that came with the onset of retirement.

He was struck by how little churches had changed since he'd attended Sunday school. He admired the Norman example in front of him, its proportions, its brickwork. There was a sturdiness about it. It had a sense of permanence. He could understand how faith gave people the answers they were looking for. Faith was like money. Both offered salvation, providing you put your trust in them. And yet if you scrutinized either, their promises fell down. Bankers believed in the invisible, pervasive power of money. Terrorists believed in the invisible, pervasive power of fear. Callow believed only in what he could touch. He stubbed out his cigarette, lit another.

Webster pointed at the throng. 'There goes the home sec,' he said.

'Quite a turnout,' Callow remarked.

'It couldn't be any other way,' Webster said. 'The service takes care of its own.'

A curious phrase, Callow thought. It conferred membership on the dead without their permission. He drew on his cigarette, blew smoke into the darkening December sky. He remembered the festive season, when he was a boy. Where did it all go? he wondered. Where did all the innocence go? When did the fear arrive? 'So,' he said.

'So indeed,' Webster said. He pulled his scarf tight around his neck. A chill was seeping across the Worcestershire countryside. There would be a thick frost overnight. The journey back to London would be a race against the gritters. 'Shall we?'

'Yes,' Callow said. 'It's getting cold. You don't get this kind of cold in London. Only the provinces.'

Webster went to push himself but then he stopped abruptly. 'This, all of it, could have been avoided,' he said, pointing at the throng pouring into the church.

'Maybe,' Callow replied. 'Maybe not.'

A light rain started to fall on the cinder path snaking through the cemetery. It sounded like radio static.

'And what have we got to show for it all?' Webster said. 'What did anyone get out of it, for that matter?'

'Diplomatic immunity, in the case of our friend the prince,' Callow murmured.

'A prosecution would have been a nightmare,' Webster said. 'I suppose in a way you could claim that we got a result. No attack on our creaking nuclear infrastructure and the muzzling of a chief recruiter to the Islamist cause. We kept the Americans onside, too. They owe us for keeping a lid on the insane things that went on at Higgs. These days, that's a considerable achievement. We punched well above our weight.'

'Hell of a cost, though,' Callow said. 'Like you once told me, you can only hold the tide back for so long. The money will continue to flow. Six tell us there's no shortage of Britons going abroad for terror training. There will be blow-back when they start returning from Syria and Iraq. They'll need new battlegrounds, all those angry young men.'

The sound of footsteps on cinders made the two men turn around. They watched the two figures approach.

'We wondered whether you'd come,' Webster said.

'It would have been wrong to stay away,' Kate said. She

nodded at the two men, kept her distance. Not for the first time she felt like the new girl in the playground.

'You look better than when we saw you last,' Callow said. He nodded at Sorrenson. 'Glad to see you're both looking a bit better, come to that.'

She shivered in the cold, pulled Sorrenson closer to her. 'We're doing OK. Any news since we last spoke?'

'There'll have to be an inquest but it'll be years down the line. The CPS are still considering charges against the other two.'

'And?'

'They'll walk,' Webster said. 'We can't charge them with anything. Not with your attempted murder or plotting to crash a plane into a nuclear reactor. We can't prove either was their intention. And, well, it would get very messy. We don't want all of this coming out in court. It would prove extremely awkward for our American friends.'

She had suspected as much. Spooks didn't like to be embarrassed. American spooks particularly. Sorrenson gave her gloved hand a squeeze. 'I thought so,' she said. 'And the Quest lot?'

'Same problem,' Callow said. 'We can't prove they were trying to rig the market. They've got good lawyers, far better than our side anyway. Don't fancy the Financial Conduct Authority or the Serious Fraud Office's chances, really. Public sector is no match for the private sector on this one. And, besides, it seems that half of Quest's employees were CIA assets. Just like half of Higgs's. Everyone was hedging their bets, straddling multiple positions, trading intel.'

She shook her head. 'With assets like that who needs enemies?'

Callow shrugged. 'True.'

'Well, don't knock the Americans too much,' Webster said. 'After all, it was their intel that convinced the home sec that, and I quote, "on the balance of probability", an attack on a British nuclear power station was imminent. If they hadn't intervened . . .'

'Yes, I know. I have the CIA to thank for the deployment of an SBS sniper team. I owe my life to the agency that basically created this entire mess in the first place.'

Callow nodded. 'Welcome to the real world.'

She shook her head. 'Still, good to know my former employer had my back all along.'

The two men remained silent.

Callow lit a third cigarette from the fading tip of the second. 'Former?'

'My secondment finished while I was convalescing. I'm now technically unemployed. And, as I've signed the Official Secrets Act, I can't really tell a prospective employer what I've been doing for the last three years.'

'Well, obviously that's just a bureaucratic oversight,' Webster said. 'It can be remedied in minutes. We can have you back in the service right now. Well, perhaps after we've given thanks for the life and work of Anthony McLure,' he added expectantly.

She stared at him, conscious that the chill in the cemetery was penetrating her clothes, gnawing her bones. A thin layer of fog was encircling the gravestones. The sound of a church organ filtered into the dusk. She was relieved that her face was in shadow. She didn't want Webster to see her anger. He wouldn't have understood it. But, then, that was the problem. The service never understood. It saw everything

343

and everyone as part of a giant machine, something that could be fixed, addressed, approached, moulded, corrected.

But the reality was that the important things – the fundamental motivations that turned people into mass murderers and homicidal pilots, put them on planes with bolt-cutters and liquid bombs, on trains with backpacks full of fertilizer, in slickly-edited videos holding knives to throats of hostages in orange jumpsuits – were not created by machines. They came from somewhere that could never be mapped with a flow chart or a diagram, somewhere liminal, a shoreline shaped by tides of love and hate that had travelled halfway across the world and back.

Ultimately, the intelligence community was just like the banking community, she thought. Both had the same flaws. They saw only structures and processes. They thought in abstract terms. They didn't see the human. They saw what they wanted to see: a world they could control, a world in which they deluded themselves that they were in charge. 'Thanks,' she said, turning to Sorrenson. 'But I'm done.'

'Done?'

She was surprised by Callow's reaction. He sounded genuinely concerned.

'People like us aren't ever done,' Webster said.

She smiled at Sorrenson. 'Well, I am. I'm moving to the coast. Shall we?' She gestured towards the church and they followed her inside. Candlelight from the Christmas tree flickered across cold grey flagstones. She stopped to put coins into a collection box. The three men looked at her curiously. She gave a small shrug.

'Insurance,' she said.

Acknowledgements

Huge thanks to Peter Buckman for risking his reputation by signing the author; Hazel Orme for spotting the howlers; Edie for being my first reader and the Sea Dog for believing even when I didn't.